RITU

Graham Masterton

About *Ritual*

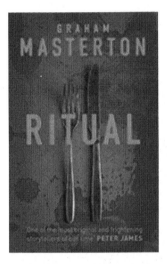

Tiny, picturesque Allen's Corner in rural Connecticut has a secret. It is a terrible one that eats at its youth, at their innocence and consumes their very souls with a twisted hunger which is never sated.

When restaurant critic Charlie McLean and his son, Martin visit the little town of Allen's Corners in rural Connecticut, little do they realise what they're letting themselves in for. In the mood to try something different they stop at Le Reposoir, unaware that most of the meals on the menu are not the a-la-carte range they're used to, but more a mixture of mundane dishes and human d'oves.

Ritual is an outrageous horror story with masterful storytelling and stomach-turning gore!

1

Outside the restaurant window, behind the trees, a huge thundercloud ballooned up, luridly orange in the afternoon sunshine, anvil-headed, apocalyptic, the kind of thundercloud from which Valkyries should have been tumbling.

'Well, then,' said Charlie, his face half hidden in the shadows. 'How long do you think this baby has been dead?'

Martin peered across the table. 'Hard to say, under all that glop.'

'This glop, as you call it, is Colonial-style Sauce,' Charlie corrected him.

'It's glop,' Martin insisted. 'Look at it. It's so gloppy.'

Charlie bowed his head so close to the lumpy scarlet sauce spread out over his plate that Martin thought for one moment that he was going to press his face into it. Charlie was sniffing it, to determine what it was made of. He was also trying to decide whether the veal schnitzel underneath had been defrosted recently enough to justify the menu's confident claim that it was 'Homestead Fresh'.

Without raising his face, Charlie said, 'This is a mixture of Chef Boy-ar-Dee canned tomatoes, undercooked onions, and Spice Islands Mixed Herbs straight out of the jar. Its primary purpose would appear to be to conceal the midlife crisis being suffered by the schnitzel beneath it.'

'Is that what you're going to write about it?' asked Martin. Charlie could hear the challenge in his voice. He sat up straight and looked Martin directly in the eye.

'I have to be practical, as well as critical. Where else is your ravenous fertilizer salesman going to eat, halfway up the Housatonic Valley on a wet fall afternoon?'

He picked up his fork, wiped it carefully on his napkin, and added, 'What I shall probably write is, "The Colonial-style Sauce was somewhat short on true Colonial character."'

'Isn't that called copping out?' said Martin. All the same, he watched with amusement as Charlie lifted up his entire veal schnitzel on the end of his fork and scrutinized first one side and then the other, as if he were trying to sex it.

'Sometimes, you have to be forgiving to be accurate,' said Charlie. 'The truth is, this veal is disastrous and this sauce is worse, but we'd be wasting our time if we went driving around looking for anything better. Besides, I've eaten far less appetizing meals than this. I was served up with steak tartare once, in the Imperial Hotel in Philadelphia, and there was half a cow's lip in it, complete with hair. The maitre d' tried to persuade me that it was something called Steak Tartare Napoleone. I said, "This is more like Steak Tartare Vidal Sassoon."'

Martin smiled, one of those odd sly smiles which fifteen-year-old boys put on to convince their forty-one-year-old fathers that they are still interested in hearing all the hoary, unfunny anecdotes that their fathers have been telling them ever since they were old enough to listen. He poked at his Traditional Connecticut Potpie.

'I haven't put you off your food?' asked Charlie.

Martin shook his head. 'I don't think you've done anything for their appetites, though.' And he nodded towards two white-haired New England matrons who were sitting at the next table, staring at Charlie with their spectacles as blind as four polished pennies.

Charlie turned in his seat and smiled at the matrons benignly, like a priest. Flustered, they attended to their fried fish. 'The food is okay here,' he told Martin. 'The vegetables are all home-grown, the breadrolls are fresh, and when they accidentally drop someone's lunch on the floor, they usually throw it in the trash. Did I ever tell you about the time they dropped a whole lobster stew in the service elevator at the Royalty Inn in Seattle? Yes – and scraped it up between two wine-lists. Yes – and served it up to a legionnaires' reunion party. No wonder legionnaires are always having diseases named after them.'

'I think you did tell me that, yes sir,' said Martin, and slowly began to eat. Outside, the thundercloud was already dredging the upper atmosphere with rain. There was a strange, threatening hush in the air, interrupted only by the sound of knives and forks squeaking on plates.

'This place has charm,' Charlie added. 'These days, you don't get to see too much in the way of charm. And, you know, for most people, charm is just as important as food. More important, sometimes. You're taking a girl out, hoping to screw her, what do you care if they only half cook the onions in your Colonial-style Sauce?'

Martin was quite aware that Charlie was trying to talk to him man-to-man. But anybody who had been sitting next to them, father and son, both silhouetted against the pewterish light of an October afternoon – anybody would have realized quite quickly that they were strangers to one another. There were too many empty pauses; too many moments of unfamiliarity and too many questions that no father should ever have needed to ask his own son.

'How's the potpie?' Charlie wanted to know. 'I never knew you liked potpie.'

'I don't,' said Martin. 'But look at the alternatives. That fish looks like it died of old age.'

'Don't knock old age,' said Charlie. 'Old age has a dignity all its own.'

'If that's true, *your* veal must be just about the most dignified piece of meat I ever saw.'

Charlie was cutting up his schnitzel with professional neatness. 'It's acceptable, given the location, the net cost and the time of year.'

'You always say that. You've been saying that since I was five years old. You said that about the very first catcher's mitt you bought me.'

Charlie laid down his fork. 'I told you. I have to be practical as well as critical. I have to remember that most people aren't picky.'

Martin said, more venomously than he had ever dared to speak to his father before, 'You'd eat anything, wouldn't you?'

Charlie looked at his son with care. At last, he said, 'It's my job,' as if that explained everything.

For a few minutes, the two of them were silent. Charlie always felt tense when they were silent. There was so much to ask, so much to say, and yet he found it almost impossible to express what he felt. How can you explain to your son that you regret every minute you missed of his growing up, when there had never been anything to prevent you from being there but your own misguided sense of destiny?

He carried a plastic wallet that was fat with dog-eared photographs, and for him they were as progressively agonizing as the Stations of the Cross. Here was Martin playing in the yard at the age of three with a bright red firetruck, his eyes squinched up tight against the summer sun. Here he was again, dressed as Paul Revere at the grade-school concert, unsmiling, unsure of himself. That picture had been taken in 1978, when Charlie hadn't been home for over four months. Here was Martin after his team had won the Little League baseball tournament, his hand raised up in triumph by some ginger-haired gorilla of a man whom Charlie had never even met.

Charlie had missed almost all of it. Instead, he had been dining in strange hotels all across America, Charlie McLean, the restaurant inspector, an unremembered ghost at countless unremembered banquets. But how could he explain to Martin why he had been compelled to do it, and what it had been like? Those solitary hotel rooms, with television sets quarrelling through every wall; those fifteenth-floor windows with soulless views of ventilation shafts and wet city streets, into which the taillights of passing automobiles had run like blood.

Every meal taken alone, like a penance.

Watching his father's face, Martin said, 'Sounds like that storm's headed this way.'

'Yes,' said Charlie. 'There's a legend up here in the Litchfield Hills that electric storms are caused by ancient Indian demons; the Great Old Ones, they call them. The Narragansett medicine men fought them and beat them, and then chained them up to the clouds so that they couldn't escape. But, you know, every now and then they wake up and get angry and shake their chains and gnash their teeth together, and that's what causes electric storms.'

Martin put down his fork. 'Dad? Is it okay if I have another 7-Up?'

Charlie said, 'You know—you can call me Charlie. I mean, you don't have to. But you can if you want to.'

Martin didn't say anything to that. Charlie beckoned the waitress. 'You want to bring me another 7-Up, no cherry, and another glass of the chardonnay?'

'You're not on vacation,' the waitress said. It wasn't a question. She wore a blue satin dress that stuck to all the most unflattering parts of her hips and her buttocks with the tenacity of Saran-wrap. She could have been quite pretty, except that one side of her face didn't quite seem to match the other, giving her a peculiarly vixenish appearance. Her hair was the colour of egg-yolk, and stuck up stiffly in all directions.

'Just making the rounds,' said Charlie, winking at Martin. There was a distant grumble of thunder, and he pointed with a smile towards the window. 'I was telling my son about the Indian demons, chained up in the clouds.'

The waitress stopped writing on her pad for a moment and stared at him. 'Pardon me?'

'It's a legend,' said Martin, coming to his father's rescue.

'You're not kidding,' the waitress remarked. She peered down at Charlie's plate. 'You really hate that veal, don't you?' she told him.

'It's acceptable,' said Charlie, without looking at her. Like each of his five fellow inspectors, he wasn't permitted to discuss meals or services with the management of any of the restaurants he visited, and it was a misdemeanour punishable by instant dismissal to tell them who he was. His publishers believed that if their inspectors were allowed to reveal their identity, they would be liable to be offered bribes. Worse than that, they would be liable to accept them. Charlie's colleague, Barry Hunsecker, paid most of his alimony out of bribes, but lived in a constant cold sweat unless he was found out, and fired.

The waitress leaned over, and whispered to Charlie, 'You don't have to be embarrassed. It's awful. Listen, don't eat it if you don't want to. Nobody's forcing you to eat it. I'll make sure they charge you for the chowder, and leave it at that.'

Charlie said, 'You don't have to worry. This is fine.'

'If that's fine, I'm a Chinese person.' The waitress propped her hands on her hips and looked at him as if he were deliberately being awkward.

'It's fine,' Charlie repeated. He could hardly tell her that he was obliged to eat it, that doggedly finishing his entire portion was part of his professional duties. *And* he was supposed to order dessert, and cheese, and coffee; and visit the restrooms, to scrutinize the towels.

'Well, I took you for a gourmand,' the waitress told him. She scribbled down '7-Up + Char' and tucked her pad into the pocket of her dress.

'A gourmand?' asked Charlie. He lifted his head a little, and as he did so the last of the sunlight caught him, and gave his age away, but that was all. A round-faced man of forty-one, his roundness redeemed by the lines around his eyes, which gave him a look of experience and culture, like a Meissen dish that had been chipped at the edges. His hair was clipped short and neat as if he still believed in the values of 1959. His hands were small, with a single gold ring on the wedding finger. He wore a grey speckled sport coat and plain grey Evvaprest pants. Perhaps the only distinctive thing about him was his wristwatch, an eighteen carat gold Corum Romulus.

That had been given to him under circumstances that still made him sad to think about, even today.

Nobody had ever guessed what he did for a living, nobody in twenty-one years. Most of the time, this anonymity gave him a slightly bitter sense of satisfaction; but at other times it made him feel so lost and isolated that he could scarcely breathe.

'Of course, this place has been going to the dogs ever since Mrs Foss took over,' the waitress said, as if they ought to know exactly who Mrs Foss was, and why she should have such a degenerative influence. She curled up her lip. 'Mrs Foss and all the other Fosses.'

'How many Fosses are there exactly?' asked Charlie. Martin covered his mouth with his hand to hide his amusement. He enjoyed it when his father was being dry with people.

'Well, there's six, if you count Edna Foss Lawrence. There used to be seven, of course, but Ivy went missing the week before Thanksgiving two years gone.'

Charlie nodded, as if he remembered Ivy Foss going missing just like it was yesterday. 'It sounds to me like too many Fosses spoil the broth,' he remarked.

'She'd burn a can of beans, that woman,' said the waitress. 'Come on, now, why don't you let me get you the snapper. I should of warned you not to have the veal.'

There was a sharp sizzling crack, and the restaurant flickered like a scene out of a Mack Sennett movie. One of the matrons pressed her hands to her face, and cried out, 'Mercy!' Everybody looked around, their retinas imprinted with luminous green trees of lightning. Then a bellowing thunderclap rattled the plates and jingled the glasses, and set the panes of the old colonial windows buzzing.

'I think God's telling me to finish my veal and behave myself,' said Charlie.

'I thought you said they were demons,' Martin reminded him.

'I don't believe in demons.'

'Do you believe in God?'

Charlie looked across at Martin, narrow-eyed. The rain began to patter against the windows. 'Would it make any difference to you if I said that I didn't?'

'Marjorie always says that you have to believe in something.'

'How come you call your mom Marjorie but you won't call me Charlie?'

'How come you never say you hate anything?'

Charlie looked down at his plate. Then, for the first time in years, he put his knife and fork together, even though he hadn't scraped the plate clean. 'You may find it difficult to understand, but when you're somebody's employee, as I am, you have to do what's expected of you, regardless of your own personal feelings.'

'Even if you don't respect yourself?'

Charlie was silent for a moment. Then he said, 'If you and I are going to be friends, you should try to get out of the habit of quoting your mother at me.'

Martin flushed. The waitress came over and set down their drinks. 'You saved your stomach some extra torture there, sir,' she told Charlie, taking his plate away.

'We'll have the apple pandowdy,' said Charlie.

'Are you *that* tired of life?' the waitress remarked.

The rain trailed across the parking lot and dripped from the yew hedges that surrounded the restaurant gardens. There was another dazzling flicker of lightning, and another furniture-moving bout of thunder. Charlie sipped his wine and wished it were colder and drier. Martin stared out of the window.

'You could have gone to stay with the Harrisons,' said Charlie.

Martin was frowning, as if he could see something outside the restaurant, but couldn't quite decide what it was. 'I didn't want to stay with the Harrisons.

I wanted to come around with you. In any case, Gerry Harrison is such a turd-pilot.'

'Would you keep it clean?' Charlie requested. He wiped his mouth with his napkin. 'In any case, what the hell is a–turd-pilot?'

'There's somebody outside there,' said Martin.

Charlie turned around in his seat and looked out into the garden. All he could see was a sloping lawn and a row of badly trimmed hedges. In the middle of the lawn stood an old stone sundial, leaning at a derelict angle; and further back, surrounded by a tangle of old man's beard, hunched a wet, half-collapsed shed.

'I don't see anybody,' he said. 'And who the hell would want to stand out there in the middle of a storm?'

'Look – there!' Martin interrupted him, and pointed.

Charlie strained his eyes. For one moment, through the rain that herringboned the windowpanes, he thought he glimpsed somebody standing just to the left of the shed, veiled like a bride with old man's beard. Somebody dark, somebody stooped, with a face that was disturbingly pale. Whoever it was, man or woman, it wasn't moving. It was standing staring at the restaurant window, while the rain lashed across the garden so torrentially that it was almost laughable; like a storm-at-sea movie in which all the actors are repeatedly doused with bucketfuls of water.

There was a third flash of lightning, even more intense than the first; and for one split second every shadow in the garden was blanched white. But whoever had been sheltering there had disappeared. There was only the old man's beard, and the dilapidated shiplap shed, and the bushes that dipped and bowed under the relentless lashing of the rain.

'Optical illusion,' said Charlie.

Martin didn't answer, but kept on staring outside.

'Ghost?' Charlie suggested.

'I don't know,' said Martin. 'It gave me a weird kind of a feeling, that's all.'

The waitress returned with their plates of apple pandowdy and a jug of country cream. She was grimacing as she came across the restaurant. Walking close behind her was a short, fat woman in a blue and turquoise tent dress. There was an air of ferocious authority about her which told Charlie at once that this must be Mrs Foss, under whose direction the Iron Kettle was going to the dogs.

Mrs Foss wore spectacles that looked as if they had been modelled on the rear end of a '58 Plymouth Fury. The skin around her mouth was tightly lined, and the fine hairs on her cheeks were dogged with bright beige foundation.

'Well, hello there,' she announced. 'I'm always glad to see strangers.'

Charlie rose awkwardly out of his seat, and shook her hand, which was soft and limp, but jagged with diamond rings.

'Harriet tells me you didn't care for the veal,' said Mrs Foss, the lines around her lips bunching tighter.

'The veal was acceptable,' said Charlie, making sure that he didn't catch Martin's eye.

'You didn't eat it,' Mrs Foss accused him. 'Usually, they polish the plate.'

The patronizing use of the word 'they' didn't go unnoticed by a man who had eaten and slept in over four thousand different American establishments.

'I'm sorry if I gave you an extra dish to wash,' Charlie told her.

'The dishwashing isn't here and it isn't there. What concerns me is that you didn't eat your food.'

Charlie lowered his eyes and played with his spoon. 'I don't think I was quite as hungry as I thought I was.'

Mrs Foss said, 'You won't find a better restaurant anywhere in Litchfield County, I can promise you that.'

Charlie was sorely tempted to say that if there wasn't anywhere better, then God help Litchfield County, but Harriet the waitress chipped in, 'Le Reposoir.'

Mrs Foss turned to Harriet wild-eyed. 'Don't you even *whisper* that name!' she barked, her jowls wobbling like a Shar-pei. 'Don't you even *breathe* it!'

'A rival restaurant, I gather?' said Charlie, trying to save Harriet from Mrs Foss's blistering wrath. Lightning crackled through the room, and for one second they were all turned white.

'I wouldn't grace that place by calling it an abattoir, let alone a restaurant,' snapped Mrs Foss.

'I'm sorry,' said Charlie. 'I can't say that I've ever heard of it.'

'Do yourself a favour, and stay well clear,' Mrs Foss said. 'Those fancified French folks, with all of their unpleasant ideas.' She betrayed an upbringing many hundreds of miles south of Litchfield County, Connecticut, by the way she said 'idee-yuhs'. 'Most of the neighbourhood children take the long way round through Allen's Corners, since that place was opened. And you won't catch any of the local clientele going to dine there, no sir.'

Charlie reached into the inside pocket of his sport coat and took out his worn leather-covered notebook. 'What did you say it was called, this place?'

'Le Reposoir,' said Harriet, leaning over Mrs Foss's shoulder like Long John Silver's parrot. 'That's Le like in Jerry Lee Lewis; repos like in repossess; oir like in –'

'Harriet! Table six!' boiled Mrs Foss.

'I'm going,' Harriet told her, lifting a hand to ward off Mrs Foss's anger. 'I'm going.'

'I have to apologize for Harriet,' fussed Mrs Foss. 'I promised her mother I'd give her a job waitressing. There was nothing much else she could do.' She tapped her forehead. 'You wouldn't say deficient, but you wouldn't say genius.'

Charlie nodded his head in acknowledgement, and tucked his notebook back into his coat. 'I guess it takes all sorts.'

Mrs Foss pointed towards his coat. 'You're not thinking of *going* to that place, are you?'

'Is there any reason why I shouldn't?'

'I could give you just about a *hundred* reasons. I know folks like that from before. I used to run a restaurant on Chartres Street in New Orleans; Paula Foss's Red Beans And Rice, that was the name of the restaurant. I used to know folks like that back in those days. Frenchified, and *suave*. We used to call them the Célèstines. Private, that's what they were; but secret's a better word. Secret.'

Martin said, 'He's there again, look.'

Charlie didn't understand what Martin meant at first. Then Martin urged him, 'Out of the window, *look*!'

Mrs Foss squinted towards the garden. 'What's the boy talking about?'

Martin stood up, and walked stiff-legged over to the wide French windows. The matrons turned to stare at him. He shielded his eyes with his hand, and peered out into the rain. Charlie said, 'Martin?'

'I saw him,' said Martin, without turning around. 'He was by the sundial.'

Mrs Foss glanced at Charlie, and then went over to stand next to Martin by the window. 'There's nobody there, honey. That's my private garden. Nobody's allowed in there.'

Charlie said, 'Come on, Martin, let's see what we can do to this apple pandowdy.'

Martin came away from the window with obvious reluctance. Charlie thought he was looking pale. Maybe he was tired, from all of their travelling. Charlie was so used to driving and eating and eating and driving that it was easy for him to forget how punishing his daily routine could be. Since they had taken the Major Deegan Expressway out of New York three days ago, heading north-eastwards, they had covered well over 700 miles and eaten at nine different hotels and restaurants, from an over-heated Family Cabin in White Plains with sticky red vinyl banquettes in the dining room to a pretentious English-style Chop House on the outskirts of Darien at which every dish had been given a Dickensian name – Mr Micawber's Muffins, Steak Dombey and Chicken Copperfield.

Martin said, in a panicky-suffocated voice, 'You won't let it in, Dad, will you?'

Charlie was ducking his head forward to take his first mouthful of apple. He hesitated, with his spoon still poised. He hadn't heard Martin talk like that since he was tiny.

'What did you say?'

Martin glanced quickly back towards the window. 'Nothing. It's okay.'

'Come on,' Charlie encouraged him. 'Eat your dessert.'

Martin slowly pushed his plate away.

'You're not hungry?' said Charlie. 'It's good. Taste it. It's just about the best thing here.'

Martin shook his head. Charlie watched him for a moment with fatherly concern, then went back to his apple. 'I hope you're not pining for anything, that's all.' He swallowed, and then reached for his glass of wine. 'Your mother won't be home for ten more days, and I can't keep you with me if you're sick.'

Martin said, with unexpected vehemence, 'It's all right, I'm not sick, I'm just not hungry. Come on, Dad, I've been eating three meals a day for three days. I never ate so much Goddamned food in my whole Goddamned life.'

Charlie stared at him. Martin's faced was hectic and flushed, as if he were running a sudden fever.

'Who taught you to speak to anybody like that?' Charlie demanded. He was quiet, but he was also angry. 'Is that what you learn from your mother, Goddamned this and Goddamned that? All I did was ask you a civil question.'

Martin lowered his eyes. 'I'm sorry. I apologize.'

Charlie leaned forward. 'What's gotten into you all of a sudden? Listen – I don't expect you to behave like the Angel Gabriel. I never did. But we're friends here, you and me. At least that's what fathers and sons are supposed to be, isn't it?'

'Yes, Dad.'

Martin kept his head bowed while Charlie made a theatrical performance of finishing his apple pandowdy. In truth, he thought it was foul. The cook had emptied what must have been half a jar of ground cinnamon in it, which made it taste like mahogany sawdust. He would describe it in his report as 'wholesome, reasonably fresh, but over-generously spiced.'

All around the building, the gutters gargled the rain away down iron throats. The French windows were as dark as the glass in a blind man's spectacles. 'You know something, it's hard enough to come to terms with this situation without either of us getting all tied up into knots about it,' Charlie told Martin.

'I said I apologized,' Martin repeated.

The garden outside was lit up by a hesitant flicker of lightning. Charlie turned towards the window again. As he did so, he felt a sensation like somebody running a hairbrush down his back. A white face was pressed against the window, so close to the glass that its breath had formed an oval patch of fog. It was peering into the restaurant with an expression that looked like a mixture of fear and longing.

It could have been a large-faced child. It was too short for an adult. Charlie was frighteningly reminded of Dopey, in Snow White, with his vacant pale blue eyes and his encephalitic head.

In spite of the child's obvious anguish, it was the most terrifying thing that Charlie had ever seen. The lightning flickered one last time and then died; the garden was darkened; the face was swallowed by shadow. Charlie sat staring at the window with his hands flat on the table, rigid. Martin raised his head and looked at him.

'Dad?' he asked. Then, more quietly, '*Dad?*

Charlie didn't look at him. He kept his eyes on the blacked-out windowpane. 'What did you see, out there in the garden?' he asked.

'Nothing,' said Martin. 'I told you.'

'You said you saw somebody,' Charlie insisted. 'Tell me what he looked like.'

'I made a mistake, that's all. It was a bush, I don't know.'

Charlie was about to bark back at Martin when he saw something in the boy's eyes that stopped him. It wasn't anger. It wasn't contempt. It was a kind of secrecy, a deep unwillingness to discuss what he had seen. Charlie sat back in his chair and watched Martin for a while. Then he raised his hand to attract the attention of Harriet the waitress.

'Don't have the coffee,' Harriet told them, as she came across the restaurant.

'I don't intend to. Just bring me a last glass of chardonnay, would you, and the bill?'

'I'll make sure that Mrs Foss doesn't charge you for the veal.'

'Don't worry about it, please.'

Harriet was just turning to go when Charlie lifted his hand again, and said, 'Harriet, tell me something. Does Mrs Foss have any children?'

Harriet sniffed. 'Three – but sometimes they seem like thousands. There's Darren, who takes care of the accounts. Then there's Lloyd, who buys all the provisions. And Henry – but the less said about Henry the better, believe me. Henry is really *peculiar.*'

'I mean *young* children.'

Martin glanced up. His sudden interest didn't escape Charlie's notice. He *had* seen that figure in the garden, Charlie was sure of it. What Charlie couldn't understand was why he didn't want to admit it.

Harriet said, 'Young children, no. You're talking about kids, toddlers? She's about two hundred years too old for that.'

On the other side of the restaurant, Mrs Foss's antennae picked up Harriet's slighting tone of voice, and she lifted her head and searched for Harriet with narrowed eyes. '*Harriet,*' she said, and there were a dozen Biblical warnings in that one word.

While Charlie was paying the bill, he remarked to Martin, '*You* may not have seen anything, but I did.'

Martin didn't answer. Charlie waited for a little while, but decided not to push him, not yet. There had to be a reason why he didn't want to talk about what he had seen, and maybe the reason wasn't any more complicated than the simple fact that he didn't yet trust Charlie enough to confide in him. And considering Charlie's record as a father, he could hardly be blamed for that.

'Where are we going to stay tonight?' Martin asked.

'The original plan was to drive across to Hartford, and stay at the Welcome Inn.'

'But now you want to go to that French restaurant they were talking about?'

'It had crossed my mind,' Charlie admitted. 'I always like trying new places. Besides, it'll give us time to spend the afternoon any way we want. Maybe we could go bowling, or take in a movie or something. That's what fathers and sons are supposed to do together, isn't it?'

'I guess.'

'Charlie attempted a smile. 'Come on, then. You go wait for me in the car. I just have to wash my hands, as they say in polite circles.'

'Oh, you mean you have to go the inky-dinky ha-ha room.' Charlie slapped his son on the back. 'You've got it, champ.'

*

The men's washroom was tiled and gloomy, with noisy cisterns and urinals that looked as if they had been salvaged from the *Lusitania.* In the brown-measled mirror over the sink, Charlie's face had the appearance of having been painted by an old Dutch master. He scrutinized himself closely, and thought that he was beginning to show signs of wear. It wasn't true what they said about life beginning at forty. They only said that to stop you going straight to the bathroom and slicing your throat from ear to ear. When you reached middle age, you started to disintegrate, your dreams first and then your body.

He bent over the sink and soaped his hands. A faint wash of watery sunlight strained through the small window over to his right. He could see treetops through it, and grey clouds unravelling. Maybe it was going to be a fine afternoon.

Outside the washroom, in the Iron Kettle's red-carpeted lobby, there was a cigarette machine. He hadn't smoked in eleven years, but suddenly he felt tempted to buy a pack. It was the tension of having Martin around him all the time, he decided. He wasn't used to demonstrating his affection on a day-to-day basis. That was why he had so rarely stayed home for very long. He had always been afraid that his love would start wearing thin, like medieval fabric.

He was still buttoning up his coat when Mrs Foss appeared, and stood watching him through her upswept spectacles, her hands clasped in front of her.

'I hope we're going to see you again' she said. 'I promise that we can do better for you next time.'

'The veal was quite acceptable, thank you.'

Mrs Foss opened the wired-glass door for him. 'I hope I've managed to persuade you not to visit Le Reposoir.'

Charlie made a dismissive face.

'It wouldn't be wise, you know. Especially not with that son of yours.'

Charlie looked at her. 'I'm not sure that I understand what you mean.'

'If you don't go there, you won't have to find out,' said Mrs Foss.

She straightened Charlie's necktie with the unselfconscious expertise of a woman who has been married for forty years and raised three sons.

Charlie didn't know what to say to that. He turned and looked out through the door across the puddly asphalt parking lot, towards his light yellow Oldsmobile. A new car every two years was the only perk that his publishers ever gave him; and considering that he covered an average of 55,000 miles a year, which meant that most of his cars were on the verge of collapse after eighteen months, it wasn't so much of a perk as a bare necessity.

He could see Martin standing on the opposite side of the car with a copy of *The Litchfield Sentinel* draped over his head to keep off the last few scattered drops of rain. He frowned. The way Martin was waving his hand, he looked almost as if he were talking to somebody. Yet, from where Charlie was standing, there didn't appear to be anybody around.

Charlie watched Martin for a while, and then he turned back to Mrs Foss, and took hold of her hand. Those jagged diamond rings again. 'Thank you for your hospitality. I'll be sure to stop by here again, itinerary willing.'

'Remember what I told you,' said Mrs Foss. 'It's not the kind of advice that anybody gives lightly.'

'Well, no,' said Charlie. 'I suppose it isn't.'

He walked across the parking lot under a gradually clearing sky. He didn't call out to Martin, but as he approached, Martin suddenly dragged the newspaper off the top of his head, turned around, and skipped in front of the car, lunging and swiping at the air as if he were d'Artagnan. *Now he's behaving just like a typical fifteen-year-old kid,* thought Charlie. *But why is he making such a song and dance about it? What's he trying to show me? Or, more importantly, what's he trying to hide?*

'You ready to roll?' he said. He glanced quickly around the parking lot, but there was nobody in sight. Just the tousled grass slope of the garden, and the quietly dripping trees. Just the sky, reflected in the puddles, like glimpses of a hidden world.

'Do you think I could learn fencing?' Martin asked him, parrying and riposting with imaginary musketeers.

'I guess you could,' Charlie told him. 'Come on, it's only three or four miles to Allen's Corners.'

He unlocked the car door and eased himself behind the wheel. The windshield was beaded with clear, shivering raindrops. Martin climbed in beside him and buckled himself up. 'They have fencing lessons at school. Danny DeMarto does it. It's fantastic.'

Charlie started up the Oldsmobile's engine and backed slowly out of his parking space. 'Maybe you should ask your mother.'

'It's only twenty-five dollars a lesson.'

'In that case, you should definitely ask your mother. Besides – what do you want to learn to fence for? You'd be better off learning how to play the stock market.'

'I don't know. Maybe I could get myself a job in the movies, if I could fence.'

'The movies? I'm not sitting next to the reincarnation of Errol Flynn, am I?'

Martin said, quite seriously, 'I thought about being a stuntman, something like that.'

'That's kind of a wacky career,' Charlie ventured.

'Well, I'm not going to be a restaurant inspector,' said Martin. There was no scorn in his voice, and somehow that made his remark all the more painful. It was a plain and simple fact.

Charlie steered out of the parking lot and turned right on the road for Allen's Corners. For two or three minutes they drove in silence. On either side of them the woods rose up like heaps of ashes at a mass cremation, smoking with mist.

As offhandedly as he could, Charlie asked, 'Who were you talking to just now?'

Martin looked baffled. 'What do you mean? I wasn't talking to anybody.'

'In the parking lot, I saw you. You were waving your hands around as if you were talking to somebody. Come on, Martin, I know when somebody's talking to somebody.'

Martin turned away from him, and stared out of the window at the woods.

Charlie said, 'I'm not checking up on you or anything. I'm just trying to take care of you. I've also got to admit that I'm curious to know who you can find to talk to, in this Godforsaken locality.'

'I was singing,' said Martin. 'You know, like pretending to play the guitar.' He demonstrated by strumming an invisible Fender.

Charlie glanced up at his own eyes reflected in the rearview mirror. He wanted to tell Martin that the guitar-playing gestures he was making now were nothing at all like the gestures he had been making in the parking lot. Those gestures had been flat-handed, chopping, declamatory, as if he had been explaining something, or making some kind of appeal. They certainly hadn't been imaginary chord changes.

Martin reached forward and switched on the tape player, instantly drowning out the car with jarring rock music. He began to sing along with it, making a *juvv-juvving* noise with his mouth that reminded Charlie of the sound he used to make when he was a small boy, to simulate a Mack truck laboriously climbing up the lid of his toybox. It hadn't occurred to Charlie when he had offered to take Martin around with him that Martin would constantly require in-car entertainment. Charlie always drove in silence. He liked to hear the sound of America passing beneath his car, mile by mile. That, too, was part of the penance.

'Tom Petty and the Heartbreakers,' said Martin, crashing out more imaginary chords.

'Am I supposed to have heard of them?' asked Charlie, and then thought, *What a hideous middle-aged thing to say. No wonder Martin thinks you're so damned old.*

Martin didn't answer. Charlie carried on driving through the golden mist. He began to feel as if he were living in another time altogether; as if somehow they had driven through to the Ninth Dimension, like travellers used to do on *The Twilight Zone.*

He glanced at Martin surreptitiously. No teenage boy could have looked more normal. He might be aggressive and sarcastic, but what teenage boy wasn't? At least he didn't wear studs through his ears and make-up. He was nothing more than your average, skinny, short-haired pale-faced boy, with preshrunk 501s and a big plaid jacket and sneakers that looked as if they had been borrowed from one of the Harlem Globetrotters.

Maybe Charlie's anxiety at forming a new relationship with his son had made him too suspicious. Maybe Martin was telling the truth, and all that he had seen out in the garden had been a bush. Yet why he had said, 'You won't let him in Dad, will you?' Nobody says that about a bush. And he *had* been talking to somebody out in the parking lot, Charlie was sure of it, even though the parking lot had appeared to be empty.

Maybe he had been talking to himself. Or maybe he had been talking to somebody too small to be visible behind the car

2

They drove into Allen's Corners just as the bell from the Georgian-style Congregational Church was beating out three o'clock. Charlie parked the car right outside the entrance to the First Litchfield Savings Bank, and climbed out into the sunshine. The air was tangy with woodsmoke and recent rain.

Allen's Corners lay seven miles from Washington and five miles from Bethlehem, in a wooded hollow where the Quassapaug tributary ran. The heart of the town was a plain, sloping green, faced on three sides by white-painted colonial buildings, and dappled by crimson maples. There was a colonial cannon standing at the lower end of the green, and in the striped shadow of its wheel spokes two elderly men were sitting on a bench, their trousers protected from the wet wooden slats by carefully folded up newspapers.

'Best thing we can do is get some directions from those two,' said Charlie.

Martin looked around, his hands tucked into the front pockets of his jeans. 'You're sure this place has a bowling alley?'

'Down on the south side of town, next to the supermarket and the railroad depot. What the folks from the historical district call the commercial district.'

Charlie tugged his well-thumbed copy of MARIA out of his sagging coat pocket, licked his finger, and leafed through it until he found Allen's Corners, population 671, one gas station (daytimes only); two restaurants, Billy's Beer & Bite and The English Muffin; one boarding house, 313 Naugatuck, six guests only, no dogs.

MARIA was the popular acronym for the guide called *Motor-Courts, Apartments, Restaurants and Inns of America.* For Charlie, it was appropriate that it should have been a woman's name, because MARIA had been the mistress that had broken up his marriage. MARIA was the siren who had lured him away from home, and sent him driving around America in search of an illusory fulfilment that he had realized years ago would never be his. He wasn't bitter about it. He knew that he would never be able to settle down, so the best thing he could do was to go on driving around until some early-morning maid in some small mid-West hotel tried to wake him up one day and found that she couldn't.

Founded in 1927 by a flannelette salesman called Wilbur Burke who had been stranded in rural communities just once too often '*sans* beefsteak, *sans* bed', MARIA had been the travelling man's Bible for twenty years. In his preface to the first edition, Burke had written, 'This guide is dedicated to every man whose Model A has let him down somewhere in the vastness of the American continent, on endless plain or wind-swept mountain, and who has been obliged through lack of local knowledge to dine on Air Pie; and to seek his rest on the cushions of his back seat.'

Lately, however, MARIA had been overtaken in stylishness and circulation by *Michelin* and *Dining Out in America*. Salesmen flew to their destinations these days, eating and sleeping high above the prairies which they once used to cross in overloaded station wagons. But MARIA still sold 30,000 copies every year, and that was enough to justify the perpetual travels of Charlie and his five colleagues, constantly updating and correcting like the clerks in George Orwell's Ministry of Truth.

MARIA's restaurant inspectors managed on average to survive their jobs for three years. At the end of three years, they were usually suffering from emotional exhaustion, alcoholism, and stomach disorders. Very few inspectors were married, but almost all of those who were went through separation or divorce. Charlie had lost Marjorie; but he had outlasted the next-longest serving inspector five times over.

Mrs Verity Burke Trafford, who owned MARIA, said without kindness that Charlie must have been born a glutton; not only for food but for punishment. Charlie, in reply, said nothing.

Charlie walked across the dappled shadows of the green towards the two elderly men, and Martin followed him. Their feet made parallel tracks in the silvery moisture on the grass. The old men watched them approach with their hands shading their eyes. One of them was ruddy-faced, and blue-eyed, with the deceptively healthy looks of high blood pressure. The other was sallow and bent, with tufts of white hair that reminded Charlie of an old photograph he had once seen of an Indian scout who had been scalped by Apaches.

'Fine afternoon,' said Charlie, by way of greeting.

'It'll rain again before nightfall,' replied the ruddy-faced man. 'You can make a bet on that.'

'Wonder if you could help me,' said Charlie. 'I'm looking for a restaurant hereabouts.'

'There's Billy's down by the depot,' said the ruddy-faced man. Although the church clock was clearly visible through the maples, he took out a pocket watch and examined it for a while as if he wasn't sure that it was working. 'Be closed by now, though. Five after three.'

'It's a particular restaurant I'm interested in, Le Reposoir.'

The ruddy-faced man thought about that, and then shook his head. 'Never heard of any place called anything like that. Sure it's Allen's Corners you want? Not Bethlehem?'

'I had lunch at the Iron Kettle,' said Charlie. 'Mrs Foss told me about it.'

'What did he say?' the white-haired man cried out, leaning forward and cupping his hand to his whiskery ear.

'He said he had lunch at the Iron Kettle,' the ruddy-faced man shouted at him.

'Well, rather him than me,' his companion replied. 'Never could tolerate that Wickes family.'

'The Fosses own it now,' the ruddy-faced man told him.

'Oh, the Fosses,' said his white-haired friend. 'I remember. That woman with the fancy eyeglasses and the stupid sons. And that daughter that went missing – what was her name?'

'Ivy,' the ruddy-faced man reminded him. 'And she wasn't a daughter, she was a niece.'

'You're a hair-splitter, Christopher Prescott,' the white-haired man snapped.

'And you, Oliver T. Burack, are a xenophobe.'

Charlie interrupted them. 'You don't know where this restaurant could be, then?'

The ruddy-faced Christopher Prescott said, 'You've been misguided, my friend, if you want my opinion. Somebody's led you astray.'

'Harriet the waitress told me about it. She even spelled it out.'

'Harriet? Harriet Greene?'

'I guess that's her name, yes.'

Christopher Prescott reached out and gently took hold of the sleeve of Charlie's coat. 'My dear man, Harriet Greene is well known in this locality for having an unusually low proportion of active brain cells. In other words, she's what you might call doolally.'

'Mrs Foss mentioned the place, too,' said Charlie. Beside him, Martin was growing restless, and scuffing his feet.

'What did he say?' Oliver T. Burack wanted to know.

'He was talking about the Fosses,' Christopher Prescott shouted.

'The Fosses of Evil,' cackled Oliver T. Burack. 'That's what I call them. The Fosses of Evil.'

'Be quiet, Oliver,' Christopher Prescott admonished him.

It was then that a young sheriff's deputy came walking across the grass towards them. He was thin and big-nosed and he had grown a drooping blond moustache in an obvious effort to make himself look more mature. His eyes were concealed behind impenetrable dark sunglasses. He came up to Charlie and Martin and stood with his hands on his narrow hips, inspecting them.

'That your car, sir? That Olds with the Michigan plates?'

'Yes, it is,' said Charlie. 'Anything wrong?'

'I'd appreciate it if you'd move it, that's all,' the deputy told him.

'It's not illegally parked,' said Charlie.

'Did you hear anybody say that it was?' the deputy inquired. Charlie – who had argued with traffic cops and deputies on almost every highway from Walla Walla, Washington, to Wind River, Wyoming – took a deep and patient breath.

'If it's not illegally parked, deputy, then I'd honestly prefer it to remain where it is.'

The deputy looked past Charlie and Martin to the two old men on the bench. 'How're you doing Mr Prescott, sir? Mr Burack?'

'We're doing fine, thank you, Clive,' Christopher Prescott replied.

'These two people bothering you any?'

'No, sir, not at all. Asking for directions, that was all.'

'Lost your way?' the deputy said, turning back to Charlie.

'Not really. I'm trying to find a restaurant, that's all. Le Reposoir.'

The deputy thoughtfully stroked at his blond moustache. He had a ferocious red spot right on the end of his nose. 'You know something, sir? There are laws and there are customs.'

'Are you trying to make some kind of a point?' Charlie asked.

'What I'm trying to say, sir, without giving unnecessary offence, is that your vehicle is parked in the place where the president of the savings bank parks. He's still out at lunch right now, but he'll be back before too long, and you can understand what his feelings are going to be if he discovers an out-of-state vehicle occupying his customary place.'

Charlie stared at the deputy in disbelief. The wind whispered through the maples, and over by the commercial district a dog was barking. At last, Charlie said, with uncompromising coldness, 'Take off those sunglasses.'

The deputy hesitated at first, but then slowly removed them. His eyes were green and one of them was slightly bloodshot.

Charlie said, 'Do you happen to know where I can find a French-style restaurant called Le Reposoir?'

The deputy glanced at the two old men. 'Is that what you asked these gentlemen?'

'Yes it is. But now I'm asking you.'

'Well, sir, Le Reposoir isn't open to the public. It's more of a dining club than a restaurant. The way I understand it, you have to make a special appointment before they'll let you in there.'

'I see. But can you tell me where it is?'

The deputy looked uncomfortable. 'The people who run Le Reposoir are not too keen on unexpected visitors, sir. A couple of times they've called us out to take away trespassers.'

'I'll deal with that when I get there, deputy. All I want to know from you is where it is.'

'Sir – believe me – it doesn't have too good a reputation. I don't know how you got to hear about it, but the people round here don't speak too well about it. If I were you, I'd take a raincheck. Billy's is probably the best place to eat in Allen's Corners, if it's good country food you're looking for. My cousin works in the kitchen, and that kitchen's so clean, you wouldn't mind them taking out your appendix.'

Charlie said, 'You still haven't given me any idea where to find Le Reposoir.'

The deputy pushed his sunglasses back on to his nose. 'I'm sorry sir, I'm not sure that I should. We do our best to divert people away from Le Reposoir, tell you the truth.'

'I'll make a deal with you,' Charlie suggested. 'You tell me where Le Reposoir is, and I'll move my car.'

The deputy didn't look at all happy about that. 'Let me tell you something, sir, Mr Musette isn't going to like it any.'

'Mr Musette? Who's he?'

'He kind of runs Le Reposoir, him and Mrs Musette. Well – I believe they run it, anyway. I never saw anybody else up there, excepting some tall fellow who was working in the garden.'

A Jeep sped noisily around the green, and the deputy glanced around with undisguised anxiety in case it was the president of the savings bank, returning from lunch to find that his sacred parking space had been usurped by a stranger.

'Come on,' said Charlie. 'A deal's a deal. And what do we have at stake here? The sheriff's five per cent mortgage?'

The deputy said, 'All I can tell you is the name Musette. You can look it up in the telephone book.'

'Come on,' said Charlie. 'You can tell me approximately where it is, can't you?'

The deputy looked over at Christopher Prescott, as if he were seeking approval. Charlie was sure that he saw Prescott almost imperceptibly shake his head, but he couldn't be certain about it.

'You'd better call Mr Musette first,' the deputy repeated. 'If you try to go up there uninvited, well – the next thing I know he's going to be yelling down the horn at me, telling me to come up and get you because you've been trespassing. Mr Musette has a real obsession with trespassers.'

Martin said, 'Come on, Dad, we won't have any time left for bowling.'

'Bowling?' asked the deputy. 'You won't be able to do any bowling around here. Nearest lanes are in Hartford. There used to be a bowl, sure, down by the railroad depot, but they closed it nine months back. Too many old folks in Allen's Corners to make a bowl pay. No youngsters any more.'

'I was here last year,' said Charlie, in surprise. 'I can remember that bowl being pecked out with kids.'

'Times change,' Christopher Prescott intervened. His voice was as dry as the wind in the leaves. 'Lot of young couples decided that Allen's Corners wasn't the place they wanted their kids to grow up in. Too quiet, you see, and nothing in the way of opportunity, excepting if a kid wanted to be a horse doctor or a country lawyer. Then, of course, there were the disappearances, all those kids going missing.'

'Including the Foss girl?' asked Charlie.

'That's right,' said Christopher Prescott. 'First young David Unsworth disappeared; then Ivy Foss; then Geraldine Immanelli. Then six or seven more. Some of the parents began to get scared. Those who lived in town moved out of town. Some of them even went back to the city. Those who lived outside of town didn't allow their children into the Corners any more. So the bowling alley died from what you might diagnose as a loss of young blood.'

'Did they ever find what happened to all those kids?'

Christopher Prescott shrugged. 'They dragged the Quassapaug. They searched the hills for fifteen miles in all directions. But I reckon those kids went to New York City; or maybe to Boston, Massachusetts. They never found one of them, not even a trace.'

A silver-coloured Cadillac appeared at the far corner of the green. Abruptly, the deputy snatched at Charlie's arm. 'You listen here now, move that vehicle of yours. That's the bank president, coming back from lunch.'

'Where does he eat?' asked Charlie sarcastically.

'He sure as hell doesn't eat at Le Reposoir,' Oliver T. Burack put in. 'He said to me the other day that Mr Musette was the closest thing he'd ever met to a goat that walks on its hind legs.'

'I thought your friend was deaf,' Charlie said to Christopher Prescott. 'I also thought that neither of you had ever heard of Le Reposoir.'

'Oh, Oliver's deaf all right,' smiled Christopher Prescott. 'He knows what people are talking about, though. He has a sixth sense. What do you call it? Intuition.'

'Are you talking bullshit about me again?' Oliver T. Burack said.

'Please,' the deputy asked Charlie, as the Cadillac came dipping over the last corner of the green. But Charlie persisted. He was beginning to get the measure of these people, and he wanted to know what was going on.

'The restaurant,' he said. 'How come you wouldn't admit that you knew about the restaurant?'

Christopher Prescott stared up at him with watery eyes 'Sometimes it's better to hold your peace, better to say nothing at all than to say something malign.'

'What's so malign about Le Reposoir?'

The deputy came back two or three paces and pulled again at Charlie's arm. The bank president's car had arrived outside the bank, and the bank president was leaning forward and peering through its windshield at Charlie's car as if he were seeing a mirage.

'You want me to book you for obstructing justice?' the deputy demanded, almost panicking.

Christopher Prescott said to Charlie, 'You'd better get along, fellow. I wouldn't want to get you into trouble.'

'All right,' Charlie agreed. He didn't want to cause too much of a disturbance. MARIA inspectors were supposed to be 'discreet and inconspicuous in their behaviour at all times'. He followed the deputy back up the grassy slope, and across the road to his automobile. The bank president was sitting with his Cadillac's engine running. His face was hidden behind a geometric reflection of sky and trees on his windshield, but all the same Charlie gave a cheerful, insolent wave.

Martin took his seat beside Charlie and slammed the Oldsmobile's door. 'You realize you're copping out again,' he said.

'Who's copping out?' Charlie protested, starting the engine. 'I made a deal.'

'Some deal,' said Martin scornfully. 'You could have found out where that stupid restaurant is without having to ask him.'

'Oh, really? How?'

'You could have asked me.'

'You? You don't know where it is any more than I do.'

Martin reached into the pocket of his jacket and produced a small white card. He passed it over to Charlie without a word. Charlie took it and held it up to the window, ignoring the contorted face of the deputy outside, who was still desperately waiting for him to move.

At the top of the card there was an heraldic emblem of wild boars, embossed in gold, with the copperplate caption 'Les Célèstines'. Underneath were the words 'Le Reposoir. Société de la Cuisine

Exceptionelle. 6633 Quassapaug Road, Allen's Corners, CT.'

Charlie turned the card over. The reverse side carried the pencilled word 'Pain'.

'What the hell is this?' Charlie asked Martin. 'First of all those geriatrics try to pretend that they've never heard of the place. Now you give me this. Where did you get it, for Christ's sake? And why the hell didn't you show it to me before?'

The deputy tapped on the window with his knuckles. 'Sir,' he mouthed, 'will you please move?'

Charlie let down his window and held up the card. 'Is this the address? Sixty-six thirty-three Quassapaug Road?'

The deputy stared at him. After all, if Charlie had known the address all along, why had he kicked up such a fuss about it? 'Yes, sir,' he said.

Charlie said, 'Okay. At least we're making some progress.' He was about to shift his car into drive and pull away when the president of the First Litchfield Savings Bank approached him – a tall, wide-shouldered, white-haired man with a head as large as a lion. He bent down beside Charlie's open window, and said, 'Good afternoon. I hope you don't feel that I'm being autocratic here.'

'Don't worry about it,' Charlie replied. 'I'm just about to pull out. My friend the deputy tells me you have squatter's rights on this parking space.'

The bank president stared at Charlie level-eyed, and then smiled. 'You could call them squatter's rights, I suppose. My family have lived in this town since 1845. We own most of it, and hold mortgages on the rest. So you'll forgive me if I tend to regard this parking space as private property.'

'I'm only passing through,' Charlie told him.

The bank president's pale grey eyes focused on Martin. 'You and your boy?'

'That's right. A single parent's tour of hospitable New England.'

'Listen, I apologize,' the bank president said. 'You stay right there. I'll have Clive park my car for me. Allen's Corners is a friendly town. I certainly don't expect its law officers to hassle visitors on my behalf.'

He reached his hand into the car, and said, 'Walter Haxalt. Welcome to Allen's Corners.'

'Charlie McLean. And this is Martin McLean.'

'Happy to know you,' said Walter Haxalt. 'Please feel free to stay here as long as you want.'

'As a matter of fact, we're on our way to Quassapaug Road.'

Walter Haxalt glanced around at the deputy, then turned back to Charlie. 'I don't know that there's anything of interest to a tourist up there. Quassapaug Road is just a road. Not much of a road for driving on, either. It's all hairpins from beginning to end.'

'We want to visit Le Reposoir,' said Charlie. He held up the card that Martin had given him.

Walter Haxalt's expression went through a subtle but distinct change. It looked almost as if his face had been modelled out of pink wax, and an oven door had been opened close by, melting and shifting it. 'I suppose Clive has told you that Le Reposoir is completely private.'

Charlie reached forward and switched off the Oldsmobile's engine.

'All right,' he said hotly. 'Would somebody mind telling me what in the hell is going on?'

'I'm sorry, I don't understand,' Walter Haxalt replied. 'I didn't mean to offend you in any way.'

'I'm talking about this restaurant, Le Reposoir,' said Charlie. 'Mrs Foss back at the Iron Kettle warned me against visiting it. Those two good old boys on the bench there said they'd never heard of it, when they obviously had. And your pet deputy here did everything he could to tell me that I wouldn't be welcome. Now you.'

Walter Haxalt said nothing. Clive the deputy stroked his moustache as if it were a small furry pet.

'What I want to know is what's so darned off-putting about this place?' Charlie appealed. Walter Haxalt's refusal to reply was quickly defusing his temper, and making him feel embarrassed. 'Is the food really that bad?'

Walter Haxalt stood up straight. 'I'm sorry, Mr McLean, I don't think that Allen's Corners can really give you the kind of welcome you expect. My suggestion is that you drive right on to Bethlehem. There's a good New England-style restaurant there. They serve home-made hams and excellent boiled beef.'

Martin said, 'Dad, come on. Please.'

Charlie hesitated, biting his lip. Then he twisted the key in the ignition again, so violently that he made the starter-motor screech. He was just about to pull away from the kerb, however, when he glimpsed something moving behind the maple trees on the far side of the green. It could have been nothing more than a cloud shadow, or a wind-blown sheet of newspaper. It had vanished in an instant. But Charlie was sure that he had seen a small figure, dressed in grubby white. A figure with the body of an infant and the fully developed head of a man.

3

They drove north-westwards out of Allen's Corners past two rows of white wooden houses. They saw nobody at all, nobody walking by the roadside, no other cars. After a quarter of a mile, they were back amongst the woods again, surrounded by the rusting funeral of yet another lost summer. Although it was still early, the sun had already dropped below the treeline, and glittered at them tantalizingly, always out of reach behind the branches.

Charlie said nothing for a while, but when Martin reached forward to switch on the tape player, he took hold of his wrist and said, 'Not now. I want to talk.'

Martin folded his arms and sat back in his seat.

'I want to know where you found that card.'

Martin shrugged. 'I picked it up at that Iron Kettle place.'

'Where? I didn't see any cards there.'

'I found it on the floor.'

Charlie lowered his sun visor. 'You're not telling me the truth, Martin. I don't know why, but you'd better start explaining yourself pretty darned quick, otherwise this trip is over here and now and you go off to the Harrisons.'

Martin said, 'It's the truth, Dad. I found it.'

'We were talking about Le Reposoir and you just happened to find one of their cards? For Christ's sake, what do you take me for?'

Martin sulkily lowered his head.

'It's over, have you got that?' Charlie told him. 'Tomorrow I'm going to call the Harrisons and then I'm going to drive you right back to New York.'

Martin said nothing.

'Have you got that?' Charlie repeated.

'Yes, I've got it,' said Martin, in his best 'anything-to-keep-the-old-man-quiet' voice.

Charlie slowed down as they approached a steeply sloping intersection with a sign saying Washington in one direction and Bethlehem in the other. He stopped the car by the side of the road and opened up his map. 'This should be Quassapaug Road right here.'

He took a right, and cautiously steered the Oldsmobile up a tight corkscrew gradient, under overhanging oaks and American beeches. The sun danced behind the leaves. Somewhere behind the thicket fence of tree trunks, there were creamy clouds and pale blue sky; but here in the woods, Charlie began to feel strangely imprisoned and claustrophobic.

'All right, admitted, I haven't been much of a father to you,' he told Martin. 'But I never told your mother one single lie. I was never unfaithful, and I always sent money. Always.'

'Well, Saint Charlie McLean,' said Martin.

Charlie swerved the car off the side of the road and jammed his foot down on the parking brake. He tried clumsily to smack Martin's head, but Martin ducked and wrestled away, and the two of them found themselves panting and glaring at each other, hands clasped tightly, a fit fifteen-year-old fighting a tired forty-one-year-old.

'Listen,' said Charlie. 'Either we try to get along together like father and son, or else that's the finish. And I mean the finish. You're old enough to survive without me, if that's the way you want it. I don't mind.'

Martin released his father's wrists and turned his face away. Charlie knew that he was crying. Someone else had once cried like this, in the passenger seat of his car, a very long time ago, in Milwaukee. Charlie felt as if the world was an ambush of endlessly repeated agonies, and here it was again. The argument, the tears, the temporary reconciliation that both of them knew would never last. He squeezed Martin's shoulder but there was no love between them. He might just as well have been squeezing an avocado to make sure that it was ripe.

'I'm sorry,' he said, although he wasn't.

He continued driving around the roller-coaster curves of Quassapaug Road. A wild turkey scrambled across the blacktop in front of them, and Charlie swerved towards it in a feigned attempt to run it down. 'You ever eaten wild turkey, barbecued with new season's squash?'

Martin said, 'We never have turkey, even at Thanksgiving. Marjorie doesn't like it.'

'Marjorie, Marjorie! Why the hell can't you call me Charlie?'

'Because you're Dad, that's why.'

They passed the entrance to Le Reposoir so unexpectedly that they overshot it by a hundred feet. Charlie caught a flash of wrought-iron gates, painted black, and a discreet black signboard. The Oldsmobile's tyres slithered on the tarmac. Then Charlie twisted around in his seat and backed up all the way to the gates, with the car's transmission whinnying.

'That's it, Le Reposoir. Société de la Cuisine Exceptionelle.'

Martin stared at the sign unenthusiastically. 'Yes, and look what else it says. No visitors except by prior arrangement. These grounds are patrolled by guard dogs.'

'We can talk to them, at least,' said Charlie. He parked the car right off the road, in the entrance-way in front of the gates, and then climbed out. There was an intercom set into the bricks of the left-hand gatepost. He pushed the button, and then turned to Martin, who was still sitting in the car, and smiled in what was the nearest he could manage to encouragement. Martin pretended that he hadn't noticed, and in the end Charlie turned away. *God,* he thought, *they're like prima-donnas, these teenage boys. You only have to raise your voice to them, and they start sulking and pouting and bursting into tears.*

He pushed the intercom button again. This time, there was a sharp crackle of interference, and then a voice demanded, '*Qui? Qu'est-ce que vous voulez?*'

Charlie cleared his throat. 'Is that Mr Musette?'

'Who is it who is wanting him?' the voice asked, in English this time, but with a strong French accent.

'My name's McLean. I was wondering if you had a table for two for dinner tonight?'

'You must have made a mistake, *monsieur.* This is a private restaurant. Reservations can only be made by advance booking.'

'Well, this is advance booking, isn't it?'

'*Je regrette, monsieur,* booking is always effected in writing, and bookings are accepted only at the discretion of the management.'

'What kind of a restaurant operates like that?' Charlie wanted to know.

'This restaurant, *monsieur*. Although I must correct you. It is a dining society, rather than a restaurant.'

'So I've been told. Is it possible to join?'

'Of course, *monsieur*, by personal recommendation.'

Charlie ran his hand through his hair. 'You people sure make life difficult.'

'Yes, *monsieur*, you could say that.'

'So somebody has to put me up for membership? Is that it?'

'Yes, *monsieur*.'

Charlie thought for a moment, and then said, 'Is everything I've heard about you true?'

'It depends what you have heard, *monsieur*.'

'I've heard that you're exceptional.'

'Yes, *monsieur*.'

Charlie had nothing more to say. The voice on the other end of the intercom refused to be drawn. Charlie took hold of the gates and shook them, just to make sure that they were locked, then he walked back to the car and climbed into it. He leaned over towards the glove box and took out a pack of Rol-Aids. The Colonial-style sauce was resisting all his stomach's determined efforts to digest it. That was the trouble with bad food, it always fought back.

'They won't take reservations unless somebody sponsors you,' said Charlie.

'What does that mean?' Martin asked.

'It means they're just about the most exclusive restaurant in the whole continental United States. It may not be easy getting into the Four Seasons, but at least they want your business. This place... who knows? How can you run a restaurant right in the middle of nowhere at all, with no advertising, no promotion, not even a signpost to tell you how to get there, and booking by personal recommendation only, in writing, in advance?'

'Maybe they're really good,' said Martin.

'What the hell do you mean, "maybe they're really good"!' Charlie retorted. 'The Montpellier is really good! L'Ermitage is really good! There are twenty restaurants in America which are really good! But, darn it, even the best restaurants have to advertise. Even the best restaurants have to let people in!'

Martin said, 'What are you getting so upset about? If they won't let you in, they won't let you in. Forget them. There isn't any point in including a restaurant in MARIA if nobody can get to eat there.'

Charlie took one last look at the implacably closed gates of Le Reposoir, then started up the car and turned back towards Allen's Corners. 'If it's that good, if it's really that good, then I want to eat there, that's all. Even my stomach can only take so much good old country cooking. I could use a revelation. Quite apart from the fact that I'd be fascinated to

56

find out what it is about Le Reposoir that upsets everybody at Allen's Corners so much.'

They drove back through the woods. Another thunderhead had swollen up in front of the sun, and the landscape had suddenly grown chilly and cheerless.

Martin said, 'Where are we going to stay tonight? Are we going to drive on to Hartford?'

Charlie shook his head. 'Tonight we're going to stay at Mrs Kemp's boarding house, 313 Naugatuck. I'm not leaving Allen's Corners until I can fix a table for two at Le Reposoir.'

'Dad—we're going to be days behind schedule. What are the people at MARIA going to say?'

'I can fudge the schedule, don't worry about that. I want to eat at that Goddamned private exclusive dining club and that's all there is to it. There must be somebody around here who belongs. That bank president, Haxalt, don't tell me that he's not a member. All I need is one person who's prepared to sponsor my reservation.'

Martin remained silent as they drove back into Allen's Corners. The light was turning to pale purple, and the streetlights had already been switched on. Christopher Prescott and Oliver T. Burack had left the green; but there were lights on the upper floor of the First Litchfield Savings Bank, and a few people were walking past the lower end of the green, on their way back from the supermarket. Birds sang in the maples, that sad intermittent song of early evening.

'I don't know,' said Charlie. 'This reminds me of something. *Déjà vu,* I guess.'

He drove around the green until they reached Naugatuck Avenue. This was one of the oldest streets in Allen's Corners, running directly west to east away from the green. At one time, before the main road had been laid at the lower end of the green, Naugatuck Avenue had been a main highway through to Hartford. English redcoats had marched drumming along here, while the people of Allen's Corners had watched them from their upstairs windows.

Mrs Kemp's boarding house stood at the corner of Naugatuck and Beech; a gaunt saltbox house with flaking weatherboard and windows blinded by grubby lace curtains. It was fronted by a paling fence, half of which was sagging sideways, and a small brick yard in which a single maple grew. Charlie drew up outside it, and eased himself out of the car. 'Are you coming?' he asked Martin.

'Are you sure it's open?' Martin frowned. 'It looks derelict to me.'

'It could use a lick of paint,' Charlie admitted. He opened the wooden gate and walked up the path. 'The last time I was here, the place was immaculate. I gave it a Gold Feather for comfort. Maybe Mrs Kemp has closed up shop.'

Martin followed Charlie cautiously up to the front door. There were two stained-glass panels in it, one of them badly cracked as if the door had been slammed during a violent argument. In the centre of the door hung a weathered bronze knocker cast in the shape of a snarling animal – something between a wolf and a demon. Charlie nodded towards the knocker and said, 'That's new. Welcoming, isn't it?'

Martin looked up at the loose tiles that had slipped down the porch in a straggling avalanche. 'This can't be open. And I wouldn't want to stay here, even if it is.'

'There's no place else, not in Allen's Corners, anyway.'

Charlie picked up the knocker. It was extraordinarily stiff and heavy, and he didn't much like the way the wolf-demon was snarling into the palm of his hand. He couldn't think why, but the knocker seemed familiar. He could vaguely remember reading about a wolf-like knocker in a book, but he couldn't remember what book, or when.

He banged it, and heard it echo flatly inside the house. He waited, chafing his hands, smiling at Martin from time to time. A stiff breeze had arisen with the setting of the sun, and Charlie felt unnaturally cold.

'Nobody here,' said Martin, standing with his hands in his pockets, 'Looks like we'll have to go on to Hartford after all.'

They were just about to turn away when they heard somebody coughing inside the house. Charlie banged the knocker again, and after a while footsteps came along the hallway. Through the stained-glass windows a small pale figure appeared, standing close behind the door. After a moment's pause, the figure reached up and drew back two bolts, and opened up the door on the safety-chain. A woman's face appeared, white and unhealthy-looking, with dark smudges of exhaustion around her eyes. Her hair was untidily clipped with plastic barrettes, and she was wearing a soiled blue quilted housecoat. From inside the house there came the vinegary odour of stale air and cooking.

'Mrs Kemp?' asked Charlie.

'What do you want?' the woman demanded.

'It says in the guidebook that this is a boarding house.'

Mrs Kemp stared at him. 'Used to be,' she told him.

'I see. You've given it up.'

'It gave itself up. I tried to keep open but nobody wanted to come here any more.'

'Is there anyplace else to stay the night?'

'There's the Wayside Motel outside of Bristol, on the Pequabuck road.'

'Nowhere in Allen's Corners?'

Mrs Kemp shook her head.

'Well,' said Charlie, 'I guess that fixes it. I might as well introduce myself. My name's Charles McLean, I'm a restaurant inspector for MARIA. I guess I can take your boarding house out of the book.'

Mrs Kemp's eyes narrowed. 'I remember you. You stayed here three or four years ago.'

'That's right, you've got some memory.'

'I remember you specially because you asked for the Brown Betty. That was always my late husband's favourite, and that was why I kept it on the menu. Maybe two people asked for Brown Betty in seven years, and you were one of them. Well, well. If I'd known you were an inspector, I would have done you better, I'm sure.'

Charlie smiled. 'That's why I never tell anybody. I want to get the ordinary treatment everybody else gets.' He stepped back a little and looked up at the house. 'Pity you've closed up, I liked it here. You ran a good cosy place.'

'Do you want to come inside for some coffee and cake?' asked Mrs Kemp. 'I mean, if you're really pushed for a place to stay, I could air a couple of beds for you. I wouldn't charge, it'd be company.'

Charlie glanced at Martin. It was quite plain from the expression on his face that he didn't relish the idea of spending the night here at all; and the truth was that Charlie didn't exactly fancy it either. But his curiosity about Le Reposoir had been aroused too strongly for him to leave Allen's Corners until he found out more about it. And maybe it would do Martin good to find out who was boss.

'We'd appreciate that,' he said.

Mrs Kemp slid back the safety-chain. 'You'll have to pardon the way I'm dressed. I wasn't expecting company.'

They followed her into the hallway. It was chilly and stale in there, and although the tables had once been highly polished, they were now covered by a fine film of dust. Old hand-coloured engravings of colonial Connecticut hung on the cream-painted walls.

Mrs Kemp brought them coffee in the best parlour, a gloomy room crowded with massive sawed-oak furniture of the Teddy Roosevelt era, when bellies and walrus moustaches had been in fashion. She had changed into a plain grey day-dress with a white lace collar, and sprayed herself with floral perfume. The coffee was hot and fresh; the

Jubilees stale and chewy. Martin sat in a dark spoonback chair silent and bored.

'I guess you could say that one bad season begets another,' said Mrs Kemp. She kept dry-washing her hands, over and over, and then fiddling with her wedding ring, as if it needed adjusting for size. 'Business was good until late last year; I used to have all of my regulars, Mr King from American Paints, Mr Goldberg the Matzoh Man – well, that's what I always used to call him, the Matzoh Man. And there was good steady family trade through the summer and fall, right past Thanksgiving.'

'What happened?' asked Charlie, setting down his coffee cup. 'They didn't build any new detours.'

Mrs Kemp looked down at her lap for a moment. When she spoke her voice sounded muffled and different. 'I don't suppose you remember, it was three or four years since you came here last, but there was a girl who used to help me in the kitchen.'

'I think I remember,' said Charlie.

'Her name was Caroline. She was my niece. My brother and his wife were killed in an auto accident in Ohio when she was seven. I'd been looking after her ever since. When my husband passed over she was all I had left.'

Mrs Kemp paused, and then she said, 'You can imagine, we were very close.'

Charlie said nothing, but waited for Mrs Kemp to continue.

'Last November 18, Caroline disappeared,' said Mrs Kemp. 'She went to New Milford to see a friend of hers, but she never arrived. Of course it was hours before I found out that she was missing. I called the police, and the police searched every place they could think of, but no trace of her was ever found. Nothing. It was just as if she had never existed, except for her clothes of course, and her personal belongings. The police said that it happens all the time, young people walking out on their parents or their guardians. They usually end up in California or some place like that, working as dancers or waitresses or – well, you know what kind of a world we live in these days, Mr McLean.'

'Call me Charlie,' said Charlie.

Mrs Kemp nodded, although Charlie wasn't altogether sure if she had heard him or not. She said distractedly, 'I suppose what happened to the boarding house after that was my fault, really. Every salesman who came here, I used to give him a printed sheet with Caroline's picture on it, and ask him to keep a look out for her wherever he went. I suppose I used to carry on about her too much for most people's comfort. The regulars stopped calling by, and then the casual trade fell off. I wanted to keep the business going, I did my best, but I wanted to find

Caroline even more, and that kind of affected everything I did.'

'It seems to me that a lot of young people have gone missing from Allen's Corners,' Charlie remarked.

'The sheriff said that it happens a lot in backwater places like this. The kids get bored, that's what he said, but they know that their parents won't let them go, not voluntarily. So they run away, and that's the last that anybody ever sees of them. Not just children of Caroline's age, neither. Some of them are not much more than nine or ten years old. Well, you've seen their pictures on the Knudsen's milk cartons. I used to look at them and wonder how any parent could possibly let their child disappear like that. But it happened to me, too, and all I can tell you about it is that it hurts a good deal, and that you can never get over it.'

They talked for a while about Caroline. Mrs Kemp opened up her rolltop bureau and produced a handful of the printed pictures that she had distributed to her guests. Charlie and Martin dutifully examined them. They showed a pretty fair-haired girl with a snub nose and a wide smile. She could have been a cheerleader or a roller-skating waitress at a drive-in soda fountain. Underneath the picture, a short appeal said, 'MISSING, Caroline Heyward, 17 years old. Last seen Allen's Corners, CT,

11/18 last year. 5′ 4 1/2″ tall, slim build. Wearing brown-and-white wool coat, brown wool hat. $500 reward for information.'

'Pretty girl,' said Charlie, offering the flysheet back.

'Keep it,' Mrs Kemp told him. 'You never know, the way you restaurant inspectors travel around, one day you might just find her.'

Charlie folded up the flysheet and tucked it into his wallet. 'Would it be too much to ask you to put us up for the night?'

'Of course not,' said Mrs Kemp. 'I'd be glad to. I can give you the big room right at the back, that's the room I always used to give to honeymooners. Well – they weren't all honeymooners. "Romantic couples", that's what I used to call them.'

'I tried to get to eat at that French place,' said Charlie.

Mrs Kemp lifted her head. In the lamplight, the dark circles under her eyes looked like bruises. 'What French place?' she inquired sharply. So sharply that she must have known exactly what he was talking about.

'Le Reposoir, up on Quassapaug,' said Charlie. 'They seem to have quite a reputation around here.'

'They're not the kind of people you'd choose to have as neighbours, if you had a choice,' Mrs Kemp replied.

'Oh?' said Charlie.

'They keep themselves to themselves, that's all. They live here, but you couldn't say they're part of the local community. They seem to do whatever they like, though. They built a whole new wing on that house of theirs, up on Quassapaug, and I never heard a whisper about zoning laws. I talked to Mr Haxalt about it – Mr Haxalt's the chairman of our community association –'

'Yes,' Charlie told her. 'I had the pleasure of meeting Mr Haxalt this afternoon. I parked my car in his sacred parking place.'

'Well, then, you'll know what he's like,' said Mrs Kemp. 'He's an expert at giving folks the brush-off. And that's what he did when I tried to talk to him about Le Reposoir. "Don't you worry, Mrs Kemp, those people are here to bring more trade into Allen's Corners." But did they bring in more trade? They certainly didn't. I can tell you – lots of people come and go, up on Quassapaug Road – lots of wealthy people, too, in limousines – but none of them stop at Allen's Corners, and even if they did, you can't imagine that they'd be the kind of people to buy cream or corn-dollies or home-cured bacon. Let me tell you, Mr McLean –'

'Charlie, please.'

'–well, let me tell you, Charlie, that place is a curse on Allen's Corners. It takes everything and gives nothing. There's people around here who won't go near it for money in the bank. And don't ask me why, because I don't know. But it has the feeling about it. Allen's Corners has never been the same since that place opened, and until it closes down it never will. This used to be a happy town, but you look at it now. Sad and lost and anxious, that's what it is. Maybe Le Reposoir isn't to blame. Who can say? It could be the way that life is going everywhere, the recession and all. But I believe that place is a curse on Allen's Corners, and that the sun won't shine here until it's gone.'

Martin said, 'It's only a restaurant.'

Charlie turned around in his chair and looked at him. Martin repeated, 'It's only a restaurant, that's all.'

'Oh, yes,' said Charlie. 'And since when have you been the expert?'

Martin pouted, but didn't answer. Mrs Kemp glanced from Charlie to Martin and smiled, as if she were trying to make peace between them.

Charlie said, with a frankness that was unprecedented for him, 'Martin and I haven't seen too much of each other—well, not for years. His mother and I were divorced. You have to make allowances on both sides I guess.'

Martin looked at his father with an expression that was a mixture of embarrassment and respect. *I wish you hadn't said that, Dad, and anyway, who was it who never came home?* But he held his tongue. There are some feelings which are mutually understood between father and son, but which are better left unspoken.

'You must know Mr Musette,' Charlie said to Mrs Kemp.

'I've seen him, yes, but no more than twice.'

'And?'

'He's charming. Very foreign, of course. He likes to be called *Monsieur* Musette. A lot of the ladies around here think he's *tray charmong.* Only from a distance, of course. He keeps himself to himself. And then of course there's Mrs Musette – Madame Musette – although I've never seen her.'

Charlie waved away the offer of another Jubilee. 'Tell me something,' he asked Mrs Kemp. 'What is it about Le Reposoir that can affect a whole community?'

Mrs Kemp said, 'What can I tell you? Maybe it's nothing at all. Your son's quite right. It's only a restaurant. Why should anybody be frightened of a restaurant?'

The atmosphere in the parlour was very strange. Charlie felt as if he had been asked to complete a sentence to which there was no logical conclusion – such as, 'I like the shifting of the tides because...' He couldn't rid himself of the suspicion that Martin had been talking to somebody back in the parking lot of the Iron Kettle, no matter how much Martin denied it, and he also felt that his conversation with this unknown somebody had been connected with Le Reposoir. After all, where had Martin found that visiting card from Le Reposoir? And why had he denied seeing that pale-faced child in the garden?

Mrs Kemp showed them up to their room. It was stuffy, high-ceilinged, with maps of damp disfiguring the plaster above their heads. The walls had been papered with huge green flowers that were supposed to be roses but looked more like efflorescing mould. In one corner loomed a gigantic wardrobe, with blistered veneer and mottled mirrors. The bed was enormous, an aircraft carrier of a bed, built of green-painted iron with brass decorations in the shape of seashells. Martin tried to bounce on it, and complained, 'Jesus, this mattress is as hard as a rock.'

'Hard beds are good for your posture,' said Charlie. 'And don't profane.'

'Do we really have to stay here?'

'Maybe you can answer that,' Charlie replied, taking off his coat and hanging it up inside the cavernous depths of the wardrobe. There were five wire hangers in there, and a dried up clove and orange pomander that looked like a shrunken head.

'I don't know what you mean,' said Martin. He went over to the opposite side of the room and stuck his head inside the carved wooden fireplace. 'Halloo–halloo–any skeletons up there?'

Charlie watched him in the wardrobe mirror. 'You still haven't told me the truth about what happened at the Iron Kettle.' He tried not to sound too petulant.

'Dad,' said Martin. '*Nothing* happened.'

Martin turned away from the fireplace, and as he did so Charlie saw in the mirror that his face had peculiarly altered. It seemed to have stretched out, so that it was broad and distorted, and his eyes had the same blind look as the eyes of a dead fox he had once found lying by the road. Charlie jerked in shock, and turned around, but Martin appeared quite normal when he confronted him face-to-face. He looked back at the mirror. It must have been the mottling, and the dirt. He remembered how old he had looked himself, in the men's room mirror at the Iron Kettle.

'Do you want to go down to the car and get the bag?' Charlie asked Martin.

Martin said, 'Okay,' but on the way out of the door he hesitated. 'Do you *really* not believe me?' he asked.

Charlie said, 'I believe you.'

'You're not just saying that to stop us from having an argument?'

Charlie unfastened his cufflinks. 'Since when did boys talk to their fathers like that?'

'You said we were supposed to be friends.'

'Sure,' said Charlie, and felt a wave of guilt. He went over to Martin, and laid his hand on his shoulder, and said, 'I've been travelling around on my own for too darn long, that's my trouble. Too much talking to myself in hotel mirrors. I guess it's made me a little nutty.'

'You can believe me,' Martin told him; although Charlie detected a strange hoarseness in his voice that didn't sound like Martin at all. 'You can believe me.' And it wasn't so much of an affirmation as a command. It wasn't really, *You can believe me.* It was more like, *You must believe me.*

He sat on the side of the bed and waited for Martin to return with the suitcase. He thought about a quiet foggy afternoon in Milwaukee, parking his car and walking up the concrete pathway to a small suburban duplex. Six or seven children had been playing ball at the end of the street, and their cries had sounded just like the cries of seagulls. He remembered pushing the bell, and then the front door opening. And there she was, her brown hair tangled, staring at him in complete surprise. '*You came,*' she had whispered. 'I never thought you would.'

Martin returned with their zip-up overnight bag. He laid it down on the bed, and said to Charlie, 'Are you okay? You look kind of logie.'

'I'm okay. Tired, I guess, like you.'

'I'm not tired.'

'Well, then, let's freshen ourselves up, and get on down to Billy's Beer & Bite.'

Martin looked around. 'There's no television here. What are we going to do all evening?'

'You know how to play cards, don't you? Let's see how much of your allowance I can win back.'

Martin said, 'Mega-thrill. If you really want it back that bad, I'll give it to you.' Charlie couldn't even smile. He wondered what he was going to say to the boy next – let alone how he was going to find something to talk about for ten more days. His tiredness was mostly caused by the strain of keeping up a long-running conversation. He wanted with all his heart to develop an easy father-and-son relationship with Martin, but right now he would have given a month's salary to be alone.

They ate in a corner booth at Billy's. A jukebox played 'Joleen' and 'Blanket on the Ground' and 'DIVORCE' and what with the rough wooden decor and the loud laughter and the red fluorescent lights they could have been in Amarillo, TX, instead of Allen's Corners, CT. Martin seemed to have rediscovered his appetite, and wolfed down a king-sized cheeseburger with mammoth fries. Charlie restricted himself to a New York steak sandwich with onion rings. Afterwards, they walked around the windy deserted green for a while, with their hands in their pockets, not talking, and then went back to Mrs Kemp's to play cards.

Before he went to bed, Charlie found Walter Haxalt's telephone number in the local directory, and called him up from the phone in Mrs Kemp's parlour. The phone rang and rang but there was no reply.

Mrs Kemp was watching him through the partly open doorway. 'Do you know anybody who goes to Le Reposoir to eat?' Charlie asked her, as he waited for somebody at Walter Haxalt's number to pick up.

Mrs Kemp shook her head. 'You'd be better off keeping clear,' she advised him. 'I don't know what's so bad about that place, but if I were you I wouldn't want to find out.'

4

It was well past two o'clock in the morning when Charlie awoke. For a moment he had that terrible vertiginous feeling of not knowing where he was, or what city he was in. But after years of waking up unexpectedly in unfamiliar rooms, he had developed a trick of closing his eyes again and logically analysing where he must be.

Usually, his sense of smell and his sense of touch were enough for him to be able to re-orient himself. Howard Johnson's all smelled like Howard Johnson's and TraveLodge beds all felt the same. This was somewhere private. This was somewhere old. *This,* he thought, opening his eyes again, *is Mrs Kemp's boarding house in Allen's Corners, CT.*

The bedroom was intensely dark. Charlie felt as if black felt pads were being pressed against his eyes. Either the moon had not yet risen, or it was obscured by thunderclouds. The room was also very quiet, except for the intermittent blowing of the wind down the chimney, and the soft ticking of Charlie's watch on the bedside table.

Charlie eased himself up into a sitting position. Gradually, he found that he could make out the slightly lighter squares of the windowpanes, and the gleam of reflected street light on one of the brass knobs at the end of the bed, but that was about all. He strained his ears to hear Martin breathing next to him, but from the other side of the bed there was no sound at all.

'*Martin?*' he whispered. There was no reply, but he didn't call again. He didn't want to wake Martin up for no reason at all. He reached out his hand to make sure that his son was well covered by the thin patchwork quilt, and it was then that he realized that Martin was silent because Martin wasn't there.

He fumbled around in the darkness of the top-heavy bedside lamp, almost knocking it over. He switched it on and it lit up the room as starkly as a publicity photograph for a 1950s detective movie. Martin's side of the quilt was neatly folded back, as if he had left the bed quietly and deliberately, and Martin's bathrobe had disappeared from the back of the chair. Charlie said, '*Shit,*' and swung himself out of bed. His own bathrobe was lying on the floor. He tugged it on, raked his fingers through his hair, and opened the bedroom door. Outside, the house was silent. Engraved portraits stared at him incuriously from the brown-wallpapered landing. There was a smell of dust and sticky polish and faded lavender; the sort of smell that dreams would have, if dreams were to die.

'*Martin?* His voice didn't even echo. The darkness muffled it like a blanket. 'Martin – are you there?'

Charlie cursed everything he could think of, and in particular he cursed himself for having thought that it would be a good idea to bring Martin along with him on his tour of New England. Goddamnit, the boy was nothing but confusion and trouble. Charlie called, '*Martin?* again, not too loudly in case he disturbed Mrs Kemp, but a whole minute passed and there was still no answer, and so he ventured out on to the landing and peered down into the stairwell.

He made his way downstairs, treading as softly as he could. The house all around him seemed to hold its breath. He could feel the string backing of the worn-out stair carpet under his bare feet. When he reached the hallway, he paused, and listened, but there was nothing to be heard. He was tempted to go back to bed again. After all–where could Martin have possibly gone? Out for a walk, that was all, because he'd eaten too much, and couldn't sleep. Out for a walk, because he wanted to think about his parents, and his fractured upbringing, and how much he distrusted his father. Charlie could hardly blame him.

But then he heard a door softly juddering, as if it hadn't been closed properly and the wind was shaking the latch. He paused, and listened, and the juddering continued. For the first time in a very long time, for no earthly reason that he could think of, he was alarmed–so alarmed that he groped around the shadows of the hallway searching for something that he could use as a weapon. An umbrella, maybe; or a doorstop. All he could find, however, was a very lightweight walking stick. He swung it in his hand so that it whistled through the air. Then he made his way along the hallway to the kitchen door.

'Martin? Are you there?' His voice sounded unfamiliar, and he turned quickly around to make sure that there was nobody standing close behind him. For one second he felt the thrill of real fright. A shadow was standing close to the front door, its huddled shape limned by the blood-red light that gleamed through the stained-glass panes. But it was only an overcoat that Mrs Kemp had left hanging on the hallstand. Coats and blankets and dressing gowns, thought Charlie. Innocent garments by day, threatening hunchbacks by night. He couldn't count the number of times he had woken up in some strange hotel bedroom to stare fascinated and frightened at his own coat, crouched over the back of a chair.

He turned the handle of the kitchen door. It grated open, grit dragging against floor tiles. The kitchen smelled of burned fat and sour vegetables. There was an old-fashioned cooking range, and a white-topped table. In the corner stood a coffee grinder and an old rotary knife-sharpening machine, like Puritan instruments of torture. Blue-patterned plates were stacked on the hatch. Charlie stayed in the half-open doorway for a moment, holding his breath, but when he heard nothing he turned away, lowering his walking stick. *Martin is fifteen years old right? He isn't a child any more. And just because you happened to miss his childhood, that doesn't give you any kind of right to treat him like a kid. If he wants to take a hike in the middle of the night, that's up to him.*

Charlie wasn't convinced by any of his reasoning, but he retreated slowly along the hallway, tapping the tip of his walking stick gently against the walls, like a man who had recently lost his sight. He was just about to return it to the cast-iron umbrella stand, however, when he thought he heard somebody whispering. He froze, his head lifted, trying to catch the faint sibilant sounds of conversation.

Maybe it's the wind, thought Charlie. But he knew that it wasn't. No wind ever argued, the way that this voice was arguing. No wind ever begged. Somebody was right outside the kitchen door, in Mrs Kemp's back yard; and that somebody was talking, quickly and urgently, pleading, the way that a lover pleads, or a man asks for money—one well-rehearsed argument after another.

Raising the walking stick, he retraced his steps along the corridor. The clouds had suddenly moved away from the moon, and the kitchen was illuminated in cold, luminous blue, knives and grinders and mincers gleaming, like some spectral abattoir. There were two panes of Flemish glass in the kitchen door, and through their watery distortion Charlie could make out the shadows of two people, earnestly engaged in conversation. A thin, boyish figure, which must have been Martin, and another smaller figure, which must have been wearing a hat or a hood, because it was strangely rhomboidal in shape, like an old-fashioned coal scuttle.

Charlie tiptoed close to the door and listened. The whispering voice went on and on, as endless and insistent as water running over a weir; yet peculiarly seductive, too, in a way that Charlie found it very hard to understand. It wasn't erotic, yet it gave him a thrill that was almost entirely physical. It was a voice that knew the desires of the flesh, and pandered to them. It was frightening, but at the same time irresistibly alluring.

You shall find happiness; you shall find joy. You shall find friends and lovers. You shall find the most complete fulfilment known to man, and the name of that fulfilment is written where nobody can find it but you.

Charlie waited for almost a minute. Then he reached out and clasped the cold brass doorknob. He wasn't sure if he could be seen from the yard or not. It depended on the angle of the moonlight. He took a breath, and then tugged the door open – at the very instant a huge grey cloud rolled over the moon and obscured it completely.

He saw something. He wasn't quite sure what it was. A face, or a mirror reflecting his own face. A white transfixed face, with eyes that glittered at him. A blue-white tongue lolling between blue-white lips. Then a white blur of fabric, a hood tugged hurriedly over, and a small crooked figure crabhopping away; then darkness. No sound, no cry, no noise at all. Only the breeze blowing boisterously over the yard, and the irritating banging of an upstairs shutter. *Squeeak-shudder-clop!*

Martin was standing in his dressing gown, his thin-wristed hands down by his sides, his face concealed by shadow. Charlie looked back down the yard, in the direction the hunched-up creature had fled, and said quietly, 'You want to tell me what's going on here?'

Martin said nothing. Charlie took two or three steps into the yard, but it was too dark for him to see very much. The moon remained hidden behind the clouds. The washing line sang a low vibrant tenor. At last Charlie turned back to Martin and said, 'Who was that? Are you going to tell me who that was?'

'It wasn't anybody.'

'Don't bullshit me!' Charlie yelled at him. 'I saw him and I heard him! A little guy – no more than four feet tall!'

'I was here on my own,' said Martin. His voice was flat and expressionless.

'Martin, don't try to kid me, I saw him for myself. It was the same boy who was looking into the window at the Iron Kettle, wasn't it? It was the same boy you were talking to in the parking lot. You didn't really think I believed that guitar stuff, did you? I saw him again this afternoon, on the green, and now here he is, in the middle of the night, at Mrs Kemp's.'

Martin lowered his head. The very faintest touch of moonlight illuminated the parting in his hair.

'Martin,' said Charlie. 'I'm your father. You *have* to tell me. It's my duty to look after you, whether I like it or not. Whether *you* like it or not.'

'You don't have to look after me,' said Martin.

'I'm your father.'

Martin raised his head. Charlie couldn't make out his face at all. 'You're a man who happened to fuck my mother, that's all,' Martin snapped at him. Then he wrenched open the kitchen door and ran inside. He left the door ajar, and Charlie standing in the dark back yard, feeling more isolated than ever before. Even in the Criterion Hotel in Omaha, Nebraska, in the middle of winter, he hadn't felt as isolated as this. He began to feel that real life was a little more than he could manage.

He turned and looked up at the moon, masking itself behind the clouds. He felt there was something he ought to do, some magic ritual he ought to perform to ward off malevolence until morning, but he couldn't think of anything else to do except to cross his two index fingers in the sign of the crucifix and hold them up to the sky. 'God, protect me,' he said, although he wasn't sure what good that would do, or even if he meant it.

He went back inside, locking the kitchen door behind him. He returned the walking stick to the umbrella stand. The house was silent. He climbed the stairs feeling very tired. One of the reasons he had been able to survive his job for so long was because he had always gone to bed early, with two large glasses of water to drink if he happened to wake up, and he had always made sure that he stayed in bed for a full eight hours.

Martin had returned to bed, and was lying with his back turned to the door. Charlie climbed between the sheets, and lay there for a long time listening to Martin breathe. He knew he wasn't asleep, but he was waiting for him to say something.

After a while, he felt Martin gently shaking. He realized with intense pain and discomfort that he was crying.

'Martin?' He laid his hand on the boy's shoulder. 'Martin, for Christ's sake, if you can tell anybody what this is all about, you can tell me.'

'I can't tell anybody,' Martin sobbed.

Charlie was silent for a very long time. The worst part of it was not having the experience to be able to think of the right thing to say. Marjorie would know; Marjorie was unfailingly good with children. Marjorie had been unfailingly good with him, too, but not good enough to know what he really wanted out of life.

Martin wiped his eyes on the corner of the pillow slip and then lay there silently, not sleeping, but perfectly still.

Charlie said, 'I don't know what any of this means.'

'It doesn't mean anything.'

'But I don't see why you have to lie to me, Martin. I don't see why you have to pretend that there was nobody there when there very obviously was.'

'There was nobody there, Dad.'

For a split second, Charlie felt angry enough to smack Martin's head. But he made a deliberate effort to turn away, and stare fiercely at the bedside table, and let his sudden burst of temper dissipate into the darkness like a tipped-over basketful of small black snakes.

'We're going to have to talk this over tomorrow,' he said.

'Okay,' Martin said, as if he didn't have any intention of discussing it again.

There was another long pause, and then Charlie said, 'Was he a dwarf, or what?'

Martin didn't reply. His breathing was regular and even. Charlie leaned over him and saw that he was asleep–or, at least, that he was pretending to be asleep. He lay back on his pillow and looked up at the ceiling and wondered what the hell he was going to do now. There were no handbooks for the estranged fathers of awkward and secretive teenage sons. There was no advisory service which could tell you what to do if your offspring started making mysterious trysts with white-hooded midgets in the middle of the night. It would have been funny if it hadn't been so distressing; and if Martin hadn't plainly been so upset.

The night went by as slowly as the great black wheel of a juggernaut. Every time Charlie checked his watch, it seemed as if the hands had hardly moved since the last time he had looked. He couldn't sleep. He couldn't even remember what it was he normally did to get himself to sleep. He thought about Marjorie, he thought about Martin. He thought about Milwaukee and the pain that he had suffered there. He half dozed for a while, and dreamed that he was eating dinner in a strange high-ceilinged restaurant with a long white napkin tucked into his collar. The waiters were all hooded, like monks, and they came and went in silence, carrying plates and wheeling chafing dishes. There was no menu, you had to eat whatever the monk-waiters set in front of you. The other diners were smooth-faced and expressionless. There was no food in front of them, and yet they waited at their tables with consummate patience, as if their meals would be worth waiting for even if they took several hours to be served. The men were dressed in evening wear – white ties and stiff collars and tail coats. The women wore extravagant wide-brimmed hats with wax fruit and flowers and ostrich plumes. They also wore glittering diamond necklaces and earrings that sparkled like Christmas trees, but apart from that most of them were nude. Looking around the restaurant Charlie saw bare breasts everywhere, some with nipples that had been rouged, others which had been pierced and decorated with golden rings. He saw a redheaded woman with a feathery hat talking to the maitre d', smiling archly as she did so. Her thighs were wide apart on her satin dining chair, and a small hairless dog was lapping with its tongue at her bushy, russet vulva. He turned. A monk-waiter had brought his meal, concealed beneath a shiny dish cover. The monk-waiter's face was as black as the inside of a clothes closet. 'Your dinner, sir,' he whispered seductively, and raised the dish cover with a flourish.

Charlie looked down at his plate and screamed.

The plate was brimming with thin, greyish soup, in which Martin's face was floating, staring up at him in silent desperation.

He opened his eyes. He was twisting the quilt in both hands, and he was smothered in sweat. He also had a taut, painful erection.

He thought for a moment that he had screamed out loud, but the night seemed so silent and undisturbed, and Martin was still breathing steadily and peacefully, and he realized then that he must have screamed only in his dream. He checked his watch. A minute and a half had passed since the last time he had looked.

He thought for a while about Martin's face staring up at him out of the plate. Then he thought about the naked women in his dream restaurant. There was no question about it, his daytime problems were catching up with him while he slept. The problems of food, fatherhood, and sexual frustration. He lay there feeling very middle aged and inadequate and tired, for hour after hour. He didn't know when he fell asleep; but shortly afterwards Martin opened his eyes and turned and looked at him, and then slid quietly out of bed and went to the window.

Martin stood by the window for almost a half-hour, while the sky gradually grew paler over the treeline towards Black Rock and Thomaston. In the yard below him, the small hooded figure stood, equally silent, its cloak ruffled by the thin, early-morning wind, its eyes fixed steadily on Martin, waiting with a patience that had been shared by the diners in Charlie's dream.

5

Walter Haxalt was smooth, patronizing, and impatient. He sat behind his leather-topped reproduction desk, his hands steepled, gently tapping his fingertips together as if he were counting the valuable seconds that Charlie was wasting, second by second, dollar by dollar.

The morning sun struck through the window of his office and illuminated, as if it were a sign from God, a gold presentation clock that stood on the bookshelf just behind him. There was a motto engraved on the clock, 'Time Driveth Onward Fast'. Strangely, Charlie could remember the verse from which that motto had been taken. It ended, 'all things are taken from us, and become/Portions and parcels of the dreadful Past'.

Walter Haxalt said, 'I can't help you, I'm afraid. My only contract with M. Musette is purely professional. He lives here and so he banks here, and that's as far as it goes.'

Charlie glanced towards the window. Martin was waiting for him outside, in the car. 'I wasn't asking for anything more than an introduction.'

'Well, I wish I could help,' said Walter Haxalt, making it quite plain by his disinterested tone of voice that he didn't wish anything of the kind. 'But I can't abuse a customer's personal relationship with the bank for any reason at all, even if that reason happened to be meaningful and advantageous.'

'Have you ever eaten at Le Reposoir?' asked Charlie.

Walter Haxalt kept on tapping his fingers, but didn't answer directly. 'I guess you'll be leaving us now,' he said. 'Travelling ever onward, in your search for culinary perfection.'

Charlie stared at him. Walter Haxalt became suddenly self-conscious about the way that Charlie was looking at him, and shifted in his studded leather chair. 'How did you find out what I do for a living?' Charlie asked.

'You told me,' said Walter Haxalt, uncomfortably.

'I never tell anybody.'

'Well, to tell you the truth, I had Clive check it out for me. He ran your licence through the computer.'

'Clive? That deputy who told me to move my car yesterday?'

Walter Haxalt nodded. 'This is a small town, it's vulnerable. We always have to take certain elementary precautions when strangers come around.'

'Did you take any elementary precautions when M. Musette set up shop?'

Walter Haxalt said, 'I can't discuss M. Musette with you, Mr McLean. If you want to know anything at all about M. Musette, I suggest you ask him yourself.'

Charlie eased himself out of his chair. 'All right,' he said. 'What can I say but thanks for nothing?'

Walter Haxalt focused on Charlie narrowly. 'We do try to be friendly, here in Allen's Corners. I want you to know that.'

'I think I've been able to make my own assessment, thank you,' Charlie replied.

'In that case, I hope you won't judge us too harshly.'

Charlie opened the office door. 'It's not my job to judge *you,* Mr Haxalt. Only your hotel and refreshment facilities. Right now, I'd say that Allen's Corners deserves the bent spoon award for service, the broken spring award for comfort, and the golden barbed wire award for hospitality.'

Walter Haxalt stood up. 'I hope you're not going to try to publish anything like that. If you do, I'm going to have to speak to your employers.'

Charlie said, 'My employers take a very dim view of bribes and threats, Mr Haxalt. Come to mention it, so do I.'

He walked out of the bank into the sharp fall sunshine. Martin was lounging back in the front seat of the car reading *Power Man and Iron Fist.* Charlie climbed in beside him and started the engine. 'Glad to see you're reading something improving.'

Martin said, 'Did he fix it up for you?'

'No. It seems to me that Allen's Corners is low on helpfulness, apart from being a poor place to get a good steak. I'm going to try the direct approach.'

'What does that mean?'

Charlie steered away from the green and out toward the Quassapaug Road. 'That means a direct frontal assault on Le Reposoir, with all guns blazing.'

They drove for four or five minutes in silence. Then Martin said, 'Dad?'

'Uh-huh?'

'We don't have to do this, Dad. I mean, it isn't totally necessary, is it?'

Charlie glanced at him. 'What do you mean, it isn't totally necessary?'

'I mean, if it's private, nobody who reads MARIA is going to be able to eat there anyway.'

Charlie nodded. 'You're right. You're absolutely right. But the argument against that is that *I* want to eat there.'

Martin said nothing more to dissuade him; but all the same Charlie began to feel that he was distinctly worried about their driving up to Le Reposoir and forcing their way into La Société Gastronomique without being invited. But the more reluctant Martin showed himself to be, the more determined Charlie became. Perhaps he was punishing Martin in a way, for lying to him last night. Perhaps he was just being stubborn and bloody-minded, like he always was.

They drew up outside the entrance to Le Reposoir and, to Charlie's surprise, the wrought iron gates were open. He hesitated for a moment, craning his head around to see if there were any security guards or parking valets around, but there was nobody there at all, neither to greet them nor to prevent them from driving inside. Charlie looked down the wide, shingled driveway, which curved in between two dense banks of maculata bushes. The house itself was out of sight, although Charlie thought he could glimpse rows of black chimneys through the bright yellow maculata leaves.

'Well,' he remarked. 'Not so reclusive after all.'

'We're not going in?' asked Martin.

'The gates are open, why not?'

'But it's private!'

'Since when have you been concerned about private?'

'Dad, we can't just drive straight in. You heard what that deputy said about trespassers.'

'We're not trespassers. We're potential customers.'

Charlie didn't really feel quite so confident about venturing into the grounds of Le Reposoir, but he was determined to show Martin that he was in complete control of everything he did, and that he was scared of nobody and nothing. If he backed out now, Martin would regard him for the rest of their vacation together as a flake and a wimp; and if that happened their relationship would be ruined for ever. He didn't mind if Martin thought he was a flake; but he had to be a *brave* flake; like Murdoch in *The A-Team.*

Charlie eased his foot off the brake and the Oldsmobile rolled forward between the gates and down the curving drive. The car windows were open, so that they could hear the heavy crunching of shingle beneath the tyres. The morning which had started sunny was now dull. The eastern sky behind them was as black as Bibles. They could hear ovenbirds and prothonotary warblers singing in the woods, but apart from that the air was curiously still, as if their intrusion into the grounds of Le Reposoir had been noticed by nature at large, and a general breath was being held until they were discovered.

They turned a bend in the driveway and Martin unexpectedly covered his face with his hands.

'What's the matter?' Charlie asked him. 'Martin? What's wrong?'

Martin turned his head away, and pushed at Charlie with his left hand, like a linebacker warding off a tackle. At the same time, the house in which Le Reposoir had been established rose up in front of them, sudden and dark and almost wickedly elaborate. It was built in the high Gothic style, the kind of house that Edward Gorey drew for *The Dwindling Party* or *The West Wing,* with spires and turrets and twisted columns, and a veil of long-dead wisteria over the porch. Charlie slowed the car as he passed between two old and stooping cedar trees, and drew up at last on a circular shingled turning space, with weeds growing up through the stones. He pushed on the parking brake and killed the engine, and then almost immediately he stepped out of the car and stood leaning on the open door, his eyes narrowed against the light wind, looking around like a man who has discovered an uncharted valley, or a garden which has been secretly neglected for fifty years.

'Now this is what I *call* a restaurant,' he said, although he was quite aware that Martin was making a determined effort not to listen to him. He stepped away from the car and walked a few yards out across the shingle, the soles of his brogues crunching in the fall silence. 'What a locale! It merits one star for locale alone. Did you ever see a locale like this?'

The house was enormous, yet for all its blackness and all of its size, it seemed to float suspended in the dark air, like a mirage, or a grotesquely over-decorated man of war. There was a central entrance, reached by wide stone steps, and flanked on either side by eight gothic pillars, each of them different in design with spirals and diamonds and hand-carved ropes. Between the pillars stood an arched mahogany door, with brass handles and engraved glass panels, all highly polished. On either side of the central entrance, the house stretched over 300 feet to the east and 300 feet to the west, with tier upon tier of glittering windows. A weather vane in the shape of a medieval dragon creaked and whirred to itself on the highest spire.

There was an odd smell on the wind, like burning fennel.

'You know something?' said Charlie, leaning back into the open automobile, 'I never even knew this place existed. Can you believe it? I'm supposed to be one of the top restaurant inspectors in the continental United States. I got an award, did I ever tell you that? So how did I get to miss a place like this?'

'Dad,' Martin begged him. His voice was odd and edgy. 'I don't want to stay here. I want to go on to Hartford.'

Charlie had heard the tone in Martin's voice but he feigned a brash, tourist enthusiasm.

'You don't want to see what goes on here? Look at this place? It's probably unique. Some of the really old colonial houses were built on designs the Pilgrims brought over from England. I'll bet you anything the place is haunted by Nathan Hale's great-grandmother.'

Martin begged, 'Dad, please.'

'What's it to you?' Charlie demanded. He felt a little cruel now; but he felt that Martin had been equally uncaring about him, refusing to talk about the small figure he had met in Mrs Kemp's back yard, and refusing to tell the truth about the visiting card he claimed he had found.

'Dad, I just don't like it here. I want to go.'

'Come on, Martin, there's nothing to get worked up about. It's a restaurant. And let me tell you something about people who run restaurants – even the worst of them have some sensitivity. You have to have some sensitivity, whether you're running an à la carte or a greasy spoon. You're dealing with people's stomachs, and there isn't anything more sensitive than that.'

At that moment, quite unexpectedly, a deep, cultured voice said, 'You're right, my friend. The alimentary canal is the river of human life.'

Charlie involuntarily jerked in surprise. He turned around to find a tall man standing only five or six feet away from him. The surprise was that the man could have approached so close without making any noise at all, especially over a shingled driveway. And the man wasn't just tall; he was unnervingly tall, at least six feet three, and he had the predatory appearance of a well-groomed raven. His black hair was slashed straight back from his hairline. His forehead was narrow and white. Beneath two thinly curved eyebrows his eyes looked like two shining silver ball bearings, and were equally expressionless. His nose was thin and hooked, although there was an angular flare to his nostrils. He sported a thin, black, clipped moustache. By his clothes, Charlie could tell that he was a man of taste, and a European. He wore a dark blue pinstripe suit in the Armani style, although obviously more expensive than Armani, a pure silk paisley-patterned necktie, and gleaming handmade shoes.

His most arresting characteristic, however, was not what he wore, but his bearing. Like the elaborate house behind him, he seemed almost to float a fraction of an inch above the ground. It was something that Charlie found impossible to analyse, and it was highly disturbing, as if the man were not quite real.

The man held out his hand and Charlie shook it. The fingers were very cool and limp, like wilted celery.

'That's your son?' he asked, nodding towards Martin.

'Martin,' said Charlie. 'And you must be M. Musette.'

'Well, well,' the man smiled. 'My reputation has reached even the ears of MARIA.'

Charlie looked at him suspiciously. 'You know who I am?'

'I am in the gastronomic business, Mr McLean. It is my business to know who you are. Similarly, I know the inspectors from *Michelin* and *Relais & Chateaux*. Forewarned, you see, is forearmed.'

'Haxalt told you,' said Charlie.

'You are being unfair on Mr Haxalt,' M. Musette replied. 'Mr Haxalt would never betray anybody's trust. Even yours.'

Charlie put his hands on his hips and surveyed the black Gothic building. 'The main reason I came was to see whether your restaurant was worth putting into the guide.'

'Le Reposoir?' asked M. Musette, with obvious amusement. 'I fear not, Mr McLean. This is hardly a roadside hamburger stand. It is a private dining association, open only to subscribing members. It would be very unfair to your readers if you were to suggest that they could obtain a casual meal here as they wandered through Connecticut looking at the autumn leaves. Or, selling their patent cleansers.' That last remark was an undisguised dig at MARIA's strong associations with travelling salesmen.

'Men who sell patent cleansers provide an honest service,' Charlie replied, more sharply than he had meant to. 'Just like most restaurateurs.'

'I'm afraid that does not include me,' said M. Musette. 'I am hardly what you could call a restaurateur. I am more of a social arbiter than a chef.'

At that moment, the mahogany doors opened, their windows reflecting the dull silvery sky, and a young woman appeared, pale-faced, in a black ankle-length cape. M. Musette turned, and gave her a wave which meant that he wouldn't be long, and that he would be with her in just a moment.

'Madame Musette?' asked Charlie.

'It is probably time for you to leave,' said M. Musette, affably but adamantly.

'There isn't any chance of eating here, then?' asked Charlie.

'I regret not. We are a very exclusive society, and I am afraid that the presence of a restaurant inspector would not be regarded by our membership with any particular warmth.'

The young woman who had been standing on the steps came closer, stepping on to the shingle driveway and watching Charlie with solemnity. She was almost alarmingly beautiful, with a fine oval face coloured by only the slightest tinge of blusher, soulful blue eyes, and very short gamine-style hair, a blonde bleached even blonder. She remained completely covered by her cape, and Charlie had the unsettling fantasy that, underneath it, she was naked, except for black silk stockings and stiletto shoes.

'Aren't you going to introduce us?' asked Charlie.

M. Musette looked at Charlie in a way which Charlie had never been looked at before. His eyes betrayed not malice but a total lack of interest in Charlie as a human being; as if he were nothing more than one of twenty thousand blurred faces in a baseball stadium crowd. 'You should not come here again without a prior appointment,' he said, and this time his tone was completely dismissive. 'Although it might appear that you can drive into the grounds unobserved, we have very attentive security services.'

Charlie looked around the grounds of Le Reposoir one last time, and then shrugged. 'All right,' he said. 'Have it your way. I must tell you, though, I could have done with a top quality French meal. This leg of the trip is always a desert, gastronomically speaking.'

'I am sure you will be able to find somewhere to satisfy your appetite,' said M. Musette. There was lightning flickering on the horizon, and a few heavy drops of rain fell on to the shingle and the roof of Charlie's car. He waited for one moment more, and then climbed back into the driver's seat, stretching over to fasten his seatbelt. M. Musette came up and closed the door for him.

'I'm sorry for intruding,' said Charlie, although he didn't sound sorry and he didn't particularly mean to.

M. Musette said nothing, but took two or three theatrical steps back. Charlie slowly swung the car around in a wide circle, and headed back the way he had come. As he did so, he glanced in his rear-view mirror at the young woman who might have been Mme Musette. Now that the rain was falling more heavily, she reached with one hand out of the darkness of her cloak to tug a large hood over her head.

The car was moving; the rear-view mirror was joggling; the morning was dark with thunder. All the same, Charlie was convinced that what he had seen was not an illusion, and he stared at Martin in amazement and perplexity, and slowed the car down for a moment. Then he turned around in his seat to stare at Mme Musette even harder.

Martin said, 'Dad? What are you looking at?'

'That Mme Musette, the woman in the cloak.'

'What about her?'

Charlie turned back again, and steered the Oldsmobile at low speed all the way up the curving driveway between the bushes. Martin repeated, 'Dad?' but Charlie wasn't sure whether he wanted to tell what he had seen or not, particularly since Le Reposoir had seemed to upset him so much. 'It's nothing,' he remarked, although he couldn't help looking back in the rear-view mirror just one more time, before Mme Musette disappeared into the house like a shrinking shadow. What had alarmed him so much had been that hand – that hand which had emerged from the blackness of her cloak.

That hand on which there had been only one finger, a forefinger, to hook down the fabric of her hood and keep away the rain.

6

By six that evening they were lying with their feet up on their beds at the Windsor Hotel in West Hartford, watching what looked like a Venusian version of *Diffr'nt Strokes* because even the black people had green faces.

'If you had to judge racial harmony in America from nothing but what you saw on hotel televisions, you'd think we were the most integrated nation on earth,' said Charlie, sipping Miller Lite out of the can. 'The red people get on with the purple people, the orange people get on with the blue people...'

Martin didn't even smile. He had heard the same remark so many times that he scarcely heard it. It was just Dad being Dad.

They watched the end of the programme, and then Charlie swung his legs off the bed, and pushed his hand through his hair, and said, 'How about something to eat? The restaurant here isn't too bad.'

'Do I have a choice?' asked Martin. A last chink of sunlight had penetrated beneath the blinds, and gilded his eyelashes.

'Sure you have a choice. This may be work for me, but for you it's a two-week vacation.'

'Then do you mind if I stay here and watch television? I couldn't eat another meal, not right now.'

Charlie shrugged. 'It's all right by me if it's all right by you. Are you sure you won't come along just to keep me company? You don't have to eat anything.'

'Dad,' said Martin, 'we haven't been getting along too well, have we?'

Charlie straightened his narrow blue woven necktie. 'It's early days yet. We hardly even know each other. I'm the father who was never at home, and you're the kid I never came home to. We'll get along. Give it some time.'

Martin said, 'Why?'

'Why what? Why give it some time?'

Martin shook his head. 'No–why didn't you ever come home?'

'There were reasons. Well–there was one big reason and then there were lots of little reasons. It isn't too easy to explain, not at one sitting, anyway. Before you go back to your mother, though, I'll tell you exactly what happened, and exactly what it was all about. People sometimes lead lives you wouldn't even guess at, do you know what I mean? That savings bank manager, that Haxalt, for all we know he goes home at night and dresses up like Joan

Crawford. And as for that Musette dude... well, he's some kind of weird character if ever I saw one.'

'What are you trying to tell me?' Martin demanded.

Charlie looked down at Martin's young, sunlit face. God, how lucky he was! Only fifteen, and all his chances still ahead of him. Old enough to be argumentative and arrogant, but not yet old enough to understand that argument and arrogance never got anybody anywhere. He said, gently, 'What I'm trying to tell you is that I had another life, apart from the life you already know about; and that one life was always fighting against the other life.'

'And the other life won?'

Charlie said, 'You don't resent me, do you? You don't still feel bad about me?'

'I don't know,' said Martin. 'That's what I came along on this trip to find out.'

Charlie was silent. It hadn't occurred to him that Martin was vetting him just as much as he was vetting Martin. He rubbed his forehead, and turned around so that Martin could see only his back, and then he said, 'What happens if you decide that I'm not the kind of father you want?'

'Then I'll go back to Mom and that will be the end of it.'

Charlie picked up his coat off the back of the chair. The hotel room was wallpapered in a brown bamboo pattern, and there were two prints on the wall of Boston & Maine railroad locomotives of the 1880s. He had stayed in rooms like this so often before that he had almost no sense of place, only of time. 'You're sure you don't want to eat?' he asked Martin. 'You could call room service and have them send you a hamburger or a sandwich or something. They do good ribs here, as far as I recall.'

Martin said, 'It's okay. I'm not hungry.'

'Well, I'm not either,' Charlie told him. 'At least, not for the kind of food they serve up here. But, that's the way it goes. Some people work so that they can eat. I eat so that I can work.'

He gave himself a last unnecessary check in the mirror, and then he went to the door. 'You can join me any time you want to, if you change your mind. I'll be glad of your company.'

'All right, sir.'

'Will you call me Charlie, for Christ's sake? My name is Charlie.'

'Yessir,' said Martin. Then – almost without pausing – 'Have you given up on Le Reposoir? I mean, are you content to go to your grave never having eaten there even just once?'

Charlie frowned. 'What? There are millions of restaurants I'm never going to get to eat in – tens of millions. I've never eaten at La Colombe d'Or in

Houston. Why should I be worried about Le Reposoir?'

'Because it's special,' said Martin; and then, with devastatingly cold observation, 'And most of all, because they won't let you in.'

Charlie stood by the door, his hand on the chain, with the feeling in his heart that if he didn't quickly take steps to make sure that Martin became his friend, he was going to finish up by being his very worst enemy. A little unevenly, he said, 'You know what Groucho Marx told that club that refused his membership application?'

'Yes, sir. "I do not wish to belong to the kind of club that accepts people like me as members."' Martin paused, and then he said, 'You told me.'

'Okay.' Charlie nodded. 'I'll catch you later.'

He walked along the red-carpeted corridor until he reached the fire door that would take him out of the Windsor's annexe, across its so-called ornamental gardens (four scrappy-looking flowerbeds and a tangle of bushes that should have been cleared away years ago), and into its Olde Hartforde Suite and the main building. He laid his hand on the fire door ready to push it open when he saw something through the smudgy wired-glass window. A white flicker in the unkempt garden. A small scurrying shape that could have been a dog or a windblown sheet of newspaper or an optical illusion created by the evening sunlight on the glass.

But he stood where he was, feeling cold and uncertain, because he suspected that it wasn't any of those things. He suspected that it was the dwarfish figure that he had seen in Mrs Kemp's garden last night, talking to Martin through the distorting kitchen window. And the figure was here, in West Hartford, in the same hotel, which meant only one thing that Charlie could think of. Real or imaginary, it was following them. Worse than following them, it was tracking them down.

For a moment, Charlie hesitated. Maybe he should go back and warn Martin that the dwarf was around. On the other hand, if Martin had been talking to it, maybe Martin *knew* that it was around. Maybe Martin had even gone so far as to tell it where they were going. Maybe it was nothing more than his own imagination, creating a demon or a devil which could take the blame for his own failure to make friends with the son he was supposed to have taken care of, and hadn't. He felt confused and uncertain, as if he had been drinking. But at last he pressed his hand against the fire door, opened it, and stepped out.

There was no sign of any creature. Only the dry hunchbacked bushes and the untidy flowerbeds.

Only the dark clouds rolling overhead as if they were hurrying on their way to some distant battle.

The food at the Windsor Hotel was relentlessly dull. In an attempt to console himself for not having been able to eat at Le Reposoir, Charlie ordered the Grande Royale menu, which started off with steamers, followed by charcoal-broiled bluefish, carpetbag steak, and peach pie. In the hands of a competent chef, any one of these traditional American dishes could have been a masterpiece. In the Windsor Hotel, they were tough, dry, slimy, and canned, in that order. Charlie sat alone at an underlit table, facing a badly painted frieze of Windsor Castle in England, chewing his way through this unappetizing menu while a four-piece band played 'Tie A Yellow Ribbon' and the six businessmen sitting next to him chain-smoked cigars throughout their meal.

When he had finished, Charlie was approached by the maitre d', who stood beside his table with his hands folded over his groin. 'You didn't care for the dinner, sir?' the maitre d' asked, with unconcealed annoyance.

'The dinner was – acceptable,' said Charlie.

'Perhaps a small glass of brandy on the house?' the maitre d' suggested. His tone of voice was almost ferocious.

'That won't be necessary.'

The maitre d' bent forward. He had huge open pores in his nose and his breath smelled of Binaca. 'It isn't my fault this place is so bad.'

Charlie stared at him without expression.

The maitre d' went on, 'I do my best, I used to work at the Hyatt Pilgrim in Boston. But what can I do with a place like this? They won't invest any money on it.'

Charlie said, 'What does this have to do with me?'

'Come on, Mr Restaurant Inspector. You can't kid me. I know a restaurant inspector when I see one.'

'You think so?'

'I was expecting you. I knew what you were, the moment you walked into the room. All restaurant inspectors have that same look. Most men who are forced to eat alone will keep their eyes on their food, or on a book. But you – your eyes are never still. You are looking at the cutlery, at the glasses, at the table linen. You are timing the waiters, you are testing the food. After you have finished your coffee you will go to the men's room to make sure it is clean. You may even try to dodge into the ladies'. I know your kind.'

Charlie slowly shook his head. 'You must be making some kind of mistake here, friend. I'm a salesman, dealing in hydraulic valves. You want to come out and look at what I'm carrying in the back of my car?'

'You can't kid me,' the maitre d' hissed at him, triumphant now. 'I was told. I was expecting you. You don't fool me for one moment.'

'Bring me the bill,' said Charlie.

'No, sir, no charge,' retorted the maitre d'.

'I want the bill,' Charlie insisted. 'In fact, if you don't bring me the bill right now I'm going to call for the manager.'

'No charge,' the maitre d' challenged him.

Charlie paused for a moment, and then stood up. 'All right,' he said. 'No charge. I'm not going to get myself involved in an argument about it.' He raised his eyes. 'All the same, I'd like to know who told you to expect me.'

The maitre d' shrugged, and flapped at Charlie's coat with a napkin to brush off the crumbs of peach-pie. 'The restaurant business is a brotherhood, sir.'

'Like the Cosa Nostra, you mean?' said Charlie sarcastically.

'No, sir. More like monks, or friars.'

Charlie looked away. The maitre d' was obviously drunk. Either drunk, or so disaffected with his job that he didn't care what he said, or to whom he said it. Monks or friars, Christ Almighty. The only possible religious ingredient in the restaurant business was the prayers of forgiveness they said when they wrote 'Fresh' and 'Home Cooked' on the menus.

The maitre d' said, 'How about that glass of brandy? Come on, friend. It's on the house.'

A little wearily, Charlie nodded. The maitre d' clapped his hands and the wine waiter came over, a stocky, unsmiling type with a tight maroon coat and a tight maroon face to match. 'Give the gentleman a glass of the Courvoisier, Arnold. You'd like it in the lounge, sir? In the lounge, Arnold. Next to the fireplace.'

Charlie sat in a high leather-upholstered library chair nursing his brandy while two large logs smouldered in the olde colonial fireplace like the last remains of a derelict building. Across the lounge, sitting in profile to him, was a thirtyish woman with ash blonde hair and a tight sapphire-blue dress and a little more jewellery than was tasteful, especially for a country mausoleum like the Windsor. Charlie surmised that she was a woman of relatively easy virtue, if not an out-and-out hooker. She made a big play of lighting a cigarette and blowing the smoke across the lounge. Charlie sipped his brandy and thought that she had a pretty impressive chest, even if her hips were on the wide side.

After about ten minutes, the woman stood up and came across to the fireplace. She stared down at the logs, the elbow of her smoking arm cupped in the hand of her other arm, her chin slightly lifted.

'I always think a real fire is so romantic, don't you?' she asked Charlie, without looking at him.

'I don't know about this one,' said Charlie. 'It looks half dead to me.'

'Ashes to ashes,' the woman remarked. Then, 'Are you travelling alone?'

'Not entirely. I have my son with me.'

'Do you usually travel alone?' For the first time she turned to catch him with a blue-eyed stare. She was good-looking, in a Hollywood kind of a way, short-nosed, broad-cheekboned, almost baby-faced; except of course that the crisscross lines were beginning to show in the corners of her eyes. A diamond brooch in the shape of a star reflected the light from one of the ceiling lamps. Charlie thought: *Genuine. This woman has been places, and done things, and men have showed their approval in the time-honoured way.*

Charlie said, 'I'm not looking for company, if that's what you mean.'

'You look unhappy,' the woman told him. 'I can't bear to see anybody looking unhappy.'

'I'm a little tired is all.'

'Would you mind if I sat down beside you and talked to you?'

Charlie nodded toward the chair next to his. 'It's a free country. I can't guarantee that you'll get any answers.'

She sat down and crossed her legs. Her blue shiny dress rode higher on her thighs than it ought to have done. She smelled of Obsession by Calvin Klein. She blew smoke over him, but he wasn't sure that he particularly minded. The top three buttons of her dress were unfastened and Charlie could see a very deep cleavage indeed. White breasts with a single beckoning mole between them.

'I saw you arguing with Bits,' she said.

'You mean the maitre d'? Is that his name?'

'It makes him sound like a gangster, doesn't it? But his real name's Arthur. They call him Bits because when he was younger he was always saying, 'For two bits I'll quit this job,' or 'For two bits I'll make that damned sauce myself.' Not that he was ever a violent man – oh no. Just a little temperamental. He says he was descended from the Borgias.'

'That wouldn't surprise me,' said Charlie. He pointed towards the woman's empty glass. 'How about a nightcap? Was that frozen daiquiris you were drinking?'

She smiled. 'You know what they say about ladies who have a taste for frozen daiquiris?'

'I can't say that I do. I hope it's polite.'

'Polite?' the woman laughed.

Charlie ignored her mockery and held out his hand. 'I'm Charlie McLean.'

'Velma Farloe,' the woman replied.

'Nice to know you, Velma. Have you been here long?'

'Here in this bar, or here in West Hartford?'

Charlie said, 'I never did feel at home in New England – Connecticut in particular. I always feel like I'm being looked at as some kind of outsider.'

'Where do you feel at home?' asked Velma.

'Illinois, Indiana. I guess I'm a small-town mid-Westerner at heart. Mind you, I was born in Elizabeth, New Jersey. My parents moved to Kokomo when I was ten, and then to Merrillsville.'

He paused, and then he said, 'I don't intend to sit here and tell you the story of my life.'

Velma dropped her eyelids in the warm, coaxing way in which some women would have dropped a perfumed scarf. 'I don't mind if you do.'

'I'm a salesman, that's all. That's the beginning and the end of it.'

'Bits said you were one of those restaurant inspectors.'

'Bits confides in you, huh?'

'Come on, Charlie,' said Velma. 'You know who I am. I'm the friendly lady who sits in the corner of every restaurant lounge from here to eternity.'

The stocky wine-waiter brought them two fresh drinks. When Charlie offered to pay, he said, 'On the house,' in a gruff falsetto that was as adamant as it was startling.

'Bits is trying to butter you up, that's all,' Velma told Charlie. 'He thinks if he gives you two or three glasses of brandy you're going to recommend the Windsor and get him a pay hike.'

'Some hope of that,' said Charlie. 'This is one of the worst restaurants between Mount Fissell and Wequetequock.'

'Well,' purred Velma. 'You sure know your geography.'

She shifted herself closer. She touched Charlie's left temple with her fingertips. He could breathe her perfume, and also that other indescribable odour known as Woman On Heat. He sipped at his brandy feeling as prissy as a boy scout. He needed a woman desperately, but for some reason he always held himself back, as if it were the right and proper thing to do. Because of Marjorie? No, he couldn't believe that. Because of everything that had happened in Milwaukee? No, he couldn't believe that either. It was far more deeply rooted. It was a glimpse of his mother fastening her stockings. It was his father's face intruding on his unconscious like a big pale blimp, roaring, 'Women should be respected, Charlie. 'Women are *holy*.'

Velma said, 'You're one of those quiet ones, aren't you?'

'I told you. I'm tired.'

'How tired is tired?'

Charlie raised his eyes and looked at her. She was mocking him, in a way; but she was also encouraging him, supporting him, in the way that only women like her knew how. They could take in travellers from the unforgiving night, men who were tired and disappointed and lonesome and very afraid of failure, and give them all the comfort they needed. One night of sex, one night of burying all of their anxieties in darkness and flesh and the pungent smell of intercourse, and they were ready to face the world again, ready to report back to J.J. on how many miles of UPVC piping they had sold, ready to drum up new business. They were as much a part of American business as Lee Iacocca or Aaron Spelling.

Charlie leaned back in the leather chair and looked around the lounge feeling drunk and detached. 'Who told you to talk to me? Was it the maitre d'? Bits? Or did you decide to proposition me off your own bat?'

'I'm not propositioning you,' smiled Velma.

'You wouldn't be smiling if you weren't.'

'Well, maybe I wouldn't.'

At that moment Charlie knew for certain that he was going to sleep with her. It was her honesty which decided him, as much as anything else. She was handsome and straightforward and big-breasted and that was all that he needed, for tonight at least. He would think about tomorrow tomorrow.

'You can't come back to my room,' he said. His voice didn't even sound like his own. 'My son is there.' He checked his watch. 'Sleeping by now. He isn't used to all of this travelling around.'

'It's okay,' said Velma, taking hold of his hand. 'I have a room. Come on.'

They left the lounge together. At the doorway, Charlie turned around and saw Bits smiling at him through the wine racks which separated the restaurant from the lounge. He turned away without acknowledging that he had seen him. Velma reached back and grabbed his hand and led him through the lobby to the main building. It was well after eleven o'clock now, and the lobby was brightly lit, red-carpeted, smelling of stale cigarettes, and completely deserted.

They kissed as they went up in the elevator. Her tongue snaked into his mouth. Her hand reached directly down between his legs and squeezed him. He wasn't sure whether he ought to feel aroused or frightened. They didn't say anything coherent. The slightest bit of logic would have broken the spell completely, like the fragment of mirror in *The Snow Queen.*

Velma's room was at the far end of a long, airless corridor. She unlocked it with the dexterity of experience. She went in first, leaving Charlie in the corridor to make up his own mind whether he wanted to follow her or not. He hesitated, and then went inside, closing the door by pressing his back against it.

It was only then that she switched on the bedside lamps. The room was almost identical to Charlie's own room in the hotel annexe, except that the prints were wild flowers instead of locomotives. Fool's parsley, and fragrant bedstraw. Velma, her back to Charlie, unbuttoned her dress. He made no move to help her. She dropped the dress on the bed and then turned around to face him. There was a strange, bright look of elation and defiance in her eyes. She was wearing nothing more than a black translucent bra, through which her nipples showed as smoky pink shadows, and a pair of patterned black pantihose, against which her pubic hair was flattened like the geographical map of a river delta.

Charlie approached her, gradually loosening his necktie. He held her, and kissed her forehead. It was cool, slightly damp with perspiration, and tasted of perfume. 'I hope you don't think I make a habit of picking up women in hotel lounges,' he said, his voice hoarse.

'I wouldn't mind if you did,' Velma replied. 'Practise makes perfect.'

She reached behind her one-handed and unfastened her bra, drawing it off her breasts and letting it fall. Her breasts were big and soft and heavy, with nipples that crinkled tight. she unbuttoned his shirt, tugging it out of his pants, and then she grasped her breasts in both hands and pressed her nipples against his bare chest, kissing him with mounting hunger. Her teeth sought out his lips and his tongue, and bit at them so sharply that he could taste the metallic flavour of blood in his mouth. 'I'm going to eat you,' she whispered.

They climbed on to the bed, struggling out of the last of their clothes. Charlie could hear himself panting. He took hold of Velma and rolled her over. Her breasts moved with slow-motion fluidity. Her white thighs parted. He saw dark hair and glistening pink. Then he had pushed himself into her, and the bedsprings began to jounce, and all he could see was Velma's hair and part of the pillow and a torn off piece of wallpaper that looked like the head of a dog. Details, blurs, gasps, and then a snuffling, snorting release.

He rolled off her, trying to catch his breath. Immediately, however, she was on top of him and straddled his stomach, so that he could feel her wetness pressed against him. 'I want more of you,' she demanded, and when Charlie squinted up at her, with one hand raised to keep the light out of his eyes, he could see that she wasn't smiling.

'No good huh?' he said. 'I told you I don't make a habit of it. Next time, I'll try to take my time.'

'I want you now,' she said, and her eyes glittered.

'Come on now,' Charlie protested. 'I'm only human.'

But Velma slid down him, and crouched like a cunning animal between his legs, and held his slippery softened penis in her hand. She stuck out her tongue, and it was very long and pointed, and she teased him by licking at the small sensitive opening. All the time she kept her hair drawn back from her forehead with her other hand, and her eyes fixed on him. Taunting him, provoking him, seeing how much she could shock him. She was irritating him with her caresses rather than arousing him. 'Can you guess how much I want you?' she said. Charlie was almost frightened to answer. 'How much do you think I want you?'

Charlie said nothing as she sucked his softened member completely into her mouth. She sucked too hard, and he said, '*Ah!*' and put his hand on her shoulder to push her away. But she opened her mouth even wider and tried to cram his testicles in as well. Her whole mouth was cram full and still she looked up at him with those taunting, glittering eyes.

'Velma–'

She bit him gently, then a little harder.

'Velma, I have to tell you that hurts.'

She didn't release him. Instead, she bent her head a little lower, and used her fingers to put his second testicle completely into her mouth. Her cheeks were swollen as if she had been gorging herself with too much food.

'Velma, come on, careful now, that really hurts when you–'

She bit him again, sharper and harder this time, and this time she drew blood. A thin dribble of it ran out of the side of her mouth. Charlie felt a peculiar empty feeling in his stomach and suddenly realized that it was panic. Here he was, lying in bed with a woman he had never met before, and she was holding everything that made him a man between her teeth. With one hard bite, she could turn him into an eunuch. She could even kill him.

'Velma, you have to listen to me now... let me go, will you, please?'

Velma snarled and dribbled and shook her head from side to side, worrying his sexual organs as if she were a young lioness who was refusing to surrender her prey. In spite of his fear, however – or perhaps because of it – Charlie began to feel his penis hardening again. It uncurled itself against the arch of Velma's palate and gradually forced her to let his testicles plop out from between her lips, one by one, two wet plums, although she managed to keep almost his entire erection inside her mouth.

She forced her head forward the very last half-inch. His swollen glans must have actually been inside her throat. Still she kept her eyes fixed on him, challenging, warning. Any other woman would have gagged or choked. Velma kept him there, on the brink between extreme erotic excitement and total terror, and it seemed to Charlie that whole minutes went past.

At last she lifted her head, allowing the shaft to slide out from between her lips inch by inch. 'Did I frighten you?' she asked him. Now she was smiling.

Charlie rolled over and got up off the bed.

'I frightened you,' she said.

'I'm just going to the bathroom, that's all,' Charlie felt as if the floor were tilting, and wished to God he hadn't accepted that cognac. He very rarely got drunk. He didn't like losing control of himself. Apart from that, the brandy fumes seemed to be rising up from his stomach like gasoline vapour, and he knew that it would take only one more drink to make him very sick indeed.

Velma stood in the doorway watching him as he urinated. 'Do you know something? I could have bitten it right off.' She stepped forward as he was finishing and held him in one hand. 'You knew that, didn't you? And you were frightened.'

'I do my best not to live too dangerously,' Charlie told her.

'You still don't understand, do you?' Her face so close to his that he could see the orange flecks in her eyes. 'I *wanted* to bite it off. I wanted to chew it and eat it and swallow it.'

Charlie stared at her. She had an expression on her face that he could only describe to himself as triumph, with a little mockery thrown in for seasoning. She released him, and he flushed the toilet and walked back through to the bedroom. 'I think I'd better get back to Martin,' he said, and reached for his shirt.

Velma came up behind him and touched the nape of his neck with her long fingernails. It gave him a shiver that was partly arousal and partly apprehension. *Maybe this is what I've always been missing*, he thought. *Maybe my life has always lacked a little danger.*

'Stay,' said Velma. 'I promise I won't frighten you again.'

'I don't know,' Charlie demurred.

'Your son will be okay. He's a big boy now, isn't he?'

'Fifteen.'

'Well, then,' purred Velma, turning him around and kissing his nose. 'He's almost big enough for me.'

Charlie opened his fingers and his shirt dropped on to the floor.

7

He woke up and there was bright fall sunshine criss-crossing the ceiling like the reflection on a fishing pond. He rubbed a crust of sleep from his eye and then turned over. Velma was lying with her back to him, still breathing deeply. The room reeked of sex and Obsession. Charlie reached over and gently untangled Velma's hair.

Beside the bed, the electric clock read 7:07. Martin had been very tired last night; he was probably still asleep. If Charlie dressed and went back to their room, Martin may not even realize that he had been away all night.

Charlie wasn't guilty about having gone to bed with Velma. He was divorced, he could go to bed with anybody he wanted. But he did feel that it might upset Martin, seeing how close Martin was to his mother. He pulled at a curl in Velma's hair and Velma opened her eyes and looked at him sideways and smiled.

'It's morning,' he told her. 'I have to go.'

'No breakfast special?'

'I think I'm just about plumb wore out,' Charlie said in an Uncle Tom accent.

'That's hard to believe,' said Velma, and turned around to admire him with eyes that were still glassy from dreams.

For the first time, Charlie noticed a deep sickle-shaped scar, just where her right breast met her chest. The scar was pale pink, and it had obviously healed well, but it looked as if something had actually taken a good sized piece out of her muscle. He didn't like to be over-inquisitive. When you met people on the road, you had to accept that they tell you as much or as little about themselves as they wanted; truth or lies; and that you had to take them for what they were. But he touched Velma's scar very lightly with his fingertips, and he asked her the question with his eyes.

'Self-inflicted,' smiled Velma.

'What does that mean?' Charlie asked.

'What do you think?'

Charlie shrugged. His guess was that Velma had stayed with a violent boyfriend just one night too many, and that he had cut her or burned her or whatever it was that violent boyfriends did these days.

'I think it's none of my Goddamned business,' he said.

'It could be,' said Velma. 'You know all about the Célèstines, don't you?'

Charlie stared at her. 'The Célèstines? You're the second person who's mentioned the Célèstines to me in a couple of days. I never heard of them before. Didn't they come from New Orleans or something?'

'Originally they came from New Orleans, yes; but now they're all over.'

'I still don't have any idea of what they are, or *who* they are,' Charlie admitted.

Velma said nothing for a moment. Then she climbed out of bed, and approached the dressing table, inspecting her naked body in the mirror. She laid one hand over the scar on her chest, and closed her eyes. 'You feel hostile towards them.'

'I don't know anything about them. How can I possibly feel hostile towards them?'

Velma opened her eyes and looked at him in the mirror. 'Do you always feel hostile towards things that you don't understand?'

Charlie swung back the covers. 'I'd better get back to my son. If I get back now, he'll still be asleep.'

'You mean he won't realize that his father has been away all night?'

'Something like that.' Charlie reached for his crumpled pants.

'Does it make you feel guilty, spending the night with a woman you picked up in a bar?'

'Not at all.'

Velma came over to him, still naked, and buttoned up his pants for him. Then she kissed him on the lips, and laughed.

'I know that some Célèstines run a restaurant at Allen's Corners,' said Charlie.

'That's right,' said Velma. 'So you do know something.'

'I don't get this,' Charlie told her irritably. 'It's like some kind of guessing game. Do you know what the Célèstines are?'

'Of course. They're like a society, a club. Every now and then they get together and they eat a special dinner.'

'Le Reposoir, they meet there,' said Charlie, and Velma nodded.

Charlie said, 'The way we got together last night, was that accidental, or was it arranged? I mean, was it arranged by somebody else? Were we *supposed* to get together?'

'You could say that,' she said. He knew now that she was mocking him.

'Do you mind telling me who arranged it, and why?'

'Are you feeling used?' she teased him. She turned her back on him and for a split second he saw a mental Polaroid of last night's lovemaking, Velma biting his shoulder, Velma sitting on his face, grinding herself into his mouth. Vicious, harsh, dangerous sex; sex with teeth and blood and fingernails.

He buttoned up his shirt, buttoned the cuffs. 'I don't know what this is all about,' he said, trying to keep his voice steady. 'I don't think I *want* to know what this is all about. I'm going back to my room and then I'm leaving. If you want some money – here –' He reached into his back pants pocket and took out fifty dollars in ten dollar bills.

Velma shook her head. 'I don't want your money. I've already been paid.'

Charlie seized hold of her wrist and twisted her around. Instantly, she slapped his face, hard, and he let her go. They stood glaring at each other, and panting. A crimson handprint gradually appeared on Charlie's cheek.

'Somebody paid you to pick me up and screw me?' he asked her incredulously.

'I was trying to help you, that's all,' said Velma. 'I was trying to make you understand.'

'Understand what? I mean, what's the connection? You, me, Le Reposoir, these Célèstine people. What the hell is it all about?'

Velma was calm. 'You approached them, didn't you? The Musettes?'

'You know about that?'

'I know the Musettes. They called me. They were under the impression that you knew something about the Célèstines and that you were anxious to join them.'

Charlie stared at Velma, narrow-eyed. 'Now, wait a minute. I went to Le Reposoir because I wanted to eat there, that was all.'

Velma dressed and Charlie watched her, feeling completely perplexed. If the Musettes had believed that he knew what the Célèstines were, and that he wanted to become one of them, why hadn't they invited him to join when he had visited Le Reposoir yesterday? And why on earth should they have gone to the trouble of finding out where he was staying after he had left Allen's Corners, and paying for Velma to take him to bed?

Velma lifted her breasts into her bra, and fastened it. 'You'd better go down to see your son. You don't want him to think that you're the kind of man he'd rather not have for a father.'

Charlie checked his watch. 'Okay. You're right. But stick around. Meet me in the lobby in ten minutes' time and we'll have breakfast together.'

'I never eat breakfast.'

'Well, I have to. You can always toy with a cup of coffee.'

Velma said nothing as Charlie went to the door. He opened it, and stood there for a moment simply looking at her. 'Ten minutes then,' he said.

Charlie went to the reception desk first of all, to see if there were any messages for him. The bell captain smirked, and said, 'One from your wife, Mr McLean. She wants you to call her back.'

'When did she call?'

'Maybe eleven last night, sir.'

'Didn't you put her through to my room?'

'You weren't in your room, sir.' The smirk grew wider.

'Not right then, no. But my son was.'

The bell captain's eyes blinked an almost imperceptible negative. 'There was no reply, sir. We did think of putting the call directly through to you, but we considered that you might not appreciate it too much, not right then, sir.'

He walked through the unkempt gardens of the Windsor Hotel and through to his room in the annexe. When he got there, he found that the door was wide open, and that there were two black maids in there, one cleaning out the bath and the other making the bed. The bedside radio was playing 'The Girl From Ipanema'.

'Pardon me,' said Charlie, 'did you see my son here this morning?'

The maid who was making the bed looked up slowly and shook her head. 'No, sir. This room was empty this morning.'

'But he was sleeping here. A boy of fifteen, brown hair. Light blue windcheater and jeans.'

'No, sir. This room was empty. There's some luggage here, sir, but that's all.'

Charlie opened the closet and there was his own overnight case, as well as two of his shirts hanging on hangers, just where he had left them. But there was no sign of Martin's case, nor of any of Martin's clothes. *Shit,* thought Charlie, *I left him alone last night and now he's run away. I failed him when he was a kid and I've failed him again. Now what the hell am I going to do?*

He went into the bathroom. Martin's toothbrush was gone, and there was no sign of any farewell message written on the mirror with Crest. Back in the bedroom, the maids had almost finished. They were performing their last ritual of laying out fresh books of matches and luridly coloured postcards of the Windsor Hotel photographed in the days when the gardens hadn't looked like a snakepit.

'Was there a note anywhere?' Charlie asked them. 'A piece of paper with a message on it?'

The maids made a desultory attempt to look through their black plastic trash bag. 'No, sir. Nothing like that.'

Charlie took one last look around, and then went to the reception desk. The bell captain was picking his teeth behind his hand.

'My son,' said Charlie.

'I'm sorry?' the bell captain asked him.

'My son was in 109 but he's gone.'

The bell captain eyed him steadily. 'Your son?'

'I left my son sleeping in 109 last night, but now he's not there.'

'Your son was sleeping in 109?'

Charlie smacked his hand flat on the desk. 'Do you have to keep repeating everything I say? I want to know what time my son checked out of here, and if he told anybody where he was going.'

'Your son sure didn't check out of here, sir.'

'You mean he left without anybody seeing him?'

'No, sir, I mean your son sure didn't check out of here. The reason being that he never checked in.'

'What the hell are you talking about?'

The bell captain looked back at him dispassionately, with the face of a man who has spent a lifetime dealing with irritable customers and pays them about as much attention as he would to a few exhausted wasps, buzzing around in a jelly-jar. 'You checked in here at 5:45 yesterday evening, sir?'

'That's correct.'

'At that time, sir, you were alone.'

'What? What is this? I mean, what kind of ridiculous joke are you trying to play here? I booked in yesterday evening with my fifteen-year-old son, and if you look at my registration card you'll see that

I've included his name. Charles J. and Martin S. McLean.'

The bell captain reached under the counter and slid out a narrow file drawer crowded with registration cards. He rifled through them until he came to the M-Mc section, and tugged out Charlie's registration card. 'This is the one, sir. See what it says?'

Charlie stared at the card in horror and disquiet. It read nothing more than *Charles J. McLean, 49 West 24th Street, New York, NY 10010.* Fastened to the card was an impression of his American Express card, and that was all. There was no doubt that the writing on the card was his. He even remembered how the pen had almost run out of ink halfway through, and how he had squiggled it hard on the bottom of the card to start it flowing again. There were the squiggles, just as before. But what had happened to Martin's name?

'I don't even pretend to get this,' said Charlie harshly, giving back the card. 'But my son arrived here with me last night, and yesterday evening before I went to dinner I left him in 109. This morning he's gone – no message, no nothing – that's not like him at all.'

'Do you want to talk to the manager about it?' asked the bell captain.

'Yes, call him. And there's somebody else I want to talk to, too. Ms Velma Farloe. I don't recall her room number, but she should still be there now.'

'Ms Velma Farloe? I'm sorry, sir, but I can tell you right off the top of my head that there's nobody by that name staying here. There's Mr Fairbrother in 412, but that's about the nearest.'

'Is this some kind of Goddamned stupid joke?' Charlie roared, and an elderly couple who had just appeared out of the elevator stared at him in shock and alarm.

'Mr McLean,' the bell captain retorted toughly, 'I've got to warn you to keep your voice down. Shouting isn't going to get anybody anyplace.'

Charlie leaned across the desk and jabbed at the bell captain's uniformed chest with his finger. 'You listen to me, wise-ass. I came here last night with my son Martin and I spent the night here with a lady called Ms Velma Farloe while my son slept in 109. This morning my son is gone and so is Ms Farloe. All I need to know from you is when my son left and where Ms Farloe is. Otherwise I'm not just going to talk to the manager, I'm going to talk to the police.'

The bell captain lifted both hands in taunting surrender. 'I'm sorry, Mr McLean. What can I tell you? There's no record of your son having arrived here. There's no sign of him now; and there's no sign of Ms–what did you say her name was?'

At that moment the manager arrived. He was tall, vague, distant, with a drawling Bostonian accent and a flaccid double chin like an elderly pelican. He listened to Charlie's story as if Charlie were trying to sell him a new brand of industrial floor cleaner. His dry, rutted fingernails played an impatient tattoo on the countertop, and then at last he said, 'I'm sorry, sir. I can't help you. If there's no hotel record that your son checked in here, and if there's no record that Ms Furlough checked in here either... well, you can understand our position.'

'Yes, I do understand your position,' said Charlie furiously. 'Your position is that for some reason best known to yourselves you're trying to fool me into thinking that my son wasn't even here last night, and that the woman with whom I spent the night was some kind of figment of my imagination.'

The manager smiled without warmth or interest. 'You said it, sir, not me.'

Charlie said tightly, 'I want my son.'

The manager didn't reply, but beckoned the bell captain to lean over the desk toward him. He whispered something into the bell captain's ear and the bell captain nodded.

'What was that all about?' Charlie demanded.

'Nothing to do with your son, sir,' said the manager. 'As I say, I'm very sorry, but we're unable to assist you.'

Charlie had always scoffed at those Hollywood movies in which unscrupulous relatives try to steal a woman's fortune by driving her mad; but he could understand now how quickly a person's sense of reality could slip away. He walked away from the reception desk for a moment in sheer exasperation; then he turned back again and said, 'Call the police.'

The bell captain glanced at the manager, but the manager shrugged in agreement. 'Of course. It's the only thing you can do. But can I ask you one favour? Be discreet. The Windsor has a reputation to keep up.'

'There's something else,' said Charlie. 'I want to talk to your maitre d'. He knows the woman I stayed with last night.'

'He won't be awake yet, sir. He doesn't come on duty until eleven o'clock.'

'Well, in that case, I'm sorry. You'll just have to disturb him. The police will want to see him anyway.'

The manager interlaced his fingers, and then said to the bell captain, 'Put a call in to Arthur. Tell him to meet me in my office in ten minutes.' He turned back to Charlie and said, 'You will allow him ten minutes, sir, to dress?'

While he waited for the police and for Arthur, Charlie went outside and walked around the hotel parking lot. It must have been raining during the night. The air was cold and damp and all the cars were bejewelled with raindrops. He opened up his own car to see if Martin had left him a message on the steering wheel or the seat, but there was nothing there at all. He slammed the car door and wiped the rain off his hands with his handkerchief.

The police took nearly fifteen minutes to arrive. Two deputies, one middle aged and as lean as a whippet, the other young and pudgy with close-bitten nails. Charlie walked up to them as they parked outside the hotel, and said, 'My name's McLean. It's my son who's gone missing.'

The lean deputy sniffed, wiped at his nose with his finger and looked around him. 'You've searched the hotel? He's not hiding or anything? Little kids do that sometimes, just to annoy their parents. Found one kid hiding in the trash once, all ready to be collected and sent off to the dump.'

Charlie said, 'He's fifteen. He's not a little kid.'

The lean deputy made a face that was obviously meant to be interpreted as *Fifteen? What do you expect from a kid of fifteen? They're always running away. It's the prime age for running away.*

'Want to give me some kind of description?' the lean deputy asked. His pudgy partner tugged out a notebook and a stub of pencil and frowned at him expectantly.

'He's a fifteen-year-old boy, that's all. Brown hair, brown eyes. Slight build. He's probably wearing a pale blue windbreaker and Levi jeans.'

The pudgy deputy assiduously wrote all this down while the lean deputy gritted his teeth in imitation of Clint Eastwood and looked this way and that as if he expected a sign from God or at least an imminent change in the weather. 'When was the last time you saw him?' he asked.

'Last night. I don't know, round about seven-thirty.'

'Here, at the Windsor?'

'That's right, in the room we were sharing.'

The lean deputy frowned. 'If you were sharing a room with your son, how come the last time you saw him was at seven-thirty yesterday evening?'

'Because I spent the night in another room.'

'You spent the night in another room?'

'I was sleeping with a lady.'

The lean deputy raised an eyebrow. 'You were sleeping with a lady and when you returned to your own room you found that your son was no longer there?'

'That's the nub of it, yes.'

The pudgy deputy scribbled in his notebook for a long time while the lean deputy peered first to the northern horizon and then to the south.

At last, the lean deputy said, 'Did you have any family problems?'

Charlie shook his head. 'His mother and I are divorced, but there isn't any hostility between us. His mother's taking a vacation right now, and so I agreed to bring him along with me. I'm a restaurant critic, I travel around eating in restaurants and writing reports.'

The lean deputy nodded his head towards the entrance to the Windsor. 'What do you think of this place? Stinks, don't it?'

'Deputy, I'm interested in finding my son, that's all.'

'Well,' said the deputy, 'the whole point is that teenage disappearances are pretty much two for a nickel these days. Kids have plenty of independence, plenty of money. They're smart, too. As soon as they're old enough to strike out on their own, they generally take the opportunity and do it. You can never tell when it's going to happen. Sometimes it happens after an argument, sometimes it just happens.'

'Thanks for the sociological analysis,' Charlie retorted.

The manager came out and said coldly, 'My maitre d' is here, as you requested. I hope you won't be keeping him for very long. He has a full lunchtime schedule ahead of him, and a Lodge dinner at seven-thirty.'

Charlie didn't answer, but led the way back into the hotel. In the manager's office, Arthur, the maitre d', was standing in green striped pyjamas and a maroon silk bathrobe with stains on the belly. He was unshaven, although Charlie could smell that he had already had a quick squirt of Binaca. He glared at Charlie with eyes like freshly peeled grapes.

'Arthur?' said the lean deputy. 'How are you doing?'

'I was doing all right before I was woken up,' said Arthur harshly.

'One of those dreams, huh?' the lean deputy gibed. 'A desert island and you and forty naked women and no rescue imminent for at least six months.'

Arthur looked away dismissively. It was quite obvious that he had no respect for anything or anybody – his employers, his customers, or the law.

'Arthur,' said Charlie, 'do you remember that woman who was sitting in the lounge with me? The woman in the blue dress?'

Arthur stared at Charlie, and then looked in perplexity from the lean deputy to the manager, and back again. 'What kind of a question is that?' he asked.

143

The lean deputy said, 'It's simple enough. Do you remember a woman in a blue dress sitting in the lounge with this gentleman last night?'

Arthur shook his head in apparent disbelief. 'If there was a woman there, she was the Invisible Woman. I didn't see any woman.'

'You mean that Mr McLean here was sitting on his own?'

'Well, that's right. He looked kind of fed up and lonesome so I made sure we gave him a cognac on the house.'

Charlie jabbed a finger at him. 'I was sitting talking to Velma Farloe and you damned well know it! Velma Farloe – she was right in front of your face.'

The maitre d' frowned at the manager for moral support. 'Velma Farloe? I don't know anybody called Velma Farloe.'

'Oh, she knew *you* all right,' said Charlie. 'She said your nickname was Bits. Now, isn't that true? Bits, that's what she said, because you used to have the habit of saying for two bits you'd do this, or for two bits you'd do that. Now – how could I possibly have known that unless Velma Farloe was real and I'd met her?'

The maitre d' stared at Charlie for a long time and then turned appealingly toward the two deputies. 'Bits?' he asked, in complete disbelief. 'What is this guy, some kind of a fruitcake, or what? I mean, *Bits*?'

Charlie glanced at the manager and then at the deputies. Their faces all wore the same expression of caution. *We've got a funny one here, guys. Let's just play along with him until he runs out of steam.*

'All right,' said Charlie. 'If you don't want to believe me, you don't want to believe me. But I can warn you here and now that I'm going to the sheriff, and if I don't get any satisfaction from the sheriff I'm going to the FBI. I have friends, don't you make any mistakes about that. I have influential friends.'

'Well, we're sure you do,' said the manager. 'But you have to see the situation from our point of view, Mr McLean. You checked in here yesterday on your own, you ate dinner on your own and, as far as I can understand it, you slept on your own. I guess the best thing we can do for the time being is to put the whole incident down to exhaustion, maybe, or to over-excitability.'

Charlie was so angry at that instant that he could have punched the manager in the face. Instead, however, he closed his eyes and clenched his fists and waited for the fury to die down inside of him. When he opened his eyes again, he caught the manager winking conspiratorially at the bell captain, and the lean deputy shuffling his feet as if he were practising his ballroom dancing. The pudgy deputy was eating the end of his pencil and staring out of the window.

'Okay,' said Charlie. 'Okay. Just give me some time to think this through. It happened because it happened and because I *know* that it happened. But I don't have any evidence to prove it and you guys obviously aren't going to break your asses in any kind of effort to help me prove it.'

'Mr McLean,' the lean deputy appealed to him, 'we aren't going to break our asses because so far we haven't seen any evidence that your son was actually here, let alone any evidence that he disappeared.'

Charlie said, 'Don't worry about it, okay? I said not to worry about it. Let me think it all through by myself. Then I'll call you, when I've worked something out.'

'We don't want you to think that we're failing in our duty,' the lean deputy said. 'But the simple fact is that we don't have anything that looks like a legitimate complaint here. I mean, this looks like your common-or-garden misunderstanding, which in a district like this is what occupies most police time. Maybe your son was here, maybe he wasn't. If he was here, he sure isn't here now, and he sure didn't leave any kind of evidence that he was. These good people here didn't even see him, didn't even check him in. So where is he now? Or more to the point, was he ever here at all?'

'It's all right,' said Charlie, as apologetically as he could. 'I guess I made a genuine mistake. I guess I thought that my son was here when all the time he wasn't. I guess that's it.'

'It has been known,' the lean deputy prompted him. 'You know, like mirages, all that kind of stuff. You're walking through the desert and what do you see but cans of cold Pabst. It's something you want, and because you want it so much, you think that you can actually see it in front of your eyes. That's what happened to you. You wanted to have your son with you, but you couldn't. So instead you imagined he was with you, but now he's gone, even though he wasn't there in the first place.'

Charlie raised his head and stared at the deputy with level eyes. The deputy was gazing eagerly at him, like a dog anticipating a reward. Charlie said, 'How dare you talk such bullshit to me? I've just lost my son.'

The deputy coughed and shuffled and looked embarrassed. 'I have to keep every possible option open, sir. You must understand that. And that includes the option that your son wasn't here at all – that he was only riding along with you inside of your own mind.'

Charlie knew then that there was only one way in which he was going to be able to find Martin, and that was by himself. These people might be right. Perhaps Martin hadn't come along with him at all. Perhaps the stress of his job at MARIA had all grown too much for him, and he had driven to Connecticut under the illusion that his son was with him. But he could live his life only by his own perceptions, and by his own reality, and he remembered Martin coming with him as clearly as he could see these people standing in front of him now. All he could think was, *If they don't believe me, that's too bad. I'll go look for Martin on my own.*

He was aware, however, how unwise it would be tell them that. The best course of action would be for him to apologize for being hasty; to make out that he was confused by everything that had happened; and to leave the Windsor with an idiot smile on his face. He knew that Martin had been with him. He knew just as distinctly that he had slept with Velma Farloe. The only possible reason why the manager and the bell captain and the maitre d' and these Laurel-and-Hardy deputies were pretending that he was deluded was because they knew where Martin had gone, and why.

And the only possible reason why they were keeping up the pretence was because they had been ordered to; or paid to; or because they were in fear of their lives if they told him what had really happened.

Charlie found it completely unreal that he was thinking this way. Yet his instinct for survival had always been strong. It had enabled him to travel around the continental United States year after year, testing and tasting, sleeping in unfamiliar beds, and to endure the long-drawn-out agonies of his divorce from Marjorie and everything that had happened in Milwaukee.

Stiffly, he raised his hand, and said, 'I'll leave it to you, then, deputy. If anybody calls and says they've seen my son – well, I hope that you'll let me know. I'll leave a forwarding number at the desk here, and I'll call you regularly so that you know where I am.'

The lean deputy nodded, and said, 'That's a real sensible way of going about it, Mr McLean. Come on – I know you're upset. Maybe disoriented, too. But we'll do everything we can to clear this little problem up pronto. You won't have to worry about a thing. Believe me, your son is probably home with his mother right now, watching television and eating popcorn and totally oblivious to all of your worries. We'll check into it. The very worst that could have happened is that he's decided to light out for a day or two. So many kids do it these days.'

Charlie reached into his coat and took out his wallet, and said to the manager, 'How much do I owe you?'

The manager shook his head. 'Let's call this one a gimme, shall we? You've had a bad time at the Windsor. I don't want anybody to drive away from here with a sour taste in his mouth, for whatever reason.'

Charlie wasn't in the mood to argue. It made no difference to him, after all. MARIA picked up all of his tabs. And he had the feeling that he wouldn't be filing a report on the Windsor Hotel; nor on any of the restaurants he had visited on this trip. In fact, he had the feeling that his time at MARIA was already over; that his career had vanished overnight, like the mist over the Connecticut River.

'This won't adversely affect your report, I hope?' the manager asked him, taking hold of his elbow and smiling at him from close quarters.

'I can't think why it should, can you?' Charlie replied. The manager's smile gradually faded, and he turned toward the bell captain and said, 'Bring the gentleman's bags, would you?'

Charlie stood by the door and waited while a black bellboy was sent to find his suitcase. The two deputies made themselves comfortable up against the reception desk and discussed football with the bell captain. When Charlie's suitcase eventually arrived, the lean deputy said, 'Don't you worry, sir, we'll make sure we keep in touch. Remember that ninety-nine per cent of all those kids reported missing return to their parents within seventy-two hours.'

Charlie said, 'What about the other one per cent?'

The lean deputy made a face. 'You want better chances than ninety-nine out of a hundred?'

Charlie stowed his case in the trunk of his car and then climbed behind the steering wheel. For a moment he regarded his eyes in the rear-view mirror. *Goddamn it, Charlie McLean, sometimes you're hopeless,* he told himself. Then he started up his engine, drove out of the parking lot, and headed towards Allen's Corners.

He was going right back to the moment when things had started going off at a tangent. Back to the Iron Kettle, back to Mrs Kemp's boarding house, and back to the place which seemed to be exerting a dark and ever-increasing influence over him: Le Reposoir.

8

He reached the Iron Kettle shortly after ten o' clock. The front door was locked, so he walked around the house on the wet stone pathway until he reached the kitchen. The door was open and Charlie could hear the brisk, sharp sound of scrubbing. He knocked on the door frame and stepped inside.

The kitchen was small but professionally equipped with stainless steel Jenn-Air hobs and Amana ovens. Mrs Foss, wearing a large floral pinafore, was down on her hands and knees scrubbing the brown quarry-tiled floor.

'Mrs Foss?' asked Charlie.

Mrs Foss raised her head like a penitent who had been interrupted in her prayers. She didn't recognize him at first, but then she said, 'Ah, you. Yes, well, hello there. I'm afraid we're not open until twelve-thirty.'

'Mrs Foss, I need to ask you some questions,' said Charlie.

'Questions? What kind of questions?'

'You remember I came here with my son? He went missing this morning.'

Mrs Foss grasped the edge of the kitchen table to help herself up. She reached for a towel and dried her hands, keeping her eyes on Charlie all the time. 'How did it happen?' she wanted to know. Charlie, briefly, told her—omitting the fact that he had spent the night with Velma. Mrs Foss listened, and nodded, and then said, 'Come through to the parlour.'

The parlour was a small gloomy room smelling of potpourri and damp. Mrs Foss obviously used it partly as an office and partly as a sitting room. There was a desk with invoices and bills arranged neatly on top of it, and two wheelback chairs with tapestry seat cushions. The window gave a view of the garden in which Martin had first seen the small, hooded dwarf-person; or claimed he had.

'Sit down,' said Mrs Foss. 'Would you care for a cup of coffee?'

Charlie shook his head. 'I want to track down my son, that's all.'

'So why did you come here?' Mrs Foss looked at Charlie directly and he could see the curved reflection of his own face in her upswept spectacles. Two desperate moon-faced Charlies searching for the same son.

'We had lunch here, during that electric storm – remember? – and Martin said he saw somebody in the garden. Well – I thought I saw somebody, too. I don't know what it was, maybe it was one of the neighbourhood children. Maybe it was nothing at all, just two tired imaginations playing tricks on each other. But from that moment on, things began to go wrong between Martin and me, and this morning he's gone.'

'You've talked to the police?'

'I talked to two deputies at West Hartford. They weren't exactly the Brains Brothers. They said that most runaway kids returned to their parents after seventy-two hours.'

Mrs Foss took off her spectacles and studiously polished them on the bodice of her pinafore. 'You have some suspicions, don't you?'

Charlie said, 'I'm probably crazy. I *feel* like I'm crazy.'

'Let me say it for you,' said Mrs Foss. 'You think that the Célèstines may have had something to do with it, don't you? Those folks at Le Reposoir.'

Charlie hesitated. He had already reached the stage where he didn't quite trust anybody. After all, if Velma and Arthur and the manager of the Windsor had all been deliberately deceiving him, why shouldn't Paula Foss be deceiving him too? It seemed quite possible that the moment he had walked into the Iron Kettle, he had entered unwittingly into a conspiracy to take his son away; and to make him believe that he was mad.

He decided to put Paula Foss to the test. 'Tell me about the Célèstines,' he said. The truth about the Célèstines. I mean, what are they? Because they have something to do with Martin's disappearance, don't they? Or don't they?'

'The Célèstines are secret,' said Mrs Foss, with considerable emphasis. 'People used to pass on all kinds of stories about them, down in New Orleans. The story goes that they came from France, originally, but they were forced to emigrate during the French Revolution. They were a dining society, that's what I heard. But they were something else besides. They were religious, too. Not religious in the way that you or I might think of it, but *mystical*.'

Charlie said nothing, but stood and listened with a face that couldn't devise any kind of expression.

Mrs Foss continued. 'They had a restaurant on St Charles Avenue, two doors down from Kolb's, but it wasn't a restaurant in the regular sense. You couldn't walk in there straight off the street, the way you could with Kolb's or the Pearl, or the red beans and rice place that I used to run. They had blanked-out windows, and a locked door, and nobody I knew ever got to eat there. They were select. They were secret. People used to whisper about them, all kinds of stories: how they were eating live monkey brains, how they were eating Pomeranian dogs. But the story most people used to tell was that they were taking stray children off the streets and fattening them up, so that they could eat them too.'

'That,' Charlie said, 'has got to be a fairy tale. I haven't heard anything like it since Hansel and Gretel.'

'All right, it's a fairy tale,' said Mrs Foss. 'But people used to tell it, all the same.'

'Why did you call them the Célèstines?'

'Everybody did. It means Heavenly People, in Cajun French. I don't know where they first acquired it, but that's what they used to call themselves. The Heavenly People. They was Cajun from centuries back, right from the time that the Spanish granted them land in the bayous. Everybody called them the Célèstines. But it doesn't just mean Heavenly People, it means something else besides. It means this secret eating society; and whether it's true or not, it means anyone who eats something they are not supposed to.'

Mrs Foss pronounced 'supposed to' in an unadulterated Deep South accent, like 'sah postah'.

Charlie said, 'I keep feeling that something's going on here and everybody's trying to explain it to me, but I still can't understand it. These Célèstines – you're not seriously trying to tell me they eat children?'

'One and one makes two. Maybe one and one makes three.'

'And what does that mean?'

'That means every time the Célèstines appear, children start to disappear. The Célèstines have peculiar eating habits, so one and one makes two, or maybe it doesn't. Nobody can prove it.'

'Children are disappearing all the time. It's a national crisis.'

'Sure they do.'

Charlie said, 'I'm sorry, I can't believe any of this.'

'Can't you?' asked Mrs Foss. 'In that case, why did you come back here?'

Charlie covered his eyes with his hand. He sat for a long time in silence, thinking about Martin, and the very last moment when he walked out of the door of his room at the Windsor Hotel. Martin had quoted Groucho Marx back at him. *I do not wish to belong to the kind of club that accepts people like me as members.* How ironic that comment would prove to be if the Célèstines really had taken him.

But the whole idea of a secret society that ate children was preposterous. How could they get away with it? and they would certainly have to be a whole lot more careful about their secrecy than the Célèstines had proved to be. Velma had appeared almost to be recruiting him to join them, and that didn't seem like the way a private society of cannibals would behave.

Mrs Foss must be prematurely senile, or suffering from overwork. 'Is that waitress of yours around anywhere?' he asked. 'What was her name?'

'Harriet. No, she hasn't been in. She wasn't in yesterday, either.'

'Do you think you could give me her address? There's just a chance that she might be able to tell me something helpful.'

'She lives with her parents on the Bethlehem Road, about three miles east of the Corners. You can't miss it. It's a square white house with a red roof almost on the road. A big maple growing right close to it.'

Charlie nodded. Mrs Foss stood quite still. 'Was that really what they say about the Célèstines?' Charlie asked her. 'They ate children?'

'Maybe it was just a bogey story,' said Mrs Foss.

'I think maybe it was,' Charlie told her.

He left the Iron Kettle and drove back to Allen's Corners. The day was windy and the trees waved at him frantically as he passed the sloping green. The two old men whom Charlie and Martin had met yesterday were sitting on their customary bench, Christopher Prescott and Oliver T. Burack. Charlie parked his car not far away from them and walked across the green with the wind in his face.

'Well, well,' said Christopher Prescott, lifting his brown fedora hat.

'Good morning.' Charlie looked around. The green was deserted except for a stray brown-and-white dog sniffing at one of the garbage baskets. 'I was wondering if you might have seen my son.'

'We certainly did,' said Christopher Prescott.

Charlie's chest tightened. 'You saw him? When? This morning?'

'Yesterday, with you,' Christopher Prescott said. 'Fine-looking boy he is, too.'

Charlie tried not to show his anger with Christopher Prescott's imbecility. 'He's gone missing,' he said. 'I was wondering if you might have seen him today.'

'Missing, huh? What's he done, run off to make his fortune? You know, that's what I did when I was a boy. I ran off to make my fortune, didn't come home for five years and two months solid, and by that time I was old enough and wealthy enough to buy my father's house out from under him. Every boy should do that. If that's what your boy's done, then good luck to him I say.'

Charlie said, 'He's only fifteen years old. He doesn't know this part of the country at all. And he left without any kind of warning. No note, no nothing.'

'Doesn't want you to find him, then. That's obvious.'

'Will you do me a favour and keep a look out for him?' Charlie asked them.

'Weather-eye open,' said Oliver T. Burack.

Charlie left them with a wave and drove out on the Bethlehem Road until he reached the white house with the red roof where Harriet lived with her parents. The house looked badly in need of paint and repair. The shiplap boards were flaking, and most of the windowsills were rotten. An avalanche of shingles had left one side of the verandah roof exposed, like bones seen through decayed flesh. From one of the overhanging branches of the big old maple tree, an old tyre swung from a fraying rope. Chickens pecked around the back door.

Charlie parked his car and climbed the creaking wooden steps to the porch. He pressed the doorbell and waited, rubbing his hands to warm them up. Dust and chaff blew in the wind; chicken feathers clung to the screen door.

After he had pressed the bell a second time, Charlie called out, 'Harriet! Are you there? Harriet!'

Without warning, the front door opened, and Charlie was confronted by a fiftyish man of slight build with thinning hair. He was wearing a carpenter's apron and he was carrying a clamp in his hand. He frowned narrowly at Charlie, and said, 'Yes?'

'I'm sorry to trouble you, sir. I'm looking for a girl called Harriet. She works at the Iron Kettle with Mrs Foss.'

'*Used* to work there. Not anymore.'

'Oh? I didn't realize that. Mrs Foss didn't tell me.'

'That's no surprise. Mrs Foss doesn't know yet.'

Charlie said, 'My name's McLean, Charlie McLean. Is Harriet here? I'd like to talk to her, if I could.'

'I'm Harriet's father, Gil Greene,' said the man. He wiped his hand on his apron and held it out. 'Been glueing a chair.'

'Is Harriet here?' asked Charlie.

'Haven't seen her since yesterday. Come on in. Would you care for some coffee? There's a pot on the stove.'

'No, thank you. It's important I talk to Harriet. Well, it could be important. Do you know where she is?'

Gil Greene shrugged, and twisted his clamp around. 'Her mother lets her do what she likes. Much against *my* better judgement, believe me. Gone off to see those French people again, that's my guess.'

'French people?'

'Them Musettes, up at the restaurant. She's always talking about them, you'd think they was crowned heads of Europe or something like that. Every now and then, they call her and she goes up to the restaurant to help out with the serving, or whatever they want her to do. Odd jobs, washing dishes, that kind of thing. She never gives Mrs Foss no notice, she just goes. She never gives us no notice neither. Sometimes she's gone for two or three days at a time, no explanations, nothing. So what can you do? Well, the point is you can't do nothing.' Gil Greene cleared his throat, and then he added, 'The last time she went, Mrs Foss said she was going to sack her if she did it again. And you can see what's happened.'

'Does Mrs Foss know where she is?' asked Charlie.

'She probably suspects. But Harriet made her mother and me promise not to tell, on account of the fact that Mrs Foss was always dead set against the Musettes right from the very beginning. I don't know whether it was anything personal but there seemed to be real bad blood between them.'

Charlie said, 'Did Harriet ever tell you what goes on at that restaurant? What they do there, or what the place is like?'

Gil Greene looked at Charlie and smiled wryly. 'You don't know Harriet. Sometimes she could talk the rear wheel off of a forty-ton truck, other times you can't get a word out of her.'

Charlie checked his watch. 'Listen,' he said, 'I'll take a drive up to the restaurant myself, see if I can get to see her. If I can't, or if I miss her, would you ask her to look me up? I'll be staying at Mrs Kemp's.'

'Didn't know Mrs Kemp was still in the boarding house business.'

'She's not. But I have to stay somewhere.'

'Rather you than me, pal.'

Charlie turned his car around and drove straight back through Allen's Corners and out on to the Quassapaug Road. A few drops of rain freckled his windshield, although it didn't look as if it were going to come down heavily. Cherub's tears, Marjorie always used to call those light sporadic showers, an occasional reminder that even the life hereafter could be unhappy, too.

The gates of Le Reposoir were locked. Charlie climbed out of the car and pressed the intercom button. There was no reply, so he pressed the button again, and kept his finger on it for almost half a minute. At last, a detached, metallic voice said, 'Please – we are closed. If you have anything to deliver, leave it at the post office in Allen's Corners. We will collect it from there ourselves.'

Charlie said, 'This is Charles McLean. I want to speak to M. Musette.'

'M. Musette is not here.'

'What about Mme Musette?'

'I regret, sir, that Mme Musette is not here, either.'

'Is there a manager? Somebody in charge?'

'Only myself, sir. I am the caretaker.'

'I'm looking for my son,' Charlie insisted, trying not to let his voice tremble.

'Your son?' asked the disembodied voice. 'I regret that I do not understand.'

'My son, Martin McLean, is missing and I have reason to believe that somebody at Le Reposoir may be able to help me locate him.'

'Sir – you must be making some mistake. There is nobody here who could possibly help you with such a matter. If your son is missing you would be advised to contact the police.'

Charlie said, 'Is Harriet Greene there?'

'I beg your pardon, sir, there is nobody of that name known to us. You seem to be suffering from some kind of misapprehension.'

'Can I come inside and talk to you? It's darned windy out here.'

'I regret that would serve no constructive purpose, sir. Besides, in M. Musette's absence, I have been requested not to admit anybody at all. There is much valuable property in the house, sir, and we have to be exceptionally careful about security.'

Charlie rubbed the back of his neck. He was feeling very stiff and very tired. 'All right,' he conceded. 'I'll go talk to the police. But I would like to see M. Musette when he comes back. Is it possible to make an appointment?'

'M. Musette has no appointments free before the end of the month.'

'The end of the month? But it's only the fourth now!'

'M. Musette is a very busy man, sir.'

Charlie controlled himself. 'I understand,' he told the voice on the intercom. 'I'm sorry if I disturbed you.'

'You are quite welcome, sir.' The voice was as faultlessly polite as it was faultlessly unhelpful.

Charlie returned to his car. For the first time he saw the remote TV camera watching him from the trees just inside the gates. He climbed back into his car, and made a showy three-point turn before taking a right along the north-west side of Le Reposoir's extensive grounds, in the opposite direction to Allen's Corners.

He drove slowly, peering between the trees that lined the roadside to see what kind of fencing protected Le Reposoir from the outside world. Every now and then he glimpsed spiked steel railings, painted green, with ceramic conductors on them. *Electrified,* he thought. *That's how much they want to keep people out. Or maybe that's how much they want to keep people in.*

After a little over a mile, however, he came to what he was looking for: a place where the grounds of Le Reposoir dipped downwards, while the verge of the road remained high. He stopped the car and got out, walking up the verge a little way to make sure that he would be able to do what he wanted to do. The wind blew across his ears like a ghostly mouth blowing across the neck of an empty bottle. He returned to his car, started up the engine again, and shifted it into first.

Carefully, he turned the Oldsmobile off the road and drove it on to the grass. The suspension bounced and bucked, and he heard the muffler scrape against the gravelly ground. But then he was able to drive at a sharp angle down towards the green spiked fence, and pull to a halt with the automobile's front bumper only an inch or two away from it. He switched off the engine and climbed out. Then – looking quickly all around him – he heaved himself up on to the hood. The sheet metal dented under his weight, but he walked without hesitation right to the front of the car to find that the green fence stood only two feet proud of the hood. He took two steps back, and then jumped right over the spikes and into the tangled bushes on the other side, tumbling over and over and tearing the elbow of his suit.

Winded, he sat up, and listened. All he could hear was the leaves rustling, and the low humming of the voltage in the electrified fence. He got up to his feet, brushed himself down, and then began to make his way through the undergrowth in the rough direction of the house.

It appeared that the woods which screened Le Reposoir from the Quassapaug Road curved in a horn shape towards the north-west side of the house; so that it would be possible for Charlie to approach the building very closely without being seen. Behind the house there were wide lawns, looking unnaturally green in the morning light, with sombre statues of naked Greek gods standing beside them, their shoulders heavy with moss, their eye-sockets blind with mildew.

The house itself was as forbidding as Charlie had remembered it. It still possessed that peculiar quality of seeming to be suspended an inch above the ground, of having infinite density, like a black diamond, but at the same time being weightless. Window upon window reflected the grey fall clouds as they hurried past, giving the extraordinary illusion that the sky was *inside* the house. Charlie came as close to the edge of the lawns as he dared, stopping and listening every few seconds in case he was being observed. The house, however, looked silent and empty. Perhaps the voice on the intercom had been telling the truth, and there was nobody here.

Charlie weaved his way in between close-set oaks and tangles of thorn that were as vicious as rolls of barbed wire. At last he reached a low stone retaining wall from which he could see into the large cast-iron solarium which ran along the back of the house. He could see potted plants and old-fashioned cane furniture, and several white marble statues of naked children. Keeping his head down, he skirted the side of the house until he came within fifteen yards of a small door. The door was carved with wooden grapes and gargoyles and studded with black iron bolts. It was impossible to tell whether it was locked or not. If it were, Charlie would not only have to risk discovery by running across the open lawn towards it, but he would have to run back again, too. He crouched down behind the retaining wall and waited to see if there was anybody around, but apart from the wind and the agitated shivering of the trees, the house and its grounds were silent. No airplanes passed overhead. No birds sang. The reflected clouds ran silently across the windows.

At last, glancing left and right, Charlie took hold of the top of the retaining wall, and prepared to heave himself up on to the upper lawn. But at the very instant he did so, the handle of the garden door rattled and turned, he ducked down just before it was opened wide. He pressed himself as close into the stones as he could, his heart beating, his face sweaty, and prayed that whoever was coming out of the garden door wouldn't come too close to the edge of the lawn and find him there. It was one thing to have driven openly into the front entrance of Le Reposoir; it was another to have deliberately breached their security and to be hiding like a would-be housebreaker in their private grounds.

He heard voices, and a noise that sounded like the squeak of badly oiled wheels. One voice was high and accented; the other was gruff, and plainly American. The high voice said, 'She should be allowed to sleep until the afternoon. You remember what it was like your first time.'

The gruff voice replied, 'I wish I could have my first time again.'

'It is the *last* time that you must look forward to now,' the high voice replied.

It sounded to Charlie as if the two speakers were moving around the side of the house and away from him. Their voices were accompanied by the persistent squeaking of wheels, as if they were pushing something. Charlie hesitated for a moment, and then edged his way about ten yards to the right along the wall until he came to a large stone urn. The urn was felted with dark green moss, and a small toad sat on its plinth, watching Charlie with yellow expressionless eyes. Charlie slowly raised his head, using the urn for cover, and tried to catch a glimpse of the people who had come out of the garden door before they disappeared.

To begin with, they were out of his line of sight behind a triangular yew bush. But suddenly they appeared quite clearly between the bush and the corner of the house, and when Charlie saw them he shivered the way a small child shivers when a grown-up shouts at him. It was surprise, and fright, but most of all it was the incongruity of their appearance, like people out of a Breughel painting of lazars and cripples.

Leading the way was the small dwarf-like figure in the white hood whom Charlie had seen at the Iron Kettle, and outside the back door at Mrs Kemp's. It walked with a swinging lurch, like an ape, yet it was distinctly human. Behind this small figure came a three wheeled invalid carriage, a kind of a Bath chair in which a pale-faced woman was lying, her eyes open, her head back, staring at the sky. She was covered up to her neck in an off-white blanket, and there was a leather strap around her waist which looked as if it was supposed to prevent her from falling out.

The invalid carriage was being pushed by the black-cloaked woman whom Charlie recognized from his first intrusion into the grounds of Le Reposoir, the woman who *might* have been Mme Musette. Her hood had fallen back, revealing her face, and even from a distance Charlie could see that she was just as striking as before, a woman of almost unbelievable beauty. Yet – remembering what he had seen in his rear-view mirror as he had driven away from the house the first time – his eyes jumped at once to the steering bar of the invalid carriage, on which the woman's hands were resting. She was wearing black cotton gloves, but only one finger of each glove was actually hooked over the bar. The remaining fingers were crumpled and obviously empty.

Charlie stared at this bizarre procession until it had disappeared from sight around the side of the house. Then he slowly slid down into a sitting position behind the retaining wall, oblivious to the green moss which smeared the back of his coat. He felt as if he had accidentally wandered into some extraordinary Victorian nightmare. *Alice Through the Looking Glass* with freaks and dwarves and beautiful women with no fingers. He wiped his face with his hands; he was wet with chilly sweat.

It was not only the weirdness of the procession that had frightened him. It was the conviction that he had recognized the pale-faced woman lying in the invalid carriage staring at the sky. Although he had glimpsed her for only two or three seconds, he could have sworn that it was Harriet Greene.

If it were Harriet Greene, though, what the hell had they done to her? She looked almost as if she were dying.

Charlie waited for nearly a minute. Then he raised his head cautiously over the top of the wall to see if there was anybody else around. But the house and the lawns seemed to be deserted, and even though ravens were circling around the spires which rose above the house like monuments in a Victorian cemetery, they were silent, as if they knew that this was not the place to cry out.

Grunting with effort, after a working lifetime of four-course meals and not very much in the way of coherent exercise, Charlie climbed up the retaining wall and then crouched on the very edge of the lawn like a middle-aged backstop who refuses to admit that he is over the hill. The grass was bright and green and springy, and felt almost like short-cropped human hair. Charlie held his breath and listened – then made his way as quickly and as quietly as he could across the lawn to the garden door. By the time he reached it he was trembling with tension, but he took hold of the handle without hesitation and turned it. It had been left unlocked, and it swung open easily, without the slightest squeal. Charlie glanced behind him to make sure that he wasn't being watched, and then stepped inside.

9

He found himself in a store room, which was gloomy but very dry. Rakes, hoes and edging-spades were hanging neatly on the walls and there were sacks of aromatic peat, of lawn-feed and rose fertilizer. Charlie edged between the sacks until he found another door on the far side of the room, a grey-painted steel door, with an automatic hinge to close it. He turned the handle, and to his relief this door wasn't locked either. He eased it open and put his head around it. On the other side there was a long oak-panelled corridor, very dark and smelling of polish, with mottled engravings all along the walls. Charlie stepped out of the store room and into the corridor, and then hesitated, wondering which direction he ought to take. If he went to the right, towards the front of the house, it would probably be easier to get his bearings. But if the Musettes were really holding Martin, it was unlikely that they would have hidden him in any of the principal rooms at the front.

He turned left, towards the back of the house. His fingers trailed along the stained oak panelling, as if he needed to touch the wall to keep his hold on reality. He glanced up at one or two of the old engravings. They were French, and they were all concerned with butchery. They showed the carcasses of cattle and sheep, and serious-faced men with big moustaches and white aprons removing with large knives the *aiguillettes* and *culottes* and *plats de côtes découverts.*

When he reached the end of the corridor he found himself at the foot of an oak staircase, which led steeply up towards a back landing. There was a large window overlooking the landing, which filled the stairwell with grey photographic light. Charlie guessed that this must have originally been used as the servants' staircase. He looked upward. There was the sound of someone vacuum cleaning in some far-off bedroom, but that was all. He began to climb the treads one at a time, holding on to the banisters.

He was halfway up the stairs when a voice said, '*Charlie?*'

He looked up in shock. Standing just above him, one elbow casually propped on the banister, was Velma, dressed in a linen kaftan so fine that it was almost transparent. She was smiling at him dreamily, as if nothing had happened between them at all; as if they were old chums who happened to have bumped into each other on a quiet New England commuter train.

'They told me you didn't even exist,' said Charlie unsteadily.

'Who said I didn't even exist?' She wouldn't stop smiling. 'Those people at the Windsor. Bits, whatever his name was. The maitre d'. He denied point-blank that he'd ever seen you. When I said that you called him Bits, he laughed in my face.'

'I expect he did,' said Velma. 'I made it up.'

Charlie said tightly, 'Is Martin here?'

'Martin?'

'My son. Was that what you were doing—keeping me busy while Martin was being kidnapped?'

'Charlie,' said Velma, 'you're not making any sense.'

Charlie took a sharp, impatient breath. 'When I returned to my room at the Windsor after I'd spent the night with you, Martin was gone. There wasn't any trace of him at all. There wasn't any trace of you, either.'

'I left,' said Velma, with complete simplicity.

'Well, sure you did. In fact, the hotel porter said you'd never even been there. So did Bits, or whatever his name is. So what was I supposed to think?'

Velma teased up her hair with her fingers. 'This is private property, you know. You shouldn't be here.'

'I want to know if my son's here, that's all.'

Velma suddenly stopped preening herself and stared at Charlie in amusement. 'How old did you say your son was? Fifteen?'

Charlie took three or four more steps up the staircase, until he was almost at the top. He was trying to be threatening but Velma didn't seem to be intimidated in the least. She cupped one hand over her left breast through the gauzy fabric of her gown, and lifted it slightly as if she was weighing it. Charlie had felt it for himself. He knew how soft and heavy it was.

'You said something about the Célèstines this morning, didn't you?'

'Did I?' Velma asked him.

'You thought that I wanted to join them, didn't you? I mean—that's what goes on here, doesn't it? Meetings of the Célèstines? You thought that I wanted to join, and that's why you kidnapped Martin.'

Velma stretched and yawned. 'You're going to get into serious trouble, you know, if M. Musette finds you here. M. Musette is very particular about trespassers. If it was legal, he'd shoot them dead. But of course he's too law-abiding to do that.'

Charlie reached the top step. He was only three feet away from Velma now. He could smell her favourite perfume, Obsession, and he could see the crow's-feet around her eyes that last night had looked like experience and excitement, and which this morning looked like the first sign of advancing age. He could see her stiffened nipples through the linen of her gown. He didn't even know whether he liked her or despised her. He didn't even know what he thought about the Musettes. All he cared about was finding Martin, and if that meant being friendly to people he despised, then that is what he would do. He couldn't help thinking of Mrs Foss, and the serious way in which she had looked at him through her upswept eyeglasses and said: '*The story most people used to tell was that they were taking stray children off the streets and fattening them up, so that they could eat them.*'

And he couldn't help thinking about his own response. '*I haven't heard anything like that since Hansel and Gretel.*'

Charlie stood close beside Velma and touched her hair. 'Is Martin here?' he asked her gently. 'I'm his father, Velma. I'm responsible for what happens to him.'

'And do you love him?' she challenged.

'What do you think? He's my only child, my only son.'

'That doesn't mean anything at all. I was my father's only daughter, and he used to beat me up every day. Well, it felt like every day. He used to burn the soles of my feet with cigarettes.'

Charlie said, 'What are you trying to do? Are you trying to make me feel guilty, or what? Your childhood is nothing to do with me. I just want to know if Martin is here, that's all. I just want to know what the hell is happening.'

Velma's eyes brightened. 'Come with me,' she said. 'You want to know what the hell is happening? Well, let me show you.'

Charlie hesitated for a moment, but then he allowed Velma to take hold of his arm and lead him away from the landing and down a long, narrow corridor that was the twin of the corridor downstairs. Oak-panelled, dark, with only occasional windows to light up the framed engravings of abattoirs and butchery. One engraving showed a selection of butcher's knives, skinning knives, sticking knives, boning knives, cleavers and splitting saws. Another showed offal being sliced, liver, kidneys, hearts, and sweetbreads. Each engraving carried a caption in French.

'Are the Musettes at home?' Charlie asked, as they made their way along the corridor.

'What makes you ask that?'

'I saw some people in the garden. Somebody in a hood, like a dwarf; and a woman in a black cloak. The first time I came here, I got the impression that the woman in the black cloak was Mme Musette.'

Velma glanced at him over her shoulder. 'Come and see this before you ask me any more questions.'

'They were wheeling a woman in an invalid carriage,' Charlie persisted. He reached out and took hold of Velma's arm and stopped her. 'Listen to me, will you? I knew the woman from before. At least, I thought I did. She used to work as a waitress at the Iron Kettle.'

Velma unexpectedly bent forward and kissed Charlie on the mouth. 'You really don't know what's going on, do you?'

Charlie said, 'Maybe you ought to tell me. I mean, you're obviously in it with them. You're obviously a part of it.'

'A part of what?' asked Velma, with an innocence that was plainly feigned, and intended to taunt him even more.

'*This*,' said Charlie. 'The Musettes. The Windsor Hotel. All of this. Martin disappearing. That Goddamned dwarf. The way that every single person I've met in the past two days has jumped like a jackrabbit whenever anybody mentions Le Reposoir. It's all tied together, and don't you try to kid me otherwise.'

Velma looked at Charlie for a very long time, and then turned her head away. He was conscious that her profile was very handsome, and that her breasts swelled up inside the thin linen of her gown in a way that provoked him, even now.

'I guess you could say they misjudged you,' she said.

'Who misjudged me?'

She gave him a smile as faint as a distant echo. 'They thought that you knew a whole lot more about the Célèstines than you obviously did. M. Musette found out you were a restaurant inspector. I guess he must have thought that a restaurant inspector knew about the Célèstines.'

'Well, as a matter of fact, I don't. Maybe I'm unusually ignorant or something. Mrs Foss back at the Iron Kettle gave me some kind of weird story about them; and that's why I came up here. I was worried about Martin.'

Somewhere deep in the building a heavy door slammed, and echoed. Velma said, 'We'd better hurry. Mme Musette will be looking for me in a minute.'

Charlie kept hold of her arm. 'First you have to tell me the truth about these Célèstines.'

'Don't you understand?—I'm going to *show* you.'

Reluctantly, Charlie followed her further along the corridor. She pushed her way ahead of him through a swing fire door and crossed a wide hallway with a yellow-tinted skylight and a highly polished linoleum floor. On the other side of the hallway, there was a solid oak door with a varnished wooden shield on it, emblazoned with a painting of a Papal crown, encircled by a halo.

Another door slammed, closer this time, and Charlie thought he could hear footsteps. 'They won't go totally ape, will they, if they find me here?' he asked Velma. He was beginning to feel seriously worried now. Velma didn't answer him, but pressed her finger against her lips and opened the door decorated with the Papal crown.

Beyond, there was another corridor, at least sixty feet long, dimly lit by small windows set into the doors which ran along either side. Velma beckoned Charlie to follow her, and she went from window to window, peering inside. The first three windows were covered by white cotton blinds. The fourth was uncovered, but the room inside was empty, except for a plain metal-framed bed and a white screen of the type used in hospitals.

'What the hell is this?' Charlie demanded, but Velma suddenly touched his arm and indicated with a nod of her head that he should look into the fifth window.

At first, Charlie couldn't quite understand what he was supposed to see. The room was almost bare, and lit only by the pale uncompromising daylight. A young girl was sitting cross-legged on the floor at a three-quarter angle to the door, so that Charlie could just see her profile. He guessed that she was about fourteen or fifteen years old. Her dark hair was bobbed, and she was dressed in the same kind of linen gown that Velma was wearing.

'I see a girl, that's all,' whispered Charlie.

'She's one of the new ones,' said Velma.

'One of the new what?'

'Devotees, that's what the Célèstines call them.'

'Velma, I don't understand. I simply don't understand. You're going to have a spell it out for me.'

Velma smiled broadly and there was something about her smile which made Charlie feel uncomfortably cold. It was a lewd, coarse smile; the smile of someone who has indulged every lust that you can think of, and many more that you could never think of.

'Look at her feet,' she urged Charlie.

'Her *feet*?' Charlie turned back to the window and peered at the girl more closely.

It was then he realized that the girl's feet were both mutilated. There was a heel, an arch, and that was all. The girl had no toes.

Charlie turned back to Velma and hissed, 'What? What is this all about?'

'It's exactly what it looks like,' she said. 'She hasn't any toes.'

'But why? Is this some kind of a nursing home or something?'

'Nursing home?' Velma laughed. 'Of course not.'

'Then what happened to her feet?'

'She cut off her toes, of course.'

'What do you mean, "of course"? What kind of a state of mind do you have to be in to cut your own toes off?'

'Devotional,' said Velma, as if that explained everything.

'Devotional?' Charlie echoed. 'That doesn't look like devotion to me. That looks like a straightforward case of insanity.'

'Believe me, she's not insane,' said Velma.

'Then why did she cut off her toes?' Charlie demanded. His voice was quivering now.

Velma looked at him with an expression that was almost pitying. 'Why do you *think* she cut them off? To eat them, of course.'

As she said that, the door opened behind them. Charlie, already shocked at what Velma had told him, turned around in alarm.

Standing in the doorway, silhouetted against the yellow radiance from the skylight in the hall, was M. Musette. He paused; and then he came forward so that Charlie could see his face. 'Well, Mr McLean,' he said. 'I don't know whether I ought to be happy to see you or not.'

Charlie cleared his throat. 'I don't care whether you're happy or not, pal. You and I have some talking to do.'

'Perhaps you're right,' said M. Musette. 'Velma, will you go to your room? I want to talk to you later.'

Velma passed them by. As she did so, she glanced at Charlie quickly, and Charlie saw such an extraordinary mixture of fear and desire on her face that he couldn't help looking at M. Musette in complete consternation.

10

Downstairs, in a drawing room with high leaded windows which overlooked the gardens, M. Musette sat back in a deeply cushioned armchair and crossed his immaculately pressed trouser legs and lit a cigarette. Charlie, sitting on the far side of the room, could hardly see him behind a circular antique table on which stood a huge pink and white ceramic planter crowded with hothouse camellias.

'I have to confess that what has happened has largely been my responsibility,' said M. Musette affably. 'I must ask your forgiveness, although I am sure you will find it easy to understand how the error was made.'

'Before you start giving me any explanations, I want to ask you one question,' Charlie interrupted. M. Musette, with a wave of his cigarette, indicated that Charlie could do whatever he wanted.

'Is my son here?' Charlie asked him. 'I want a straight answer, yes or no.'

'My dear sir, let me put it this way: nobody ever comes here except of their own free will. Therefore you must search in your heart and ask yourself whether it is *likely* that your son is here.'

'I said a straight answer, not a Goddamned riddle.'

M. Musette blew smoke, and smiled. 'Then I promise that I will answer you before you leave. But first, I want you to understand what is happening here, and why you should not be so fearful.'

'I'm not sure that I want to understand. Was it right what Velma was telling me—that girl actually ate her own toes?'

'You're running ahead of me,' said M. Musette. 'You came here to find out more about the Célèstines. Let me tell you about them.'

'Okay,' Charlie agreed. 'But don't take all day about it.'

M. Musette said, 'Do I have to remind you that you are trespassing on my property and on my time and that I am not obliged to say anything to you at all? It would be far easier for me to call for the sheriff and have you thrown out of here.'

Charlie didn't answer, but clasped his hands together and sat with his head bowed waiting for M. Musette to speak. M. Musette stood up, and walked across to the windows in a wafting cloud of Turkish cigarette smoke. He gazed out over the garden for a while, obviously calming himself, and then he said, 'The Célèstines were originally members of a religious order created in the year 1260 by Saint Célèstine V, Pietro di Murrone. Célèstine was elected Pope in 1294, after the two-year interregnum that followed the death of Nicholas V. He was a saintly man, but too politically weak for the duties demanded by the Papacy, and later the same year, he abdicated in the face of opposition from Cardinal Gaetano, who was to succeed him as Pope Boniface VIII.'

M. Musette paused, and inhaled smoke, and went on: 'The Célèstines flourished during their founder's lifetime, and at their height they had over 150 houses throughout Europe. But at the time of the French Revolution they declined, and many of the French members of the order fled abroad, some to England and some to the Caribbean. It was on the Caribbean island of Sainte Desirée that the remnants of Saint Célèstine's devotees were transformed into the predecessors of the present-day Célèstines.'

M. Musette turned, and watched Charlie carefully as he spoke. 'What happened was a remarkable mixing of two cultures. Sainte Desirée is a wild and desolate island about fifteen miles off the coast of Guadeloupe. Its sole inhabitants before the exiled Célèstines arrived were native fishermen, who barely managed to make a living out of their labours. The fishermen, however, were Caribs, members of that fierce and alarming tribe who before the days of Columbus had indulged themselves in orgies of cannibalism. By the time the Célèstines reached Sainte Desirée, their ritual eating of human flesh had long since died out; but somehow, they were inspired by the religious enthusiasm of the new arrivals to revive it. There were close similarities, you see, between the ritual of the Holy Communion, with its eating of the Lord's flesh and the drinking of the Lord's blood, and the eating of human beings which had once been the Caribs' speciality.'

Charlie kept his head lowered, but the feeling that was beginning to penetrate his consciousness was one of extreme dread. He felt almost as if he were being lowered against his will into a bath of chilly water; helpless to resist.

'It is quite extraordinary how cultures can intermingle,' said M. Musette. 'There are natives in New Guinea who worship aeroplanes as gods, because their only experience of them is to see them flying high overhead. There are many pagan rituals inextricably woven into the so-called Christian calendar. The very day on which we say we are celebrating the birth of Christ our Lord was in reality one of the darkest and most magical days of rejoicing in the times of the Druids. What happened to the Célèstines as they lived in isolation on Sainte Desirée with the Caribs was that they came to believe that true communion with God could only be consummated by the eating of human flesh and the drinking of human blood.'

Charlie looked up. 'Is this true? Is this authentic history, or are you putting me on?'

'Do you think I would waste my valuable time playing practical jokes?' M. Musette retorted. 'I am talking about the achievement of oneness with God, and complete oneness with your fellow human beings. Does that sound like a put-on, as you call it?'

Charlie said tautly, 'Go on.'

M. Musette crushed out his cigarette in a large crystal ashtray. 'Over a period of 150 years, generation after generation, the Célèstine Order gradually evolved into what it is today.'

'And what is it today? A club for well-heeled cannibals?'

'Cannibalism is a word we prefer not to use; even though it describes us aptly. The word 'cannibal', after all, is derived from *Canibales*, which is the Spanish variant of the name Caribs. Cannibalism also implies that we are involved in the violent or forceful eating of the sacred flesh. While the Caribs often murdered their enemies and sometimes their friends in order to make a meal of them, the Célèstines introduced to them the Christian principle that thou shalt not kill. Instead, the eating of the sacred flesh became a *self-sacrificial* communion, in accord with the very highest tenets of Christianity.'

Charlie stared at M. Musette in complete horror. He was at last beginning to realize that he was being told the truth – that M. Musette in all seriousness was explaining to him that the Célèstines really did eat human flesh.

Unperturbed, M. Musette went on, 'Did not Jesus say, "*Take, eat, this is My body*"? And did he not say, "*Drink... for this is My blood of the new testament*"? The whole essence of Christianity is concerned with the sharing of flesh and blood. Not murderously, of course, but *voluntarily*—the devoted giving of one's body for the greater glory of all. That girl you saw upstairs—as Velma told you, she is a new Devotee. So far she has amputated only her toes.'

'And *eaten* them?' Charlie asked, his throat constricted.

'Only five of them. The rest she shared with her Guide and with other Devotees.' M. Musette pressed his hands together as if he were saying grace. 'A small and simple meal, but one of tremendous emotional and religious significance as far as she is concerned.'

Charlie said, 'I'm sorry, I'm finding it difficult to believe what I'm hearing. I cannot even begin to comprehend how a pretty young girl like that can voluntarily mutilate herself and eat her own flesh. Not for the greatest religious cause known to man. Not for any reason whatsoever. It's barbaric.'

M. Musette shook his head. 'Barbaric? No. It is the most highly developed act of religious devotion that I can think of. It demands the greatest degree of devotion to God that you can possibly imagine. It shows in real terms the conquest of the spirit over the flesh. To devour the very body that God gave you is the closest that you can ever get to true holiness.'

'You're out of your tree,' said Charlie. He stood up, and his legs felt as if they were about to fold up like a cheap camera tripod. 'All I want to hear from you is that Martin isn't here, and then I'm going to go straight to the police. You ought to be locked up. Jesus Christ, I don't know how you've gotten away with it for so long. And so openly!'

'The reason is quite simple,' said M. Musette. 'While it may be against the law to eat the flesh of others against their will, it is not against the law to eat yourself; neither is it against the law to eat the flesh of another person if that flesh is offered without any form of coercion. We have had the status of a religion for nearly eighty years now, and while the law may not approve of what we are doing, they know that they cannot touch us. We live with the law in relative harmony. They do not harass us, and we in turn carry out our rituals as discreetly as possible. As you yourself know, we do not exactly encourage visitors.'

'But you present this place as a *restaurant*,' Charlie said.

'As a dining society, rather than a restaurant,' M. Musette corrected him. 'In that way, we do not arouse the unwelcome attention of those Godless media people in whose eyes every religious sect is a target for scandalous exposé. In order to perform our rituals, we require much of the apparatus and many of the supplies that would be used by a dining society, and so to present to the outside world the image of a restaurant is useful camouflage. The name Le Reposoir was carefully chosen because it has two different meanings – one for our devotees and one for the outside world. Le Reposoir means 'the resting place'; but it also means 'the little altar'.

'Then the police know about this place? They know what you do? And they haven't taken any action to stop you?'

'My dear sir, the whole surrounding community is aware that there is something special about Le Reposoir. Many consider us frightening; at least until they have the opportunity to see for themselves the true significance of our rituals. I suppose you could say that there is a parallel with World War Two, when many German citizens living close to concentration camps were aware that there was something of great drama happening in their district, but preferred on the whole not to investigate too closely. Of all creatures, man is the most incurious, believe me.'

Charlie said, 'Haxalt knows, doesn't he? The president of the savings bank?'

M. Musette nodded. 'Almost all of those with senior civic positions in Allen's Corners are aware of what we are, and what we do.'

'Then *why*—?'

'Because many of their sons and daughters have joined us. Because many of *them* have joined us. There are fifty-eight Devotees here at the moment; some of them are the children of families whose names you would recognize. Others may not have come to us from such celebrated homes, but their parents nonetheless have considerable influence in the community.'

Charlie slowly rubbed the back of his neck to ease the tension. 'Is Haxalt a Devotee? He's not eating himself, is he?'

M. Musette smiled. 'There are two levels of Devotion. There are the Devotees, those who attain spiritual perfection through self-ingestion. Then there are the Guides, who participate in the rituals by eating the flesh of the Devotees—only, of course, when that flesh is freely and openly offered. The Guides are both mentors and servants to the Devotees. They must assist them to reach spiritual perfection by discussing the scriptures with them; they must also do anything that the Devotees ask of them, no matter what. To give you an example, we had a Devotee in New Orleans who fell in love with his Guide, who was a woman. A very striking woman, I might tell you, a real Cajun beauty. One day the Devotee demanded that she take out his eyes and eat them, so that he would no longer be tempted by her looks.'

'You're telling me this to frighten me off,' Charlie said, 'I don't believe any of it.'

'Well, believe whatever you wish,' said M. Musette.

Charlie hesitated, and then asked, 'Did she?'

'I'm sorry?' said M. Musette, his head on one side.

'Did she eat his eyeballs?'

'Oh, that! You must use your own imagination. But I have been told that there is something very special about the human eyeball, especially when it has been freshly gouged out, and snipped quickly from its optic nerve. You can do it with very little pain indeed, provided you are careful; and I understand that there is no sensation on earth like biting into an eyeball when the optic fluid inside is still warm from its living owner... Ha! Do you think I'm trying to frighten you now? Maybe I am. Maybe, rather, your own inhibitions are frightening you. You eat other animals, don't you? You eat slices of cattle and lumps of lamb. Why should there be any difference when it comes to humans? Especially when you think that those cattle and those sheep and those pigs that you eat—you aren't Jewish, are you?—are all *murdered*, so to speak. None of them would *volunteer* to be eaten if they had the choice. Whereas the humans who are eaten here are eaten because they want to be, of their own free will. Isn't that far more moral?'

Charlie said, 'I've heard enough of this garbage. I want you to tell me if my son is here, and that's all.'

M. Musette lifted both hands. There was a gold ring on his right middle finger in the shape of two snakes, entwined, with emeralds for eyes. 'You are like most Americans, I regret,' he said smiling. 'You have no sense of humour whatsoever.'

'I can laugh when something's funny. This isn't funny.'

'Very well,' said M. Musette. 'I appreciate your anxiety. Your son *is* here. He came here early this morning of his own free will, and asked whether he might be initiated into the order of the Célèstines.'

Charlie had been almost certain that Martin couldn't have been here – not after all that fantastic nonsense about people eating themselves. He was so shocked when M. Musette casually admitted that he *was* that for one fragmented moment he was unable to think of anything to say. He stared at M. Musette with one clenched fist held tightly against his chest. Then he managed to say, 'You'd better show me where he is, and pretty damn quick.'

'He did ask that you should be kept away,' said M. Musette. 'At least until he's had time to settle himself in.'

'You're crazy! This is kidnap! This is a capital offence! Now you show me where my son is or else I'm going to be doing some damage around here!'

'Please, Mr McLean, keep calm. Losing your temper isn't going to solve anything.'

Charlie seized hold of M. Musette's lapels and tugged him forward until their noses were almost touching. 'You show me where my son is *right now* or else I'm going to break your arms.'

M. Musette said quietly, 'I don't think so,' and grasped Charlie's wrists. With almost no effort at all, he prised Charlie's hands away from his coat, and lowered them. Then he fastidiously brushed his lapels and gave Charlie a nod that was more of a warning than an acknowledgement of what he had done.

Charlie was breathing deeply. 'Let me get this straight. Martin came to you of his own free will?'

'That's what I said.'

'How did he get here? He doesn't have any transportation.'

'He arrived by taxi at about midnight last night. He paid the fare out of his own money. He was unaccompanied, so there was no possible question of kidnap. I talked to him myself when he arrived. He said that he had decided to join us, and that he was prepared to become one of our Devotees.'

'And what did you do?' snarled Charlie. 'Give him a knife and fork and tell him to get on with it?'

'As a matter of fact, my dear sir, I tried very hard to dissuade him from becoming a Devotee. I always do when I am approached by volunteers. I explain that it is a difficult and painful road to heaven, a road that is often beset by terrible doubts, and which can bring despair as well as ecstasy.'

Charlie said, 'He listens to rock music and reads comic-books. How the hell was he supposed to understand anything like that?'

'Your son is far more perceptive than you think. He sees you and your weaknesses quite clearly. For himself, he wants something better.'

'Cutting your own toes off and eating them is better? What kind of a cockamamie crock of shit is that?'

'Just listen to yourself,' M. Musette said. 'Listen to the sound of your own voice. You are a man of impulse and vulgarity, a man with no spirituality whatsoever. You have spent your whole life in the empty pursuit of something you can never find, which is yourself. Those endless meals you eat, those endless miles you drive, you are looking for something which you left behind with your wife and your son. Your soul is what I am talking about, Mr

McLean. Your spirit.' He paused briefly, and then he said, 'Your son came here because he didn't want the same fate to befall him. He has accompanied you on your travels for only a few days, but he has already seen the tragedy of your life. It was you who precipitated his decision to come here, not I, nor any of my Devotees.'

'This is bull,' Charlie retorted. 'If it hadn't been for Harriet Greene and that damned dwarf of yours, he never would have known about Le Reposoir.'

'Oh yes, dearest Harriet,' said M. Musette. 'Harriet has wanted to join us ever since I first employed her as a waitress. A little too enthusiastic, I'm afraid; a little too talkative. She never should have mentioned our name. And of course David was waiting to collect her from the Iron Kettle and bring her here. He couldn't help noticing such an obvious candidate as Martin.'

'Who's David?' Charlie demanded.

'The one you call the dwarf. David was a Devotee, too; but at the very height of his initiation, he decided that he could no longer continue. It was impossible for him to return to the outside world, of course; but to atone for his lack of faith he acts as our gofer. His punishment for doubting the reality of heaven is the lifelong humiliation of having to live in that part of his body which he denied to the Lord.'

'And Velma? You got me involved with Velma deliberately, didn't you, so that Martin would have time to escape?'

'Nobody obliged you to get involved with Velma, Mr McLean. You did it of your own free will. You put the beastly desires of the flesh before your spiritual involvement with your son, and that is why he left you. If you had stayed with him that night, then the chances are that you could have convinced him that you are not the man he perceives you to be. You might have won his heart for ever. As it is... he is here now, and he is preparing himself for a physical and spiritual journey whose end is glory.'

'Take me to him, now,' said Charlie. 'This is your last warning.'

'He has no wish to see you.'

'I don't give a damn. He's my son, he's a minor, and I'm legally responsible for him. I'm taking him away with me, and what's more I'm going to make sure your ass is thrown straight into jail, for kidnap, and unlawful imprisonment, and unnatural practices, and anything else that the law can throw at you.'

M. Musette laughed out loud. 'Very well, you can see him if you want to. What else can I do, but bow to such a terrifying threat? Let me call my wife, she will take you.'

He went across to a rococo-styled telephone and picked it up. 'Aimée, this is Edouard. Yes, that's correct. I have Mr McLean with me, and Mr McLean is anxious to see Martin before he leaves.'

M. Musette's familiar use of Martin's Christian name was not lost on Charlie. Nor was the implication that Charlie would be leaving alone.

'My wife will be with you directly,' said M. Musette. 'I hope very much that you will not be excessively angry with us, my dear sir. Our beliefs are deeply rooted, and tenaciously held, but we always do our very best to live in peace with those who do not revere the body and blood in the same way that we do.'

He opened his case and took out another cigarette. Charlie watched him in fascination and loathing. M. Musette seemed so single-minded, his view of the world seemed so complete; and Charlie felt that M. Musette had tipped open *his* brain like a worn out carpetbag cluttered with fear and prejudice and stubborn odds and ends. M. Musette lit his cigarette placidly, and returned Charlie's grim stare with the most courteous of smiles.

After a minute or two, the doors opened, and Mme Musette stepped into the room. Charlie had been right. She was indeed the beautiful fingerless woman in the black cloak. Now, however, she was wearing a watered silk day dress in misty blue, and she looked even more beautiful than before. Her eyes were startlingly wide; her skin glowed; her lips were infinitesimally parted in unconscious sensuality. All that betrayed her involvement with the Célèstines was the gloves she wore: wrist-length cotton gloves in blue to match her dress.

'Mr McLean,' she said softly, and inclined her head. 'Our security people have found your car. If you will let me have the keys, they will return it to the front entrance for you, so that you may leave here in comfort.'

Charlie reached into his pocket and handed over his keys. 'Just don't be too anxious to get rid of me, Mme Musette. I'm not leaving here without my son.'

'Well, we shall see,' she said. 'Would you care to come with me? Your son is upstairs, where all our new Devotees stay.'

'Please,' said M. Musette, and indicated with a smart click of his heels that Charlie should follow his wife.

Mme Musette led Charlie across the echoing marble-clad hallway. A thin youth with close-cropped hair and a suit that looked as if it had once belonged to Buddy Holly stood at the foot of the stairs. Mme Musette handed him Charlie's car keys. The youth gave Charlie a quick, insolent smile that Mme Musette either failed to notice or ignored.

She mounted the stairs and Charlie followed close behind her, smelling her perfume. He couldn't identify it. It wasn't anything as modern as Obsession. It could have been Chanel No. 5, but on Mme Musette's skin it seemed to have acquired a flowery aura all her own. Halfway up the stairs, Charlie said, 'Are you a Devotee, too?'

'I was; but Edouard decided that I could better serve the order if I were to assist him.'

'So you stopped at a few fingers, is that it?'

Mme Musette turned her head and glanced at him. 'That's it. You have it exactly.'

'Are you all headcases or what?' Charlie asked her.

'I don't know what you mean, headcases.'

'I mean are you mad? In my book, self-mutilation is the act of a lunatic. As for eating yourself, that's so far out I don't even know where it is.'

'Didn't Edouard explain our beliefs to you?'

'Oh, yes, sure he did. But I notice that Edouard hasn't started making himself into Edouardburger yet, whatever he says about his beliefs. And he stopped you before you got to the best bits.'

'You cannot make sport of us, Mr McLean,' she replied. 'Edouard is our Supreme Guide, and like all of the Guides in the Célestine order it is his duty to remain whole until the end of his natural life. It is a *duty*—not a privilege. The truly privileged members of the Célestines are those who manage to devour so much of themselves that there is scarcely anything remaining to make a meal for their mentors.'

They had reached the landing. Charlie said, 'You know something? If any of this is true, it's criminal and it's maniacal and it's totally disgusting. I thought James Jones was nuts, but you people are unreal.'

'Come see your son,' said Mme Musette gently. 'But may I warn you not to upset him? He is in the early stages of self-preparation, and if you try to bully him into leaving Le Reposoir you may cause him lasting psychological damage. You will certainly lose his affection for ever.'

'Don't let's make any mistakes here,' said Charlie. 'That boy is coming away with me right now.' He was angry; but he still wished that he didn't sound so much like Archie Bunker. The Musettes were bringing out his blue-collar Indiana background and there was nothing that he could do to stop it.

They walked down the same corridor to which Velma had taken him, all the way down to a door at the end. Mme Musette raised her deformed hand and knocked. There was a short delay, and then the door opened and a girl's face appeared. Dark, Latin-looking, with unplucked eyebrows.

'This is Martin's father,' said Mme Musette. 'He wishes to speak to Martin before he leaves.'

The Latin-looking girl glanced quickly at Charlie and then shook her head. 'It is not possible, *madame.* He is already preparing himself.'

Charlie stepped forward and pushed the door. 'Come on, honey, just get out of the way will you? I want to talk to my son.'

The girl tried to resist him, but Charlie gave her a sharp dig in the breast with his elbow, and she released her hold on the door. Mme Musette cried, 'No, Mr McLean!' but Charlie ignored her and barged into the room.

A white cotton blind had been drawn across the window, so the room was dim. There was a plain bed, covered by a white cotton sheet, a tubular steel chair, a white-painted bedside cupboard with a Bible on it, and that was all. Martin lay on the bed staring at the ceiling. He was naked.

'Martin! For Christ's sake!' said Charlie, and his eyes filled with tears. 'Martin, it's Dad here!'

He went up to the bed and took hold of Martin's hand. Martin's eyes slowly turned to look at him as if he had all the time in the world. 'You came,' he whispered. His voice sounded as if he were drugged.

'Of course I came. What did you expect? Why didn't you talk to me before you left? You didn't have to come to a place like this.'

Martin smiled. 'This is the only place, Dad. This is really and truly the only place.'

'Martin?' Charlie asked. 'Did they give you any kind of injection? Any pills, or dope, or anything like that?' Before Martin could reply, he turned around to Mme Musette, who was standing in the open doorway and he waved his finger at her threateningly. 'Believe me, lady, you're in deep trouble. Where are his clothes?'

'He has renounced his clothes,' said the Latin-looking girl.

'I'll renounce you in a minute!' Charlie roared at her. 'Just bring me his fucking clothes!'

'Mr McLean,' put in Mme Musette, 'I did warn you that it would do you no good to lose your temper.'

Charlie ignored her. 'Martin,' he said, 'you're coming with me, and you're coming now. The car's outside. You can put on something of mine.'

'I'm not coming with you, Dad,' said Martin. He seemed to be completely unperturbed.

'Am I hearing you straight? Do you know what these people expect you to do?'

'I know all about the Célèstines, David told me. That day in the parking lot; and that night at Mrs Kemp's. We talked about it for hours. I know what they do and I know why they do it and I want to do it, too.'

'You want to eat yourself? Are you bananas?'

The absurdity of what his father had said made Martin chuckle. It was that chuckle that unsettled Charlie more than anything else. His own son could lie here and laugh because he had said something stupid; when all the time he was volunteering to commit suicide, slowly and ritualistically and obscenely.

Charlie grabbed hold of Martin's wrists and tried to wrench him off the bed. But Martin twisted away from him, and kicked him in the ribs with his bare foot, and then seized the rails at the head of the bed and glared at Charlie defiantly.

'Dad, this is my life and this is my decision.'

Charlie turned on Mme Musette again. 'You've hypnotized him, right? Is that it? Am I right? You've hypnotized him!'

Mme Musette was holding the hand of the Latin-looking girl in order to restrain her. The girl was obviously distressed, and kept tugging at her hair and mewling. 'There is no question of drugs or hypnosis or any artificial stimulant,' Mme Musette said. 'We believe in the sanctity of the body, we believe in its purity. We would never allow anything to taint the flesh which we ourselves must eat.'

'Martin, come with me!' Charlie ordered him, but Martin's hands remained clenched on the rails at the head of the bed, and he shook his head in adamant refusal.

Charlie took a deep breath. He looked at his son and could see by the expression on his face that, for now, the Musettes had won. He couldn't pick Martin up bodily and carry him out of Le Reposoir, he simply wasn't strong enough. And that was supposing M. Musette and his staff would allow him to carry Martin out of the house without any opposition at all.

'All right,' he conceded. 'I'm going to leave you for now. But let me tell you right here and now that the first stop I'm going to be making is the county sheriff's office, and if necessary I'm going to inform the FBI, too. Then we'll see who makes a meal out of whom.'

Charlie contemptuously brushed Mme Musette aside and began stalking back down the corridor. 'Mr McLean!' she called after him. 'It won't do you any good!'

'I'll let the sheriff be the judge of that,' Charlie retorted. 'And one more thing—if Martin is missing even one fingernail by the time I get back here, I'm personally going to take the law into my own hands and I'm going to kill you. You and your husband both—slowly!'

He ran down the stairs, across the hallway, and out of the huge front doors. As promised, his car was waiting for him, with its hood dented and clumps of grass still clinging to its wheel-arches. He cantered down the stone steps and across the gravel, and as he did so a flock of ravens rose cawing from the spires of Le Reposoir, the first birds that he had heard since he trespassed here. They sounded harsh and triumphant, and they circled around and around above his head as if they were gloating over his defeat.

He got into the car, slammed the door, and switched on the engine. As he did so, Mme Musette came down the front steps of the house after him. She stopped only a few feet away, and Charlie let down his window.

'I'm going straight to the police,' he warned her.

'I know that,' she replied. 'It will do you no good.'

'Maybe it will and maybe it won't.'

'Don't you think every parent who finds out that their son or daughter has come to join the Célèstines feels the same way?'

'Every parent?' For some reason the thought that he might just be one worried father out of a thousand hadn't occurred to him.

'Of course. Parents always have their own ideas about how they wish their children to be brought up, both morally and spiritually. But they must understand that their children are not their property; that their children are entitled to pursue happiness in any way they wish. The Rev Moon and his followers were regarded with the same suspicion as the

Célèstines. Many parents tried desperate measures to rescue their children from Moonie settlements, and to persuade them never to return. But most did; and those who didn't were unhappy for the rest of their lives. Remember, Mr McLean, your son came to the Célèstines of his own free will. You will never get him back now. Physically, perhaps—although that is unlikely. But never, never, spiritually. You have lost him now, for ever.'

Charlie stared at Mme Musette with a ferocity that he had never experienced in his whole life. Then he said, vehemently, 'Fuck you,' and drove off up the gravelled driveway with his tyres spinning and the rear end of his Oldsmobile snaking from side to side.

11

He found the Sheriff much more quickly than he had expected. There had been a traffic accident on the steeply sloping road to Allen's Corners. An elderly farmer in a station wagon had tried to overtake a slow-moving delivery truck on a blind bend, and collided head-on with another car coming the opposite way. The road surface was mushy with blood and broken glass, and the damaged cars were being towed away like injured dinosaurs.

The sheriff was standing by the side of the road with his hands on his hips as if he found the stupidity of his fellow men impossible to believe. He was short and sandy-haired, with a big curving belly in front and a big curving bottom behind. He wore designer sunglasses that didn't suit him at all. Not far away, the deputy who Charlie had first met when he drove into Allen's Corners was taking down an eye-witness statement from a highway worker who had been clearing out ditches only fifty yards away from the smash.

Charlie parked his car on the grassy verge and climbed out. The sheriff turned to him as he approached, then leaned sideways a little so that he could see past him to his car.

'This is an accident here, fellow,' he told Charlie, in a voice made harsh by smoking and Connecticut winters. 'You're going to have to move that vehicle out of here.'

'I was coming to your office,' Charile told him. 'I have a serious crime to report.'

Somehow, out here by the roadside, Charlie thought that his words sounded weak and unreal. The sheriff gave a short, hammering cough, and eyed Charlie through his green-tinted lenses as if he wasn't sure whether to shout at him or hit him.

'What nature of serious crime?' he inquired.

'Kidnap, maybe worse,' said Charlie.

The sheriff asked, 'Where? And when? And who got kidnapped?'

'It happened last night. My fifteen-year-old son Martin was abducted from the Windsor Hotel at West Hartford.'

'Outside of my jurisdiction,' said the sheriff. 'You should of reported it in West Hartford.'

'But they brought him here.'

'Who brought him here? You mean you know who did it?'

'M. and Mme Musette, at Le Reposoir, back on the Quassapaug Road. I saw him there not more than ten minutes ago.'

The sheriff said, 'Hold on, now. You've seen him *since* this alleged kidnap took place?'

'That's correct. I tried to get him away, but I couldn't.'

The Sheriff looked thoughtful. Then he called to his deputy, 'Clive! You want to wrap this up? I have to talk to this gentleman here for a while.'

Clive came over with his thumbs in his belt. 'How do you do,' he greeted Charlie. Then he said to the sheriff, 'This is the gentleman who parked in Mr Haxalt's space the other day.'

The sheriff said, 'Sounds like you're the kind of man who likes to live dangerously.'

'Where can we talk?' asked Charlie.

'You'd better follow me back to my office. You and I have got some discussing to do.'

The sheriff eased his bulky bottom into his car, and drove off, with Charlie following close behind. His office was cater-corner from the church, overlooking the sloping green at Allen's Corners. He parked in a space marked 'Sheriff' and Charlie parked beside him in a space marked 'Coroner'.

'You sure do like to live dangerously,' the sheriff remarked, indicating the slot in which Charlie had parked. 'Our county coroner has a rare temper.'

'I'm not in the mood for worrying about people's private parking spaces,' said Charlie.

The sheriff grasped his shoulder. 'I know you're not. Just trying to lighten the atmosphere a little. Come on in. Maybe you'd care for some coffee.'

Charlie sat in the sheriff's office under a tired-looking flag and a crest with the Connecticut state motto, *Qui Transtulit Sustinet.* There was also a comprehensive selection of colour photographs of the current sheriff shaking hands with almost everybody from Ronald Reagan to Jimmy Breslin. The sheriff sent his work-worn, bespectacled secretary to bring them two Styrofoam cups of what turned out to be remarkably good coffee. Then he kicked the door closed, and settled himself down behind his desk.

'You'd better give me some of the salient facts,' he said. 'Your boy's age, description, what he was wearing, all that kind of thing. You'd better tell me how it happened, too.'

'But I know where he is,' Charlie insisted.

The sheriff pulled a tight face. 'Sure you know where he is. The difficulty is, if he's staying with those people voluntarily, we're not in any kind of a position to go crashing in there with all guns blazing to rescue him.'

'He's a minor. Don't tell me that you can't get a warrant to go in and get him. Listen—I can prove that his life is in danger. Do you know anything about those people at all? Do you know what they're *doing* in that place?'

'Well, sir, as a matter of fact I do.'

'You know about the rituals?'

The sheriff nodded, squashing his double chins like an accordion bellows.

'And you've been content to sit here and let them get on with it? For Christ's sake, sheriff, they're cannibals! They're worse than cannibals! They're actually persuading young people to hack themselves to pieces and eat their own bodies!'

'Yes,' said the sheriff.

'*Yes?*' Charlie exploded. 'Is that all you can say? *Yes?* I'm talking about my only son, sheriff. My boy is lying on a bed in that place stark naked and preparing himself to do God alone knows what. He's probably going to cut off his own fingers and eat them. Or worse.'

The sheriff sipped his coffee and then set it back on his desk. 'Whatever I'm going to say to you now, Mr McLean, you're going to feel that it falls far short of the kind of response you've been expecting from the law on this matter. But there are what you might call ramifications.'

'I don't see how any ramifications can allow the law to turn a blind eye while my son is allowed to remain in the hands of people like that.'

The sheriff said, 'The problem is, the law and the ramifications are kind of tied up together. You see, those Célèstine people used to be nothing much more than a small secret society, maybe twenty or thirty people, no more than that, centred on New

Orleans. They were two separate bodies in those days, the same way that the Irish Republican movement is split up into the IRA, which is technically illegal, and the political wing, Sinn Fein, which is technically legal, although who knows where one begins and the other ends? You understand me? The Célèstines in New Orleans were divided between their religious order, which was recognized as an official religious body, and their secret society of flesh-eaters. In those days, the flesh-eating side was kept totally under cover. Several FBI agents tried to penetrate it and couldn't. All the law-enforcement agencies knew that it was going on, but there was no way of proving it. The *National Enquirer* printed a story about it, and all that happened was nobody believed it and the Célèstines Order successfully sued them for four and a half million dollars.'

Confused, Charlie said, 'What are you trying to tell me?'

'I'm trying to tell you that for years the Célèstines had to carry on this cannibalism business in total, one hundred per cent secrecy. Their people used to walk the streets of New Orleans. They'd meet up with young, disaffected runaways, get to talking to them, then introduce them to the legitimate side of their religion. When they were sure that they weren't dealing with undercover cops masquerading as runaways, they'd introduce them to the other side of what they were doing. One secret FBI report estimated that between 1955 and 1965, more that eighteen per cent of all young people who went permanently missing in the New Orleans area became Célèstine followers, and finished up as their own Last Supper.'

'If the FBI knew all this, why didn't they stop it?' Charlie asked.

'They almost did, more than one time. But the Célèstines had first-class lawyers, and since nobody could prove kidnap, abduction, imprisonment, or any criminal act either local or federal, they had to let them go. There is no law in any state which says that it is a criminal offence to devour yourself; nor is it an offence to offer parts of yourself to other people for no charge for whatever purpose they may care to put it. I guess the legislators just didn't envisage anybody wanting to do things like that.'

'But people who want to eat themselves must be mentally incompetent,' said Charlie. 'Surely somebody tried to put a stop to the Célèstines with mental health legislation.'

'Oh sure. There was a test case put before the Louisiana Supreme Court on 11 May 1967. It was held in camera, so it never got reported. They called expert witnesses to testify as to the sanity of a nineteen-year-old girl who had eaten both of her arms. They had psychiatrists, priests, social workers, theologians, anthropologists, the whole cast of thousands. Not one of them could tell the court with any conviction that the girl was nuts. She had mutilated herself for an explicable religious reason, in accordance with the teaching of a recognized church. Her lawyer pointed out that millions of young boys all over the world are mutilated every year—circumcised, that is—for religious reasons that are far less profound that those embraced by the Célèstines. The case for committal to a mental institution was dismissed, and the girl went back to New Orleans and ate the rest of herself.'

'Is that why they're so brazen about what they're doing?' said Charlie.

The sheriff nodded. 'That's part of the reason. They know now that anybody who tries to challenge them in the courts is going to have a real difficult time—apart from attracting all kinds of very unwelcome publicity. Women don't like to tell the police they've been raped; you think parents like to come along and admit that their children have been eating themselves?'

'What's the other part of the reason?'

'The other part of the reason is that the daughter of a very senior member of the United States government died two years ago at a Célèstine house in South Carolina. The scandal would have been a doozy, believe me. The FBI undertook a six-month covert investigation and found out that the sons and daughters of countless socialite, celebrity and big-business families were also Célèstine Devotees. Worse than that, at least four top-ranking politicians and at least two members of the Joint Chiefs of Staff were involved. Several of them were Guides. Do you know about Guides?'

Charlie nodded numbly.

The sheriff sucked up some more coffee. It was too hot to drink without making a lot of noise. 'The government decided that so long as the Célèstines never actually committed any illegal acts, they were to be left alone. They have what you might call diplomatic immunity. It's national legislative policy, my friend, all the way down from the Oval Office to yours truly, the sheriff of Litchfield County.'

'Why are you telling me all this?' asked Charlie. 'If it isn't true, I'm bound to find out that it isn't. If it *is,* then I would have thought that it wasn't the kind of story you would want to spread around.'

The sheriff shook his head. 'I have a very good reason for telling you, and that reason is that right now you're feeling mad. You want the law to go busting in to Le Reposoir and rescue your son, Rambo-style. And if the law won't do it for you, then by God you're going to take the law into your own hands and do it yourself. Am I right? Am I reading you right?'

'How would you feel, in my position?' Charlie asked him.

'My friend,' said the sheriff, 'I *was* in your position. My own daughter of twenty-one years old was one of the first Célèstine recruits around here, and believe me I did everything I could to get her out of there. I got hold of a search warrant, and I went through that building like you wouldn't believe. And I found her; and do you know what she'd done? She'd already cut off her own hand.'

He stared intently at Charlie just to make sure he wasn't missing the point of what he was saying. Just to make sure that Charlie didn't believe that he was the only father in the world who had ever been through agony and doubt and grief because of the Célèstines.

'Let me tell you something,' he went on, and his voice was as soft as tissue now. 'I sat down by my little girl's bed and I pleaded with her to come home with me before she hurt herself more. And do you know what she did? She touched me with her one hand, and she smiled at me, she *smiled*, and she said, "Daddy, for the very first time in my life I'm truly happy." That's what she said.'

The sheriff paused. He obviously found this bitterly painful to remember. 'That was when I used my authority, or rather my gun. I took my little girl and I got her out of that place by force. They didn't try to stop me, they just smiled at me the same way that my little girl had smiled at me, and they said, "See you later, Susan," – that was my little girl's name. I'll never forget to my dying day the way they said that. They were so fucking cheerful.

'Susan came home for two and a half weeks. That was as long as I could persuade her to stay. You don't know what those two and a half weeks were like. She was so depressed I had to take her to the doctor and the doctor put her on tranquillizers. By the end of the second week things were so bad she was begging me to let her go back there. Do you know what she said? She said that what the Célèstines were doing was showing her the way to heaven, and that even if I kept her chained up to her bed for the rest of her life, she would never be happy in this physical, material world that the rest of us have to endure. That's just what she said. "I've broken free," she told me. "Free of any kind of physical need. All that's holding me back now is my earthly body, and I'm going to eat that."'

The sheriff ran his hand through his scrubby red hair and said, 'Jesus! How do you cope when your daughter tells you something like that?'

'What did you do?' Charlie asked him, in a haunted voice.

'I didn't do anything, except to make sure that Susan was handcuffed to her bed every night. Then one morning we woke up and she was gone. She had bitten away all the flesh around her hand and wrist so that she could get out of the handcuff. The pillow was plastered in blood and bits of flesh. I knew then that I was never going to get her back. Those Célèstines had won her over and that was it.'

'Didn't you take it any further?'

'Oh sure. I took it all the way to Hartford. But in the end I was quietly taken aside and told to lay off. That's when I found out everything that I've just told you. I made one last effort and took the story to the media, and I found one reporter on the *Hartford Courant* who was prepared to take a risk. But after about a week he called me back and said the story wouldn't stand up and that was all there was to it.'

Charlie looked at the sheriff coldly. 'So what you're telling me is that I have to accept Martin's kidnap—I have to accept the fact that those people are going to persuade him to eat himself alive – because of some national conspiracy of silence?'

The sheriff said, 'That's part of the story, sure. But the other part—the real important part—is that no kid goes to that place unless they want to. I found that part the hardest of all to accept, when Susan went. She *wanted* to go.'

'Did you ever get to see her again?'

'Yes.' The sheriff nodded. 'Just once. I went up to Le Reposoir against the specific instructions of my superiors and I forced them at gunpoint to let me see her. They were so damned polite they gave me the creeps. I mean, they were even *humorous* about it. They took me into the room and there she was, or what was left of her. I wish to God that I'd never gone. Did you ever see that old movie *Freaks*? There's a guy in it who's just a head and a kind of a caterpillar body in a cotton sock? Did you ever see that? Well, that's what Susan was like. I never knew that anybody could lose so much of their body and still live. There was her face, that same face I loved so much, still with that wavy red hair, and underneath that face there was nothing at all but a body no bigger than a leg of pork, all wrapped up in a white cotton stocking.'

Charlie swallowed. His throat was dry; but he knew that if he tried to swallow any coffee he would probably gag.

The sheriff said, 'You may not believe me, but that wasn't the worst of it. The worst of it was that she lay there in the sunshine and she smiled at me and said, "Daddy", and I knew that she was completely contented. They called me about two weeks later to tell me that she was gone. I didn't say anything. I didn't trust myself. I took a week's vacation that was owing to me and I stayed drunk from Friday evening to the following Sunday night.'

'How am I going to get my son out of there?' Charlie asked him.

'I don't think you've been listening to me, my friend. Your son is there because your son *wants* to be there, and you're not going to get him out of that place without the US Marines.'

'And the same thing happened to you, to your only daughter, and you just accept it?'

'Tell me what I can do about it!' the sheriff said, his jowls shaking. 'Tell me just one thing that I can do about it! Short of killing the Musettes outright, and burning the whole damned house down—and, believe me, that wouldn't help either. There are nineteen Célèstine houses in the continental United States; there are more in Europe. If you burn down one, there will always be scores of others. You'd be pissing in the wind.'

Charlie stood up. He laid one hand on the sheriff's desk and looked him steadily in the eye. 'Is this what it's come to?' he said. 'The country that was founded on the principles of life and liberty?'

The sheriff gave him a defeated, sideways look. 'Sometimes the price of life and liberty is pretty high.'

'Tell me who else in Allen's Corners has lost a child.'

'Apart from Mr Haxalt, there must have been eleven or twelve. Some of them know where their children have gone, others don't.'

'Like Mrs Kemp, you mean?'

The sheriff nodded. 'We don't tell 'em if they don't find out. We don't want to cause any more distress than we have to.'

Charlie rubbed his eyes. He felt as if he were dreaming all this; but the dream was so procedural that he knew it was true. Apart from that, he couldn't wake up, no matter how hard he tried.

The sheriff said, 'I'll tell you what I'll do. I'll go on up to Le Reposoir myself, and talk to them about your son. Martin, is that what you said his name was?'

Charlie said, 'You've got to get him out of there, sheriff.'

'More parents have said that same thing to me than I like to recall.'

'I promise you—if you don't do it—then I will.'

'I can't stop you from making promises, my friend. But it's my elected duty to uphold the law, and I'm telling you right here and now that if you attempt anything in the way of aggravated assault on those people, or damage or intrude on their property, then I'm bound to give them assistance.'

Charlie said, 'What's your name, sheriff?'

'Podmore,' he replied.

'I mean your given name.'

'What do you want to know that for? It's Norman, as a matter of fact.'

Charlie said, 'I want to be able to say to you, "Norman, this is Charlie. You've lost your daughter, I'm in danger of losing my son." I want you to think about that, Norman, what that means. And you tell me something else, Norman. That boy's mother doesn't know what's happened yet. You tell me what I'm supposed to say to *her*.'

12

Grey-faced with rage and frustration, Charlie drove back up the corkscrew road to Le Reposoir, the tyres of his Oldsmobile howling and squittering on the blacktop. He swerved into the entrance and collided at nearly ten miles an hour with the front gate, with a noise like the gates of hell being clanged shut. Two or three of the gate's iron uprights were bent, but the locks held, and all Charlie ended up with was mild whiplash and two shattered headlights.

He climbed out of the car and stabbed furiously at the intercom button. M. Musette – who must have inspected the damage to his gates through his closed-circuit television camera – answered almost immediately.

'Mr McLean, what can I do for you? You seem to have suffered an accident.'

'Open up,' Charlie demanded. 'I want my son back.'

'Mr McLean, you know as well as I do that your son wishes to remain here.'

'I don't give a shit, Monsewer Musette. I want my son back and I want him back now.'

'Do you always treat your son's wishes with such contempt?'

Charlie yelled, 'Don't you start getting fancy with me, you Goddamn cannibal! Now open up, and give me my son back!'

'I'm sorry, that's impossible. If your son has a change of heart, then obviously I shall be glad to let you know. But at the moment he is very happy where he is. Why don't you talk to the sheriff?'

Charlie said, with more control, 'I already did that, thank you.'

'I hope he was sympathetic.'

'Yes, he was. Yes, he was sympathetic. That's all that anybody seems to be good for, around here: being sympathetic.'

'Well, I quite understand your feelings, my dear sir. You don't want sympathy, do you? You want your son's affection.'

'I'll worry about his affection when I get hold of him again.'

'He's not a dog, *monsieur*. He's an intelligent human being—quite capable of making his own decisions.'

'And what are you?' Charlie wanted to know.

The intercom clicked once, and then remained silent. Charlie returned to his car, started the engine, slammed into reverse, then back into drive and collided again as hard as he could with the gates. Then he backed up and crashed into the gates a third time, and then a fourth, until he could hear his radiator fan clattering against its cover, and a grinding sound in the transmission like a Cuisinart full of broken glass.

He sat in his car and screamed at the gates of Le Reposoir in helpless rage. Then he crossed his arms over his steering wheel and bent his head forward and sobbed. He stayed like that for almost a quarter of an hour, while the emotionless eye of the remote-control camera watched him from the trees.

Eventually, he sat up and dug out a crumpled handkerchief and wiped his face. It was clear to him now that a frontal assault on the Célèstines was not going to work. Nor was any appeal to the police, or to the media. The Célèstines had won for themselves the kind of charmed lives that only true fanatics seem to be able to achieve. If he wanted to get Martin out of Le Reposoir, he was going to have to do it alone. What's more, he was going to have to make sure that his plan was properly thought out. Martin would have to be taken someplace secure, where it would be impossible for him to escape and return to the Célèstines. And there was no doubt that he would need deprogramming, either by a psychiatrist or by one of those people who made it their business to deprogram Moonies and other adolescent victims of obsessional cults.

It was very hard for him, but he reversed his car away from the entrance to Le Reposoir and drove slowly back towards Allen's Corners with his transmission crunching and his suspension complaining at every bump. The sun, which for most of the day had been enveloping itself in hazy grey clouds, now suddenly decided to make an appearance, and it lit up the coppery fall leaves for miles around. There was a tang of woodsmoke in the air, and Charlie knew that he would never be able to come up to Connecticut again, in fall, whether he was able to rescue Martin or not. It would always remind him of mutilation, and self-inflicted pain, and the Célèstines.

He returned to Mrs Kemp's. Mrs Kemp herself was standing at her front door, almost as if she had been waiting for him; but in fact she was lifting her face to the sun. Her eyes were closed and her fists were clenched and there was an odd little smile on her face as she basked her wrinkles.

She opened her eyes as Charlie walked up the front path.

'Mr McLean,' she said.

'How are you doing, Mrs Kemp?'

'I'm enjoying this sunshine. It'll be winter before you know it. You're back soon. I didn't expect you for at least a year; if ever. Your boy not with you?'

'Martin's... having a break.'

'I thought you said you were taking him to Boston with you.'

'Well, I was.'

Mrs Kemp frowned at him, and touched his arm. 'Something's wrong, isn't it? I can tell.'

'Everything's fine, Mrs Kemp. I just need a place to stay for the next few days. Some place quiet, where I can think.'

He tried to step into the porch but Mrs Kemp stopped him. 'He's gone, hasn't he? Your Martin?'

'Yes, Mrs Kemp,' Charlie admitted. 'He's gone.'

'What's the matter? Did you have an argument? Did his mother come to take him back?'

Charlie shook his head. He was about to make an elaborate excuse, but then he thought, *What the hell? Mrs Kemp lost Caroline, so at least she'll understand what I'm going through. And maybe it's time she knew that Caroline hasn't gone off to live in California; nor has she been raped and murdered and her body left in some nameless ditch. It's about time the parents of all those children who have been lost to the Célèstines got themselves together and did something dramatic.* If what Sheriff Podmore had told him was true – if the government and the law refused to admit that what the Célèstines were doing was wrong; and if the television and the newspaper people did nothing but turn a blind eye – then it was time for the nation's bereaved parents to take a stand on their own.

Because if they had no other rights, as far as their children were concerned, parents at least had the right to see them live.

'Come inside,' he told Mrs Kemp. 'I want to talk to you.'

They sat together in the front parlour and Charlie told Mrs Kemp everything that had happened since he and Martin had left for West Hartford. Then he told her what Sheriff Podmore had said about Susan. He watched her carefully as he explained that Caroline had probably died in the way that all Célèstine Devotees eventually died. Her eyes betrayed no expression at all, as if somehow she had known that this had happened all along.

When Charlie had finished, she stood up and walked with mechanical steps to the bureau. 'I think you and I had better have a drink,' she said. 'I still have some Chivas Regal left, from the time that Jerry Kogan used to stay here. Everybody used to say, "Do you know Jerry? He's in alcohol."'

'Thanks,' said Charlie. He watched in silence as Mrs Kemp poured them each a hefty three fingers of whisky. Mrs Kemp raised her glass and said, 'To the ones we love. In memory, and in hope.'

Charlie said, with a catch in his throat, 'To the ones we love,' and drank.

They shared another drink, and then Mrs Kemp said that she had to go to the market to buy supplies for supper if Charlie was going to be staying. Charlie opened up the sagging doors of her garage for her, and backed out her old tan Buick wagon. He stood at the front door and watched her as she drove off in a cloud of oily smoke on her way to the shopping mall. Then he stepped back into the airless house, and went up to the room in which he had slept only two nights ago with Martin. He knew now that he had lost Martin then, after the dwarf-like David had talked to him. If only he could go back forty-eight hours in time; to that fateful instant when Harriet had let slip the name of Le Reposoir, the resting place, the little altar.

On impulse he wrestled the Connecticut telephone directory out of the bedside cupboard, and looked up the *Litchfield Sentinel.* With the directory balanced on his knees he dialled the number and waited while the call tone purred. After a long while, a young woman's voice said, '*Sentinel?* If you want advertising I'm afraid they're gone for the day.'

'I wanted the editor,' said Charlie.

'Oh, well, I'm sorry, he's not here, either. There's a big business meeting in Danbury.'

'In that case, forget it. I'm sorry I troubled you.'

'Is it news?' the young woman asked him. 'I'm a reporter. I can take your story if that's what you want.'

'I'm sorry, I really wanted to speak to the editor.'

'Okay, have it your way. He'll be back in the morning. You're sure I can't help?'

Charlie lowered the directory on to the floor. 'I don't know, maybe you can. My son's gone missing in pretty unusual circumstances. I thought it might help if I could locate other parents whose children have gone missing.'

'Well, that's incredible,' the woman told him. 'That's exactly the story that I've been working on. You know the *Denver Post* won a Pulitzer Prize for their investigations into the missing children statistics; well, I've been assigned to do a follow-up, because we've had so many kids missing in Connecticut lately.'

'Do you know any other parents who have lost their kids, apart from me?' asked Charlie.

'Sure I do, dozens. The number of children who have gone missing in the Litchfield area in the past five months is way up – forty-two per cent higher than it was for the comparable period last year, and seventy-eight per cent higher than it was the year before.'

'And the police keep telling you it isn't a problem – just like the *Denver Post* won that Pulitzer Prize for saying it wasn't a problem.'

'That's right,' said the young woman. 'How did you know that?'

Charlie said, 'For once in my life I seem to have gotten lucky. My name's Charlie McLean, and I think that you and I ought to meet.'

'Well, sure thing. My name's Robyn Harris. Where are you calling me from?'

'Allen's Corners, but I don't want to meet you at Allen's Corners. Do you know a restaurant in Watertown called the Loving Doves? How about meeting me there at six-thirty? I'll book a table in the name of Gunn.'

'Gunn?'

'You know, like Ben Gunn, who was marooned on Treasure Island. You won't miss me, I'm forty-one years old and I look like I've spent my life driving from coast to coast and back again.'

'All right, Mr McLean. You're on. I look forward to meeting you.'

Charlie called the restaurant and made the reservation, then cradled the phone and sat for a while in thought. He wasn't at all sure that he was doing the right thing, in talking to the Press, but if he was careful he might be able to use Ms Robyn Harris to make contact with other parents; and then there was a possibility of concerted action – something to bring the Célèstines to the attention of ordinary people, and to quarantine them for ever, if not kill them off.

As far as Charlie was concerned, the Célèstines weren't a religion, they were a disease. They were nothing better than a spiritual form of AIDS.

He eased off his shoes, then peeled off his socks. The day's tension had made him feel sweaty and sticky, and he needed a shower. As he stood under Mrs Kemp's rattling brass shower faucet, he tried to work out a plan for snatching Martin out of Le Reposoir, and getting him clean away. He made himself assume that Martin wouldn't have started eating himself already. His mind couldn't cope with the idea that he might already have cut off his own fingers or his own toes, and swallowed them.

He recognized that he was going to need help, if only to drag Martin physically out of the building. A man would be preferable, but a woman would do if she were determined enough.

He also recognized, reluctantly, that he was going to need a gun. Even though Sheriff Podmore had told him that the Musettes had made no effort to stop him when he had rescued his daughter, it was obvious that Le Reposoir had at least two security staff and probably more.

He would need a third person, too – somebody who was not necessarily involved in breaking into the building and heisting Martin out, but a getaway driver who was waiting to speed them out of trouble and take them to the nearest airport.

Because that was the last essential. There had to be air tickets ready. First, a flight to somewhere within the continental United States, because Martin hadn't brought his passport with him, then a car or a boat ride to Mexico.

After that, exile for both of them, for a while at least, while Martin was deprogrammed, and while Charlie tried to find another way of making a living.

Charlie stepped out of the shower and towelled himself with one of the rough, cheap towels that Mrs Kemp had left folded on the hot pipe. He knotted the towel around his waist and walked across the landing to his room. He heard the front door open and shut again, and leaned over the banisters and called, 'Mrs Kemp? That you?'

Mrs Kemp looked up. She was standing in the hallway looking peculiarly wild-eyed, her hair dishevelled and a button hanging off her coat. She carried no shopping.

'Mrs Kemp?' asked Charlie. 'Is there something wrong?'

'It's all right,' she said, tugging her coat tightly around herself. 'I'm fine. I'll go fix you something to eat.'

'Did you go to the market?'

'I... forgot.'

Charlie looked at her sharply. 'What's wrong, Mrs Kemp? Where have you been?'

But Mrs Kemp disappeared into her kitchen without answering; and Charlie heard the door slam behind her as an unequivocal warning that she did not want to be followed.

Charlie waited for a moment, then shrugged to himself, and went to his room to get dressed. He watched his face in the mirror on top of the bureau. He looked tired, and there was a look in his eyes which he had never seen before. Wounded, but determined. The look of a man who wants revenge.

He was tying up his shoelaces when he heard the scuffing of tyres outside in the street. A moment later, there was a ring at the doorbell. Then another ring. He finished tying his shoelace and went out to the landing. 'Mrs Kemp?' he called, but there was no reply. The doorbell rang again and so he went downstairs to answer it.

It was Sheriff Podmore, and he didn't look pleased. He pushed the door open wide and stepped into the hallway without being invited. 'What did you tell her?' he demanded.

'I don't know what you're talking about,' said Charlie.

'Don't play the stiff with me, my friend. You told Mrs Kemp what happened to Caroline, didn't you?'

'So what if I did? She has a right to know.'

'Jesus, McLean, what kind of a cretin are you? The reason I didn't tell her before was because she doesn't

237

have the mental strength to accept anything like that. At least she used to have hope that Caroline might still be alive. Don't you understand that? Until they know what's happened to their children for sure, all parents believe that they may still be alive. Hence the great myth about them all running off to California to become go-go dancers or whatever. One per cent of one hundred per cent stay away for good. One per cent of that one per cent make a living as exotic dancers or porno stars. The rest of them get killed, one way or another; or else they end up as Célèstines and kill themselves.'

Charlie said, 'I still think she has a right to know.'

'Is she here?' Sheriff Podmore asked him.

'She just came in. She's in the kitchen.'

Sheriff Podmore stomped down to the end of the hallway and rattled the door handle. 'Ida!' he shouted. 'You in there?'

'Go away!' Mrs Kemp shouted back. 'You lied to me, Norman, I don't want to see you and I don't want to talk to you ever again!'

'Ida, will you be reasonable?' said Sheriff Podmore.

'Go away! I don't want to be reasonable!'

Sheriff Podmore waited outside the kitchen door a little longer and then came sashaying back down the hallway again, all belly and gunbelt. He lifted his hat to adjust it, and said to Charlie. 'You know what she did?'

'I have the distinct feeling that you're going to tell me.'

'She came down to the sheriff's office while I was out and she ripped the place apart. Broke the windows, emptied out the file cabinets, and then she wrote 'Norman Podmore Child-killer' on my wall. So, what do you think about that?'

'I think maybe you deserved it,' said Charlie, in a level tone.

Sheriff Podmore looked at Charlie thoughtfully. 'I hope you're not thinking of causing me any trouble,' he said.

'You'll soon find out if I am.'

Sheriff Podmore jerked his thumb back toward the kitchen. 'All I'm asking you to do is keep your eye on her. She's pretty overwrought. There's no knowing what she might do.'

Charlie opened the front door. 'I think you'd better leave,' he told the sheriff.

At that moment, however, the kitchen door opened and Mrs Kemp appeared, 'Norman!' she screeched. The sheriff turned around. 'Norman, you be warned! This isn't going to be the end of it! I'm going to kill those people if it's the last thing I do! They took my Caroline, and I'm going to kill them!'

'Ida,' said Sheriff Podmore, 'you have to know that it's illegal to make threats against people's lives.'

'And it's not illegal to let people slaughter your children, is that it?' Mrs Kemp shrieked at him.

'Ida, you take care.' Sheriff Podmore turned to Charlie again. 'I'm just telling you, my friend, anything happens here and I'll hold *you* responsible.'

Charlie said nothing, but let the sheriff out and stood by the door as he walked down the path. Mrs Kemp stayed where she was, wringing her hands. Her cheeks were running with tears. Charlie said, 'I'm sorry, Mrs Kemp. It looks like I made a mistake.'

'No, you didn't,' she said shakily. 'You were right to tell me. Up until now, I've been feeling grief, but there was no way of telling if I had anything to grieve about. I've felt angry, but I've never known who to be angry with. Now I know, and now I can do something about it.'

'You're not going to try to kill the Musettes, not really?'

'Try?' she said. 'I'm going to succeed.'

'Can I dissuade you?'

For a fleeting moment, Mrs Kemp almost smiled. 'You wouldn't *want* to dissuade me, would you? You want to see the Musettes dead just as much as I do, if not more.'

Charlie came up close and laid his hand on Mrs Kemp's shoulders. 'Can I ask you just one favour?

Don't do anything without telling me first. I'm going to try to get Martin out of there before anything happens to him. If you get in there on your own, all you're going to succeed in doing is make them tighten up their security. At the moment, they're complacent. They're inside the law, however much you and I may hate them, no matter how disgusting we think they are. Let them stay complacent, huh? – at least until I've managed to get Martin out.'

Mrs Kemp reached up and touched his cheek. 'Is this a punishment, do you think, for the way we treat our children?'

Charlie tried to smile. 'Maybe. Maybe some people have a different way of looking at life and death.'

'Will you want supper?' she asked. 'I'm afraid that I didn't quite make it to the market. I got overtaken by the impulse to wreck Norman's office.'

'I'll go out to eat,' said Charlie. 'Do you think the sheriff is going to press charges against you?'

'Norman? He'd better not. I've known him since he was a big, fat, unpopular kid. He gave me cough-candy once and asked me if he could marry me. Thank God I didn't.'

Charlie spent the next half-hour straightening out his car – scraping the clumps of grass from underneath the wheel-arches and bending back the cover that protected the radiator fan. He managed to kick the front bumper reasonably straight, and fit new bulbs in the headlights. The Oldsmobile still looked as if he bought it second-hand from a family of deranged Mexicans, but at least it went along without making too much noise. The transmission was okay provided he drove in second.

He left Mrs Kemp sitting in her parlour with the last of her bottle of Chivas Regal, and drove over to Watertown. Once the sun had gone, the evening was unexpectedly cold. The Oldsmobile's climate control had been damaged, and he wished he had worn a sweater underneath his coat. It occurred to him as he drove that it was time he called Marjorie to tell her what had happened – or at least to tell her that Martin was missing – but he couldn't even begin to think of what to say.

'Marjorie, listen, we've got a problem here. Martin wants to eat himself.'

'I'm sorry, Marjorie, but Martin has decided to join a society of cannibals.'

'Marjorie—'

He arrived at the Loving Doves. It was a small self-conscious restaurant in the centre of Watertown, with gilded lettering across the facade and two gilded doves pecking at each other's beaks perched on the porch. Its style was New England *nouvelle cuisine,* if such a thing were imaginable. Perhaps its most characteristic dish was a dinner that consisted of

242

three thin slices of brisket, four baby onions, three miniature carrots, two tiny beets, and a decoration of tenderly cooked cabbage, all laid out on a circular pool of delicate broth.

Charlie went inside. The decor was candlelight, brass, and dark green tablecloths. 'You have a six-thirty reservation for Mr Gunn,' he said. The tall, blonde waitress smiled at him as if life were still ordinary, as if restaurants still mattered, and led him across to a table in the corner. There, a young woman was waiting – a handsome young woman with long well-brushed brunette hair and wide dark eyes and big dangling earrings. She wore a fashionable suit in pale grey, with a white cotton sweater underneath it. The multi-pocketed purse slung over the back of her chair was the only give-away that here was a career woman pursuing her career.

'Mr Gunn?' she said, rising from her chair and extending her hand.

13

It was almost eleven o'clock when they left The Loving Doves. They stood in the entrance for a while, sheltering from the wind.

'What are you going to do now?' Robyn asked Charlie.

'Go back to Mrs Kemp's, I guess. I feel I have a duty to keep an eye on her.'

'You won't come back to my place for a drink? I still want to talk to you some more.'

Charlie tugged up the collar of his coat. 'I'm not sure there's any more to say. The Célèstines have got hold of my boy, and I want to get him back. End of story.'

Robyn took her spiral-bound notebook out of her pocket and leafed through it. 'I'll talk to two other parents in the morning. I may be able to get hold of one of them tonight. Then I'll talk to my editor.'

'Remember the agreement, though,' said Charlie. 'No publicity until Martin is safe. If M. Musette gets the idea that I'm going to try to break him out of there, he won't even let me through the front gate.'

Robyn closed her notebook and put it away. 'I hope I haven't been too sceptical this evening.'

'About what?'

'The whole thing. The Célèstines. It *is* pretty hard to believe.'

Charlie made a face. 'I guess the answer is that the Célèstines are absolutely no different from any other fanatical religious sect. They all have a magnetic appeal for young people, and the reason they do is because the way of life their parents lead has absolutely no appeal at all. If these sects flourish, it's our fault, the parents' fault. I mean, what have we given our children that has any spiritual value whatsoever? I'm not just talking about materialism, either. I'm talking about a lack of spirit. A lack of self-respect.'

Robyn eyed him over her red mohair scarf. 'You're talking like somebody who's been there.'

Charlie took her arm. 'Let me walk you back to your car.'

'I didn't bring my car. My photographer dropped me off. I was hoping maybe you could give me a ride. I don't live far: Waterbury.'

'What if I'd turned out to be a seventy-year-old hunchback with halitosis and axe-murderer's eyes?'

'In that case, I would have called for a taxi.'

They walked across to the parking lot under the trees. 'I was telling you the truth about driving into their gates,' Charlie remarked, pointing to the front-end damage. He helped her into the car.

'I didn't doubt that you were.'

'But you find the Célèstines difficult to believe in?'

'I accept what you're telling me, but I find it hard to accept that so many people know about it, the government, the FBI, and yet they let it carry on and nobody says a word.'

Charlie drove out toward Waterbury. 'It's nothing unusual, when you think about it. The Scientologists and the Moonies and the Masons are all run openly – to the extent that they don't try to conceal their existence. But who knows what they really do? Provided it's nothing overtly illegal, they're going to be left alone. And it's the same with the Célèstines. The media don't want to touch the story because it's too grisly and the risks of a libel action are too high. The police don't want to know because they don't believe that they'll get a successful conviction. And the government certainly isn't interested because too many people in high places have embarrassing connections with them.'

'It's such an incredible news story,' said Robyn.

Charlie made a face. 'Sure it is. But what's the story? That some psychopathic sect is encouraging our children to eat themselves in the name of the Lord? – or that this nation has such a low regard for human life that they're letting them get away with it? Do you know something, there comes a time when the principle of liberty for all has to be circumscribed. The right to bear arms is one example. I don't mind people exercising that right just so long as it doesn't intrude on *my* right to a safe existence, free from fear. And I don't challenge anybody's right to worship whatever God in whatever way they choose – except when it threatens my son's life.'

They drove into the outskirts of Waterbury, and Robyn directed Charlie to a small frame house painted white and green. There was a bronze station wagon parked in the driveway, and there were lights on in the living room window.

'You live with your parents?' Charlie asked her.

'That's right. I came back home to recuperate after a spectacularly messy love affair. My mom wants me to stay for ever, but I guess I'll be looking for my own place pretty soon. You can't be somebody's child all your life. Sooner or later you have to be yourself.'

'Maybe I won't come in,' said Charlie.

'Oh, do, they won't mind. And I do have a room of my own, kind of an office. They're very proud that their only daughter is a newspaper reporter.'

Charlie blew out his cheeks. 'Okay, then, just for a while.'

Mr and Mrs Harris were sitting in front of the television when Robyn brought Charlie into the living room. Mr Harris was skinny and unsmiling; he ran a dry-cleaning business in the centre of

Waterbury and, according to Robyn, thirty years of other people's dirty clothes had permanently crippled his sense of humour. But Mrs Harris was warm and motherly and fun, and Charlie could see where Robyn had gotten her looks and her figure from. She asked them if they wanted coffee, or maybe some fresh-baked pound cake, but Robyn smiled and shook her head, and said, 'This is work, mother. W-O-R-K.'

'Still,' said Mrs Harris, beaming at Charlie as if he were a potential son-in-law. 'It's always good to meet the people that Robyn works with.'

'Oh, I don't work with her, Mrs Harris. I'm just a news story.'

'Good news, I hope?' said Mrs Harris.

'I hope it's going to turn out that way.'

Robyn took Charlie through to the small converted bedroom at the back which she called her office. It was decorated in pale beige colours, and furnished with a modem pine desk, an angular couch, and two cheese-plants in basketwork jardinières. There was a large Mucha poster on the wall, of the kind that used to be popular in the days of flower-power and 'Blowin' in the Wind'.

'Can I tempt you with a glass of wine?' asked Robyn.

'Just half a glass. I don't want a hangover tomorrow.'

Robyn took off her jacket and hung it over the back of her chair. Charlie sat down on the couch and watched her as she went across to her cupboard and took out a bottle of Stag's Leap chardonnay. Under happier circumstances, he would have been very interested in her. Her personality was incisive and bright; she had an irrepressible sense of humour; and she was very good-looking indeed. She poured out two glasses of wine and Charlie found himself wondering about her 'spectacularly messy' love affair. It seemed axiomatic that nice girls like her always got themselves involved with brutes.

'You said you might be able to contact one of the other parents tonight,' said Charlie.

'Surely. I'll give him a try.' Robyn checked through her Roladex to find the number, then picked up the phone and punched it out. 'His name's Garrett,' she said, covering the mouthpiece with her hand. 'He lost his daughter just after the Christmas holiday. She was eighteen or nineteen, if I remember rightly. She was driving through Allen's Corners to visit her brother in Bethlehem. They found her car abandoned by the side of the road.'

At that moment, the phone was picked up at the other end. Robyn waved to Charlie to pick up a second phone next to the couch, so that he could listen in.

'Hallo?' said a deep, slurred voice.

'Is this Mr Robert Garrett?' asked Robyn. 'This is Robyn Harris from the newspaper. Do you remember me? I came up to your house about four weeks ago to talk about your daughter.'

'I remember,' the voice replied, guardedly. 'What do you want?'

'Well, Mr Garrett, it seems like we may possibly have some kind of new theory about your daughter's disappearance.'

'Oh, yeah?' Still the voice was defensive.

'Mr Garrett, I was thinking today about what you told me... the way you described your daughter's disappearance... and I remember being puzzled.'

'What do you mean, puzzled? She disappeared, that's all. They found her car and she was gone.'

'But you said to me—here, I have it in my notebook—you said to me, "She's at peace, anyway." And—do you know something?—that isn't at all characteristic of the parents of missing children.'

There was a pause, and then the voice said, 'What in hell are you talking about? I hope you didn't call me up after eleven o'clock at night just to tell me that, because if you did—?'

'Mr Garrett, I've been working on this story for weeks, and so far I've talked to two dozen parents of missing children. Apart from one other parent, you're the only one who hasn't shown any signs of hope whatsoever that your daughter is still alive, and you're the only one who has categorically said, "She's at peace", even though no body has been recovered and you haven't been able to give her a proper funeral.'

'What are you trying to suggest? Are you trying to suggest I killed her or something? Is that it? You're trying to say that I murdered my own daughter?'

Robyn said, 'No, sir, Mr Garrett, I am not. But what I am saying is that you know what happened to her.'

'This is bullshit,' the deep voice growled. But its owner didn't put down the phone. Charlie glanced across at Robyn and Robyn gave him a little wave of her hand which meant, *This is it, we're making headway.*

'Mr Garrett,' said Robyn, 'have you ever heard of a religious order called the Célèstines?'

Charlie kept his eyes on Robyn. From the other end of the phone, there was a silence, followed by a quick, sharp intake of breath, that was almost an admission in itself.

'Mr Garrett?' Robyn repeated. 'Did you hear what I said?'

'I heard you.'

'You know what I'm talking about, don't you? You know about the Célèstines? You know what they do, and how they do it?'

'Maybe.' The voice was on the brink either of losing its temper or bursting into tears.

'Mr Garrett, the Célèstines took your daughter, didn't they?'

There was a silence so lengthy that Charlie began to think that Mr Robert Garrett had let go of the telephone receiver and left it hanging. At last, however, the deep voice said, 'The sheriff said I wasn't to talk about it. He said it would make things worse for other runaways. They didn't want to publicize the Célèstines because other kids would get to hear about them and the last thing they wanted was an epidemic of kids joining up.'

There was another silence, and then the voice said, 'The sheriff told me that nobody could have done more. I went to the place, I talked to her, they didn't stop me talking to her, those bastards, they just stood around and smiled. She wouldn't change her mind, though. She said it was the way to heaven, for Christ's sake. The way to heaven!'

Charlie spoke for the first time. 'Mr Garrett, my name is Charlie McLean, I've been listening in.'

'Who are you? Are you a cop, or what?'

'I'm nobody. I'm a parent, like you. The Célèstines just got hold of my fifteen-year-old son.'

'Well, in that case, I'm very sorry,' said Robert Garrett. 'What else can I say? I'm very sorry.'

'Did you try to get your daughter out of there?'

'Are you kidding? I went to that place with a sawed-off shotgun and I threatened to kill the whole lot of them unless they let my daughter go. They called the police and the police locked me up on a charge of threatening behaviour and illegal possession of a firearm. After that I went to my lawyer and I spent $12,000 of savings trying to get a writ to have her released into my custody. The courts turned me down flat. The judge said that she had joined the Célèstines voluntarily and that there was no evidence of mental disturbance. The rituals may have been unusual but they were entirely voluntary and undertaken without any persuasion or compulsion whatsoever. Furthermore, if he were to rule against the Célèstines he would be setting two dangerous legal precedents. One would be to make it possible for parents to interfere legally in the chosen worship of their children. The other would be to diminish the individual's rights in respect of his or her own body. Parents could legally prevent their children from having cosmetic surgery, or indeed any surgery at all, and might even be able to reverse a child's wishes to have his or her organs used after death for transplant purposes.'

'You sound like you've memorized that ruling,' said Robyn.

'Memorized it? I didn't have to memorize it. It's engraved on my heart in letters an inch deep. I asked my attorney if it was worth going to appeal. He took me aside and said the word was that the Célèstines were well within the law and that they were supposed to be left alone. In fact, I'll tell you how brightly the sun shines on those bastards. I went to your newspaper the *Litchfield Sentinel* with my story of what had happened and your editor listened very politely and do you know what happened? Well, you know what happened.'

For the first time, Robyn was taken by surprise. 'You actually talked to Ted Fellowship about the Célèstines? And he did nothing about it?'

'Have you ever read a story about the Célèstines in any newspaper, or any magazine? Have you ever heard them mentioned on television? No, sir. Because the law can't touch them, that's why, and the law is too embarrassed to admit that they can get away with what they do.'

Charlie said, 'Robert? Can I call you Robert?'

'You can call me Bob, that's what everybody else calls me.'

'Bob—my son's in that place. I want to get him out.'

'I sympathize, Charlie, believe me. I've been there. But you won't stand a cat in hell's chance.'

'I got in there before.'

'Sure, just like I did, when I first went looking for my daughter. They let you in on purpose, so that they can show you just what you're up against. They want you to hear your own child saying no, I'm not coming back with you, dad, I'm staying right here, and there's nothing you can do about it.'

'Bob,' said Charlie, 'I have to try.'

'You can try,' Bob told him. 'Nobody can stop you trying. But what can I tell you? There isn't any future in it.'

'Will you help me?' Charlie asked him.

Silence again. Robyn looked across at Charlie and Charlie could see the tension on her face.

'Bob?' said Charlie.

'I don't know,' said Bob. 'The Célèstines are something I've been trying to forget.'

'Bob, I understand, I really do. But with two of us, and somebody to drive a getaway car, I'm sure that we can do it. If you want money for doing it, I'll pay you whatever I can. Bob, I have to get my son back. Nobody gave you any help, but if they had done, maybe you could have got your daughter out. Think about it, Bob. Those Célèstines have to be stopped sometime, by somebody. Maybe this is the time and we're the people to do it.'

Bob replied, 'It's late. Do you have a telephone number where I can reach you?'

'Call here,' put in Robyn. 'If I'm not in, my parents will tell you where you can contact me.'

'All right then,' said Bob. 'I want to toss this over in my mind. I'll give you a call by eleven o'clock tomorrow morning, yes or no.'

'Bob,' said Charlie, 'thanks for listening.'

'You got it,' Bob told him, and hung up.

Robyn picked up her glass of wine and came to sit next to Charlie on the couch. 'I'm still in a state of shock,' she said.

'Because your editor knew about the Célèstines and didn't print the story?'

Robyn nodded. 'I've suddenly found that my whole world has been turned upside down. How can I ever trust Ted again? I mean – what other stories has he spiked? I thought the press was free and fearless.'

'I don't think any of us is free and fearless,' said Charlie. 'Anyway, look at the time. I've got to get back to Allen's Corners. I'm working on the assumption that Bob Garrett is going to help me, and that means I've got to make some arrangements. Plane tickets, and a rental car, and a gun. The gun's going to present some problems.'

Robyn said, 'I can get you a gun.'

Charlie set down his glass of wine. 'Where is a sweet, innocent newspaper reporter like you going to get a gun?'

'My editor keeps one in his desk. Some outraged reader came into his office with a knife once, and threatened to cut out his kidneys. He's kept a gun ever since.'

'He's not about to lend it to you, is he?'

'I can borrow it. He doesn't get into the office until ten, and I know where he keeps the keys.'

'Supposing he finds out? That's not going to do your career any good, is it?'

Robyn shrugged. 'I don't think I'm really too worried about working for a newspaper whose editor cans crucial stories just because they don't happen to suit his personal convenience.' She lowered her head so that Charlie could see the parting in her hair. 'Listen,' she said, 'I'll get you the gun, and I'll drive the car, too. A friend of mine has a Shelby Cobra, we can borrow that.' She hesitated, and then she looked up at him. 'Charlie, I want to help.'

'You know the risks? It's not just your job, there could be bullets flying around.'

'I want to help. Don't preach.'

Charlie reached across the couch and took hold of Robyn's hand and squeezed it. 'In that case, I accept. Listen—I'll get back to Allen's Corners now. You have my number. Call me as soon as you hear from Bob Garrett. I'll fix the plane tickets. You get hold of the gun and the car. Provided Bob Garrett agrees to help—and, God, are you listening up there? Please lean on Bob Garrett and make him agree to help—we should be able to break into Le Reposoir at about noon tomorrow.'

Robyn said, 'Do one thing for me. Book three plane tickets.'

'We're going to California, and then to Mexico. I hope you understand that. I'm not at all sure we're ever coming back.'

'Ever since Carl, I've learned to take one day at a time.'

'Carl was the spectacularly messy love affair?'

'Carl was Adolf Hitler reincarnated as Robert Redford.'

Charlie knew at that moment that something was happening between Robyn and himself; that they were both strongly attracted to each other. With luck, and a little prayer, the time might come when they could let that feeling of attraction loose. But right now, Charlie's overwhelming priority was rescuing Martin. He did nothing more than lean forward and kiss Robyn on the forehead, and squeeze her hand again, and tell her, 'I'll be waiting to hear from you, right? And thanks for everything. Thanks for listening. Thanks for being sane.'

'Carl never said that I was sane.'

'Human society is riddled with bozos.'

Charlie said goodnight to Mr and Mrs Harris and Robyn came to the kerb to see him off.

'Don't stay out here,' he told her. 'You'll catch cold.'

'Tomorrow we're going to rescue your son like the Three Musketeers, and tonight you're worried about me catching cold?'

'Goodnight, Robyn.' He smiled, and blew her a kiss. He U-turned in the road, and drove off. He glanced in his rear-view mirror as he reached the intersection, and she was still standing by the fence watching him go. He didn't know whether to feel happy or apprehensive. He switched on the radio and listened to Tina Turner.

He reached Allen's Corners at half past midnight. The sloping green was silver under the full moon. The streets and the buildings were silver, too. Charlie was reminded of a poem his schoolteacher used to read when he was small, about the moon turning everything to silver. He parked outside Mrs Kemp's house, switched off the radio, and dry-washed his face with his hands. For the first time since he had discovered that Martin was missing, he allowed himself to admit that he was totally exhausted.

He was about to climb out of the car when he thought he saw something flicker beside the house. He frowned, and peered into the shadows. There was nothing there. He got out, closed the car door as quietly as he could, and locked it. It was then that he heard a rustling, scurrying sound, only about thirty or forty feet to his left, beside the trees. He froze, and stared, and listened intently. *Slowly, silently, now the moon / Walks the night in her silver shoon—*

He took one step towards the front gate. Without any warning, the dwarfish hooded figure rushed out of the shadows straight towards him, in a hopping, tumbling, headlong gait, and collided with his legs. He fell backwards against the car, jabbing his hand up as he did so to push the dwarf away. But then he saw the hooked machete lifted in to the moonlight, and he twisted sideways just as the metal blade clanged against the hood of the car, and rolled across the sidewalk into the gutter.

The dwarf hissed, and came rushing after him again. Charlie kicked at him, and felt his foot strike at the solid meat of his stubby thigh. The machete whistled, but Charlie heaved himself away, and the blade jarred against the sidewalk.

With one more roll, Charlie somehow managed to scramble up on to his feet. The dwarf advanced, swinging the machete from side to side as if he were cutting grass, panting and whispering under his breath. All that Charlie could see inside the shadow of his hood was a pale nose and two glittering eyes.

'You bastard,' Charlie breathed at him. 'You sawn-off runt.'

The dwarf let out a piercing, effeminate shriek, and rushed at Charlie yet again. Charlie backed and dodged sideways, but the machete sang into his left thigh, *wheeooo-smakk!* and even though Charlie felt no pain, he knew that he was cut. He pivoted around and punched the dwarf in the side of his hood, so hard that the dwarf somersaulted over on to the ground.

'Come on, you runt!' Charlie yelled at him. 'Come on, if that's what you want! You want blood? All right, then, you can have some blood! Come on, runt!'

The dwarf clung on to the side of Charlie's car in an effort to heave himself back up on to his feet. Charlie kicked him mercilessly in the ribs, and he dropped to the sidewalk again. Then Charlie stepped on to his arm and knocked the machete out of his reach with a sideways sweep of his foot, and then reached down and seized hold of the dwarf's robes.

'You Goddamned half-assed –!' he began. But the dwarf suddenly lifted his arms and dropped right out of his robes, falling heavily on to the ground with a noise like a sack of beets.

'*Scaaaarrccchh!*' the dwarf screamed, and glared at Charlie in venomous hate. Charlie stood where he was, paralyzed, still clutching the dwarf's discarded robes. The dwarf – the creature that M. Musette had called 'David' – was standing in front of him wearing nothing but a tight cotton waistband.

David was hideously white-faced, but his head was normal size. He was a mature young man of twenty-four or twenty-five, with wiry mid-brown hair. It was the sight of his body that had stopped Charlie dead, however. His arms had been severed below the elbows. He had been holding his machete by means of a leather strap around his right stump. His legs had been severed halfway down his thighs, and his stumps were protected by leather cups padded with the fibrous material that lined the hoods of cars. There were ugly scars and indentations all over his torso, where he must have cut out flesh for the Célèstine rituals; but worst of all, his genitals were missing. There was nothing but a bush of pubic hair, beneath which Charlie glimpsed a grotesquely twisted scar, a male vagina made out of purple knots. He took in every horrifying physical detail of this thing called David in the same way that he had made an instantaneous check of ten fingers and ten toes the moment that Martin had been born.

'I will murder you, I promise!' the dwarf shrieked at him, all teeth and spittle. Then he snatched at his robes, tearing them out of Charlie's grasp, and hopped off into the shadow of the trees. Charlie stood where he was, breathing deeply. His left trouser leg was stained dark with blood, and glistening in the moonlight. He picked up the dwarf's machete, and limped slowly up to the house.

The front door was slightly ajar. Charlie knew straight away that something was wrong here, because Mrs Kemp had always been security conscious. He pushed open the door and hobbled inside, hefting the machete in his right hand. 'Mrs Kemp?' he called. 'Are you okay? It's Charlie, Mrs Kemp! Charlie McLean!'

There was no reply. Charlie listened for a few seconds, then limped into the kitchen to see if Mrs Kemp was there. He switched on the fluorescent lights. They flickered and jolted and then came on full. The kitchen was deserted, but there was a smear of blood across the worktop, next to the rice jars.

'Mrs Kemp?' He went back to the hallway and climbed the stairs. The moon looked in through the window. *One by one the casements catch / Her beams beneath the silvery thatch.* Charlie reached the landing and hesitated, listening, listening, but there was no sound to be heard except a gurgling in the plumbing, and the faraway drone of an aeroplane.

'Mrs Kemp, it's Charlie,' he said, although his voice was so hushed now that nobody could have heard it.

He said 'Mrs Kemp' for the very last time as he opened her bedroom door and saw what the dwarf had done to her. After that, there was no point at all in calling her name.

Mrs Kemp's brass bed was a grisly raft of blood and chopped-up flesh. The stench of bile and blood and faeces was stunning. Mrs Kemp's head had been almost completely severed, and was wedged between the side of the bed and the nightstand, staring wildly at nothing. All that connected her head to her torso was a thin web of skin, like the skin of a chicken's neck. Her chest had been hacked apart, her breastbone broken, and her heart and her lungs and her liver chopped into glistening ribbons. Her arms rose stiffly up on either side of her ribcage as if she were still trying to protect herself from the frenzied blows of the dwarf's machete.

Charlie couldn't quite work out what had happened to the rest of her, and didn't want to try. He could see heavy loops of pale intestine wound around the brass bedhead, and he could see one of Mrs Kemp's feet lying on its side by the bureau, severed, but still wearing its pink slipper. He closed the door and then he stood on the landing and closed his eyes. He told himself that he was probably entering a state of shock; but that he had to keep on functioning, no matter what. The machete dropped out of his fingers on to the floor, and of course it didn't occur to him that the handle now bore his fingerprints; and that the last person who had been seen in Mrs Kemp's house, by no less a witness than Sheriff Norman Podmore, was him.

All he could think of was the Célèstines; and the fact that they were prepared to kill people in order to protect themselves. Mrs Kemp, and him, too. And nobody would protect him against them, not even the police.

He stumbled downstairs, and went out of the front door, slamming it hard behind him. Somehow he found himself sitting in the driving seat of his car. He started up the engine, turned around, and headed out of Allen's Corners in the direction of Waterbury.

The moon was gone now. Shock and exhaustion began to overwhelm him. He swerved from one side of the road to the other, and the Oldsmobile's suspension groaned with every swerve. It was dark out there, he couldn't see anything. Then he narrowly missed a roadside tree, his wheels bumping over grass hummocks and slews of gravel, and he pulled the car to a stop beside the road.

'You're going to kill yourself,' he told his reflection in the rear-view mirror.

Hm, retorted his reflection, *They're going to kill you anyway. It depends what kind of death you prefer. A highway accident – restaurant prodnose dies in auto smash – or a homicide – food scrutineer chopped into American steak.*

He wanted to go on, but he forced himself to switch off the engine and douse the headlights. He needed sleep and he needed it badly. He shifted himself into the passenger seat and reclined it. Then he loosened his necktie and tried to make himself comfortable. Even an hour's sleep would be better than no sleep at all.

He dozed and dreamed. He was trying to find his way through a furniture store, heaped high with musty antique tables and bureaux and chairs with twisty legs. His face was reflected in a dozen dusty mirrors. His feet made a reluctant swishing noise on the parquet floor. Out of the corner of his eye, he glimpsed a small figure in a hood, and for an instant he caught the shine of a curved machete. He began to hurry between the stacks of furniture, turning left and then right and then left again. A high voice kept screaming, '*Daddy! Daddy! Save me!*' In one of the mirrors he saw the machete lifted up and down in a brutal chopping motion, and fingers go flying through the air.

He woke up shouting. He sat up. He must have been sleeping for three or four hours, because the sky was already pale. He opened the door and climbed stiffly out of the car and stretched. The morning air felt cold on his sweaty underarms. He would have done anything for a hot cup of coffee and a shower. Maybe Robyn could oblige when he reached Waterbury.

He sat behind the wheel and started up the Oldsmobile's engine. He thought about Mrs Kemp and wondered whether he ought to go back to Allen's Corners and report her murder to the sheriff. But a small voice in the back of his head warned him off. If he went to the sheriff now, the sheriff would delay him all day with questions and police procedure, and that was the last thing he wanted.

Apart from that, he wasn't sure how much he could trust Sheriff Podmore. Who else, apart from Charlie himself, had known that Mrs Kemp was out for revenge against the Célèstines?

His most urgent priority was not a murdered woman whom he had scarcely known, but his son Martin. He steered back on to the road again and headed for Waterbury.

Driving through Thomaston, he was observed from the roadside by two police officers in a parked patrol car. He kept checking them in his rear-view mirror as he headed south, but they stayed where they were, and made no attempt to follow him. The chances were that Mrs Kemp's body hadn't been found yet; and with any luck Charlie would be able to rescue Martin and get clear away from Connecticut before it was.

He switched on the car radio. Bob Seger and the Silver Bullet Band were playing 'Hollywood Nights'. Charlie sang along with it for a while. '*Oh, those Hollywood nights... in those Hollywood hills...!*' but as he approached the outskirts of Waterbury he fell silent, like a man who recognizes that his destiny is about to turn, and that life and death are sitting on his shoulders like a pair of predatory hawks.

14

They drew up outside a plain 1930s house with maroon-painted shutters and a scruffy front yard and Bob Garrett appeared almost immediately on the front porch in a blue Sears suit with a fawn raincoat folded over his arm. He walked quickly towards them with his free arm swinging. Charlie climbed out of the Cobra and folded the front seat forward so that Bob could climb into the back seat.

Robyn pulled away from the side of the road and headed north toward Hotchkissville. Bob leaned forward from the back seat and introduced himself. 'You're early,' he said, with a nervous laugh. He had a simple, uncomplicated face with pale blue eyes and a cow's-lick fringe combed back from his forehead and a neatly-clipped moustache.

'I'm real glad you decided to come,' Charlie told him.

'I knew I was going to, the second you asked me. I just had to think about it, was all. I had to think whether I wanted all those memories brought back. It's the memories that hurt the most.'

'I'm sorry,' said Charlie. 'Maybe this is your moment to get your own back.'

'Do you have a gun?' asked Bob.

Charlie reached forward to the glove compartment and produced it. A hefty weapon for a newspaper editor: a Colt .45 automatic, capable of blowing a hole through five men standing in a line.

'Do you know how to use it?' asked Bob.

'I think so,' Charlie told him. 'You point it at anybody who happens to be annoying you, and you pull the trigger. Every American kid knows that.'

'Well, you've just about got it,' said Bob. 'The question is, will you have the *courage* to pull the trigger?'

He sat back, and watched the Connecticut countryside flashing past the window. Charlie looked at Robyn and made a face. 'Rambo the Second,' she whispered.

Charlie gave her a philosophical smile. 'Maybe that's what we need.'

'Have you worked out how we're going to get into Le Reposoir?' asked Bob.

'We're going to walk in,' said Charlie.

'Walk in? You think they're going to let you?'

'They're not going to let me break my way in, are they?'

'Well, I guess not,' said Bob, in that deep, hesitant voice. 'I guess if you can swing it, walking in is the best way. That's the way I did it, anyhow.'

'The most important thing is to take them by surprise,' said Charlie. 'It shouldn't take more than a couple of minutes to get hold of Martin and drag him out of the house, but we have to be fast and we have to work together.'

'So tell me what you're planning to do,' said Bob.'

'I'm going to walk straight in there and tell them that I've seen the light, and that I want to join the Célèstines, too.'

'You think they're going to buy that?' asked Bob, leaning his elbows on the front seats.

'Is there any reason why they shouldn't? They have two major weaknesses – their fanaticism and their over-confidence. Fanatics always find it hard to believe that other people don't agree with their point of view. They find it a great deal easier to accept the idea that you've seen the light, and been won over. And that's exactly what I'm going to tell them. If eating himself alive is good enough for my son, then it's good enough for me.'

'I'm glad you can joke about it,' said Robyn.

'I'm not joking,' said Charlie. 'If those people think for one moment that I'm threatening them, they'll kill me.'

'You sound like you know something that we don't,' Bob said.

Charlie said, 'Let me put it this way. I didn't get this cut on my leg by accident.'

Robyn glanced at him as she drove. 'You told mom that it was an accident.'

'Sure I did, I didn't want to upset her. And she bandaged it up so well.'

'What happened? Did somebody attack you?'

'That dwarf – you remember the one I was telling you about? He was waiting for me when I got back to Allen's Corners last night.'

'Why didn't you tell me straight away?'

'With your parents straining their ears? Come on, I'm not saying they're interfering or anything, but they *are* interested in finding out what kind of a man their daughter is working with, all of a sudden. I didn't want them to get upset, that's all.'

'I've seen that dwarf, too,' said Bob. 'Well he's not exactly a dwarf, is he? He wasn't born like that. He cut off his arms and legs.'

'That's right,' Charlie nodded. 'And he's a mean son-of-a-bitch, believe me.'

They drove through Allen's Corners without stopping and made their way up towards the Quassapaug Road. Charlie managed to catch a glimpse of Mrs Kemp's house; but there were no police cars outside, no crowds, and no ambulance. Mrs Kemp's body probably hadn't been discovered yet, and that suited him fine, although the guilt and the pain that he felt for Mrs Kemp were as red-raw as fresh-cut meat. He didn't allow himself to think about her hacked-up body, soaking into the mattress. He didn't allow himself to think about her arms, still raised in rigor mortis, fighting off an assailant who had long since hurried away.

The Cobra's tyres complained as they climbed the corkscrew towards Le Reposoir. The sky was as dark as a Rembrandt painting; the trees were as pale as faces. Robyn said, 'Just about now, my editor's going to look in his desk and realize that his gun has gone.'

'He won't suspect you, though, will he?'

'Not to begin with. But one of our advertising people came into the editorial offices while I was looking through his desk.'

Charlie patted his breast pocket. 'Don't worry. I bought three tickets to San Diego. After that, we can make our way down to Baja, and thence into oblivion. Your editor won't be able to find you in a thousand years.'

They reached the gates of Le Reposoir sooner than Charlie expected. Robyn slewed the Cobra around in a wide curve, and shut off the engine. Charlie took the .45, turned it one way, then the other, then pushed it into his inside pocket. He looked back at Bob. 'Are you ready? We want to take this real easy, a step at a time.'

'I'm ready,' Bob told him.

Charlie got out of the car, and went over to the intercom. He pressed the call button and waited for somebody to answer. This time, he didn't have to wait long.

'Mr McLean? I'm surprised to see you back so soon.' It was the voice of M. Musette, but careful this time, and suspicious.

'M. Musette,' said Charlie, 'it seems that I owe you an apology.'

'An apology, Mr McLean?'

'Last night I had a run-in outside Mrs Kemp's house with that assistant of yours, David.'

Cautiously, M. Musette said, 'So I understand. You weren't hurt, I hope?'

'A slight cut, but I think I can forgive him for that.'

'Did you... see Mrs Kemp?'

'She wasn't at home,' Charlie lied. The last thing he wanted was for M. Musette to know that he had found Mrs Kemp's body. 'I stayed overnight at the Bethlehem Motel.'

'You have my regrets,' said M. Musette. 'David can be impetuous. I think it was after he lost his hands, you know. He started to throw tantrums, and act rather violently. He's not altogether to be trusted.'

Charlie paused for a moment, and then he said, 'The fact of the matter is, M. Musette, that I began to wonder why I was fighting you. I sat in that motel and I bandaged up the cut that David gave me, and then I sat there and said to myself, "Charlie, these people are religious, they believe in happiness and goodness and the life everlasting." And do you know what else I said to myself?'

'Do continue, Mr McLean.'

'Well, M. Musette, I said to myself, "If my son has chosen the Célèstines as the way to heaven, then perhaps there's something in it. Perhaps I've been the one who's been blind. Perhaps there really is something in all of this business, after all." Because what have I seen? Sights that have shocked me, sure, I have to admit. But a new way of looking at the word of the New Testament, and that's for sure. A new way of taking communion, the flesh and the blood of Our Lord Jesus Christ.'

'What are you trying to tell me, Mr McLean?' M. Musette asked him with unconcealed impatience.

'I'm trying to tell you, M. Musette, that I've been saved. I'm trying to tell you that I've seen the light. Your way is the only way, and I don't want my son to go to heaven without me. I want to go with him. Damn it, M. Musette, I want to volunteer.'

M. Musette was silent for what seemed like five or ten minutes. After a while, however, he said, 'I find it very hard to trust you, Mr McLean. You have been nothing but hostile ever since I first met you. I am inclined to think that you are feigning this sudden enthusiasm in the Célèstines in order to gain access to your son.'

'M. Musette, my son can make his own decisions. If he wants to dedicate his life to the Célèstines then that's all right by me.'

'You *are* singing a different song, Mr McLean.'

'That's the nature of religious conversions, M. Musette. Suddenly, you see the light. Saul did that, didn't he?'

There was another long pause, and then M. Musette said, 'Wait there. I'll send my security guard to open the gate. But, please—remember that you are on your honour to conduct yourself with propriety.'

Propriety, thought Charlie, with bitterness. *You can talk to me about propriety after slaughtering Mrs Kemp?*

The intercom clicked off, and Charlie was left waiting in the wind. The dry trees rustled like the voices of gossiping ghosts. There was a smell of smoke in the air, smoke and fall and sadness.

Eventually, a black Chrysler appeared between the maculata bushes, and the thin youth with the close-cropped hair and the Buddy Holly suit climbed out and unlocked the gates.

'Mr McLean?' he said, in a nasal voice. 'Drive your vehicle slowly down to the house. I'll be following right behind. And, please, no faster than ten miles an hour.'

They drove at a crawl down to the gravelled turning-circle in front of Le Reposoir. Robyn looked at the house in amazement. 'You know something, I never even knew this place *existed*, and I was brought up around here.'

M. Musette was waiting for them in the doorway. 'All we need now is speed,' said Charlie. 'We walk straight up to him, push him aside, and then go straight up the stairs to the corridor where all the new Devotees go. I know which room they're keeping Martin in. We force our way in, take one arm each, and frogmarch him out of there. Bob, you take his left arm, I'll take his right. That way, I can have a hand free to hold the gun.'

'You realize Musette is going to recognize me straight away,' said Bob.

'Just keep cool. Speed, and surprise, that's what we need. Robyn—as soon as we're inside, you turn the car around and get ready to burn rubber.'

'I'm terrified,' said Robyn.

Charlie reached across and squeezed her hand. 'It's going to work like a charm, just so long as none of us loses our nerve.'

'A charm, he says.'

'We're all right so far,' said Charlie. 'I mean, we got in here, didn't we? And they didn't close the gates behind us. That was one thing I was afraid of.'

The thin youth came up and tapped on the window. 'Will you follow me, please?'

Charlie glanced tensely at Robyn, and then at Bob. He had been so busy reassuring *them* that he hadn't realized how tightly his own nerves were wound up. He gave the youth a salute of acknowledgement and climbed out of the car. Bob followed close behind him, keeping his face to the ground so that M. Musette wouldn't recognize him until it was too late.

M. Musette extended his hand as Charlie came up the steps. Charlie's heart seemed to have leaped up and caught itself on one of his ribs. He was breathing in short, shallow gasps. He could feel the weight of the .45 in his inside coat pocket, and he was sure that M. Musette could see it bulging out.

'Well, Mr McLean,' M. Musette greeted him with a diagonal smile. 'Perhaps I can congratulate you on your conversion.'

Charlie's mind snapped into overdrive. He swung his left shoulder forward and knocked M. Musette sideways. He felt M. Musette's collarbone jar against his arm. Then he was running across the hallway with Bob right behind him. As he reached the foot of the stairs he heard M. Musette shouting, 'Harold! *Harold!* Lock off the upstairs landing!'

Charlie turned around, tugging the .45 out of his coat, and tearing the lining as he did so. He pointed it directly at M. Musette and yelled at him, 'You try to stop me, and I'll blow your head off!'

'It's no use, Mr McLean!' M. Musette replied. 'You can't get away with it! Martin is out of your reach now! You can only get him back by killing us all!'

'If that's what it takes,' said Charlie. 'Come on, Bob!'

Together, they climbed the stairs. They crossed the landing, but when they reached the door which led to the corridor where the new Devotees were kept, they found that it was locked. Charlie wrenched at the handle, but the door was solid steel, and he couldn't budge it.

'What are you going to do?' Bob asked him.

'Musette,' Charlie replied fiercely. He ran back downstairs, but M. Musette had disappeared. He went out through the door. Apart from Robyn waiting in the car, the grounds were deserted. Bob said, 'They've locked it all up and left us to it.'

'Round the back,' said Charlie.

They ran around the side of the house to the garden door which Charlie had used to enter the house the first time. That, too, was locked. Charlie cocked the .45 and pointed it at the lock, but Bob said, 'Forget it, that only works in movies. You'll probably end up with a ricochet right between the eyes.'

'God damn it, how do we get in?' Charlie raged.

He ran back to the front door, back up the steps, and back inside. He tried a downstairs door but that was locked too. Solid oak, with a five-lever lock. He kicked at it, but it didn't even rattle. He turned back to Bob in anger and frustration.

'I've blown it, damn it! I should have taken Musette hostage!'

'We'd better just get out of here,' said Bob. 'Let's go back and work out some other way of getting in.'

Charlie was almost in tears. His vision of bursting into Martin's room and dragging him out had been foiled by the simplest expedient of all. M. Musette had done nothing more than lock his doors and disappear, so that he could neither be reached nor threatened.

'Come on,' said Bob, taking hold of his arm. 'This is one of those times when discretion is the better part of valour.'

Charlie looked up at the florid Victorian stained-glass window at the head of the stairs. It depicted Sir Gawain on his way to do battle with the Green Knight, a brightly coloured scene of valleys and lakes and bulrushes. Charlie lifted the .45 and fired at the window. There was a deafening, echoing bang. Charlie had never fired such a heavy calibre handgun before, and his arm was painfully jarred. All that he succeeded in doing was blowing out one small pane of blue glass. Bob looked at him, and said, 'Are you satisfied now?'

'I'm going to get my son back if it kills me,' said Charlie.

He left the house, and walked down the steps. They were probably being covered by guns from M. Musette's security men, but Charlie didn't care. He stood at the bottom of the steps and shouted out. '*M. Musette! If you hurt my son, it's going to be your head next time, not just your window!*'

There was no reply. The ravens croaked amongst the rooftops, the trees shushed and rustled like the sea. Bob climbed back into the car and Charlie followed him.

Robyn said, 'What happened?'

'They locked the doors. Come on, we'd better get out of here.'

'I'm sorry,' said Robyn. 'I'm really sorry.'

They drove back to the gates, and exited on to the Quassapaug Road. As they did so, however, a huge Mack truck appeared, as suddenly as a nightmare, bellowing down the hill from the direction of Bethlehem. Charlie yelled, '*Go!*' and Robyn slammed her foot down on the gas so that the Cobra slithered away from Le Reposoir with a shriek of tyres and a cloud of dust and rubber smoke.

Charlie twisted around in his seat. The truck's front grille filled up the entire rear window. Robyn kept her foot hard on the gas, steering the Cobra from one side of the road to the other as she negotiated one curve after another. But the truck held on, tailgating them only two or three feet away. As they reached the corkscrew curve that would take them to Allen's Corners, the truck bumped them in the back, and Robyn juggled frantically with the steering wheel as she momentarily lost control.

They slid round the corkscrew with their tyres screaming like strangled cats. Their offside rear wheel jolted against a large stone at the side of the road, and then they were sliding sideways the opposite way. The truck barged them again and again. Charlie heard glass and metal grind, and the *whup-whup-whup* of something scraping against one of the rear wheels.

The truck shunted right up close to them, and as they came out of the corkscrew it was actually pushing them along, madly, uncontrollably, like a roller-coaster. Robyn cried out, '*Charlie! I can't hold it!*' and then Charlie saw a row of trees rushing at them and the Cobra hurtled right off the edge of the road, flying for nearly twenty feet clear through the air. It collided with two massive pines with a noise like a bomb going off. Charlie was thrown violently against the glove compartment, his head hitting the windshield, and something burst over the top of him and glass exploded.

Behind them, the truck bellowed around the corner and out of sight.

Charlie tried to sit up. Robyn was sitting with her head slumped forward but she was wearing her seat belt and he could see that she had been only jolted and shocked. There was a large red bruise on the left side of her forehead, but otherwise she looked all right. It was only after he had looked at Robyn, however, that he realized what had hurtled over him when they hit the trees. Bob – fired out of the back seat and through the windshield. The whole of the upper part of his body had gone through the laminated glass, and he now lay face down on the Cobra's hood, amidst a slush of broken glass. Blood ran slickly across the metal.

Charlie managed to kick the passenger door open, and heave himself out of the wrecked car. There was a strong smell of petrol, but there didn't seem to be any immediate danger of fire. He walked around to the driver's door and tugged it open after three or four strenuous yanks. Robyn was just coming round, and she stared at him with widely-dilated pupils. 'Charlie?' she asked him, her voice slurred. 'Charlie, what happened?'

He unfastened her seat belt and helped her out of the car. She said, 'Bob—is Bob all right?' but Charlie wouldn't let her turn around and look. He guided her back up the slope to the side of the road and made her sit down on a rock. 'Give me a minute, okay?' he told her. 'Bob's been hurt pretty bad.'

He went back down to the car. He had been almost sure that Bob was dead, but as he approached he heard him groaning. He came up close and said, 'Bob? Bob, it's Charlie. How do you feel?'

Bob raised his head from the hood of the car, and Charlie could see what had happened to him. The broken windshield had caught his forehead as he had hurtled through it, and sheared the skin off his face, from his eyebrows right down to his chin. He stared at Charlie with one white swivelling eyeball set in a livid oval of scarlet. His teeth snarled bloody and bare, without lips or gums. What was left of his face hung from his jaw in fatty folds, his cheeks, his nose, and his chin – as if his features had been nothing more than a latex Hallowe'en mask which had suddenly been ripped from his head.

Extraordinarily—and terribly—he was still conscious.

Charlie said, 'Bob? Bob, can you hear me?'

Bob nodded, and his eyeball turned and glistened.

'I'm going for an ambulance, Bob. You'll just have to stay where you are for a minute or two.'

Bob tried to say something but his mouth had been too badly mutilated for him to do anything but grunt and gargle.

Charlie clambered back up the rocks to the road. Robyn was still sitting there, white-faced and tearful. 'I couldn't hold it,' she sobbed. 'I tried so hard, but I couldn't.'

'We have to call an ambulance,' said Charlie. He felt weak at the knees and almost on the point of collapse. The day seemed to crowd in on him as if the clouds were determined to press him down into the ground and the trees all around him were trying to entangle him and choke him.

'Is Bob badly hurt?' asked Robyn.

'As bad as anybody I've ever seen.'

'It looks like there might be a house down there,' said Robyn, pointing further downhill. Charlie peered through the trees and he thought that he could make out the angular grey gable of a house or a barn.

'I guess it's worth a try,' he told her. 'Why don't you stay here, just in case somebody drives past, and you can flag them down?'

'What if that truck comes back?'

Charlie wiped the chilly sweat from his forehead with the back of his hand. 'I don't know. He was deliberately trying to run us off the road, wasn't he?'

Robyn held his arm. 'Don't worry about it. I'll duck down and hide if I see it. You go call that ambulance.'

Charlie began to jog down the hill. He had only gone about a couple of hundred feet however, when he heard a bursting, crackling roar from the hollow where the Cobra had crashed. He turned around and saw an orange fireball roll up from the trees and vanish like a conjuring trick. The car was already blazing from end to end.

He ran slopewise through the whiplashing bushes and the drifts of dried leaves. By the time he reached the car it was too late for him to do anything at all. The flames were so fierce that he couldn't get within twenty feet. He couldn't see Bob at all.

Robyn came running down the hill to stand beside him. They stood together, helplessly watching the fire gradually die down, leaving a hulk of an automobile burned brown and rainbow mottled. Bob's body still lay on the hood, but it had charred and shrunk into a little black figure no larger than a nine-year-old child. Charlie could see white bones gleaming through charcoal flesh. He could see something else, too, although he didn't mention it to Robyn. The metallic shine of a cigarette lighter, tightly clasped in Bob's burned-up hand. He must have ignited the car's leaking gasoline himself.

'We'd better get out of here,' said Charlie. 'There's nothing we can do now.'

'We can tell the police, can't we?'

'I'm not so sure that's a good idea.'

'But we can't just walk away!' Robyn protested.

'I think we can,' said Charlie. 'In fact, I don't think we have any other alternative. Not if we want to stay alive ourselves. That truck was waiting for us. I told you what the sheriff and Mr Haxalt told me: M. Musette doesn't suffer trespassers gladly.'

'I have to get to a phone,' said Robyn.

'What? To call your office? Come on, Robyn, think about it. If the Célèstines have as much of a hold on the media as they appear to, then the best thing we can do is disappear for a while, try to work this out undercover.'

'Do you really think they were trying to kill us? Maybe that truck just had brake failure.'

'Brake failure my rear end. They want us dead. And they've succeeded with Bob, haven't they? A poor uncomplicated guy who was only trying to help me out.'

Robyn was shaking. They were both so shocked by what had happened that neither of them really knew what they were talking about. At least bickering seemed to be real.

'We can cut across country,' said Robyn. 'If we keep on going downhill, we'll get to the Quassapaug River. Then we can follow it all the way down to Allen's Corners. That way, nobody will see us.'

Charlie took her arm. 'Let's go. As soon as they find out that we're still alive, they'll go straight to

Mrs Kemp's, and then I'm going to be in really serious trouble.'

'I don't understand.'

'They killed Mrs Kemp, too. That dwarf did it – the one they call David. Before he attacked me last night, he broke into her bedroom and chopped her up.'

'Are you serious?' Robyn demanded, staring at Charlie in disbelief. 'Why didn't you tell me this morning?'

'I didn't want to scare you out of driving for me.'

'God, I wish you had... Did you report Mrs Kemp's murder to the sheriff?'

'Are you kidding?' Charlie retorted.

They made their way along beside the Quassapaug River for almost a mile. It was quite narrow here, splashing busily down between the rocks, sometimes disappearing under layers of russet-brown ferns. Occasionally, they heard a police siren wailing along the road from Allen's Corners; and once they saw a police helicopter heading at top speed for Bethlehem, or maybe towards Le Reposoir. Charlie had to assume that Sheriff Podmore was looking for them now; and just in case the police brought in tracker dogs he made sure that they crossed and recrossed the Quassapaug whenever it was shallow enough for them to take off their shoes and wade. The clear-rippling water was intensely cold, but after each crossing they rubbed their feet with Robyn's pale blue sweater to dry them and warm them up.

It was almost two o'clock in the afternoon by the time they reached the outskirts of Allen's Corners. The small community was almost completely deserted, but Charlie took the precaution of approaching Mrs Kemp's along the narrow alleyway which ran along behind the back yards of most of the houses on Naugatuck Street. David must have used this alleyway when he had come to visit Martin during the night; and escaped along it, too.

All the yards were empty and silent. Robyn stayed close behind Charlie, but she was growing increasingly nervous, and kept glancing over her shoulder. 'What are we doing here?' she asked.

'First of all I want to find out if they've discovered Mrs Kemp's body yet. If they have, then I'm going to be wanted for questioning – if not for actually doing it, if I've learned anything about M. Musette. Second of all, we need Mrs Kemp's car. We'll never make it anywhere on foot, not if they get dogs out. She keeps her car keys in the hutch in the kitchen.'

They reached the back of Mrs Kemp's house, and Charlie eased open the gate. There was nobody to be seen in any of the other yards, except for a woman hanging washing about eight houses away, and there was no sign of police – not even barriers or warning notices or seals on the door to protect the evidence inside.

'They haven't found her yet,' Charlie whispered; but Robyn said, '*Look!*' and pointed up to the back bedroom window.

At first, the window simply appeared to be dark. But then a faint wash of early-afternoon sunlight came out, and Charlie could see a dull blue light reflected from it, as if the glass were tinted. But it was only when the blue light began to ripple and swirl that he understood what he was looking at. Inside the bedroom, blowflies were swarming, thousands of them, and scores of them had settled on the window. The dull blue light was the shiny colour of their bodies catching the sun.

Charlie said nothing, but ushered Robyn up to the back of the house. He tried the kitchen door and it was locked; but he picked up an edging-stone from Mrs Kemp's flower-bed and used it to crack open one of the panes of glass. The key was still in the door, so he reached in and turned it.

'God,' he said, as they stepped cautiously into the kitchen. 'You can smell it even down here!'

'Do I have to come in?' Robyn asked.

'No, you wait there,' said Charlie. 'But keep your eyes peeled, okay? And don't let anybody see you.'

Charlie crossed the kitchen, trying not to breathe in too much of the cloying, sweetish smell which now permeated the entire house. He opened up the hutch, and found Mrs Kemp's car keys straight away. Underneath her keys was a roadmap of Litchfield County, two bank books, a spare pair of spectacles, and a half-finished embroidery sampler with the message 'Home Is Where The Heart Is'. *That's ironic,* thought Charlie. *Not only the heart, but the lungs, the spleen, the liver, and the stomach, not to mention twenty-eight feet of intestine.* He was about to close the drawer, however, when his attention was caught by two leaflets which had been stuffed into the back of it. He coaxed them out, and unfolded them, and held them up to the light so that he could read them.

One was cyclostyled on yellowish paper, and bore a drawing of Christ crucified. Beneath it, Charlie could make out the words *L'Église des Pauvres, Société des Gourmands, Acadia, LA.* There was a lengthy text underneath in that curious Cajun mixture of French and English. Most of it seemed to be an exhortation to love God *avec votre esprit et avec votre corps* and to serve him *avec all your heart.*

The other leaflet was almost incomprehensible, but seemed to be something to do with *Le Recreation.* There was a New Orleans address at the bottom of it: 1112 Elegance Street. But it was what was pencilled on the back of the leaflet that interested Charlie the most. *Norman, for information. M.*

Mrs Kemp must have taken both of these leaflets out of Sheriff Podmore's office when she vandalized it yesterday. She had crammed them into the drawer along with her car keys when she came home and locked herself in the kitchen. Charlie frowned at them again. They were definitely something to do with the Célèstines, but right now he couldn't work out what. Maybe L'Église des Pauvres was another 'dining society' like Le Reposoir.

And maybe the 'M' who had signed that note to Sheriff Podmore was Edouard Musette; or even his wife.

Robyn called, 'Charlie? Did you get those keys? I'm feeling distinctly nervous out here.'

'I've got them,' said Charlie, 'and something else besides.'

He handed Robyn the leaflets. She glanced through them quickly, and then shrugged. 'I'll have to sit down with a French dictionary. I've forgotten everything I learned at school.'

Charlie tucked the leaflets into his pocket. Then he led Robyn around to the garage at the front of the house. The street was deserted. There wasn't even a dog in sight. Charlie eased open the garage doors, and together they climbed into Mrs Kemp's old Buick station wagon. 'It smells like lavender,' said Robyn.

Charlie started up the engine. It rattled and coughed, and produced a thick black cloud of smoke. 'Not exactly the ideal vehicle for a discreet getaway,' Charlie remarked.

'Where are we going?' Robyn asked him. 'We're not on the run, are we?'

'You could say that. I mean—the justice around here may be corrupt, but we're fugitives from it.'

They backed out of the driveway, and then headed for the ring road which would take them around by the supermarket and out of Allen's Corners by the railroad depot and the warehouses, where they were less likely to be spotted by sheriff's deputies or over-enthusiastic disciples of Le Reposoir. Charlie said, 'Once we make it out of Connecticut, we have a fair chance of getting away clean.'

Robyn looked at him narrowly. 'You know where you're going, don't you? You're not running away from anything; you're running *to* something.'

Charlie said, 'I'm trying to save my boy, that's all.'

'Trying to play Rambo didn't work,' Robyn commented.

'Does it ever? You can never solve anything with a sweatband and a gun. It was my fault, I didn't think it out properly and it was totally amateurish. I'm just grieving that Bob was killed.'

'So what are you planning on doing now?' asked Robyn. She touched his shoulder, a small affectionate gesture of communication; a signal that no matter what he wanted to do, she would help him.

'You see these leaflets? All in Cajun French. Well––that's where this cannibalism started, among an isolated sect of the Cajun French. Sheriff Podmore told me it began in New Orleans, and if that's where we have to go to find out more about the Célèstines, then that's where we'll go. Leastways, that's where *I'm* going. You're not obliged.'

'Do you seriously think that I'll allow you to leave me behind?' Robyn told him. 'And besides, you need somebody to take turns with the driving.'

'Do you want to drop off home and pick up some clothes?' Charlie asked her. 'We should be reasonably safe until the police find Mrs Kemp. Then it's going to be like all hell was let out for the weekend.'

Robyn shivered, partly out of cold, partly out of anticipation. 'When you called the *Litchfield Sentinel*,' she said, 'my life changed for ever.'

Charlie steered the Buick out towards Waterbury. 'Don't start blaming me. You could have said no. You can say no now, if you want to. You can see how dangerous these people are.'

'Wild horses couldn't stop me coming with you.'

Charlie reached over and switched on the station wagon's radio. 'Wild horses I'm not worried about. It's these Goddamned cannibals.'

15

They crossed the state line into New York shortly after four o'clock. There was no sign of any police pursuit, and Charlie crossed his fingers and hoped that they had gotten away. Now he settled himself down for nearly 1,400 miles of driving, all the way through eight states to Louisiana, and to New Orleans. He estimated that if they kept going, taking turns at the wheel, they could reach the Mississippi delta in thirty-six hours. That was if Mrs Kemp's oil-burning Buick behaved itself; and if they weren't stopped anywhere along the way by the police.

As they headed towards New York City, Robyn tried to translate the leaflets that Mrs Kemp had stolen from Sheriff Podmore's office. It was *Le Recreation* text which interested her the most. It was dense and obscure and smudgily printed, and neither she nor Charlie could decide why Mrs Kemp had decided to take it.

'It could be that it just happened to be lying on his desk, and she picked it up because it looked important,' Charlie suggested.

'I don't know,' said Robyn. 'It looks like it's been folded and kept in an envelope. Maybe the envelope was marked confidential or something, and Mrs

Kemp thought that it might contain something which would incriminate him.'

They made a short detour off the parkway to White Plains, and stopped at Macy's on Mamaroneck Avenue to pick up a Concise French Dictionary in the book department. While Robyn paid for the dictionary, Charlie found himself glancing left and right like a criminal. Afterwards, they picked up two Big Macs and some hot black coffee, and they ate and drank as they drove south-westwards on the Hutchinson River Parkway towards New York.

Robyn said, 'I thought I'd never be able to eat anything again, after what happened this morning. Now all of a sudden I'm starving.'

'It's delayed shock,' Charlie replied. 'Just make sure you chew it properly.'

'You're the food expert. Although it beats me how you can be a food expert and still eat a Big Mac.'

Charlie swallowed, and sipped coffee. 'Let me tell you something, if you compared the hygiene in most high-class international restaurants with the hygiene at McDonald's, you'd never want to eat anything but Big Macs for the rest of your life. After about five years as a restaurant inspector, you realize that in spite of all the cockroach bodies and the rat droppings you might have been eating along with your veal parmesan and your chicken a la whatever, you're still alive and still comparatively healthy and you haven't had a day's sickness since you can last remember. I guess that's when you begin to understand that the human constitution is pretty resilient, and that you could probably eat a codfish pie out of some Bowery bum's back pants pocket without any noticeable ill effects.'

Robyn stared at him for a long time and then returned her Big Mac to its polystyrene carton. 'I'm not sure that I can eat the rest of this.'

They drove through New York and the spires of Manhattan glittered grey and silver in the last light of the day. Then they were heading south-westwards through Jersey and Pennsylvania, along Route 22 to Harrisburg. At Harrisburg, Robyn would take over the driving, but meanwhile she pored over Mrs Kemp's leaflet with her French dictionary open on one knee.

As they drove through the Musconetcong mountains, she closed the dictionary and said, 'Do you know what this is?'

'I wouldn't have asked you to translate it if I did,' Charlie replied. He glanced in his rear view mirror. So far he was pretty sure that they weren't being tailed.

'This is a kind of Célèstine newsletter. It gives a list of some of their up-and-coming meetings as well as their calendar for the year.'

'When do they have their church cookout?' asked Charlie bitterly.

'They have more important dates than that. In fact—according to this—the whole year is significant. This is the year of *Le Recreation*.'

'What does that mean? Sports, games, that kind of thing?'

'You've got to be joking. *Le Recreation* literally means The Re-Creation. This is the year they attempt actually to recreate Jesus Christ in physical form.'

Charlie looked at her. He was more tired than sceptical. 'Go on,' he said. 'Tell me what it says.'

Robyn angled the leaflet so that it was illuminated by the Buick's interior light. 'Brothers and sisters, Guides and Devotees...' Something something – I don't quite understand that bit. 'This is the year when the Prophecies of Sainte Desirée come to pass; when the Lord and Master will rise again, as was promised in *les temps anciens;* when the Body and Blood of Christ the Lord will be formed again out of the sacrificial flesh of all who worship Him. For three centuries, Devotees have devoured themselves, and what has remained of them has been devoured in turn by other Devotees until *au bout de ses vies* – at the end of their lives – these Devotees are devoured by their Guides.'

Charlie overtook a westbound livestock truck, and then turned to Robyn and said, 'Go on, I want to hear it.'

'It's so *bizarre*,' said Robyn. 'I find it hard to believe that it's true.'

'Go on, it's important. This may give us the information that we've been looking for.'

Robyn rubbed her eyes. Then she lifted up the leaflet again, and read, '"Each human soul which has been devoured has been recorded in the Ledger; and now we are approaching at last the sacred number that forms the very centre of the Prophesies of Sainte Desirée. That is, one thousand times one thousand souls."'

Charlie whistled. 'Do you know what that means? Since the Célèstines got started, nearly a million people have eaten themselves. A million! It's a holocaust!'

'Wait,' said Robyn, 'there's more. It says here that on the holiest of all weeks the Célèstines will gather together and observe a last sacrificial convenant. All of the remaining Devotees will devour as much of themselves as they can... and the remaining Guides will devour what's left. At the very end there will be nobody left but one Devotee, who will become the Last Supper for the Master of Guides. When he has eaten the last of the Devotees, the Master will be transformed into the Lord Jesus Christ incarnate, whose body is the all-embracing temple of human souls. That's kind of a free translation, but it's near enough.'

'And when is this last supper scheduled?' asked Charlie.

'Whenever they reach the sacred number, I guess,' said Robyn. 'The leaflet doesn't give a specific date.'

'Well—that's one of the things we're going to have to find out in New Orleans,' said Charlie.

Robyn switched off the car's interior light and watched Charlie driving through the darkness. 'I still don't really understand why we're going to New Orleans at all. I mean—aren't you wasting time?'

'If I'm supposed to interpret that as 'Martin could be chewing his own fingers and toes by now', then I get your point. But you saw how things worked out this morning. I'm not cut out for that kind of a rescue. If I tried it again, I'd almost certainly wind up killed, and that would leave Martin completely at their mercy.'

He paused, and then he said, 'For most of my working life, I've been eating at other people's tables without them realizing who I am. I guess you could say that my greatest asset is my anonymity.'

'So what are you going to do?'

'I'm going to New Orleans and I'll join the Célèstines, in disguise. A moustache and tinted spectacles and a haircut should do it. Then I'm going back to Le Reposoir and get Martin out from the inside.'

Robyn said, 'I suppose that's as good a way as any.'

'For me, it's the only way.'

'I don't quite see where I'm going to fit in.'

Charlie reached across the seat and held her hand. 'I'm going to need somebody on the outside to keep in touch with. At the very last moment, I'm going to have to get out of that place like Roadrunner with his ass-feathers on fire, and there has to be somebody there to do the driving.'

'You still want to me to drive, after the crash?'

'The crash wasn't your fault.'

'What happens if the Célèstines discover who you really are, and kill you? What am I supposed to do then?'

Charlie made a face. 'You forget you ever heard about the Célèstines, or Martin, or me, and you go back to your job and your parents and maybe a new boyfriend who doesn't give you a hard time, and you live out the rest of your life in peace and happiness.'

'You're suggesting that I never mention it, ever again?'

'Not if you want a long life.'

Robyn thought about that for a moment, and then said, 'There's one thing more. If you join the Célèstines, won't you have to start eating yourself?'

302

'I was actually hoping that I could be a Guide, rather than a Devotee. I don't know what qualifications a Guide is supposed to have, but I guess I could fake them.'

'But then you'd have to eat other people.'

Charlie gave Robyn a tight smile. 'Let me cross that bridge when I come to it, huh? I'm hoping to get away without eating any human flesh at all.'

'This scares me,' said Robyn.

'You don't think it scares me too?'

*

Robyn took over the wheel just past Harrisburg, and drove into the night while Charlie lay on the back seat of the station wagon and tried to sleep. It took him until two o'clock in the morning to close his eyes. The smell of the vehicle was unfamiliar, so was the way it jolted over every bump and join in the highway, and the songs that Robyn was playing on the car radio all seemed to be songs of regret. He thought of Martin, lying naked on that plain bed at Le Reposoir, and he tried to touch him with his mind. *I love you, Martin, don't despair. Don't let them take you away.*

They stopped for an early breakfast at Buchanan, VA, a few miles short of Roanoke. They sat in a small drugstore drinking black coffee in silence and staring at themselves in the mirror behind the counter. They both looked exhausted.

'Are you sure we're doing the right thing?' Robyn asked, as they stepped out into the chilly morning air, and climbed back into Mrs Kemp's old Buick.

Charlie said, 'We could use some more gas. There's only quarter of a tankful left.'

Robyn leaned across and kissed Charlie's unshaven cheek. 'Don't worry,' she said. 'I'm with you.'

*

They drove into New Orleans on a humid, thundery morning, with the clouds hanging low over the city, and lightning flickering out over Lake Borgne and the Gulf beyond. Charlie had taken the wheel at Meridian, and Robyn was lying asleep in the back. For the past hour, the radio had been turned to a Louisiana station playing plangent Cajun and Zydeco music – high, shrill voices and accordions and fiddles double-bowed.

Charlie had called from Atlanta the previous evening to make a reservation at the St Victoir Hotel, which was quoted in MARIA as being 'inexpensive, discreet, and authentic'. He knew that after more than thirty-eight hours of driving, the first priority for both of them was going to be sleep. It was no good regretting the time that they would lose. Their exhaustion had reached the point where they could see the highways unravelling in front of them even when they closed their eyes.

The St Victoir was a narrow-fronted nineteenth-century building between Bourbon and Royal, but it lacked the distinctive cast-iron balconies that characterized the finest architecture in the French Quarter. It was wedged between an over-expensive art gallery and a Creole restaurant called Jim's Au Courant. Inside, there was a cool air-conditioned lobby with potted palms and a marble floor and old sofas upholstered in damp green velvet that could almost have been moss. A fat lady in a floral frock sat behind a curved mahogany counter and smiled at Charlie and Robyn like Jabba the Hutt.

'Mr and Mrs McLean,' said Charlie. 'I made a reservation yesterday from Atlanta.'

The fat lady opened up her file drawer and picked her way through the reservation cards with tiny hands. 'That's right,' she said. 'Double room, looking to the back, for three nights provisional. May I take an impression of your card?'

Their bags were taken up by a black porter in a peaked cap who said almost nothing but hummed all the time. Robyn had brought a change of clothes from her parents' house; Charlie, of course, had taken his travelling-kit out of his Oldsmobile, before parking it right at the back of the Harris house and

305

covering the licence plate with a plastic shopping bag so that it couldn't be identified by any passing police patrol.

Charlie had told Mr Harris that he and Robyn were taking a few days' vacation together in Canada. He had winked at Mrs Harris and Mrs Harris had obviously been pleased that Robyn had found somebody so quickly. Especially somebody so *nice*.

Charlie tipped the black porter and then closed and chained the door. The room was high-ceilinged and cool, with a huge mahogany bed and two massive mahogany chairs. There was a view from the back over the St Victoir's courtyard, shaded by layers of foliage. It had already begun to rain, heavy warm drops, and the palm leaves nodded in acknowledgement of the coming storm.

Robyn lay back on the bed and kicked off her shoes. 'I don't think I ever felt so tired in my whole life.'

'Do you want anything to eat?' Charlie asked her. 'How about some *beignets* and a pot of coffee?'

'I think I just want to sleep,' said Robyn.

Charlie went into the large tiled bathroom and slowly undressed. He took a long shower, standing for almost five minutes with his eyes closed, letting the hot water spray into his face. He shaved, but he took care not to shave the bristling beginnings of his moustache. Then he wrapped himself in a towel and went back into the bedroom. Robyn was already asleep, lying on her side with one hand against her cheek as if she were thinking. Charlie sat on the bed beside her and dried himself. She was a pretty girl. Even though she was wearing a crumpled checkered shirt and faded jeans and her hair needed washing, she had a femininity about her which Marjorie had always lacked. He rested his hand on her sleeping hip for a little while, and then returned to the bathroom to find himself a robe.

He lay on the bed and tried to sleep, but he couldn't. His mind was still crowded with thoughts of Martin, and M. Musette, and that grotesque living gargoyle they called David. He closed his eyes and heard the thunder booming over the delta, and the rain whispering through the leaves, and somebody playing the piano through an open window.

For a moment, he didn't know whether he was wakening or dreaming; but then he heard a door slam and footsteps in the corridor outside, and someone saying, 'Take those drapes down with you, don't forget.' He sat up, and looked at Robyn, She was still sleeping. He opened up his brown leather travelling bag and found himself a clean blue shirt and a pair of fawn non-crease slacks. He dressed, and then he wrote a quick note for Robyn on a damp sheet of Saint Victoir notepaper: *Gone to locate*

Elegance St, back soon, don't worry. He signed the note, *Affctly, Charlie.*

By the time he reached the street, the worst of the rain had passed over, although the sidewalks still reflected the white-painted lacework balconies and the red and yellow horse-drawn carriages taking tourists around the Vieux Carré, and the sky was the colour of dynamite smoke. He approached a wizened-faced black man on the corner of Royal Street and asked him the way to Elegance Street. The man said, 'Elegance aint so much of a *street* as an *alleh.* But you don't want to go theuh. It's all churches and cat-houses.'

All the same, he directed Charlie westward on Royal, telling him to pass nine alleyways and courtyards on the left before he took the tenth, and that would be Elegance Street. Charlie thanked him and offered him a dollar. The black man took the money, but told him, 'Druthah a cigarette,' his eyes elderly, bloodshot, either drugged or drunk or too old to care about either.

Charlie walked along Royal Street, smelling rain and damp and gasoline and cooking, and jazz was playing on the wet morning wind, that pompous, stilted highly traditional jazz that the tourists come to hear but never really like, 'Didn't He Ramble' and 'St James' Infirmary' and 'Mahogany Hall Blues Stomp', musical relics of a day long past. He came at last to the narrow courtyard called Elegance Street, a shaded alleyway of old-fashioned brick that was overlaid with dripping palm leaves and overlooked by green-painted cast-iron balconies. Charlie passed the Crescent City Antiques Gallery and the Beaumonde Tearoom featuring clairvoyant readings by Madame Prudhomme. There, at the very end of the alleyway, stood a pair of black iron gates, with a plaque announcing L'Église des Anges. Charlie approached it with trepidation, and stood for a long time staring through the railings into the inner courtyard. There was a stone fountain, and a stone bench, and some wrought-iron garden chairs that somebody had knocked over sideways. But there was no sign of life, *pas âme qui vive* as the French would say. Not a soul alive.

Charlie dragged at the wet cast-iron bell pull. He didn't hear the bell ring, but after a very long time, a stocky man in a black monk's habit appeared. His hair was white as transparent noodles and his eyes were as blank as two mirrors. He approached the gates and stood staring at Charlie with the expression of a man of very little patience. Charlie said, 'Is this the church of the Célèstines?'

'This is the Church of the Angels. Some call us Célèstines.'

'A friend of mine used to belong. I've come to the conclusion that it's my turn.'

'Did your friend attend this church?'

'No. He went to the church in Acadia, L'Église des Pauvres.'

'That is our sister church,' said the man. 'Can you tell me what your friend's name was?'

There was a faraway protestation of thunder. Charlie said, 'I only knew him as Michel or maybe Michael.'

The man said, 'You can't do better that that?'

'He never told me his surname.'

'What did he tell you about his beliefs?'

Charlie glanced around, pretending to be furtive. Then he leaned closer to the gates, and said, 'He told me all about the self-sacrificial communion. He told me all about the body and blood.'

'I see,' said the man, his expression unchanging. 'And what was your response to that?'

'My response was that it sounded pretty extreme. You know, the idea of actually—' Charlie leaned closer forward and whispered, '*eating your own body.*'

The man eyed him coldly. 'Much of what we teach is metaphorical, you know. Not to be taken too literally.'

'But the whole core of your religion is this communion, right? The Last Supper, with real body and real blood.'

'You'd better give me your name,' the man told him. Rain began to sprinkle the courtyard again, and whisper through the leaves.

'Dan Fielding. I'm a chef.'

The man suddenly looked interested. 'A chef? Of what description?'

'I used to work for the South Western Hotel chain, mainly in their prestige restaurants. I could cook anything.'

'Did you ever cook... meat?'

'Are you pulling my leg? I was taught high-grade butchery as well as cooking. I can cut and trim a prime beef carcass in less than twenty minutes. And when I cook it, let me tell you this, nobody holds a candle to Daniel DuBois Fielding, believe me.'

The man said, 'You're not an Acadian.'

Charlie managed a smile. 'Of course not, I'm a Hoosier. Does it make any difference where I come from?'

'Strictly, no,' said the man. 'Although we *do* have a church near Lafayette, Indiana.'

'Really? I have cousins in Lafayette. I have cousins in Kokomo, too.' Charlie was deliberately acting naïf. The man listened to him patiently and the rain began to patter down heavier, until there were droplets shining on his soft black hood.

'Listen,' he said, 'why don't you come back here this evening? Maybe you'd like to talk to our chief

Guide. Do you know about Guides? Did your friend from L'Église des Pauvres tell you anything about them?'

'I know about Guides,' Charlie said. He paused, and then added, 'I know about Devotees, too.'

'Well, you could be useful to us,' the man told him. 'Come back at nine. Where are you staying?'

'With friends, on Philip Street. Have you heard of the Courvilles?'

'There must be five thousand Courvilles in New Orleans. But you come back at nine. Come alone, mind, just like you are now.'

'I understand. So long for now.'

'*Au revoir, monsieur.*'

Charlie walked out of Elegance Street not at all sure if he had deceived the black-hooded man into believing that he was a genuine recruit for the Célèstines or not. He had learned from his encounters with the Musettes that the Célèstines were remarkably open and unafraid. This was not only because what they were doing was technically legal, or at least not technically *i*llegal – but because like those who dealt in narcotics and heavy duty pornography and extortion, they had many influential friends.

He returned to the St Victoir Hotel to find that Robyn was still asleep. He was beginning to have swimmy sensations, like jet-lag, but he was too agitated to sleep. He sat by the window in an upright chair looking out over the misty courtyard and listening to the sounds of New Orleans. Robyn murmured something, and turned over, but still didn't wake up.

Charlie's eyes began to close or maybe he was only dreaming that they were closing. His head nodded, and jerked. He could hear the rain trickling along the gutters. That piano was playing again, some high-stepping piece of music that sounded like Mussorgsky if Mussorgsky had ever written jazz. Some feeling made Charlie open his eyes again, a scarf of fear being laid gently over his shoulders. He looked down into the courtyard and he was sure that he glimpsed a small hooded figure disappearing amongst the palm fronds.

He was suddenly awake. Involuntarily, he said, 'Unnhh!' out loud, and Robyn lifted her head off the bed and stared at him.

'Charlie? What's the matter?'

'I was dozing. I frightened myself, that's all. It was only a dream.'

Robyn looked around the room with the glazed eyes of someone who has fallen deeply asleep in unfamiliar surroundings. 'I've been dreaming, too. I thought we were still driving. All those cotton fields. All those girder bridges. I thought I saw you standing in a field by the side of the road, calling me. But when you turned round, it wasn't you at all. It had a face like the Devil.'

Charlie eased himself up from the chair and walked over to the bed. The light in the room was the colour of pewter. 'It's so dark,' said Robyn. 'What time is it?'

'A little after twelve. It's been raining most of the morning.'

'Did you go out?'

'I found the Church of the Angels on Elegance Street. It's only three or four blocks from here. I'm supposed to be going back there at nine to meet the head honcho.'

'You should have woken me.'

Charlie sat down on the bed beside her and took hold of her hand. 'You needed your sleep.'

'And what about you? Aren't you tired?'

'In my job, fatigue is a way of life.'

Robyn combed through her hair with her fingers to loosen the sleep tangles 'Didn't you ever think about doing anything else? I mean—you didn't want to be a restaurant inspector when you were a little boy, did you?'

Charlie smiled. 'When I was a little boy, I wanted to be a zoo keeper.'

'That's a pretty smelly job, zoo keeping.'

Charlie laughed. Then he stopped laughing, and sat there silently with a smile on his face thinking about wanting to be a zoo keeper. He could remember all of those model animals, the tigers and the monkeys and the elephant with the broken ear. Robyn touched his shoulder and looked closely into his eyes, and he thought, you can always tell whether you're going to fall for somebody or not by their eyes. Love is retinal.

He kissed Robyn's forehead. It was still warm from sleeping. She closed her eyes and he kissed her lips. It was a long lingering kiss that was more romantic than passionate. Charlie hadn't kissed a woman like that in years. Not since Milwaukee.

In the midday twilight of a thunderstorm, Charlie unbuttoned Robyn's checkered shirt and bared her breasts to the touch of his fingertips. They were soft and heavy, and they fell to each side of her chest in full, pale curves. Her areolas were the palest pink, and as wide as pink-frosted cookies. Charlie bent forward and kissed her nipples and they stiffened between his lips. Robyn whispered something that could have been words of love; or maybe the words of a song.

He unfastened her jeans. That high-stepping piano music slowed down now, and Robyn's breathing was as soft as the rain. Underneath her jeans she wore French lace panties, peach-coloured, transparent, so that the dark delta of her pubic hair showed through. Charlie slipped his hand into the leg of her panties and felt a thin slippery line of wetness that almost made him feel as if all his emotions were going to self-destruct.

They made love for over an hour. He kissed her neck, kissed her shoulders and watched as the shining shaft of his erection slid in and out of that perfect dark delta. Feelings washed over him like bayou water, muddy, warm, and blinding, but always moving with a slow, strong current. Robyn sang that little song again, softly as a memory. At the very last she opened her thighs as wide as she could and he touched and tasted her, and then put his fingers to his lips and anointed her nipples so that they glistened for a moment like diamonds.

Robyn showered, then they ventured out of the St Victoir to the Café du Monde on Decatur Street, where they indulged themselves in a late lunch of beignets dusted with powdered sugar and piping hot *café au lait.*

Charlie could afford to relax, because he had done all that he could possibly do; and all that was left was to wait until nine o'clock. He didn't forget about Martin. He couldn't, because Martin was the reason he was here. But he allowed himself to walk hand in hand with Robyn through the French Quarter, around Jackson Square, where the twin Pontalba Buildings shone oddly orange in the afternoon light, and along Pirates Alley, where they stopped to look at paintings of nudes and bayous and old black men with wrinkled faces and straw hats, art for the tourist trade.

They reached the end of Pirates Alley, and emerged into an unexpected slice of sunshine, when Charlie caught a glimpse out of the corner of his eye of something white and small, fluttering like a flag. He stepped back to see what it was, and trod on the foot of an old lady who had been walking close behind him.

'You watch where you're treading!' she squawked, and lifted her stick as if she were going to strike out at him.

Charlie said, 'Please—I'm sorry. I thought I saw somebody I knew.'

Robyn took hold of Charlie's hand. 'What is it?' she asked him. She could see that he was upset.

'I'm not sure. I glimpsed it before, in the courtyard at the back of the hotel. At least, I *thought* I glimpsed it. I thought I was dozing off that time, but maybe I wasn't.'

'What?' asked Robyn. 'What was it?'

'The dwarf, the one who killed Mrs Kemp. The one who cut my leg.'

'But nobody could have followed us here. Nobody knew where we were going.'

Charlie shaded his eyes from the misty sunlight and tried to peer between the constantly changing patterns of passers-by. 'No,' he said. 'He's gone; if he was ever there.'

'You're over-tired, said Robyn. 'You've started hallucinating.'

Charlie nodded. 'Maybe you're right. Let's go back to the hotel.'

They walked back to the St Victoir. The fat woman like Jabba the Hutt beamed at them as they passed the reception desk.

'Everything *va bien*?' she asked them.

'Fine, thank you,' said Charlie. 'We're very comfortable.'

'*Les haricots sont pas salé,*' the woman sang, as they walked across to the elevator.

Charlie was opening the decorative sliding elevator gate. He turned when he heard the women singing and said, 'What was that?'

'Just a song, *monsieur.*'

'Charlie?' Robyn frowned.

'I don't know,' said Charlie. 'Not only am I suffering from *déjà vu*, I'm suffering from *déjà écouté.*'

Robyn kissed him as the elevator rose up to the fourth floor. 'It's all this Cajun French. It's having an effect on your brain.'

Charlie checked his watch. It was almost four o'clock. Robyn saw what he was doing and covered the face of his watch with her hand. 'Don't think about it,' she said, with great gentleness. 'Don't think about it until you have to.'

16

The rain had cleared by nine o'clock but the streets were still steamy and wet, so that the lights of Bourbon Street glistened and gleamed on the sidewalks and on the rooftops of passing cars and brightly in the eyes of those who had come to listen to jazz, or those who had come to eat at Begue's or Mike Anderson's, or those who had come simply to gawp, or to score.

Against his will, Robyn had made Charlie sleep for two hours during the afternoon, and then join her downstairs in the St Victoir's restaurant for a meal of blackened redfish and rice, with ice-cold beer. There were two musicians playing under the single large palm that dominated the St Victoir's old-fashioned dining rooms: a toothless old black man of about eighty playing a fiddle and a pale, pimply boy of no more than thirteen or fourteen sitting on a stool and playing a piano accordion. They played several Cajun *complaintes*, with the boy singing in a high, weird voice. Then they played 'Les Haricots Sont Pas Salé' which was the song that had given Zydeco music its name – *les haricots* repeated over and over until it was slurred. Charlie had the feeling that he had woken up in the wrong century, on the wrong continent.

He had checked his watch at a quarter to nine, and given Robyn a tight, anxious smile. 'Time I was going,' he told her. She had reached across the table and taken hold of his hand and said, 'Take care. Just remember that whatever happens, you've got somebody to come back to.'

They walked together to the corner of Royal Street. Then Charlie kissed her and made his way along the crowded sidewalks to Elegance Street. The little courtyard was lit by a single 1920s lamp standard, and from the main street it was impossible to see the gates of the Church of the Angels. Charlie hesitated for a moment, listening to the noise of traffic and laughter and music, and then walked through the shadows until he reached the gates. He pulled the bell and waited. He wore only a lightweight grey tweed jacket, a short-sleeved shirt, and a pair of pale grey slacks, but he still felt sweaty and hot. He heard a clock strike nine; he heard a jet scratch the sky. They were like his last reminders of the real world.

The man with the black hood and the hair like Japanese rice noodles appeared so suddenly and so close to the gate that he made Charlie jump. 'You are very punctual, Mr Fielding,' he remarked. 'You'd better come on in.'

Charlie thought: *This is it. This is the moment of decision. I can back out now if I want to.* But then he thought of Martin. He thought not only of the Martin he had come to know in the past few days, before the Célèstines got hold of him, but the Martin he had known on his rare visits back home, when he was small. Suddenly, a dozen images of Martin that he had long forgotten came crowding back to him, and by the time the man in the black hood had shot back the bolts and unlocked the locks, he was ready to go, carried on a floodtide of emotional memories.

The man made a noisy performance of relocking all the locks and rebolting all the bolts. Then he said to Charlie, 'Come this way,' and led him across a courtyard that was so dark that Charlie could see where he was going only by the faint gleam of wetness on the paving stones. Soon, however, they reached the back of a large old house, which Charlie guessed must have fronted on to Royal Street, although where and how he couldn't quite work out. It was three storeys high, with black-painted cast-iron balconies, and black shuttered windows from which no light penetrated whatsoever. The man in the black hood led Charlie up a flight of stone steps to the front door.

'This house has quite a history,' he remarked, as he produced a key and turned it in the lock. 'It was originally built by Micaela Almonester de Pontalba, who also built the Pontalba buildings on Jackson

Square. It was said that she had a secret admirer, and this was the house she built for their romantic trysts.'

'Interesting location for a church,' said Charlie.

The hooded man said nothing, but admitted Charlie to the hallway. Charlie was immediately struck by the smell, which reminded him strongly of Le Reposoir. It was a curious blend of herbs, and cooking, and dead flowers, and something else besides which was unidentifiable but slightly unsettling. The smell not of death but of *pain.*

The hallway was decorated with a mustard-coloured dado and wallpaper that looked as if it had been chosen from the Sears catalogue of 1908. A chandelier of black cast iron had a dozen bulbs but gave out very little light. There was a heavy bow-fronted bureau, with a black bronze statue of Pope Célèstine on it, lifting his hand in benediction. The man in the black hood led Charlie up to a pair of double doors, and said, 'You are about to meet the chief Guide and his council of Guides. The chief Guide here is Neil Fontenot. Some of the council you may recognize. But the etiquette among the Célèstines is for members not to acknowledge each other's existence outside of the church. Your friend probably told you that.'

Charlie gave him a quick-dissolving smile.

'Very well, then,' said the man, and opened up the doors.

Inside, there was a large plain room in which a dozen middle-aged men sat at a long mahogany dining table. The dining table had been polished so deeply for so many years that the men sitting on the opposite side of it were reflected upside down from the waist, so that they looked like kings and knaves on playing cards. The men were dressed in long black robes, with hoods cast back. As Charlie and his escort entered, they were all looking attentively towards the far end of the room, where a tall man with a cadaverous face was reading the Bible from a lectern.

In a rich, resonant voice, he was reading the Parable of the Dinner, in which a man invited his friends to eat with him, only to be met with repeated excuses and refusals. 'And the master said to his slave, "Go out at once into the streets and lanes of the city and bring in here the poor and crippled and blind and lame. Compel them to come in, that my house be filled. For I tell you, none of those men who were invited shall taste of my dinner."'

The chief Guide raised his head, and said, 'What do we learn from that? That Jesus believed in our divine mission. That Jesus taught us to fulfill our hunger. And what is our hunger? The *real* hunger, to which most men dare not confess. The hunger for the body; the hunger for blood. The hunger for the only food of which man is worthy. Were we ever supposed to eat pigs? The Jews say no! Were we ever supposed to eat cattle? The Hindus say no! My friends, when you read the New Testament today and consider the words of Jesus, you know in your hearts that there is only one true way.

'For what did he say at the Last Supper? He said, "*this is My body, given for you; do this for a commemoration of Me*," and he said, "*This cup is the new testament in My blood.*"'

At last, the chief Guide turned to Charlie. He smiled, and came over, extending a long-fingered right hand. 'My friend. Welcome to the Church of the Angels. Xavier told me that you were coming.'

'I feel like I'm interrupting,' said Charlie.

'Interrupting? Of course not! We are always pleased to greet new members. I understand from what Xavier told me that you used to have a friend who was a Célèstine?'

Charlie gave an equivocal shrug. 'I never really knew what they were. All I know is, Michael was happy. Well—we called him Michael. I think his real name was Michel.'

M. Fontenot draped his arm around Charlie's shoulders, and led him down to the head of the table. There was a large mole on M. Fontenot's right cheek, and his nose was peppered with blackheads. He said affably, 'Your friend Michael was a Devotee, was he?'

Charlie said, 'That's right, a Devotee.'

'And are you fully aware what happened to him?'

Charlie glanced around. 'Can I say it here?'

'Of course you can,' smiled M. Fontenot. 'Openly.' He looked around at the other Guides assembled at his table and beamed in the way that a father beams at other fathers when his son has said something cute.

Charlie said, 'The fact is, Michel told me everything that he was going to do. He said he was going to eat his own body, as much as he could, and that was the way to find Jesus.'

'And now you want to find Jesus in the same way?' M. Fontenot asked. The Guides at the table broke out into spontaneous but ragged applause.

Charlie nodded his head in what he hoped looked like idiotic acknowledgement. 'Michel said it was the only way. Michel said that if you wanted to follow Jesus, you had to do whatever Jesus did. What was the very last thing that Jesus did, before He was arrested and tried and crucified? He ate His own body and His own blood. And that was His secret! The secret that gave Him eternal life, the secret that nobody else understands. That's what Michel told me, anyway.'

M. Fontenot took hold of Charlie's hand, and said, intently, 'Yes! *Yes!* And that is why they call us the Célèstines, the Heavenly Ones. Those who are chosen by God. Because only the Célèstines understand what you have to do to sit at the right hand of Jesus. You have to devour the flesh of your own creation. That is the secret of winning God's approval. And that is the secret of everlasting contentment and perfect peace. "I am the bread of life," that's what Jesus said. "Eat me," that's what Jesus said. And Jesus ate the bread and drank the wine, too. Jesus devoured his own body and his own blood, and that was his way to heaven; just as ours is.'

Charlie said, 'I understand you're close to some kind of big occasion.'

M. Fontenot didn't seem particularly pleased to have been interrupted. 'Occasion? I'm sorry?'

'The sacred number. You've almost reached the sacred number. Isn't that right?'

'Who told you that?' asked M. Fontenot, narrowing his eyes. He stared at Charlie for a moment, and then turned to the man in the black hood called Xavier. 'Did *you* tell him that?'

Xavier shook his head. 'Not me, M. Fontenot. But his friend was a Célèstine, M. Fontenot. He knows what we do, and he's sympathetic. Believe me—I think we can trust him. He's not an FBI agent. We checked it this afternoon with FBI records. Quite apart from that, just look at him. He's not exactly FBI material, is he?'

Charlie put in, 'You can trust me, I promise. You want me to cut my throat and hope to die? Here, look – here's my wallet. You can check me out as much as you like. Driver's licence, credit cards. Here.' He prayed that they wouldn't actually look. 'My friend was a Célèstine; and I want to be one, too. Tell me—what else is there, in a world full of bombs and guns and ultimate weapons? To see God! To sacrifice yourself, and to see God! Don't you think that's the greatest trip of all?'

M. Fontenot seemed a little pained by the word 'trip', but Charlie was fairly sure that he had already won him over. His evangelical enthusiasm had helped; but it was obviously far more important to the Célèstines that he was a chef, and an experienced butcher. (Not that he was, of course; but he believed that he could keep on bluffing for long enough to rescue Martin.)

M. Fontenot turned to Xavier and between them they had a short, whispered conversation. At length, Xavier said, 'M. Fontenot is prepared to accept you as a Devotee, monsieur. However—' (and here he smiled as innocently as a small boy) '—he is anxious that you should be able to press your talents as a butcher into the service of the church; and for that reason he is asking you not to embark on your self-ingestion straight away. There will be need of many men with talents like yours when the Great Day comes, men who can quickly cut and prepare good meat, and he begs you not to start mutilating yourself until this Great Day is over.'

Charlie tried to look as if this were a disappointment. He lifted his fingers in front of his face, and wiggled them, and said, 'Oh, well, whatever you want. If you can tell me how I can serve the Lord some other way, some different way, then I'll be listening.'

M. Fontenot said, 'You will be allowed one finger.'

Charlie's face tightened. 'What did you say?'

'You will be allowed one finger. You can cut it off and cook it and eat it as soon as you wish.'

In a brittle voice, Charlie said, 'That seems kind of a small offering, don't you think, for my initiation as a Devotee? Maybe I should wait until the Great Day is over. Then I can make a proper job of it and eat my whole arm.'

M. Fontenot smiled at the other Guides, and some of them laughed. 'If only all of our new Devotees had the same spirit!' he proclaimed.

But straight away he turned to Charlie, and said, 'Now. You say you can butcher; you say you can cook. You say you are one of us. Xavier, bring me the knife. Bring me the pan, and the spirit-lamp. You like your flesh with herbs, monsieur? Xavier will bring you some fennel.'

Charlie felt a prickling surge of fright. 'You want me to do it *now*?'

M. Fontenot laid his arm encouragingly around Charlie's shoulders. 'We do what we can do to check the credentials of those who wish to join us. As you may have gathered, we have friends who give us access to the records of the FBI. But there is no simpler test of your faith and your good intentions than to have you take part in the sacred communion, the holy ingestion of your own flesh.'

He lifted up his left hand and Charlie saw for the first time that two of his fingers were missing. His smile was like a deep crack in a dried-out cheese.

'People are either for us, Mr Fielding, or else they're against us. There's never two ways about it. So despite the fact that we're a registered church, and despite the fact that we enjoy the patronage of some of the most influential men in the country, we still take care to protect ourselves against saboteurs and extremists and other ill-advised folk.'

As he said this, Xavier came back into the room wheeling a small trolley draped with a white cloth, on which was embroidered in purple the Lamb of God and a crucifix made from two crossed keys. M. Fontenot beckoned to Xavier to wheel the trolley right up close, and then he nodded and said, 'Thank you, Xavier.' Charlie's throat was as dry as glasspaper and his heart was beating in huge, irregular bumps.

'You may be feeling a number of things,' said M. Fontenot. 'You may be feeling elation. You may be feeling trepidation. But let me tell you this, if you're afraid, you have no need to be. The human body is a miracle in itself. It has wonderful powers of self-healing. Why, I was reading just the other day that a man had his leg knocked off by a locomotive, and dragged himself two miles to look for help. And that was his *leg* we're talking about. All you're surrendering here this evening is your finger.'

With a small flourish, M. Fontenot drew the white embroidered cloth away from the top of the trolley. Neatly laid out on the trolley's stainless-steel top was a spirit-burner, of the kind used in restaurants to flambé steaks, two plain white plates, a glass bottle of what looked like olive oil, a small china jar of fresh fennel leaves, a knife and a fork, a scalpel, and a small stainless-steel hacksaw. Neatly folded on the lower shelf of the trolley were three white towels, some gauze bandages, and some surgical adhesive tape.

Charlie tried to swallow. He wanted to say something but he was almost completely incapable of getting the words out. M. Fontenot said, 'It's the simplest act in the whole world, my friend. If your heart is in it, if your spirit is in it, your pain will be part of your joy. Believe me, we have brothers and sisters here who have to be restrained from cutting more from themselves that their nervous systems could tolerate; such is the holy joy they derive from self-amputation and self-ingestion. Now—we will say a prayer for you, to welcome you into our church, while Xavier lights the burner.'

Charlie thought: *They're going to kill your son, McLean. They're going to kill Martin. One of your fingers is a pretty small price to pay for the whole of his life.* But another voice inside of him said: *This is going to be agony. This is going to be more than you can take. And just remember that it's two days now since you last saw Martin alive. They could have killed and eaten him already.*

Xavier came forward and lit the burner—rather irreligiously, Charlie thought, with a flickering Zippo lighter. Xavier lifted the small copper chafing pan from the top of the burner, and adjusted the flame until it was hot and blue. Then he laid a folded white napkin on the table in front of Charlie, and beside it set the scalpel and the saw.

'Amputation is a simple matter,' he murmured. 'Feel where the lower joint of your chosen finger is, then cut through the skin with the scalpel until the bone is bared. Then use the saw. It will take you no more than a matter of moments.'

'Please—sit,' said M. Fontenot, and drew out a chair so that Charlie could sit down. All around the table, the Guides were smiling at him like old friends at a testimonial dinner. Charlie found their calmness and their good nature to be the most alarming part of the whole ritual.

'I think we should remember the words of St Paul in his letter to the Romans,' said M. Fontenot. 'And, as we do so, we can join with our brother Daniel DuBois Fielding as he enters the order of the holiest of Popes, St Célèstine.'

Xavier took hold of Charlie's left wrist and gently guided his left hand until it was lying on top of the white folded napkin. Then he took hold of his right wrist, and laid his right hand beside it. Into the open palm of Charlie's right hand he pressed the scalpel. The ridged metal handle felt intensely cold. The triangular blade winked in the light from the chandelier.

'"*One man has faith that he may eat all things,*"' M. Fontenot intoned. '"*But he who is weak eats vegetables only. Let not him who eats regard with contempt him who does not eat, and let him who does not eat judge him who eats, for God has accepted him.*"'

Charlie spread the fingers of his left hand wide on the napkin. Which one do I choose? Not the index finger, that would cripple me. I'd never be able to use a typewriter again. What about my middle finger? That would be even more disfiguring.

'Are you prepared?' asked M. Fontenot. 'Have faith, brother David. Do not hesitate. Hesitation may reveal you as one who does not truly believe.'

Charlie glanced up at him. There was an expression on M. Fontenot's face which may have seemed benign to everyone else in the room, but which Charlie read as an unmistakable warning. He looked down at his hand again, and made an instantaneous choice. The ring finger. The finger which still showed that he had been married to Marjorie. He slowly tugged off the plain gold wedding band, and set it down on the shiny mahogany table. There was a murmur of approval from the assembled Guides, and Charlie could see some of them staring at his hand with expectancy that approached lasciviousness. In Charlie's mind, there was no doubt at all that the rituals of the Célèstine church were tightly intertwined with the rituals of religious and sexual masochism; that the ecstasy of self-mutilation was orgasmic as well as spiritual.

'*Now,*' whispered M. Fontenot.

Charlie said his own silent prayer. Then he adjusted his grip on the scalpel and scratched a hesitant line around the base of his ring finger. He scarcely drew any blood; but it stung, badly. Everybody in the room was watching him in silence.

He clenched his teeth together, and cut more deeply into the top of his finger. Surprisingly, he felt almost no pain at all, but the sensation of sharp steel touching his bare bone made him shiver in his seat.

"'*If your enemy is hungry, feed him,*'" M. Fontenot quoted, as the bright red blood suddenly welled up out of the gaping slit in Charlie's finger. "'*If he is thirsty, give him a drink.*'"

Charlie's hand was trembling wildly, but he knew now that he had passed the point of no return. He cut into the side of his finger until once again he could feel the blade up against the bone. Then he lifted his hand and cut around the far side, and the underneath, while the blood pumped out of the wound like water out of a badly fitting plumbing joint. He laid the gory scalpel back down on the table, and took hold of his ring finger, tugging the flesh a little way upward to make sure that it was cut through to the bone all the way around. He could actually see the bone, and he was surprised how white it was, just like bone of a real skeleton.

The pain was extraordinary. His finger hurt so much it seemed to roar out loud. Added to that, he could feel that he was close to going into shock; stunned by the gruesomeness of what he was doing to himself. But one part of his mind remained completely detached. One part of his mind concentrated on finishing this amputation as quickly and as cleanly as possible. One part of his mind was already thinking of what the wound would look like when it was healed. He didn't want any splintered or mutilated flesh.

M. Fontenot said, in a voice that now seemed to Charlie to be echoing all around him, "'*Nothing is unclean in itself; but to him who thinks anything to be unclean, to him it is unclean. For if because of food your brother is hurt, you are no longer walking according to love. Do not destroy with your food him for whom Christ died.*'" Charlie pressed his bloody left hand flat on the folded white napkin, staining it instantly and heavily. His mouth was tightly closed, and the breath jerked in and out of his nostrils like the breath of somebody sobbing. But there were no tears in Charlie's eyes. His agony was too total for him to be able to cry.

He picked up the small saw. Wincing, he nudged the blade into the open wound on his finger. When he felt the sawblade against the bone, he hesitated, and looked up at M. Fontenot once again. 'Go on,' said M. Fontenot, encouragingly.

Charlie drew back the saw, and then rasped it forward over his finger bone. He didn't know whether he screamed out loud or not. When he opened his eyes and looked at the assembled Guides, who were all watching him in fascination, he could tell that he probably hadn't. But he had bitten the inside of his mouth: he could taste the blood.

'Go on,' M. Fontenot urged him. 'Only a few more strokes, and it will all be over.'

Mechanically, Charlie sawed at his fingerbone again, and then again. The pain was extreme, but the vibration of the saw teeth all the way through the nerves of his hand and up the lower part of his left arm was even worse. He sawed and sawed and then suddenly he felt Xavier's hand on his shoulder. 'You should stop now. Your finger is off. We don't want you to damage the table. It's antique, you know.'

Charlie stared at his left hand. His ring finger was completely severed, and lying in between his middle finger and his little finger at a peculiar angle, as if it were a joke finger that you could buy in a Mardi Gras carnival store. Slowly, stiffly, Charlie set down the saw. Then he raised his hand, and said to Xavier, 'Do you have... something to stop the bleeding?'

'Of course, brother,' said Xavier, and reached down to the lower shelf of the trolley to find a large gauze pad. Charlie held the pad over his pumping wound while M. Fontenot walked around the table, nodding to his Guides and smiling to himself. 'It is always an occasion, the very first cut,' he said. But then he came back around the table to stand over Charlie so close that Charlie could only see the ebony crucifix that hung low on M. Fontenot's chest. He laid an unwelcome hand on top of Charlie's head. 'But very much more of an occasion, of course, is the very first taste of one's own flesh.'

Xavier had now returned the small copper pan to the top of the spirit burner. He poured a little olive oil into it, and deftly tilted it so that the whole of the pan was evenly coated. As the oil began to bubble, Xavier leaned forward to Charlie and said, 'Your finger, please?'

Charlie stared at him, uncomprehending.

'Your finger,' Xavier repeated; and at last it registered in Charlie's shocked brain what he was supposed to do. He picked up his severed finger and held it up. It felt hard and strange and very dead. Xavier indicated with an encouraging nod that he was supposed to drop it into the pan, and so he did. There was a brittle sizzling noise, and Xavier quickly rolled the finger from one side of the pan to the other so that the outside of it was sealed by the heat of the oil. To Charlie's disgust, even the red flesh where he had cut the finger off turned the colour of cooked pork, a light whitish brown.

'Human flesh is rich, and it should be thoroughly cooked,' said M. Fontenot. 'However, one must be careful not to overdo it, otherwise it quickly becomes tough.'

Charlie sat where he was, silent, unable to take his eyes away from the finger which was frying in front of his face. The skin was turning crisp, especially around the edges of the fingernail, and because the fat was now dissolving, the finger slowly bent of its own accord, as if it were beckoning to him from the frying pan.

Charlie had anticipated all the horror of this ritual for days. In some ways, he was prepared for it. It was almost a relief that he had found out what the Célèstines did and how they did it. But what he could never have prepared himself for was the smell. It was similar to frying pork only it was quite unmistakably *not* pork. It was strong and meaty and (in a nauseating way) almost appetizing.

Xavier added a little fennel to the pan, and stirred the finger around to make sure that it was properly cooked. M. Fontenot watched Charlie with dark eyes that never once deviated as one of the white plates was set in front of him and the finger, still steaming, was placed on it like a small morsel with which to begin a very much grander dinner.

'Your contribution to the holy covenant,' said M. Fontenot. 'Your sacrifice, your very first; and let us hope you will give many more.'

Xavier took the bloody gauze away from Charlie's left hand, and replaced it with a clean pad. Already the wound was beginning to clot, and Charlie had to admit that M. Fontenot was right: the human body did have extraordinary powers of recovery.

'Do I... share it?' asked Charlie, trying not to look down at the crisply fried finger.

M. Fontenot shook his head. 'This one is all for you. Later, perhaps, when you wish to have your legs removed... then you can share your flesh with your brothers in Christ. For this evening, however, your meat is your own. For what you are about to receive, may the Lord make you truly thankful.'

It was a long time before Charlie could pick up his fork and prod at the finger on his plate, but M. Fontenot and the rest of the Guides remained silent, watching, giving him as much time as he needed. Charlie had the feeling that they had watched such reluctant ceremonies before. The room was filled with such expectancy that it almost seemed to exert a gravitational pull, as if the rest of the world would be irresistibly drawn towards it like nuts and bolts to a powerful magnet.

Charlie stuck his fork into the fleshy underside of the finger. The crisp skin made a slight popping noise as it was penetrated by the tines of the fork. Then Charlie lifted up the finger and somehow managed to guide it towards his mouth. His stomach made an audible groaning noise, and he could feel the back of his throat tighten up.

'Xavier, bring brother David some wine,' said M. Fontenot. 'I know how it is! Very difficult to bite, very difficult to swallow. But just remember, my friend, the human body is the greatest of all foods, because the human body is the vessel of the human spirit; and no other creature on earth has a spirit. This meat that you are about to eat is the food not of the gods but of the One True God. Think how much you will be offending Him if you refuse it. Think how much you will be offending all of us.'

Again, the implicit warning. Charlie knew that he was going to have to eat his finger if there was going to be any chance at all of him rescuing Martin.

He bit. The flesh came away from the bone quite easily. His mouth was filled with the taste of meat and fat; and the terrible part about it was that it was meat that needed to be steadily chewed. With rising nausea, Charlie swallowed a half-masticated piece – a piece that would have seemed tiny if he had been eating chicken or beef, but which felt as if it were the size and texture of a small hessian-covered sofa.

Xavier held a glass of red Californian wine in front of him. He swallowed, and nodded in appreciation.

The Guides of the Church of the Angels sat and watched Charlie for almost twenty minutes as he slowly ate the flesh of his own ring finger. At the end of that time he was sweating, and very close to vomiting; although the bone that now lay on his plate was bitten quite clean, even around the fingernail. It didn't look like Charlie's finger any more: it looked like a broken piece from a biology lecturer's skeleton.

Xavier took the plate away, and wheeled the trolley out of the room. M. Fontenot drew up a chair next to Charlie and sat smiling at him with his legs crossed and his fingers laced together. 'Well,' he said, 'you have done exceptionally well. You have crossed the threshold into the Church of the Célèstines. How do you feel now about the so-called horror of horrors – the eating of human flesh? Have you changed your opinion?'

Charlie wiped his mouth with his napkin. The wound on his left hand where he had severed his finger was throbbing so painfully that he found it difficult to think straight.

'I guess it was a shock,' he told M. Fontenot.

'But a *good* shock, wouldn't you agree?' M. Fontenot pressed him. 'Good for the spirit, and – dare I say it – good for the palate, too?'

'I've never experienced anything like it,' said Charlie, quite truthfully.

M. Fontenot paused for a moment, and then he said, 'Not even at the Napoleon House, or Le Tour Eiffel, or Pascal's Manale?'

'I'm sorry?' Charlie asked him. He really didn't understand what M. Fontenot was talking about. Not unless he meant—

'They're all restaurants, aren't they?' M. Fontenot asked him.

'That's right,' Charlie acknowledged.

'And that's what you do, isn't it? You travel around the country, under various assumed names and aliases, testing restaurants?'

Charlie's eyes were half closed with pain. He was gripping his left wrist with his right hand as tight as a tourniquet, in an effort to deaden the throbbing. 'You must have me mixed up with somebody else,' he told M. Fontenot. 'I'm a chef, not a restaurant inspector.'

M. Fontenot shook his head. 'You were never a chef, my friend. Nor were you ever a butcher. Both a chef and a butcher would have cut through that finger joint in two quick *coups*. You didn't even know where the joint was, not properly. Look how badly you have injured yourself.'

He turned to the Guide sitting closest to him, and leaned forward and whispered something. The Guide said, '*Certainement, M. Fontenot*,' and got up from the table, leaving the room by the same door through which Xavier had wheeled the trolley. M. Fontenot then leaned back towards Charlie, and said, 'You should have known that we suspected you from the ease with which we admitted you to this assembly. As a rule, no lesser church officials are permitted to intrude on these meetings, and no Devotees are allowed anywhere near. This is what that old radio programme used to call the inner sanctum.'

Charlie held up his left hand, swathed in bloody gauze. 'If you suspected me right from the beginning, then why—?'

'Why did we let you amputate your own finger? My dear Daniel – or perhaps I should call you my dear Charles—if you thrust your head into the lion's mouth, you should occasionally expect a nip or two around the neck. If not complete decapitation.'

The door opened again, and back came the guide whom M. Fontenot had sent out of the room. Beside him, waddling on his stumps, came the hooded dwarf who had murdered Mrs Kemp. He made his way around the table and heaved himself up on to a chair. Charlie watched him in dread and fascination. So he hadn't been mistaken. He had seen the dwarf at the back of the St Victoir hotel, and at Pirates Alley.

'We found it quite astonishing that you thought you could get away from us,' said M. Fontenot. 'Also, that we would dream of letting you go. You made one attempt to break into Le Reposoir to take your son away from his chosen destiny. You would surely make another. This, one supposes, is it. A clumsy effort to infiltrate the church of the Célèstines, in the hope that you might be able to snatch your son away at a moment when our guard was relaxed. And where were you going to go then? To Canada, perhaps?

Some of them go to Canada. But most try Mexico. It's a pity for them that we have such a close arrangement with the Mexican police. *La mordita,* that's what they call it. The bite. They will do anything for money.'

Charlie stood up, unsteadily. 'I think you'd better let me leave.'

'I'm sorry,' said M. Fontenot. 'That is absolutely out of the question.'

'You can't keep me here against my will.'

'You came here voluntarily.'

'Sure I did. But now I want to leave, and there's nothing you can do to stop me.'

M. Fontenot turned around in his seat and gave the dwarf a quick summoning wave. The dwarf rolled himself off his chair and came swinging up towards him. He stayed close to M. Fontenot's knee, his eyes gleaming malevolently out of the shadows of his hood.

'You have seen what David can do with a machete,' said M. Fontenot blandly.

Charlie said nothing, but stared back at the dwarf with equal enmity,

'As I say,' said M. Fontenot, 'You came here voluntarily. During the course of the evening's proceedings, you suffered an unfortunate accident to your finger, and since I have all the necessary medical facilities right here at L'Église des Anges for the treatment of such a wound, I suggested that you stay. An offer, of course, which you readily accepted.'

Charlie went suddenly white. He could feel the blood draining from his face just like a bucket being emptied. 'I have to throw up,' he told M. Fontenot. His stomach was churning and twisting and his mouth was flooded with bile and bits of chewed-up flesh.

Xavier took him to the bathroom along the hall and he was violently and painfully sick. He used his left hand to support himself as he leaned over the toilet and it left a wide smear of blood on the white paint. Strings of meat dropped from his stretched open mouth. He spent almost five minutes in there before the spasms in his stomach began to subside.

M. Fontenot was still waiting for him when he returned. 'You will stay here in this house until Friday. Then you will come with us to Acadia, to L'Église des Pauvres. That was the mother church in the early days when the Célèstines were still outlawed. It is there that we will be holding our Last Supper.'

Charlie lowered his head. His eyes were watering and the taste in his mouth was greasy and filthy and reeked of the aniseed flavour of fennel.

M. Fontenot reached forward and tapped him on the shoulder. '*Monsieur*, I advise you not to try to escape from us, not to make trouble.'

17

In the small hours of the night, when the pain became intolerable, a nurse appeared in a white winged wimple like the ghost of an albatross flying out of the darkness. Through half-closed eyes he saw the glint of a needle. Then she had injected him; and it was only a few minutes before the pain ebbed away, and dark waves of relaxation began to lift him buoyantly into the ocean of the night.

He dreamed about the strange high-ceilinged restaurant again, with the waiters who were hooded like monks, just like he had at Mrs Kemp's, and even though he was asleep he was conscious that the dream had been curiously prophetic. He saw the men in their starched shirt fronts and immaculate tail coats. He saw the mysterious and alluring women, some veiled, some wearing masks made of bird's feathers, most of them naked. One woman was standing by the doorway, her thighs and genitals tightly bound with thin leather straps, her large breasts completely covered with tattoos. She turned and looked at Charlie, and her face was the face of Mme Musette. In front of his eyes, she fell apart in great lumps of human clay.

A monk-waiter brought his meal, underneath a shiny dish cover.

'Your dinner, sir,' he whispered, and lifted the cover. Charlie knew what he was going to see there, and screamed.

He screamed, but he was drugged with morphine, and he didn't wake up. Instead, one dream closed and another dream opened. He found himself driving along West Good Hope Road in Milwaukee. It was snowing. Everything was white. The snow pattered against the windshield and the wipers had trouble coping with it. The world crept around in silence.

He could see her on the front steps of the single-storey house as he approached. Her husband was with her. He knew what was happening even before he reached the end of their block. He could see her husband's arm rising and falling, rising and falling, like a man trying to chop down a tree. He watched her fall to the porch floor, then try to get up again.

And in his dream, he was condemned to do what he had done in real life. He drove past slowly because it was snowing, staring all the time at the one woman he had really loved being beaten by her husband. And as she had tried to struggle to her feet, she had turned, and looked towards him, and recognized him through the partially misted window of his car, driving past without stopping as if he were a helpless passenger on a passing train. And their eyes had met and they had both known that was the very end of their love affair, and then he had turned the corner and when he managed to back up the car and turn and drive past the house again, they were gone. In his dream, he stopped his car and got out and went up to the front door and beat at the knocker, just as he had done in real life. In his dream, the knocker turned into the wolf-knocker on Mrs Kemp's front door, and he could feel its bristles in the palm of his hand. Then the door was hurtled open and there stood Velma from the Windsor Inn, her face hideously white, her eyes red-rimmed, both arms severed at the elbows and spraying blood like fire hydrants.

He screamed again, and this time he woke up. It was light.

There was a woman in black sitting beside his bed. She pushed back the hood that covered her face and he saw that it was Mme Musette. She was smiling at him.

'I had a nightmare,' he croaked.

She nodded. She took a glass of water from the small table beside his bed, and passed it to him with a hand that was nothing more than a thumb and an index finger. He hesitated, and then accepted it, and drank. When he returned the empty glass, he looked down at his own hand. Sometime during the night it had been expertly bandaged, and although it still ached, the most severe pain seemed to have subsided.

'Where am I?' Charlie asked. He looked around the plain whitewashed room. There was a high window through which he could see the branches of a large live oak, and a crucifix carved out of ebony was hanging on the wall, but apart from that the room was completely bare. Charlie was naked, but he was covered by a single white sheet.

Mme Musette said, 'You're upstairs, at L'Église des Anges. We have a nurse here. She's been taking care of you.'

'My finger,' said Charlie.

'A brave sacrifice,' said Mme Musette. 'You won't miss it.'

'Is my son all right?' Charlie wanted to know.

'Martin? Of course. Martin is very well.'

'He hasn't–?'

Mme Musette shook her head. 'He hasn't yet begun the act of self-ingestion, if that's what you mean. He's being saved, you see, for the great Last Supper.'

'I don't understand you people at all,' Charlie snarled at her.

'We know that. That is why I am here. The Last Supper is to be held on Friday at L'Église des Pauvres in Acadia. We want you to be there, to participate in our ceremonies. When you were trying to gain access to Le Reposoir, you talked to my husband of Saul on the road to Damascus. Well, we want you to play that part for real. We want you to be our Saul. We want you, our persecutor, to be our ultimate convert.'

Charlie said, 'You're going to try to convert me to cannibalism? That's the worst joke I've heard all year.'

'We're going to show you the truth and beauty in what we do,' Mme Musette replied.

Charlie fiercely held up his bandaged hand. 'Truth and beauty? Does that look like truth and beauty? That looks to me like deliberate mutilation of God's own creation.'

Mme Musette smiled again. It unnerved Charlie, the way that Célèstines kept on smiling, regardless of how insulting he was to them. It made him realize that they believed without question that their grisly re-enactment of the Last Supper had been ordained by Christ. They really believed it.

Mme Musette said, 'Do you remember the quotation from Paul's letter to the Romans that M. Fontenot read to you yesterday evening? "*Nothing is unclean in itself; but to him who thinks anything to be unclean, to him it is unclean*". When we come to our Last Supper, when a thousand thousand have devoured themselves and been devoured, then you will see the divine truth of what the church of the Célèstines has been doing. Do you remember what the angels said to the Apostles? "This Jesus, who has been taken up from you into heaven, will come in just the same way as you have watched Him go.'"

Charlie stared intently into Mme Musette's eyes for a moment, and then said, 'I want you to let my son go. Do you understand that? If you want to keep me, well, we can talk about that. But you have to let Martin go.'

'I'm sorry,' said Mme Musette, 'but that would be quite impossible. He has already been blessed. He has already been numbered. *He* – by great good fortune – is the thousandth thousandth Devotee. When he is devoured, my husband will become the fleshly temple of a million soles, the embodiment of a million self-sacrificial communions. My husband will become at last a worthy vessel on earth for the return of Christ the Saviour. On Friday, Mr McLean, you will witness the event for which the world has been waiting for almost two thousand years, the second coming of the Son of God, as it was foretold in the Acts of the Apostles.'

'For Christ's sake,' Charlie protested.

'Exactly,' replied Mme Musette, her beatific smile unwavering. 'For Christ's sake. He gave His body and blood in order that the human race might survive. In return, a million human souls have willingly given *their* body and blood in order that He might return.'

'And this is why the government and the police and the press have left you alone? Because *they* believe it, too?'

Mme Musette nodded. 'The turning point came ten years ago when the then President's son became a Devotee. The President tried, as you have tried, to talk his son out of self-ingestion. But at last the President himself was persuaded. Not to join the Célèstines himself, but to leave us unharassed by the law as we approached our ultimate Last Supper. As he said himself, Jesus Christ may come to us, or He may not, but if there is even the remotest chance that the second coming takes place on American soil, then that chance must be nurtured. To us Célèstines, of course, the joy will be purely spiritual. But the Administration were not so blind that they could not see the political advantages of the Son of God choosing the United States for his triumphal return. America would become the Holy Land, even above Israel.'

'I don't believe what I'm hearing.' said Charlie.

'How can you *not* believe it? You have seen for yourself the people of Allen's Corners, Mr Haxalt and Sheriff Podmore and all the others. If the Célèstines did not have government approval, would we be able to recruit so openly, would we be able to discuss our religion with such freedom? The government of the United States believes that Christ will come again, Mr McLean. Why don't you?'

Charlie lowered his eyes. He looked down at his left hand, and stiffly opened and closed his fingers. 'If Christ returns to earth because you kill my son, then let me tell you this: He's not the kind of saviour that I want to know about.'

'Now you're being petulant,' said Mme Musette.

'Petulant! You've kidnapped my son, you've forced me to cut off and eat my own finger, and you have the gall to call me petulant!'

Charlie tugged away the sheet, and swung his legs off the bed. Mme Musette made no attempt to stop him.

'Where are my clothes?' Charlie demanded.

'Burned, I expect. That's what they usually do.'

'Then get me something to wear!'

'I will if you wish,' said Mme Musette. 'But before you attempt to escape, perhaps you ought to remember that there is nothing at all you can do to stop us. Apart from having government approval, we have friends and supporters in all of the law-enforcement agencies. Besides which, it would be *very* unwise of you to go to the police or the FBI. There is a Federal warrant out for your arrest, on a charge of homicide in the first degree.'

'What the hell do you mean?' Charlie sat down on the side of the bed, and pulled the sheet over to cover himself.

'The Connecticut police want you in connection with the murder of Mrs Kemp. She was discovered hacked to death by a machete, and the fingerprints on the machete were yours.'

Charlie said, 'What have you done to me? And *why*?'

Mme Musette laid her one fingered hand on Charlie's knee, making him recoil. 'We have done nothing, Mr McLean. Everything that happened to you has been a consequence of your own actions. If you had simply accepted that your son has chosen a different path from yours, then you would have been free to continue your life unharmed and unmolested. We are a religious order; not terrorists.'

She stood up, and drew her cloak tightly around her. 'I shall be back. We have much more to talk about. By Friday, I want you to believe.'

'You can want what you like, you won't get it from me.'

'Mr McLean,' said Mme Musette. 'I want you to believe not for my sake but for yours. You are a man whose existence has no meaning. You stumble through life as if you are wearing a blindfold. You allow yourself nothing: no purpose; no love. Even when you attempt to indulge yourself, as you did with Velma, it brings you nothing but difficulty and pain. Think about it, Mr McLean, I am talking about having a goal. I am talking about bringing back the Saviour Jesus Christ in order to save the entire world. Your son is already part of that. In fact, your son is the ultimate part of that. You could be part of it, too.'

Charlie said, 'I think you'd better get out of here.'

'Very well,' said Mme Musette. To Charlie's complete surprise, she leaned forward and kissed his forehead. 'I shall come later, some time this afternoon, when you have rested some more.'

She left, and closed the door behind her. Charlie didn't hear a key turn in the lock, but when he went across and tried the handle, he found that he couldn't open the door even by wrestling with it. He went back to the bed and sat down.

So – the Célèstines had sewn him up. He couldn't go to the police for help, nor to the media – and that was supposing he was able to escape, stark naked, in the middle of New Orleans. On Friday the Célèstines were going to sacrifice Martin in the deranged belief that his death would bring about the second coming of Christ, and there was nothing at all that he could do about it.

He lay back on his pillow and cursed himself for handling the Célèstines so clumsily. Their friends in the FBI and local police forces must have been tracking him and Robyn all the way from Waterbury to New Orleans; and the Musettes must have flown to New Orleans yesterday. Some private investigator he turned out to be.

About a half-hour later, the nurse in the wimple came in and re-dressed his wound for him. She gave him another pain-killing injection and took his pulse, watching him all the time with eyes as blue as water.

'Do you really work for these freaks?' Charlie asked her, but she didn't answer. She packed up her black leather medical case and straightened his sheet and left him lying alone in his plain whitewashed room with only the nagging ache in his missing finger for company.

Charlie began to think about Mme Musette. Did it really show that badly, that he was living a life without purpose? There had never been very much purpose to begin with, but he had lost it for ever when he had driven past her house that day when her husband was beating her. Why hadn't he stopped? Why hadn't he jumped out of the car and run across the snowy sidewalk and beaten up her husband and claimed her for his own?

Maybe he had realized that, for her, he was just a dream, and that she never would have been happy leaving her husband. He beat her, but she belonged to him. She had *told* Charlie about the beatings, but she had never *complained* about them. Charlie had always been so tender towards her, bringing her flowers, treating her like a princess. Maybe that wasn't what cocktail waitresses wanted out of life. Maybe tenderness without pain had no meaning.

He could see her in his mind's eye as clearly as if he had only just turned away from her. Her name was Dolores. He had met her in the bar of what had then been called the Sheraton Schröder, in Milwaukee. He had been drunk and she had been desperate to hide the bruises on her cheek. They had fallen genuinely in love. It had been one of those sad stories, played on an off-key piano. '*When I fall in love... it will be for ever... or I'll never fall in love...*'

Dolores would haunt him for ever more. He would see her face the day he died, watching him in desperation as he drove past her.

He slept for a while. The drugs made him feel incredibly dopey. When he woke up, there was a tray on his bedside table, with cold chicken and salad and a glass of mineral water. The sky outside the small, high window was intensely blue, as if somebody had spilled ink across a drawing pad. The live oak shone gold. He drank the mineral water but he couldn't face the thought of eating. His throat was still sore from yesterday's vomiting. And chicken! How could he possibly eat anything that had once been alive?

Later, when the sky was beginning to pale, Mme Musette reappeared, wrapped in her cloak like a

Bedouin, with only her eyes showing. She sat in her chair beside his bed, and said nothing at all for five or ten minutes; simply watching him, and waiting to see what he would do.

'You've been thinking,' she said at last.

'Of course I've been thinking. There's nothing else to do.'

'No – I mean thinking *seriously*. Thinking about yourself.'

'What if I have?' Charlie challenged her.

Mme Musette allowed her eyes to register amusement. 'It's good for you, to think about yourself. Perhaps you're beginning to understand that you need some purpose in your life. You can't spend the rest of your life aimlessly wandering from one restaurant to another, until MARIA decides that you're past your prime. Because what will you do then? Will you kill yourself? Or will you simply allow yourself to fall to pieces, little by little, piece by piece, until there is nothing left of you but unfulfilled longings and curled up credit card slips?'

Charlie said, 'You'd better go. You're not going to convert me. You're wasting your time.'

Mme Musette stood up. She drew back her black cloak. Underneath it, she wore a severe black dress, and black stiletto shoes. 'I promise you, Charlie, you will kneel down in front of me, before this week is finished. You will kneel down in front of me and kiss my feet and profess your love for Jesus, the resurrected Saviour, and for Saint Célèstine, and you will tell me that you adore me.'

'I don't think so,' said Charlie.

Mme Musette came closer. Charlie could smell her perfume, which was rich and exotic; but he could also smell her womanly body. There was a hint of that honey-and-bleach odour about her, as if she had very recently had sexual intercourse. She kissed his forehead, even though he turned away, and said, 'You are such a fool. The whole world is lying in front of you, stretched out at your feet. It could be yours.'

'I insist that you release my son,' said Charlie.

'How can we release him, if he has never been captive? He came to join us of his own free will; he remains here of his own free will. Yesterday, he was flown down to Acadia with my husband, M. Musette, and the remaining Devotees from Connecticut. The moment of ultimate fulfilment is fast approaching! We want you to share in it, Charlie. We want you to participate! We want you to understand at last what belonging can mean, and the joy of joining with others in the name of Jesus Christ!'

Charlie said, 'You have to let him go. I'm his father. You can do what you like with me, but you have to let Martin go. I mean it, Mme Musette. He has his whole life in front of him. I'm not going to allow him to waste it on some oddball sect like the Célèstines.'

'So you *do* believe in self-sacrifice,' said Mme Musette triumphantly.

'What do you mean?' Charlie demanded.

'You would give up your life to save your son.'

'If there were no alternative, yes.'

'But your son is offering to give up his life for the Son of Man. Is that any different? How can you approve of one kind of sacrifice and deny the validity of another?'

Charlie rubbed his eyes. 'If you think you're going to be able to persuade me with that kind of argument, you're wrong.'

Mme Musette said nothing for a very long time. Charlie, for his part, volunteered no further questions and no further comments. He had nothing to say to Mme Musette except that he wanted Martin to be released, not only from his physical bondage but from his mental bondage, too.

At last, Mme Musette said, 'Do you wish to leave?'

Charlie looked up. 'What do you mean?'

'You can leave here if you want to, and take your chances in the world outside.'

'You'd let me?' asked Charlie suspiciously.

'If you really feel that there is nothing for you here, yes.' Mme Musette looked incomparably beautiful in the late afternoon light that fell through the window. Her dark hair shone like the wing of some rare desirable bird of paradise.

'All I want is my son.'

'You cannot have your son. Your son is not a possession. He does not belong to you, any more than he belongs to us.'

'Then there isn't any point in my leaving, is there? I might as well stay here.'

'The choice is yours, Charlie. I don't want anyone to say that we held you here against your will. How does your finger feel?'

'It still hurts. Maybe not as badly as it did before.'

Mme Musette kissed him again. This time, he did not recoil. Her kisses were strangely alluring, and consoling, too. Her lips were very cool, and somehow he didn't mind being held by those hands which had only one finger and a thumb. Mme Musette left the room, closing and locking the door, but for a long time her perfume lingered in the air, like a memory that refused to die.

Charlie eased himself off the bed and went to the window. If he stood on tiptoe, he could see the edge of an adjacent rooftop, and the back of a brick facade. The clouds rolled by, curdled and lazy and trailing skirts of misty rain.

He seemed to have reached an impasse – a point in his life at which he was equally unable to go forward or to go back. Ahead lay the horrors which –

even though they had been graphically described to him – were still unimaginable. Behind him lay indecision, confusion, and a lack of fulfilment so complete that it yawned in his life like a chasm. He stood naked looking out of the window of the cell from which he had been invited to escape, and tears ran down his cheeks and on to his chest.

When it was dark, they brought him a supper of grilled white fish and wholemeal bread. He asked if he could take a bath or a shower, but the girl who brought him the food didn't reply. Close on midnight he lay on his bed and fell asleep, his finger still throbbing with every pulse as a reminder of his own folly.

18

It was scarcely dawn when he became aware of somebody moving around in his room, and the rustling of fabric. He opened his eyes just as the door closed, but he was sure that he glimpsed the swirl of a long black cloak, like a shadow disappearing under a bridge. He sat up in bed and saw that his clothes had been neatly laid out on the footboard of his bed, his shirt and his pants and his sports coat, although there was no underwear or socks.

He climbed out of bed, and went directly across to the door. He tried the handle and it was unlocked. He opened it as quietly as he could, and peered out into the corridor. He could smell flowers, and flesh, and floor polish, but the house seemed silent and the corridors appeared to be deserted. He closed the door, and quickly went back to his room to dress. A few hours of sleep had done wonders for his optimism. If Mme Musette was offering him a chance to get out of here, then he was prepared to take it – even if it was just another ambush. He pulled on his pants and his shirt, slung his sports coat around his shoulders, and stepped out of the room barefooted.

They're watching me, he thought, as he hurried along the corridor towards the stairs. *They know exactly what I'm doing but for some reason they want me to go. Well, I won't disappoint them. I want to go too. This place is making me mental.*

He took the softly carpeted stairs three at a time. The staircase led directly down to the main hallway, which was panelled in Cuban mahogany and hung with impenetrably dark oil paintings. The huge front doors were locked but only from the inside. Charlie slid the bolts one-handed, and turned the latch. Quite abruptly, and without any difficulty at all, he was out on the street.

It was Royal Street, as he expected. The air was cold and damp and there was very little traffic around, except for a garbage truck toiling from one restaurant to another, collecting sackfuls of trash. Charlie closed the door of the Célèstine house behind him, and crossed the street. On the opposite sidewalk, he turned around and looked back at the house. Its black balconies were empty; its black shutters were closed tight over its windows. If anybody was watching him, they were keeping themselves well out of sight. Charlie hesitated for just one moment, then turned the corner and made his way back to the St Victoir Hotel.

He crossed the lobby and went up in the elevator to the third floor. He tapped on the door of his room, and waited. When there was no answer, he tapped again. 'Robyn? It's me, Charlie! Open up!'

Still there was no reply. Charlie knocked again, very much louder, and said, 'Robyn? Robyn? Are you there?'

At that moment, a voice behind him said, 'If you're looking for your wife, Mr McLean, you're out of luck.' Charlie turned around to find the fat woman like Jabba the Hutt standing behind him with her hands on her hips.

'She was booked to stay another day,' said Charlie.

'Sure she was. But she said she had to check out, didn't say why. She paid for the room on her credit card and went. But she left you this letter. Said to make sure that nobody else got to know about it.'

'Well, thanks,' said Charlie, and took the letter with a frown.

The fat woman said, 'You hurt your hand?'

Charlie said, 'What?' And then, 'Yes, oh yes. I got it caught in the door of my car.'

'Your wife took your car. And your baggage, too, such as it was.' The fat woman smiled as if she expected to hear some rare scandal when Charlie opened his letter.

Charlie tore open the envelope with his teeth, and tugged out the enclosed sheets of paper. In Robyn's deft, sprawling handwriting, he read:

Dearest Charlie, I have been followed ever since you left me and I am worried that they might be Célèstines. I have tried to shake them off several times but they always pick up my trail again which suggests that they know that I am staying here. I am moving to the Hotel Pontchartrain on Canal Street and will stay there until I hear from you. I am registered under the name of Batger which was my mother's maiden name. If they are still following me I will move again but I will leave you a forwarding letter. Love, love, love, Robyn.

Charlie folded up the letter and tucked it into his pocket.

'Not bad news?' the fat woman asked, with considerable relish.

'No, no. My wife had to go back to New York. Her father suffered a stroke.'

The fat woman said, 'You didn't stay here the last two nights, did you?'

Charlie looked at her, but didn't answer.

'I'm not being nosy,' the fat woman told him, 'but there was some gentlemen asking after you. Tall, polite. Frenchmen, I'd say.'

Charlie took out Robyn's letter again and held it up. 'You didn't show them this?'

'My dear sir, I didn't even tell them I had it. I may tattle now and again, but I don't break the confidences of my guests, believe you me, that's more than my position is worth.'

Charlie said, 'I'm sorry, I can't tip you, I don't have any money.'

The fat woman wobbled her jowls. 'Never you mind. Your wife paid me good. And when you do get yourself some money, the first thing you'd better get yourself is some shoes.'

Charlie looked down at his bare feet. 'I guess you're right. One pair of Gucci loafers, urgently required.'

'There's some plastic sandals in the closet under the stairs,' the fat woman told him. 'You can borrow them. The cleaning man uses them when he's sluicing the lobby.'

So it was that Charlie set out west along Bourbon Street at six o'clock in the morning wearing blue plastic flip-flop sandals. A cruising police car followed him slowly for a couple of blocks, making him sweat, but after a while it turned south, and he was alone again. An elderly black was wheeling a pushcart slowly along Royal Street and calling out, 'Ragaboon! Ragaboon!' It reminded Charlie of that song. '*Rags and old iron... rags and old iron... all that he wanted was rags and old iron.*'

He reached the intersection of Royal and Canal, opposite Shoppers World and the tall balconied building of Leonard Krower & Son. He crossed over, and headed north towards the Hotel Pontchartrain. He felt tired and thirsty and his finger joint was beginning to hurt again. His plastic sandals flopped on the sidewalk, and once he almost tripped over them because they were two sizes too small.

In spite of its grandiose name, the Hotel Pontchartrain was a small modern hotel that had been built on the site of the old Tessler building. Charlie pushed his way through the bronze-tinted revolving doors and into the brown-carpeted lobby. It was chilly inside; the air conditioning was down to fifty-five degrees. As he waited at the reception desk for the smooth-faced black receptionist to finish checking in a pair of British students who were determined to make sure that they took advantage of everything that was included in the price of their package vacation, Charlie began to shiver, like a man close to the end of his endurance.

'Ms Badger?' the receptionist repeated. 'I'll call her room number for you.'

'Batger,' Charlie corrected him.

'Badger,' the receptionist dutifully agreed.

At last, Robyn answered the phone. The receptionist nodded to Charlie, and said, 'She says to go on up. Room 501.'

Charlie leaned against the side of the elevator with his eyes half closed, ignoring the stares of the British students, for whom his dishevelled appearance had obviously confirmed everything they had ever heard about violent America. Blood was seeping into the gauze around his left hand, and his face in the elevator mirror was ash-grey, like a zombie.

'Do you think we ought to ask him what's wrong?' the girl student asked, in a stage whisper.

'I don't think so. This isn't exactly Dorking, is it?'

He knocked at 501 and Robyn immediately opened the door. 'Charlie, my God, I didn't expect to hear from you for days. What's happened? You look terrible!'

Charlie limped into the room and sat down heavily on the bed. It was only a single room, decorated in ginger and mustard, with a bed, a television, a crowded bathroom, and a view of Canal Street. Robyn closed the door and then came to kneel down beside Charlie and take hold of his hand.

'Charlie, what happened?'

'They were on to me all the time. They've been keeping tabs on us all the way from Connecticut.'

'Your *hand*—'

'Uh-uh. Don't touch. It's still throbbing.'

'But what happened?'

Charlie took a deep breath. For some inexplicable reason he was close to tears. It was probably delayed shock. 'They pretended that they were fooled. They made me go through a little Célèstine initiation ceremony. I had to cut my finger off. Then they cooked it and made me eat it.'

'Oh, my God,' said Robyn. She ran her hand through Charlie's tousled hair, and held him close. 'Oh, my God, Charlie.'

'I could use a drink,' Charlie told her. 'Do they have room service here?'

'Sure they do. It's a little slow, but willing. What do you want? Don't you think I ought to take you to the hospital? You don't want that finger to go septic.'

'A Scotch first, with a Michelob Lite. Then the hospital, okay?'

'Okay,' said Robyn shakily, and kissed him, and went to the phone to call room service.

'I don't know why they let me go,' said Charlie. 'They had me locked up in a room on the top floor of that building. They even took away my clothes, and told me they were burned. Mme Musette was there. She kept coming in and trying to persuade me that my life had no meaning and that I ought to join the Célèstines to save my soul. Then for no reason at all, she came up this morning and gave me my clothes back, and left the door unlocked.'

Robyn knelt down beside him again. 'Maybe they decided you were beyond conversion.'

Charlie gave her a wry smile. 'They believe in the second coming. That's what all this cannibalism is supposed to be leading up to. They think that if you eat yourself, and then somebody else eats what's left of you, then that person acquires your soul. So when *they* eat themselves, and somebody else eats what's left of *them*, two souls get passed on, and so forth, until they reach the divine number of a thousand times a thousand.'

'That's what that leaflet was all about,' said Robyn.

Charlie nodded. 'The last of the Last Suppers. The final communion. And according to Mme Musette, it takes place Friday, in the town of Acadia. They're all going to be there, all the Célèstines.'

Robyn looked at Charlie closely. His eyes were brimming with tears. 'There's something else, isn't there? Tell me.'

Charlie swallowed. 'It's Martin. I guess I should be glad that they haven't harmed him yet. But the way it's worked out, he's going to be the thousandth thousandth soul. "Great good fortune", that's what Mme Musette called it. On Friday, her husband is going to kill him and eat him, and that supposedly is going to make M. Musette into a fitting vessel for the second coming.'

'I don't think I understand that,' frowned Robyn.

'Me neither. The whole Goddamned lot of them are only playing with half a deck. But the trouble is they *believe* in it. They believe in it so Goddamned sincerely that they've even managed to persuade the

US government to turn a blind eye to what they're doing. According to Mme Musette, the administration is more than willing to give them a shot at bringing Christ the Lord back to earth, because it'll be such a boost for America's international standing, not to mention the tourist trade.'

'Can anybody be that cynical?' asked Robyn.

'What do they care?' said Charlie bitterly. 'A few missing kids stay missing, that's all. Serves them right for running away from home in the first place. The police don't mind. If they know for sure that the kids have been recruited by the Célèstines, they don't have to waste time and manpower looking for them.'

'What are you going to do?' asked Robyn.

'I don't know yet,' said Charlie. 'I want a drink first, then a bath, then I'm going to have this hand fixed. It hurts like all hell.'

'They actually made you *eat* it?' said Robyn.

'Yes, they actually made me eat it. Why? Do you want to know what it tasted like?'

'I'm sorry,' Robyn told him, ruffling his hair again. 'I didn't mean to upset you.'

Charlie touched her cheek. 'I'm sorry, too. I guess I'm over-tired, that's all.'

'Maybe we could get some help, a private detective or somebody like that,' Robyn suggested. 'They have agencies that specialize in snatching back children from divorced fathers, don't they? Maybe one of them could snatch Martin back. Have they brought him down to Louisiana yet?'

'Yes. Mme Musette told me. They're holding the Last Supper at L'Église des Pauvres, in Acadia.'

'All right, then. Let's get you fixed up. Then let's see if we can find one of those people to help us. There's bound to be somebody in the yellow pages.'

Charlie lowered his head. He started to laugh; but his laughter quickly turned to sobs of exhaustion. 'God, you're so practical,' he told Robyn. 'Who would have thought of looking in the yellow pages to find somebody to save my son from being eaten alive?'

'Come on, Charlie, rest,' said Robyn. 'They'll be up with your drink in a minute.'

Charlie eased off his plastic sandals and lay back on the bed. 'I have to admit, I feel dreadful,' he said. 'Do you want to turn on the television? I could use some light relief.'

Robyn went across and switched on *The Flintstones*, and then changed channels to a local news bulletin. A black woman was complaining about teenage dope dealers in Audubon Park. Robyn said, 'I'll run your bath, okay?'

Charlie closed his eyes for a moment, and said, 'I don't know what I would have done without you.'

'You would have survived. You're a survivor.'

There was a quick knock at the door. Robyn called, 'Coming!' and she came out of the bathroom. 'That'll be room service.'

She opened the door and instantly it was banged wide. In came a wide-shouldered half-caste with tight curly hair and a face like pitted oak. He was followed by M. Fontenot, in a crumpled, fawn summer-weight suit; and behind him, wearing a silky white gown, came Mme Musette.

'What in hell are you doing here?' Charlie demanded, sitting up.

Mme Musette closed the door behind her. 'You will have to forgive us, Charlie. It was the only way.'

'What do you mean, "the only way"?'

'The only way in which we could quickly locate your lady companion,' said M. Fontenot, with the same benign smile that had disturbed Charlie so much in the Church of the Angels. 'We had her under observation yesterday evening, but she disappeared, and so obviously the most expedient way of finding her was to let you find her for us.'

'Who are these people?' Robyn wanted to know.

Mme Musette closed and opened her eyes like a cat. 'Charlie will introduce us, won't you, Charlie? Although you haven't yet met Henri, have you? Henri is what you might call my argument of last resort.'

Henri patted his bulky seersucker sports coat, to indicate that he was wearing a shoulder holster. Mme Musette said, 'Sometimes even the most persuasive of words are not enough.'

'What do you want?' Charlie asked her.

M. Fontenot said, 'You must return with us now to Elegance Street. The Last Supper is too important to us for it to be jeopardized in any way. You are still not persuaded, you see, of the truth of what we believe, and you are still intent on taking your son away from us. This lady is your accomplice. And so, you see, we must insist that you remain with us until after the second coming.'

'I'm not going anywhere,' Robyn insisted.

'But my dear, it is imperative,' said Mme Musette. 'Not only imperative, but in your own personal interest, too. There is an FBI warrant out for your arrest, as an accessory to first-degree homicide, and as an accomplice to interstate kidnap. And a stolen vehicle has been found at your parents' home in Connecticut, and you are wanted for questioning in connection with that.'

'You're completely cracked,' said Robyn.

Mme Musette smiled. 'You will never forgive yourselves if you miss the second coming. And *we* will never forgive you if you do anything at all to interfere with it. You must be there, Charlie! Imagine it! And your own son will be the final sacrifice to restore the Lord Jesus Christ to His throne on earth.'

Charlie gave Robyn a sideways glance, but said nothing.

Robyn said, in a challenging voice, 'Does it have to be Charlie's son? Can't you see what you're putting him through?'

Mme Musette came up to Charlie and gently stroked his cheek with her one finger. 'Charlie's son is already numbered and blessed in preparation for the Last Supper. It is an honour, not a punishment. Charlie will understand that soon, when the Lord Jesus Christ reappears in front of us, and so will you. I told you that you would kneel down before me and kiss my feet, didn't I, Charlie? And so you shall.'

Charlie jerked his cheek away and looked up at Mme Musette defiantly.

She pretended to be offended, and then laughed. 'I'm offering you everything, Charlie. Purpose, meaning, success. If you stay with the Célèstines, who knows?—you could become an executive of the church. You could be an administrator, an overseer, spreading the word of the Célèstine order all over the world. You could be the kind of man people admire.' She turned to Robyn. 'As for you, my dear, we always have vacancies for trained communicators.'

'Stick it in your ear,' said Robyn. 'I'm not going anywhere, not with you, and neither is Charlie.'

M. Fontenot said, 'I regret that you have no choice. I am quite prepared to give Henri the instructions to do away with you. Of course, I would rather not.'

Charlie eased himself up off the bed. 'All right,' he said. 'We'll come. But on the strict condition that you don't hurt Miss Harris here. No finger-chopping ceremonies, do you understand me?'

Mme Musette bowed her head. 'Nobody at the church of the Célèstines has ever had even the smallest morsel of their body removed without their full consent. Remember, Charlie, even you cut your finger off voluntarily. If you had admitted that you were not genuinely interested in joining us, we would not have obliged you to do it. Every act of self-amputation and self-ingestion is done willingly and joyfully.'

Charlie lifted his left hand. 'Do you call this joyful?'

'I call it appropriate,' said Mme Musette. 'A sort of poetic justice.'

'Now, let's go,' put in M. Fontenot.

'I don't have any shoes,' Charlie reminded him.

'You have the plastic sandals you wore to walk here. Besides, our limousine is right outside. You won't have to walk far.'

Charlie sat down on the edge of the bed and picked up the sandals. 'It's a pity about Mrs Kemp,' he said, as he tugged them on, one-handed.

Mrs Kemp, thought Robyn. *What on earth is he talking about Mrs Kemp for?*

'Mrs Kemp lost everything,' Charlie went on. M. Fontenot and Mme Musette weren't really listening. 'Her niece, her boarding house business. Her car.'

As he said this, Charlie looked intently at Robyn, almost as if he were trying to transmit his thoughts by telepathy. 'She lost her car,' he went on, 'and then she lost her life. Poor Mrs Kemp. All she has now are the keys to heaven.'

Robyn suddenly realized what Charlie was trying to say to her. *The car keys, make sure you take the car keys with you.*

'Are we ready?' asked M. Fontenot impatiently. 'The last thing I want is another parking ticket.'

'May I take my purse?' asked Robyn. 'It's there, on the bedside table.'

M. Fontenot picked up her small, red-leather purse, opened it up, and quickly rifled through it to make sure that it didn't conceal a gun or a canister of Mace. Charlie heard the keys jingling in the bottom of it, and lowered his head a little to hide his tension. M. Fontenot passed the purse to Robyn, and said, 'Now perhaps we can go back to Elegance Street.'

They left room 501 and walked along the corridor towards the elevator. Apart from Charlie's plastic sandals, they could have been delegates to the Pontiac Dealers of Illinois' Fall Convention, which was taking place at the Hotel Ponchartrain all this week – executives and secretaries. They went down to ground level without speaking to each other, although Henri kept clearing his throat.

Together they crossed the lobby, making their way through a milling crowd of over-enthusiastic motor-dealers. M. Fontenot went through the revolving door first, followed by Robyn and Mme Musette. Charlie hesitated, but Henri said to him. 'Go on, you go ahead,' and the expression on his face wasn't the kind of expression that gave him much leeway for argument.

Charlie pushed his way around; but just as he reached the street he suddenly forced himself backwards against the glass behind him, arresting the door's momentum. Then he quickly knelt down, preventing Henri from pushing forward by keeping his back against the glass, snatched off one of his plastic sandals, and wedged it underneath the bottom of the door. Henri shouted out loud, and tried to heave the door around further, but all he succeeded in doing was wedging the shoe more tightly, and imprisoning himself in his own section of the door.

'The car!' Charlie shouted, hopping across the sidewalk.

M. Fontenot, seeing what had happened, rushed to the revolving door and tried to drag the sandal out, but Henri kept on pushing the door, not realizing what was holding it. Several convention delegates tried to turn the door, too, and one of them started arguing with M. Fontenot and telling him to get out of the way.

Mme Musette rushed up to Charlie and clung on to his jacket with her mutilated hands. 'Charlie! This is madness! You can't go! Stay, Charlie, don't be such a fool! What kind of a life can you possibly have without us?'

Charlie tried to pull her away from him, but she held on. Robyn came up behind her, hooked her arm around her neck, stuck out a leg behind her, and ju-jitsued her on to the sidewalk, flat on her back. Mme Musette screamed. M. Fontenot, turning around, jostled his way through the conventioneers and approached Charlie with his fists raised. Charlie swung his arm around and gave him a stupefying open-handed slap on the side of the head.

Charlie kicked off the other sandal and he and Robyn ran along the sidewalk, dodging passers-by. They collided with two elegant young black men in matching berets, and knocked over a sack of trash that was waiting for collection. 'Where's the car?'

Charlie hollered, as he sidestepped a woman with a baby buggy.

'Basement!' Robyn panted. 'Just down here!'

They reached the entrance to the hotel's underground parking lot, and ran down the dark concrete ramp. Charlie's feet stung but he scarcely noticed. When they reached the bottom of the ramp, Charlie looked around wildly, and said, 'Where is it? Where did you park it? I don't see it anywhere!'

'They parked it for me!' Robyn told him. 'It has to be here somewhere!'

They heard footsteps running at the top of the ramp. 'For Christ's sake, where is it?' Charlie yelled.

'There!' said Robyn. 'Look! Over in the corner! Behind that white car!'

Charlie peered into the far corner of the parking lot. He could just make out the bronze roof of Mrs Kemp's station wagon, parked behind a new white Lincoln Town Car. 'Come on!' he said, and together he and Robyn vaulted over the hoods of three cars to reach the station wagon. Robyn fumbled the keys out of her purse and gave them to Charlie, and he unlocked the door. The hotel's parking-jockeys had wedged the cars in so tightly that he had to bang the door hard against the BMW parked next to it in order to give them enough space to squeeze their way into the front seats.

'How are we going to get out?' Robyn asked him, panicking.

Charlie slotted the key into the ignition, and twisted it. He had seen so many TV movies in which fugitives tried unsuccessfully to start up their cars just as a murderer was catching up with them that he was amazed when the engine immediately roared into life.

'They're here!' said Robyn. Charlie glanced towards the entrance ramp and saw that Henri and M. Fontenot had reached the parking area, and were dodging their way towards them between the cars. Henri had his right hand lifted, and Charlie saw the sharp glint of a nickel-plated handgun.

Charlie tugged the station wagon's shift into second, and jammed his bare foot down on the gas. The station wagon bucked forward with a scream of tyres, and hit the Lincoln hard in the trunk. Charlie kept his foot down, hoping to push the Lincoln forward, but somebody had applied the Lincoln's parking brake, and all he managed to do was shove it two or three feet, with a long squeal of protesting rubber.

Henri scrambled over the BMW, and out of the corner of his eye Charlie saw him aiming his revolver. He yanked the gearshift into reverse, and the station wagon screeched backward, so violently that it collided with the parking lot wall. Robyn bent forward and covered her head with her hands, in the emergency position recommended by airlines. Charlie yelled, 'Hold tight!' and threw the station wagon into second gear, so that it roared forward and collided with the Lincoln yet again, a deafening crash that sent the Lincoln front first into a new Mercedes 350 parked opposite, and the Mercedes into a Thunderbird behind it.

Henri fired, but the noise of the cars crashing together was so loud that Charlie didn't realize they were being shot at until a hole burst through his windshield, the size of a man's fist, surrounded by a spiderweb of crazed glass. He backed up yet again, with the station wagon's tyres screaming on the polished concrete, and then stepped on the parking brake, so that the station wagon slewed around, facing the exit.

Henri leaned forward, holding his revolver in both hands, and fired at point-blank range. The bullet thumped through the driver's door, passed under Charlie's calves, and buried itself in the carpet that covered the transmission hump. 'Go!' screamed Robyn, and Charlie pressed his foot flat on the floor. The station wagon shot out of the parking area, skidded sideways at the bottom of the exit ramp, and then surged up toward the street like an Apollo rocket out of control. Charlie glimpsed Mme Musette's white distraught face right by the entrance to the parking lot. Then the station wagon flew clear of the sidewalk, hurtling right into the middle of Canal Street with a crash of ruined suspension, and hitting a taxi on the offside fender.

Before the taxi driver could get out of his vehicle, however, Charlie had backed up, stopped, twisted the wheel violently sideways, and roared northwards on Canal Street in a cloud of oil and rubber smoke. Slewing the station wagon from side to side to avoid slower traffic, glancing quickly in his rear-view mirror to make sure that he wasn't being pursued by the police or by Mme Musette, Charlie headed for Interstate 10, the quickest route out of New Orleans.

The station wagon shuddered and complained as he turned eastwards on I-10, but he kept his foot pressed down hard on the floor. Ahead of them, the sun shone directly in their eyes. Off to their left, Lake Pontchartrain glittered like an early morning mirage. Smoke poured out of the back of the station wagon, and the suspension was making a noise like a bucketful of spanners, but they kept going at eighty m.p.h., and Charlie wasn't going to let up for anything.

'Where are we going?' Robyn wanted to know.'

Charlie checked his rear-view mirror again. The last thing he wanted was to be stopped by the Louisiana Highway Patrol. If Mme Musette had been telling the truth, and the Célèstines really were thick with every law-enforcement agency between here and Connecticut, they would find themselves back at the Church of the Angels on Elegance Street before they knew it.

'We're getting the hell out of New Orleans,' said Charlie. 'Then we're going to make our way to Acadia. But we have to get rid of this car. Every cracker-barrel deputy between here and Bogalusa is going to be on the look out for a bronze station wagon with Connecticut plates and smoke coming out of the tailpipe. We won't stand a chance.'

'We can't *buy* a new car,' said Robyn.

'How much money do you have?' Charlie asked.

Robyn checked her purse. 'About one hundred fifteen dollars, that's all.'

'And credit cards?'

'Sure. Visa, American Express, Mastercharge. But we can't use credit cards, can we—not for buying a car? The FBI are bound to have circulated our charge-card numbers. They'll jump on us straight away.'

Charlie checked his mirror. There was nobody behind them, not for miles, but they were blowing out so much smoke that they were bound to attract attention before long.

'We could always liberate a car,' said Robyn.

'You mean steal it?'

'I saw it in an Elliott Gould movie. It's easy. All you have to do is drive along until you come across a car-dealer, then stop. I'll do the rest. Make it a Cadillac dealer, if you can.'

Charlie said, 'If you think I'm going to steal a car, you're out of your mind.'

'For God's sake,' Robyn retaliated. 'You're already wanted for homicide in the first degree, as well as kidnap and grand theft auto. What difference is one more stolen car going to make? It's the farm for you, whatever.'

'Yes, damn it, and you too.'

They crossed the north-eastern corner of Lake Pontchartrain, and then Charlie turned off Interstate 10 on to Route 11. They limped smokily into the outskirts of a town called Slidell, and Charlie steered the station wagon off the road and parked it on a dusty patch under the shade of some overhanging oaks. He climbed out, tugging his sweaty shirt away from his back, and said, 'I almost feel like putting a bullet through its hood, so that it doesn't suffer.'

Robyn said, 'There's a Chevrolet dealer down there, look, two blocks away.'

'And I'm supposed to walk up to him, without any shoes, and persuade him that I want to buy a car?'

'Charlie, for Christ's sake, stop being so defeatist! We'll buy you some shoes at Woolworth's. *Then* we'll go get the Chevrolet.'

They went into Woolworth's and Charlie bought himself a pair of grey leather casuals with a silver chain across them, which was about the most tasteful pair of shoes he could find. Then together they walked into the corner lot of Gramercy Chevrolet, under lines of fluttering bunting, to the small concrete office where Dean Gramercy himself sat in his shirtsleeves behind a bare desk, smoking a bright green cigar and talking on the telephone. There was a citation on the wall from the Slidell Chamber of Commerce, and a Vargas calendar. Dean Gramercy was stubby and big-bellied and ginger like a hog.

'Be with you folks right away,' he told them, covering the mouthpiece for a moment. 'That's right, Wally. You bring those spares over by Monday. Then we can talk about price. But I gotta see them first. You know me, Wally. I pay good but I like to see what I'm paying for.'

Dean Gramercy hung up, and extended his hand to Charlie as if he were his favourite cousin come visiting. 'Good of you to drop by,' he beamed. 'If it's a quality automobile you're after, you've come to the c'rect location.'

'We were looking for a late-model sedan,' said Charlie tentatively.

'Well, now, I've got maybe a dozen that would fit the bill. But there's one special that I know you're going to love. You come down to the lot and take a look.'

Obediently, they followed Dean Gramercy to the front of the lot. With a flourish, he showed them a silver Caprice Classic with a silver vinyl roof.

'Now you just take a look at this baby,' he enthused. 'Genuine '85 model, fully loaded, 5.7 litre gasoline engine, only 9,000 miles, one owner who was so careful she didn't even take off the plastic seat-covers.'

'Sounds perfect,' said Robyn. 'Do you mind if we take it for a drive?'

'Well, sure thing. All I have to do is turn the key in the office door. Not that there's anything to steal, apart from my calendar.' He snorted in amusement, and waddled off to lock up.

Charlie said, 'I'm sweating. Do you think we can pull this off?'

Robyn said, 'Easy. When I say *go*, just make sure that you go.'

Dean Gramercy came back, and opened the Chevrolet's passenger doors so that Charlie and Robyn could climb in. Then he settled himself in the driver's seat, adjusting the steering wheel so that it didn't press into his belly, and started up the engine. They drove sedately down the sun-gilded street between the overhanging live oaks, and all the time Dean Gramercy puffed affably at his cigar and rattled on about the pleasures of living in Slidell and what a desahrable vee-*hickle* this was, and how they couldn't do better anywhere for Chevrolets than good old Gramercy, and what's more he was going to throw in a Toshiba microwave oven as a fall bonus.

Eventually, just north of Slidell, he pulled the car over to the side of the road and said to Charlie, 'You want to drive her back? Just slide over.'

He climbed out of the car. Charlie slid over behind the wheel and re-adjusted it while Dean Gramercy walked around the front. He was just about to take hold of the passenger door handle when Robyn shouted out, 'Lock the doors! And *go!*'

Charlie flicked the central locking switch, shifted the car into gear, and kicked his foot down on the gas. The Caprice roared forward, leaving Dean Gramercy with his mouth open and his hand just about to curl round a door handle that wasn't there any more. The car's tail snaked a little as Charlie accelerated around a long curving bend. Then they were out on the open highway, heading northward into St Tammany County, with the sunlight flashing through the trees and the day dusty and bright.

'Wow,' breathed Charlie softly.

'What did I tell you?' Robyn laughed. 'You drive like Bullitt.'

Charlie checked his rear-view mirror, then turned around in his seat to make absolutely certain that they weren't being followed. 'Anything's possible, isn't it, if you've got the nerve?'

'You've found that out.' Robyn smiled and squeezed his arm. 'So believe me, if you can liberate a late-model Chevrolet, you can liberate your son, too.'

Charlie slowed the car and kissed her. 'I do believe I'm beginning to love you more than a man should.'

'Nobody ever loved anybody more than they should.'

Charlie said, 'I located Acadia on the map. It's way over to the west, in St Landry County, between Normand and Lebeau, right in the middle of Cajun country. If we keep to the side roads, we should be able to make it there without too much danger of being picked up by the police. You know what I should have done, don't you? I should have taken the licence plates off Mrs Kemp's station wagon, and changed them over.'

'You're getting to sound like a professional car thief,' Robyn teased him.

They drove throughout the morning through the flat Delta countryside, under a pale bronze sky, heading westwards, in the general direction of Baton Rouge and Lafayette. At times they could easily have believed that they had the whole of Louisiana to themselves. They saw no highway patrol cars, no helicopters, nothing. Just shining bayous and girder bridges and water oaks, and glistening muddy banks thick with black-shelled mussels. They kept the Chevrolet's air conditioning turned off to save gas, and drove with the windows open. The air flowed in humid, smelling of vegetation and slow-moving water.

They stopped for wheat Po-boys and shrimp-on-a-stick at a breezeblock roadside restaurant called Frugé's All-Day. There were cheap sunglasses for sale on a card, and they each bought a pair. They sat on the Chevrolet's hood eating their shrimp and watching the clouds slowly come apart at the seams. A Cajun music station played 'Laisser les Amis Danser'.

'Well,' said Charlie, when they had finished eating, and wiped their hands on their paper napkins, 'I guess we'd better be moving along. Acadia's a good fifty miles.'

'I hope we can find someplace to stay the night,' said Robyn. 'I could use a shower and a change of clothes.'

'We're going to need somewhere to stay for two days. The Last Supper isn't till Friday.'

'Maybe you should ask,' Robyn suggested.

Charlie went back into Frugé's All-Day and approached the grizzle-haired black man behind the counter. He was watched with unabashed interest by an old man with a Jim Beam golfing cap who was making his way steadily through what the proprietor advertised as a seven-course Cajun meal – a six-pack of beer and a one-pound boudin.

'I'm headed toward Lebeau,' said Charlie. 'You don't happen to know anyplace quiet I could stay for a few days?'

The black man stopped rag-wiping the counter and pressed his hand thoughtfully over his mouth. 'You could try Eric Broussard. He lives about six miles shy of Lebeau back from the road by the Normand Bayou. He used to take in guests from time to time, back when his wife Nancy was still alive, though whether he still does it now, I can't say. Tell him that Jimmy Frugé sent you and everything's okay.'

'That's generous of you,' said Charlie.

The black man looked at him with his eyes narrowed into cynical slits. 'You're running from the law, *mon ami*, so don't talk to me about no generosity.'

Charlie was about to protest, but the black man waved his hand dismissively. 'I know a fugitive when I see one. I've been selling Po-boys beside this highway for thirty-two years. You get along now, and good luck, and don't try driving along these back roads at night, lessen you want to go swimming inside of your car.'

Charlie hesitated for a moment. Jimmy Frugé was the first person to have offered them help since they had left Connecticut. He wanted to tell him how much this meant, but he couldn't find the words, and in any case Frugé wouldn't have understood what he was talking about. So he just said, 'Thanks,' and left the restaurant, and walked slowly back to the car, where Robyn was waiting for him in her $3.75 sunglasses, looking as if she had just stepped out of 1963.

19

Eric Broussard was sitting on the verandah of his house soaking in the late-afternoon sunshine as they came bumping and jolting down the muddy track that led through the fields to the Normand Bayou. They could see his bifocal spectacles reflecting the marmalade-coloured light.

His house had two storeys and was clad with weatherboarding that had once been painted red. There was still red paint to be seen in the nooks and crannies and knotholes; and the redness of the house was increased by the redness of the light and by the stand of cypress trees that surrounded it. Eric Broussard didn't wave as they approached, or give any indication that he had seen them, but when they drew up in front of his verandah and climbed out of the Chevrolet, he stood up, walked to the top of his steps, and stood facing them, an old black man in a warm plaid shirt whose sleeves were too short for his long accordion-player's wrists. He must have been very handsome once. Now his moustache was grey and most of his front teeth had gone, and of course he wore those heavy horn-rim spectacles with two kinds of lenses in them, so that he could see to read the sports pages in the *Times-Picayune* and also to scrutinize whoever was driving through the fields towards his house.

Charlie mounted the first step. 'Mr Broussard?' he said. A north-westerly wind was blowing off the bayou, and it made the pages of Eric Broussard's newspaper stir and flap.

'Who wants him?' Eric Broussard demanded.

'Mr Broussard, my name's Charlie McLean. This is Robyn Harris. We're travelling hereabouts and we've been looking for some place to stay. Jimmy Frugé suggested we come to you.'

'Jimmy Frugé? That boll weevil? He didn't have no business sending you here. I don't take in guests no more. You're wasting your time.'

Charlie wiped the sweat from his forehead with the back of his hand. 'Mr Broussard, we're kind of desperate.'

'Desperate? What does that mean?'

'It means we don't have anyplace else.'

Eric Broussard scratched his black, wrinkled neck. His skin had the quality of dark-dried tobacco leaves. 'There's a Howard Johnson's over at Opelousas. Whyn't you stay there?'

'Because we're having a misunderstanding with the police,' put in Robyn boldly.

Eric Broussard frowned. 'A misunderstanding? Who's misunderstanding whom?'

'They're kind of misunderstanding us,' Charlie explained. 'They think we're guilty of one or two rather unpleasant misdemeanours, and the fact is we're not, but at the moment we're having a difficult time persuading them of that.'

'You was framed,' Eric Broussard suggested.

'Something like that.'

Eric Broussard slowly shook his head. 'I didn't never meet no lawbreaker who wasn't framed. You go talk to all of the men on all of Louisiana's state farms, and the amazing thing about it is they're *all* innocent, every last one of them. They was all framed by ill-wishing associates who of course are still free. So what manner of state do we live in, that sends innocent men to prison, and allows guilty men to walk the streets unmolested?'

Charlie said, 'Believe me, Mr Broussard, we're not criminals. But we do need somewhere to stay. Only a couple of days, that's all we need. Then we'll leave and you won't ever see or hear from us again.'

Eric Broussard sucked at his gums and thought about this. 'Jimmy Frugé sent you, hey? That boll weevil.'

'He seemed okay to me,' Charlie ventured.

Eric Broussard shrugged and sniffed. 'He's okay. He and me used to be the best of friends once upon a time. We fell out over some fiddle-playing and we haven't hardly spoke since then.'

Charlie said, 'We really do need someplace to stay, Mr Broussard.'

'Well, I can understand that,' said Eric Broussard, 'but the fact of the matter is that I don't take people into my house no more. I've grown too old, and to tell you the truth I don't care too much for anybody excepting myself.'

'We don't expect meals, or any looking after,' said Robyn. 'And we can certainly make our own beds.'

But Eric Broussard kept on shaking his head like a man who has spent far too long alone, sitting on his verandah and watching the hawks circle around the cypress trees.

'Come on, Charlie,' said Robyn. 'I think we're wasting our time.'

Charlie stepped back from the house and lifted up both hands in resignation.

'Hurt your hand there,' Eric Broussard remarked.

Charlie nodded. 'Did you ever hear of the Célèstines?'

The effect of this question on Eric Broussard's face was astonishing. He stared at Charlie until his eyeballs looked as if they going to press against the lenses of his spectacles. His mouth dragged itself downward, and he took two or three epileptic steps backwards across the verandah. Charlie said, 'Mr Broussard? Mr Broussard? What did I say?' But Eric Broussard kept on stepping backwards until he was flattened against the weatherboarded wall of the house.

'Mr Broussard,' Charlie said, 'I don't know what you know about the Célèstines. Maybe you support them, I don't know. But let me tell you that they're holding my son in captivity, and that they're planning to kill him. That's why I need someplace to stay – at least until Friday.'

'You say *Friday*?' asked Eric Broussard, with unconcealed dread.

'That's right. They're holding a special ceremony. A special Last Supper.'

'It's come so soon?' Eric Broussard asked.

Charlie climbed the verandah steps and stood just a few inches away from Eric Broussard. Robyn came up close behind to give him moral support. She tried to smile at Eric Broussard, to reassure him that they didn't mean him any harm, but he stared at them both with unmasked fear.

'Mr Broussard—*we're* not Célèstines. You don't have anything to be afraid of as far as we're concerned. But if you know something about the Célèstines, anything at all, even if it's nothing more than hearsay or rumour, I really have to know what it is.'

Eric Broussard crossed himself. 'What I know about the Célèstines ain't hearsay or rumour,' he whispered. 'I lost my dear wife to the Célèstines, let me tell you that, and the manner of her passing was too terrible for me to want to think about.'

'Your wife was a member of the Célèstine church? She was a Devotee?'

'She was a Devotee, God bless her poor soul.'

Charlie said, 'Mr Broussard, we've come here to St Landry County to try to put a stop to the Célèstines, one way or another. Friday is their great Last Supper. Friday is the day that the thousandth thousandth Devotee gets eaten – or is supposed to; and Friday is the day that Jesus Christ is supposed to come back down to earth.'

'Those people,' Eric Broussard said, shaking his head from side to side. 'Those people. You know what those people are? They're voodoo, that's what those people are! They talk about Christ Jesus, they talk about the second coming, they talk about Jerusalem builded in Louisiana! But all they are is descendants of the voodoo people, the people that point the baby's bone, and curse you to death! All they are is stealers of other men's souls! I swear to God I thought I'd heard the last about the Célèstines, but when I saw your automobile come through the fields, I thought to myself, I've got a bad feeling about these people coming, I'm going to be hearing about things I don't want to hear about.'

'Mr Broussard, they've got my son,' Charlie appealed. 'My son is supposed to be the thousandth

thousandth Devotee, and on Friday they're going to eat him alive so that the Lord can be resurrected in the body of their Chief Guide.'

Eric Broussard raised his head, and there were tears sliding down his cheeks. 'They took my Nancy, those people. They took her away. They took people from all over St Landry County, from Krotz Springs and Bayou Current and Ville Platte. They took people from Acadia County, too, from Iota and Evangeline. Those people went to their meetings and never came back. And if you tried to persuade them to come back, all they did was smile at you and say, "Never you mind, we've found the Lord." That's what my Nancy said: "I've found the Lord." But what kind of a Lord is it that ends a good woman's life by having her cut open her own stomach and take out her own liver and eat it while her eyes is glazing over? My Nancy ate her own liver, Mr Misunderstanding-with-the-Law, and you tell me why I should give you a room, just to be reminded of that?'

Charlie said gently, 'Can we talk inside? I think I'm going to need your help.'

'Ain't you been listening to me?' Eric Broussard shouted at him. 'Ain't you been listening to one single word I've been telling you?'

'Let's go inside,' said Charlie, taking hold of his arm. 'Please, we have to talk about it. Otherwise my son's going to die on Friday, the same way that your

Nancy died, and the Célèstines are going to go on causing misery and pain for ever and ever.'

Eric Broussard lowered his head. He was silent for a long time, but then he said, 'Well, I suppose you're right. You'd better come along in. There's some beer in the icebox, no wine like there used to be. I'm sorry if your lady drinks wine.'

Robyn said, 'Don't mind me. I could finish a beer in five seconds flat.'

Inside the house the blinds were all drawn down and the stuffiness was oppressive. Eric Broussard led them through the kitchen to the front parlour, and offered them a large brown sofa to sit on, while he found them a glass of beer. Charlie and Robyn sat side by side in silence, looking at the green diamond-patterned wallpaper and the shelf above the fireplace clustered with framed photographs of Eric Broussard's family, solemn and formally dressed, and all bearing the distinctive Broussard likeness. The breeze that came across the bayou lifted the blind away from the window every now and then, so that it tapped against the windowsill, but it wasn't a strong enough flow of air to penetrate the room.

Eric Broussard came back with a tray and three glasses of cold beer. 'When I first walked out with Nancy, I used to drink it by the neck. But she would never allow me to do that. With Nancy, everything had to be just so. You don't meet too many women like that any more. These days, anything goes. Women don't have no pride any longer.'

'You must be lonely, living out here all by yourself,' Robyn remarked.

Eric Broussard sat down in a large armchair with dark varnished arms and seat cushions that had been pressed over the years into grotesque, wrinkled shapes. 'People say that you can get over losing somebody you love. Give yourself time, that's what they say. But, you know something, I've given myself years and years, and I still can't get myself used to living without Nancy. It was worse than losing a leg.'

Charlie said, 'Tell me, Mr Broussard, how much do you know about the Célestines?'

Eric Broussard drank beer, and made a face. 'As much as anybody I guess. Right at the very beginning, Nancy used to tell me all about them. She tried to persuade me to join her. We could eat each other's flesh, that's what she said. We could share each other's body and blood, just like the holy communion. But, my God, that made my blood run cold, that's all. I could never understand how she could believe in it all so much.'

'Do you know anything about the second coming ritual?' asked Robyn.

'I know they believe that when a thousand thousand people have gotten themselves all eaten up, their Chief Guide is supposed to eat the thousandth

thousandth person, and when he does that the Lord's going to come down and inhabit his body, and a new age is going to start. I seem to recall the Chief Guide don't have to eat all of the thousandth thousandth person, only their brain.'

'Is that all you know?'

'I know a lot, my friend,' said Eric Broussard. 'But it all depends on what you want to hear.'

'I want to know what they actually do, on the day of the second coming.'

Eric Broussard said, 'I don't have any notion whatsoever. As I say, the Célèstines used to make my blood run cold. Once Nancy joined up with them, that was our marriage gone for good. Even before she went off to stay with them permanent, she seemed like she was *possessed*, you know what I mean? She used to say the strangest things, and sometimes she used to be sitting at the dinner table and deliberately bite her own arm, just lift it up and bite at it, and there was blood going everywhere and me not understanding a word of what she was trying to explain to me. "I seen God!" she used to call out. "I seen God!" All you could say about her was, she was a woman possessed.'

'Did you ever try taking her to a doctor?' Robyn asked him.

'Oh, surely, I *tried*. But the doctor said she was fine; just a little overwrought, that's all. He prescribed her some Valium tablets and charged me a hundred-ten dollars.'

Eric Broussard eyed Robyn with bloodshot eyes. 'Let me tell you what I'm going to do. I'm going to go upstairs and find my Nancy's Célèstine Bible. Then you can look up anything you want to your heart's contentment.'

Charlie said, 'The Célèstines have their own special Bible?'

'Sure they do, just like the Latter-Day Saints. They brought it round for me when they came to tell me that Nancy was gone. I was tempted to drop it in the stove, but then I thought that I might need it someday, just to prove to the world what Nancy had to go through. Otherwise, who'd've believed me?'

'We believe you,' said Robyn gently.

Eric Broussard lifted his head. The muted sunlight caught a fingerprint on the lens of his spectacles, setting it glowing like a tiny spiderweb. 'Whatever I do to help you,' he said, 'it ain't never going to bring my Nancy back.'

Nonetheless, he lifted himself out of his armchair and shuffled off to look for the Célèstine Bible. Charlie sipped his beer, and said, 'We need to find out *when* they're going to hold the ritual – whether they're supposed to do it at any special time of the day or night – and we also need to know what happens, so that we don't make fools of ourselves by bursting in to rescue Martin at the wrong moment, before they've brought him out of his room, for instance.' He didn't add, 'or after they've eaten him', but he didn't have to. Robyn knew that their chances of getting Martin away from the Célèstines were extraordinarily slim, especially since the police and the FBI and anybody with any political or commercial influence seemed to support them, or at least to turn a blind eye to what they were doing.

Eric Broussard returned with a thin book about the size of the New Testament, bound in cheap red leather with a white mitre embossed on the front. 'Nancy said the red leather was supposed to represent the blood, and the white hat was supposed to be the body.' He passed the book to Charlie, and Charlie opened it up, while Robyn leaned closer so that she could read over his shoulder.

On the title page, it said, '*The Book of Célèstine*', and underneath: '*Being the holy words of Saint Célèstine V, Pietro di Murrone 1215–96, concerning the communion of the Last Supper.*'

Charlie flicked through the text. There were 120 pages of closely printed text. 'Mr Broussard,' he said, 'it's going to take us some time to read all this; and we do want to study it really well. I'd truly appreciate it if you'd allow us to stay.'

Eric Broussard slowly rubbed the back of his neck. Then he said. 'All right, if that's what you want. But in return, you can go to Sidney's Store for me out on the Normand highway and fetch in some steaks and some groceries and maybe a couple of bottles of liquor.'

'Mr Broussard, you've got yourself a deal.'

'Not quite,' said Eric Broussard. 'You've got to stop calling me "Mr Broussard" and start calling me "Eric" instead. Either that or "Tabac-Sec".'

Charlie reached over and shook Eric Broussard's hand. 'Eric, I think we're in business.'

They lifted their beer glasses and drank a silent toast to an adventure that would probably prove to be dangerous, painful, and frightening.

Eric Broussard wiped his mouth with the back of his sun-wrinkled hand, and said, 'You want a double bed or two singles? I've got clean sheets for both of them. The double bed creaks pretty bad, on account of all the weekending couples we used to have here, but in times of stress I always say that it's better to have somebody to hold on to, don't you?'

*

They ate a supper of steaks and fried eggs and Bulgar wheat salad, with straight Jack Daniel's as an accompaniment, and then after supper Eric Broussard produced his German accordion and sat on the kitchen chair and played slow, bluesy, but inarguably Cajun melodies of love and dancing and crayfish, and many other subjects close to the Cajun heart.

'I play better out of doors,' he said, when he had finished. 'There's something about the plein-air that makes the music resonate. I like to play out of doors wearing a big wide hat to keep the sun off of my face and the rain off of my cigareet. That's why they call me "Tabac-Sec".'

They thanked him for his cooking and his music, and then they went upstairs and showered and undressed and climbed into the big double bed which creaked as friendly and amusing as anybody's honeymoon bed in any honeymoon hotel. Charlie sat propped up with pillows drinking the last of the whiskey and reading the Célèstine Bible. Robyn lay close to him and closed her eyes and rested. The north-west wind blew across the bayou and whistled lightly through the cracks in the window frame, a soft *complainte* of its own.

Most of the Célèstine text was rambling evangelism and complicated prophecies about 'the Lord who smiteth all those whose faces are set against His Glory; and all those who worship artifice and deceit,' and 'in the Days of the Ethiopian whose descendants shall number fifty times fifty millions, a drought shall descend upon the lands of their forefathers and their suffering will be heard in all corners of the world.'

It quickly became clear, even under Charlie's inexpert scrutiny, that the Célèstine Bible had certainly not been written by Saint Célèstine himself, but possibly as much as five hundred years later – even as late as 1775. There was a reference to the 'Lands that were given by deed to those who had been cast out of Acadie.' If Charlie remembered an article he had read not too long ago in the *Reader's Digest*, those who had been cast out of Acadie could only mean those French colonists in Nova Scotia who had been dispossessed by the British after the Treaty of Utrecht in 1713. In those days, Nova Scotia had been called Port Royal, or 'L'Acadie', meaning pastoral paradise on earth. The French had been uprooted from their paradise and sent back to France, or to Guadeloupe; or even as far as the Falklands; but they had been invited back to America in 1775 when the French sold Louisiana to the Spanish. The new Spanish governor had been worried that his small population would not be able to resist a takeover by the British, so he had offered the one-time Acadians a free passage back across the Atlantic and free land deeds so that they could settle in the south-west.

Charlie found another more glaring anachronism. Although there was no direct mention of cannibalism, there was an endless obsession in the text with human flesh and blood and its relation to the words of the Last Supper. From what M. Musette had told him at Le Reposoir, the Célèstines had only taken to eating real flesh and real blood after their sojourn with the Caribs on the island of Sainte Desirée – and that had been after the French Revolution in 1789. So it was conceivable that the Célèstine Bible had been written in the early part of the 1800s, or even later.

Robyn fell asleep, and Charlie felt her breathing softly and deeply against his arm. Eric Broussard had been right: it was good to have somebody to hold in times of stress. He finished his whiskey, and went on reading, although he would have given anything to be able to close his eyes. A little after one o'clock in the morning, he came across the passage that he had been looking for. *The Return to Earth of Our Lord Jesus Christ as Prophesied by the Angels.*

The verses read: '*And the Day shall come when one thousand times one thousand shall have taken communion with Christ our Lord, save only for twelve disciples, one disciple from each parent church. And the twelve shall be brought to the appointed place known as the place of the poor, in the company of elders and Guides, and there they shall take communion with Christ our Lord in solemn memorial to the Last Supper. And they shall take communion one upon the other, until there is*

*but one; and he shall be numbered one thousand
times one thousand.*

'*Then shall the elder of the Guides take
communion with the twelfth of these disciples, and
he shall become the vessel in which those souls now
reside, one thousand times one thousand. And in so
doing he shall become a worthy vessel in his turn for
the second coming on earth of Christ our Lord, and
he shall be transformed. And all of those who have
kept the faith of the true communion shall be
rewarded on this earth as well as in the next.*

'*For know you by these secrets that the fifth day
was the one on which he was vanquished, but* his *day
is the sixth day, and on that day you shall be given
your just reward.*'

Charlie read the verses again and again. There was
no doubt that they were referring to the ceremony
that was supposed to be taking place on Friday at
L'Église des Pauvres, the Church of the Poor. Twelve
Devotees from twelve Célèstine churches would be
brought down to Acadia as representatives of the
twelve disciples – only the Last Supper was going to
be worked in reverse. Instead of the Master giving
them *His* body and *His* blood, they were going to
give Him theirs, and the process that had led up to
the Crucifixion and the Ascension was going to
happen backwards. At least, that seemed to be the
Célèstine theory.

The last verse puzzled Charlie a little, because it was the only verse that didn't appear to make explicit sense. It had the character of a riddle, but there was something about it which sounded peculiarly like a warning as well, although Charlie couldn't quite analyse what it was.

Certainly there was a mention of 'secrets'. And the next phrase was odd – 'the fifth day was the day on which he was vanquished.' Presumably this meant Good Friday – but no Christian believed that Christ was vanquished on Good Friday – rather that he finally triumphed over evil. It was also noticeable that in this one paragraph 'he' was spelled with a lower case 'h'. And what did the writer mean by the sixth day being 'his day' – the day on which you will be given your just reward?

Maybe it was that term 'just reward' that Charlie found vaguely threatening. It seemed to have the quality of 'on Saturday, you'll get what's coming to you.'

When it came to rewards, too, there was another line that bothered him: '*And all of those who have kept faith with the true communion shall be rewarded on this earth as well as in the next.*' To be given a material reward as well as a spiritual one seemed peculiarly at odds with anything that Christ would have promised or a Christian would have expected.

At a quarter of two, Charlie finally put down the Célèstine Bible on the bedside table. He switched off the light, and snuggled up close to Robyn. In fact, the bed dipped so much in the middle he didn't have any choice.

By two o'clock he was asleep. He didn't dream. But the north-west breeze stiffened during the early hours of the morning, and rattled the window even more frantically, and one by one it leafed over the pages of the open Bible, one whispering page after another, until it came to rest at the page which said, '*But the sixth day is* his *day, and on that day you shall be given your just reward.*'

While only two miles away, in the darkness, a car turned off the Normand highway and began to make its way purposefully along the dirt track that led to Eric Broussard's house on the bayou.

20

Charlie was awakened by a bony hand shaking his shoulder. Involuntarily, he shouted in fright, and sat up so fast that he knocked heads with Eric Broussard, who was leaning over him. Eric Broussard said, 'Shit, Charlie, that hurt.'

'What's the matter?' Charlie asked him. 'What's wrong?'

'I'm not too sure,' said Eric, in the darkness, 'but there's a vehicle parked in the cypress grove, about two hundred feet off to the east. I heard it coming. Your ears acquire a sensitivity for things like that. But it didn't come right up to the house, like you'd expect. It parked in the trees and now it's just waiting.'

Charlie switched on the light. Eric Broussard was wearing a wonderfully ancient pair of red-flannel longjohns, and big, old, frayed carpet slippers. Eric said, 'If it's the po-lice, I don't want no shooting.'

Charlie climbed out of bed. In doing so, he allowed Robyn to roll into the dip in the middle of the mattress, and that woke her up. She blinked and stared at them and said, 'What time is it?'

'Five o'clock,' Eric told her.

Charlie went to the window and drew back the blind, but it was too dark outside for him to be able

414

to make out anything. All he could see was his own face, as pale as a ghost floating in the night. 'If it's the police, or the FBI, it seems pretty weird that they should park in the trees like that. They know I'm not armed.'

'Who else could it be?' asked Eric.

'Célèstines?' Robyn suggested.

Charlie dressed himself. 'The only way to find out for sure is to go out there and see for ourselves.'

'Charlie,' said Robyn, 'they'll kill you.'

'I don't think so. I don't think they meant to kill us the last time.'

'They shot holes in our car and they didn't mean to kill us?'

Eric stood up. His belly hung slack in his longjohns like a giant canned tomato. 'I can think of a better way. Let me send my dog Gumbo, he'll roust them out. He's half Doberman, half German shepherd, and half bird-dog.'

'That's a dog and a half,' Charlie remarked.

'Sure it is, and that's what Gumbo is, a dog and a half.'

Charlie said to Robyn, 'You'd better get dressed. If the Célèstines are really here, we may be in for some trouble.'

Eric went off to find himself a yellow plaid shirt and some bleached-out blue denim overalls, while Robyn dressed in the same skirt and blouse that she had been wearing this morning. She had washed the blouse and it was still slightly damp. 'What are you going to do if it *is* them?' she asked.

Charlie shrugged. 'Try to give them the slip, I guess. Maybe Eric knows another way out of here.'

'There can't be another way,' said Robyn. 'The house backs right on to the bayou.'

Charlie gave her a wry smile. 'What kind of a swimmer are you?'

Just then, Eric came in to tell them that he was ready to let Gumbo off the leash. They all went downstairs, keeping the lights off, feeling their way across the kitchen to the back door. Eric unlocked it, and opened it up as quietly as he could, and stuck his head out to listen to the sounds of the night. Charlie whispered, 'Anything?'

'Nothing; but there's somebody there. I can feel it in my bones.'

'Where do you keep your dog?'

'He's around the side, in his doghouse. Come on, Charlie, you follow me. Miss – you stay here. Keep the door locked. Don't open it to nobody, only to us. But when it *is* us, you make sure you open it real quick.'

Robyn gripped hold of Charlie's sleeve in the darkness. 'For God's sake, Charlie, be careful.'

'You can count on it,' Charlie told her.

He and Eric stepped out on to the verandah and Robyn turned the key in the lock behind them. Dawn was not far off. All along the banks of the bayou, the trees and the bushes seethed in agitation, and Charlie wondered how Eric could distinguish any kind of noise amidst it all, but when they reached the top of the steps Eric stopped for a moment, listening, and then said, 'Come on. It's okay for now.'

Keeping close together they skirted the northern side of the house until they came to a ramshackle collection of outhouses and derelict chicken coops. Gumbo, the dog and a half, growled deep in the back of his throat as they approached, and his tail started to lash against the planks of his doghouse. Charlie had never seen a doghouse built like this before. It was more like a miniature fort. Eric unfastened the padlock that held the doghouse door, and Gumbo launched himself at them like a jet-black, bristling drag racer. Charlie instinctively jumped back, but Gumbo was chained up and, with a jingling of solid steel links, he was arrested only a foot away from Charlie's ankles. He snarled and slavered and twisted, but Eric let out a sharp whistle between his teeth and said, 'You mind your etiquette, Gumbo, this is a houseguest,' and the dog quietened down a little, and allowed Eric to approach him, although Charlie still felt uncertain about his lolling tongue and hungry panting, and decided to keep well back. 'Now, you stay polite, boy,' Eric kept soothing Gumbo. 'You stay polite and keep your fangs to yourself.'

Eric caught hold of the dog's chain and released it. Then, with the dog leaning away from him as if it were being pulled by a giant magnet, its breath scraping in its half-strangulated throat, he led it across the yard toward the edge of the fields. 'You see them trees,' Eric told Charlie, indicating the dark, sad spires of the cypresses. 'That's where they're at. I heard them drive off the track and across to them trees and they haven't stirred since. But old Gumbo'll roust them, won't you, Gumbo? Gumbo's the best rouster that ever was. Chickens, rats, turtles, catfish, gars. He'd roust anything on land or water, would Gumbo – wouldn't you, Gumbo?'

As if he had been given his cue by an off-stage prompter, Gumbo said *grrooowwrrrr* and scrabbled at the grass with his claws.

Eric knelt down and let Gumbo off his chain. 'Go fetch them, Gumbo. You go fetch them.' Gumbo dashed off madly towards the left, abruptly stopped, and then barked loudly and tore off toward the cypress grove. They saw him running like the shadow of a passing storm cloud across the grass, and then he had disappeared into the darkness. Eric slowly stood up, and placed his hands on his hips and listened.

'That's some dog,' said Charlie, mainly because he was nervous.

'That's a dog and a half,' Eric agreed. Charlie liked to hear him say it, because of his Cajun pronunciation of *hay-uff*.

They waited. The wind blew through the trees, making the cypresses bow and curtsey like dancers at a midnight ball. Eric sniffed but kept his hands on his hips and said nothing. Charlie surreptitiously checked his watch. He didn't like to say that, for the best rouster that ever was, Gumbo was taking his own sweet time about rousting. It was quite clear that Eric worshipped his dog and a half; and Charlie would no more have thought about criticizing Eric's wife, if she had still been alive.

After about five minutes, Eric placed his finger and thumb in his mouth and let loose a sharp, ear-splitting whistle. 'Dog's taking too darn long,' he said, by way of explanation.

Charlie strained his eyes to penetrate the pre-dawn darkness. 'Give the poor fellow a chance.'

'Fellow?' said Eric. 'That ain't no fellow. That's my dog.' And to prove the point, he let out another piercing whistle.

The wind blew and the night began to lighten a little, a faint grey light that outlined the world without colouring it. Eric hummed 'Les Blues du Voyager' and Charlie could tell that he was worried now. 'Maybe that dog forgot to stop running,' he said.

'Maybe there's nothing in those woods to roust,' suggested Charlie.

'Oh, I heard them all right.'

Charlie said, 'Do you want to go take a look?'

Eric was silent for a long while. Then he said, 'I don't know... this ain't like Gumbo one bit. That dog's the best rouster that ever was.'

Charlie peered into the gloom. He was sure that he could see something move, over to the left of the trees. Something small, and pale, like a child running through the long grass. He took hold of Eric's arm and said, 'Look – do you see that?'

Eric looked, with his glasses and without them, but in the end he shook his head. 'I guess I could use a new pair. I haven't had my eyesight tested since Nancy went. I guess I haven't been looking after myself too well in lots of ways.'

Charlie said, 'Come on. Let's take a look for ourselves. It's the only thing we can do.'

He began to walk toward the cypress trees, and Eric reluctantly followed behind him. They were almost halfway there, however, when Eric said, 'Ssh – listen! I heard something! That's Gumbo, I swear it!'

Charlie listened but all he could hear was the wind. Eric said, 'He's mewling or something, like he's been hurt.'

Without any further hesitation, Eric began to run stiffly across the field, his long arms and legs waving like a semaphore. Charlie called, 'Eric, for Christ's sake be careful!' but Eric had heard his dog calling and that was all he cared about. Charlie had no choice but to go running after him. He glanced behind him only once, just to make sure that the house was still deserted and unlit, apart from the single lamp that he had switched on in their upstairs bedroom.

'Eric!' Charlie shouted. He didn't care if there was anybody there to hear him. If there was, they would have seen them and heard them by now in any event.

He had almost caught up with Eric when they saw a huge ball of orange fire suddenly ignite in the shadow of the trees. The flare up was immediately followed by a high stomach-lurching scream – a scream that sounded human at first – but which was even more horrifying to Charlie when he realized that it wasn't.

The fireball came rushing towards them through the grass, zigzagging as it came, and it was shrieking unbearably – high and harsh and agonized, like somebody dragging their fingernails down a dry chalkboard. Charlie and Eric stopped where they were, both of them, and stared at the running, tumbling flames in helpless fright. They knew what it was but they couldn't bring themselves to believe it. It was Gumbo, and he was ablaze from head to tail, and screaming in agony as he ran.

'Watch out!' Charlie told Eric. 'He's coming straight for you! He wants you!'

Gumbo ran burning through the grass and the fire that engulfed him rippled like a cloak. Eric was paralysed for a second, but then he turned and began to stumble away. Gumbo in his death agony was running for the one person he could trust; the one person who had always protected him and fed him and kept him from harm.

Eric tried to escape, but Gumbo was too fast for him. Gumbo was driven by the pain so intense that he was running faster that he had ever run in his whole canine life, faster than he had ever chased chickens or catfish. He passed within two feet of Charlie and Charlie felt the heat of his blazing fur, and smelled gasoline and burning flesh.

Eric tripped, and cried out, and fell to his knees. Gumbo leaped on top of him, still screeching, still blazing, like a dog from hell. Eric rolled over and over trying to beat him off, but Gumbo's flesh and fur came off in burning chunks, and seemed to stick like napalm to Eric's clothes. Eric yelled out hoarsely for help. 'Charlie! Charlie! For God's sake, Charlie! He's killing me!'

Charlie ran through the grass and kicked Gumbo hard in the side. The dog rolled off his master with a roar of flames, then rolled over again and lay quivering on his back, only barely alive, his blackened paws drawn up like spider's legs. Charlie tugged off his coat and covered up Eric's shoulders and chest with it, and brushed the smouldering dog fur away from his face. He glanced at Gumbo but the dog must surely have been dead now. The flames had died down, and all that Charlie could hear was the crackling of his fire-shrunken tissues.

'Eric, are you okay?' Charlie asked him.

Eric shook his head. 'He's hurt me bad, Charlie.'

'Come on, Eric, I'll call for the ambulance. You'll be okay.'

'It's not the burns, Charlie. The burns hurt but the burns ain't nothing.'

'What are you talking about?' Charlie demanded. 'If you let me call the ambulance right now, we can have you in hospital in fifteen minutes.

'Don't,' Eric whispered. In the growing light of the morning, Charlie could see how grey his face had become. 'I don't want to die in no hospital. I want to die here, by the Normand Bayou.'

'Eric, you've been burned, but only superficially. You're not going to die.'

Eric cleared his throat, and looked up at Charlie with an odd smile. 'It's my heart, Charlie, it's been giving up on me for years. I had a bad attack last year, the doctor said I was lucky as all hell to be still alive. I'm going, Charlie. I can feel it closing in. Old man death, creeping in. Old Baron Samedi, that's what my mother used to call him.'

'Eric, I'm not going to let you die in some field,' Charlie protested. He squeezed the old black man's hand very tight.

'Well, you don't understand, this isn't no ordinary field, this is the field where I lived, me and my Nancy. This is the field where we danced, and delighted ourselves. So, this is a good field to die in, if you're talking about dying in a field.'

Charlie said, 'Somebody set fire to Gumbo on purpose.'

'Them Célèstines.' Eric nodded. 'They're out there now, you take my word for it. They came after you, didn't they, even though you thought you was clean away?'

'Eric, what can I say? If it hadn't have been for us, this wouldn't have happened.'

Eric laid his head back in the scorched grass, and let his eyelids droop a little as if he were tired. 'Every man has to go some time, Charlie, and none of us chooses the way. It wasn't your fault. My heart was ready to take me at any time. I could of been brushing my teeth, I could of been dancing. I just thank the Lord that it wasn't in bed, when I was asleep, because then I wouldn't have known nothing about it.'

Charlie said, 'Do you think you can make it back to the house, if I carry you?'

Eric shook his head again. 'Don't move me, Charlie. I want to stay here. I want to see the sun rise, if I can.' He grunted, and then he smiled and said. 'It's a funny thing, that yours should be the last human face I ever see. My father ain't going to be too pleased with me, when I get up to heaven. He sent the doctor out of the room when he was dying. He said he didn't want no white ghost faces looking at *him* when *he* died.'

'I have to move you,' Charlie insisted.

'Don't you dare try. Those people who burned my dog are out there somewhere and believe me they want to do the same to you, or worse. The best thing that you can do is get the hell out of here, you and your lady friend, and not come back. There's a skiff down by the landing. You can row south-westwards from here, if you keep the sun off'n the right side of your back all morning, and off'n the left side of your chest all afternoon, you shouldn't get lost.'

'Eric, you're coming with us,' said Charlie.

'No,' said Eric. 'Leave me here, Charlie, and leave me now. I'll only slow you down.'

Charlie stood up. He looked towards the cypress grove, following the zig zag path of scorched grass which Gumbo had left behind him as he chased after his master. It was light enough now for him to be able to see the quick glint of chrome from an automobile bumper, and the small pale flicker of a hooded child.

They had sent David the dwarf after him. Now he knew for certain that the Célèstines meant business. They were determined to catch him, and they were probably determined to kill him, too. He bent forward to give Eric's hand one last squeeze, and then he began to jog towards the house. He had no intention of leaving Eric out in the field unattended, but with the Célèstines closing in on them, he figured that the best idea would be to call for an ambulance as quickly as he could.

He ran up the verandah steps and knocked at the kitchen door. The curtain was tugged back and he saw Robyn's frightened face. 'It's okay, it's me. Let me in.'

She frantically unlocked the door. 'Where's Eric? What's happened?'

'Eric's been hurt. The Célèstines are here. I have to call an ambulance.'

'Oh, my God! What are we going to do?'

Charlie picked up Eric's old-fashioned telephone and dialled for the operator. While he waited for an answer, he told Robyn about the skiff moored on Eric's jetty. 'We won't stand a chance if we try to get out by road. They've probably got the track blocked back by the highway.'

'Do you know how to row?' Robyn asked him, aghast.

'It's easy, it's like anything else. You can pick it up as you go along.'

Robyn watched him, biting his lip, as he talked to the operator. 'Listen—there's been an accident out at Eric Broussard's place, on the Normand Bayou. Eric's suffered a heart attack. He's in the field about seventy feet to the east of his house. I offered to move him into the house but he didn't want me to touch him. Can you make sure an ambulance gets here quick... You don't have to worry about my name. I'm just passing through. All right, then, yes. I surely will. Thank you.'

Charlie hung up the telephone and said, 'That's the best I can do. Right now, you and I have to get out of here.'

They went upstairs to gather up the few possessions they had left there, including the Célèstines' Bible. Then Charlie went all around the house, peering out of the windows, to see if there were any signs of an ambush. 'It looks quiet,' he said, as he let the parlour drapes fall back. 'Maybe they've decided that we're too scared to come out again.'

They opened the kitchen door, and Charlie leaned this way and that to make sure that the verandah was deserted. He listened – but, like before, his untrained ear could hear nothing at all but the wind and the rattling of dry leaves across the yard.

'All right,' he said. 'I guess it's now or never.'

They tiptoed along the verandah and down the steps, checking from right to left with almost every step they took. Robyn clung on to Charlie's sleeve, and kept nervously coughing, a little dry cough of sheer fear. They crossed the yard, and there was a sudden gush of wind which made the dust sizzle against their ankles. Robyn said, 'Is that somebody singing? I'm sure I can hear somebody singing.'

Charlie listened, and when the wind died down he could hear the high quavering voice of Eric Broussard still lying on his back in the field where his own dog had brought him down, singing 'Laisser les Cajuns Danser'. There was something infinitely sad about it, a man lying dying in a field, singing his own requiem, but there was something infinitely eerie about it too.

The crouched their way along the back fence until they reached the path which led to the jetty. The sky was light enough now for them to be able to see Eric's skiff outlined black against the bronze surface of the bayou. Frogs croaked, katydids chirruped, and steam rose from the surface like a graveyard scene in a horror movie. 'Come on,' said Charlie. 'I don't think they've managed to figure out where we are yet. They're probably still watching the car.'

Running now, they headed for the jetty; but just as they did so they heard the roaring of a car engine, echoing around the side of the house, and a pale-coloured Buick came sliding around the corner in the dry black dirt, its headlights full, cutting them off from the entrance to the jetty.

'This way!' Charlie shouted, and took hold of Robyn's arm and dragged her away from the jetty and back towards the house. They ran in between the outbuildings, their footsteps thudding, while behind them the Buick revved up its engine again and came slewing around the yard. Charlie pressed Robyn against the wall and then breathed. 'They have to go all the way around the house. Come on – let's get back to the bayou.'

They could hear the car's tyres sliding and howling as it circuited the house once more, hunting for them like an enraged beast. They ran without a word towards the jetty, along the wooden duckboards, and out on to the rickety wooden structure itself. They were only halfway along it when the Buick reappeared, its headlights blinding them, its engine screaming. It headed straight towards them, the duckboards clattering and thundering under its wheels.

'*Dive!*' yelled Charlie, and they tumbled off the jetty into the water. The Buick flashed past them with its brakes shrieking like strangled pigs. Although there was fifty more feet of jetty to go, the Buick's driver must have been heading towards them a fraction too fast, and the boards were slippery with moss and early-morning damp.

Charlie, tossing his head up out of the water, saw the huge car go flying off the end of the jetty in a bloody blaze of brakelights, and crash into the bayou. Immediately, weighted down by the engine, the front of the car dipped under the water, and the trunk reared up like the stem of a sinking ship. A wave of chilly brown water slapped against Charlie's face, and he felt as if he had swallowed half of the bayou. He frantically trod water, then mud.

'Robyn!' he shouted. 'Robyn! Are you okay?'

'I'm here!' Robyn called back. 'I'm right by the boat!'

Charlie touched the oozy bottom of the bayou, and managed to wade a little way closer to the shore. Grabbing hold of the tough grass that grew on the bank, he pulled himself hand over hand toward the jetty, and at last managed to climb back up on to the planks, where he lay chest down for a moment, panting with effort, his trouser legs glistening black with mud from the knees down. After a few seconds spent getting his breath back, he stood up and squelched along to the end of the jetty, and looked down into the water. Robyn was clambering into Eric Broussard's skiff, tilting it sideways as she did so.

'You sure you're okay?' he asked her.

'What about those men in the car?' said Robyn.

Charlie looked towards the bayou. Already there was nothing to be seen of the Buick but its red taillights glowering under the surface. Charlie wiped his hands across his mouth to clear away some of the mud, and said, 'Fuck them.'

'But they must be still alive.'

'They wanted to run us down, didn't they? They were trying to kill us!'

But before Robyn could say anything else, Charlie took a deep breath, ran a short distance along the jetty, and dived back into the bayou. He knew just as well as Robyn that he couldn't leave the car in the water without making at least a token effort to save the men inside. Fighting for your life was one thing. Letting people die was another.

He felt his clothes clinging heavily around him as he swam below the surface towards the submerged car. The water was so murky that he found it impossible to see anything except the vehicle's lights until he was almost on top of it. It was tilted downward, with its nearside bumper already buried in the ooze, its passenger compartment still half full of air, giving it a lumbering buoyancy. Charlie could hear the blurting of bubbles, however, as the air steadily poured up to the surface, and he guessed that it couldn't be more than a matter of seconds before the car filled up completely. He swam around it, short of breath now, staring as wide-eyed as he could.

He heard thumping, and something that must have been a shout for help. He kicked himself around to the car's offside, and saw M. Fontenot, his white face pressed against the driver's window, a mask of absolute terror. In the passenger seat, the big-shouldered man called Henri was sitting, his face equally strained, but making no effort to open the Buicks' doors. Charlie tried to snatch at the driver's door handle, but he was out of oxygen now, and he had to thrash himself up to the surface.

Robyn was sitting in the skiff watching for him. Charlie gulped for air, and doggy-paddled around in a circle. 'Did you find them?' called Robyn. 'Are they still alive?'

'They're alive all right. But they don't have long. It's that Fontenot guy from the Célèstines, and the other one, the big one. But they don't seem to be making any effort to get themselves out.'

'Can you open the doors?'

'I don't know,' Charlie gasped. 'I'm going back to give it a try.'

He took two more giant breaths, then plunged back under the surface of the bayou once more. He had never been a good underwater swimmer, and it took him several strenuous strokes of his arm to get himself back down to the car. Even then he had to tug himself further down by holding on to the drip-rail around the car's roof.

M. Fontenot and Henri were still sitting where they had been before. The water had already filled up to M. Fontenot's chest. His eyes were bulging and his teeth were clenched, as if the skull that had been hidden inside his head for so many years had caught the scent of freedom. Henri's expression was extraordinary, and even more frightening because it was so resigned. Charlie wrenched the door handle, but the door was either locked or jammed, or too heavy to open because of the water pressure. Charlie banged on the window, and gestured frantically that M. Fontenot should try to open it from the inside. That way, the pressure inside and outside the car would equalize.

But M. Fontenot shook his head, and screamed, 'I'm trapped! I'm trapped behind the wheel! My legs are trapped!'

Charlie realized with cold dread what he was witnessing. M. Fontenot refused to open the Buick's doors because he was unable to get out; and obviously he had ordered Henri to remain where he was, too, so that he could have just a few more seconds of life. Henri's lungs must have already been bursting for air, but obediently he remained where he was, drowning for the sake of his master. Because the car was tilted towards the nearside, the water would reach Henri's face first. It was already filling up to the side of his chin, but he made no attempt to lift his mouth clear of it.

Charlie banged on the door again, and gestured towards the door locks. But M. Fontenot did nothing but stare at him in desperation. Charlie couldn't stay down any longer, and he released his hold on the car and kicked himself up to the surface.

Robyn had untied the skiff and brought it closer. Charlie, coughing, spitting up water, clung gratefully on to the side of it. 'Tried,' he choked. 'No damn good. Fontenot's legs are trapped.'

Robyn leaned forward and took hold of his hand. 'Just get on board, Charlie. If there's nothing you can do, there's nothing you can do. I don't want *you* to drown too.'

'One more try,' said Charlie, but just as he was taking his second deep breath, there was an abrupt and noisy rush of bubbles from below the surface, and the Buick's lights went out.

'It's no use,' said Robyn. 'God knows you did your best.'

Charlie trod water for a few minutes, waiting to see if Henri had managed to get out, but after a while the bayou returned to steamy stillness, and the frogs took up their regular chorus as if nothing at all had happened. 'Okay,' said Charlie. 'I'm coming aboard.'

With Robyn tugging at his soaking shirt, he clambered into the wildly rocking skiff, and sat on the plain plank seat, with water running from his clothes, his head bowed, trying to cough up as much of the Normand Bayou as he could.

'Well,' he said, 'we licked them, didn't we? And all *that's* going to look like is accidental death. Come on, let's get back to the jetty. I want to see if Eric's okay. Then we can take the car and get the hell out.'

Robyn balanced her way to the middle of the skiff and picked up the paddle. She leaned forward and kissed Charlie's wet tangled hair. 'You were fantastic,' she whispered. 'You were better than Lloyd Bridges.'

Charlie gave a wry, slanting smile. 'Can't you ever love me for myself?'

They began to paddle their way back toward the jetty. As they did so, however, they heard the warbling sound of an ambulance siren in the middle distance. They heard something else, too – the whip-whipping of a police siren.

'Shit,' said Charlie.

'Do you think we can make it to the car in time?' Robyn asked him.

'Oh sure. But there's only one way out of here by road, and what do you think the police are going to do when two fugitives from justice come steaming toward them in a stolen vehicle? Come on – we don't have any choice. We're going to have to paddle our way out of here. Eric said to keep heading south-west.'

Charlie quickly checked the contents of the skiff. At the prow, there was a heap of clumsily folded rubberized sheeting, which Eric had presumably used to cover himself up with when it was raining. There was a broken fishing basket, a collection of baling-hooks and rusty screwdrivers and some piece of machinery that looked as if it had once belonged to an outboard motor. There was also a spare paddle and a bottle that contained about half a pint of clear liquid. Charlie uncorked it and sniffed. 'Bad Eric,' he remarked. 'This is raw corn whiskey.' He wiped the neck, took a cautious swig and swallowed it.

'Benedict Arnold,' he swore, as it soaked down his throat like lighted kerosene.

They took up their paddles, nudged the skiff around, and began to splash their way south-westward along the bayou. They bayou was nearly sixty feet wide here, but Charlie could already see that it narrowed up ahead. The steam enveloped them in mysterious swirls, floating over the brown surface of the water like the ghostly hands of all those who had lived and died on the Normand Bayou. It seemed to clutch and cling at their paddles, and then whirl away as they splashed into the water. The sound of the police siren soon became muffled and distant. After a while they could hear nothing but the frogs and the watery guttural noise of their own paddling. They didn't speak for a long time. They were both tired and shocked, and Charlie was beginning to feel chilly and uncomfortable in his soaking wet clothes. He thought of Eric dying in his field. Perhaps Eric's spirit was travelling with them now, in the skiff from which he had fished so often, with his bottle of raw corn whiskey and his broken basket full of catfish. Charlie began softly to whistle 'Laisser les Cajuns Danser', although he had never realized that he had picked up the tune.

The morning passed and the steam thickened and then began to clear; so that by eleven o'clock they were paddling on water that was livid yellow-ochre in colour, and sparkling with sunlight, in between high levees where catalpa and willows draggled their roots, and mud-turtles basked at the water's edge. Charlie in his damp-dry clothes suddenly lowered his head and said, 'I'm just going to have to rest up for a while. Why not let's pull under that bridge?'

About a quarter-mile up ahead of them was a wooden bridge; not much of a bridge, because here the bayou was comparatively narrow, but closely surrounded by water oaks, thick with dangling vines, so that the underneath of the bridge was curtained off like a dark, private room. They gently bumped the skiff into the cool shadow, stowed away their paddles, and sat for a while in the gloom looking at each other. A few chinks of sunlight penetrated the wooden walkway of the bridge above them, and played on the water and on Robyn's hair. Turtles splashed and plopped; catfish finned by in swirls of grainy silt. They felt so far away from the rest of the world that they could have been children again.

'Today's Thursday,' said Robyn, as if to remind them both of the urgency of what they were doing, and why they were here.

Charlie nodded. 'It shouldn't take us very much longer to get to Acadia.'

'Go on rest up,' Robyn told him soothingly. He smiled at her, she smiled back and he realized without any fear whatsoever that he loved her.

He eased himself down into the well of the skiff, resting his head on her lap. She straightened his tousled hair with her fingers. 'We're not exactly the world's best dressed couple, are we?' she said.

Charlie closed his eyes. All that diving into the bayou to try to rescue M. Fontenot – on top of the shock of seeing Gumbo burn and Eric Broussard lie there dying began to overwhelm him, like a cloak of lead. He could feel the skiff dipping and bobbing beneath him. He could feel Robyn's fingers stroking his forehead. He wasn't sleeping, but he was already in that strange anteroom to sleep, where reality and illusion intertwine, and so he didn't pay any clear attention to the slight shifting sound in the back of the skiff, where the rubberized sheets were stored.

Nor did he open his eyes when the sheets were gradually nudged back, and the dull blade of a machete appeared from underneath them, like the claw of some monstrous crab.

21

Charlie began to dream about the dark monkish restaurant again, although this time the dream seemed to be subtly different. He was sure that he could hear chanting, from the direction of the kitchen doors. It sounded like a Gregorian chant, disciplined and sweet, and yet he could also hear the dull erratic thumping of a primitive drum.

He left his seat and began to walk between the tables towards the kitchen. Other diners turned to watch him as he passed. All of the men were dressed in formal evening wear, although not all of them appeared to be real. Some of them had faces that were as smooth as wax, and others had eyes that burned in their heads like coals. The women wore decorative masks, covered with mother-of-pearl and gleaming peacock feathers and glass jewellery; as well as heavy bodices embroidered with gold and silver thread. From the waist down, however, almost all of them were naked, and they sat with their thighs wide apart in order to expose themselves to whoever was passing. They giggled and tittered beneath their masks as Charlie walked towards the kitchen. He had a terrible feeling that they knew something he didn't – something frightening and dire.

The kitchen doors came nearer and nearer – as if they were gliding towards him instead of him walking toward them. They were stainless steel with circular porthole windows in them. The windows were totally black, impenetrable, like tunnels to nowhere at all. As he approached, Charlie's heart began to tighten with fear, and his feet began to drag on the carpet, as if his shoes where soled with Velcro. *Don't go inside,* his sense of survival cried out to him. *It's the ritual kitchen, don't go inside!*

He stopped walking, but the kitchen doors continued to glide nearer, until he was standing right up against them. He put out his hand. The stainless steel was utterly cold. He knew there were faces watching him through the porthole windows, but he didn't dare to look at them. They were blind faces – faces with eyes like the eyes of freshly boiled fish.

Don't go inside! his sense of survival screamed. *It's the ritual kitchen, don't go inside!*

One of the women approached him. She wore a mask like a hawk, with a solid silver beak and glossy black feathers. The eyes that looked out at him through the apertures in the mask were Velma's. Her breasts were covered in a sleek black bodice with silver fastenings. A plaited cord of black silk was pulled tight between the lips of her vulva, so that they pouted vivid pink with shining black pubic hair. She reached out and touched his lips with her fingers, and whispered, '*You're one of us now, my darling. You've tasted the holy bread now. You're one of us.*'

Then silently, her fingers dropped off, and fell pattering on to the floor, leaving her with nothing but a mutilated paddle instead of a hand. Her eyes smiled at him through the mask, '*You're one of us now,*' she repeated, and screeched with laughter. '*One of us now! One of us!*'

And then...

...with a sinister swishing sound, the kitchen doors swung open. Charlie screamed. But instantly, he understood that it wasn't *he* who had screamed at all. He was splattered all over with something wet, and the skiff was rocking wildly, and then Robyn tumbled over him, still screaming, and fell heavily into the stern.

Charlie glimpsed a dwarfish, hooded figure, and eyes that stared malevolent and pale. He glimpsed a curved upraised machete, strapped to a stunted arm. He twisted around, tried to get up, overbalanced, and then the machete sang like a bird and hit the plain plank seat. Charlie stood up, crouched, breathing hard, facing the dwarf with both hands held out in front of him. His good right hand, and his left hand, from which one finger was missing.

'Robyn!' he snapped. 'Robyn! Are you okay? Did he hurt you?'

The dwarf cackled and danced, deliberately rocking the skiff from side to side. 'Stupid bastard! Stupid bastard! Running away! Running away!'

'Robyn?' Charlie repeated. 'Robyn, for Christ's sake!'

Robyn said, in a high voice, 'He hit my shoulder.'

Charlie stared at the dwarf with renewed fury. 'You runt, David,' he breathed, taking two awkward steps forward in the bottom of the skiff. But David laughed, a ridiculous hysterical laugh, and swished his machete from side to side, and taunted Charlie as if he were taunting a dog.

'Come on then, bozo. Come here and get it. You think I'm a runt? I'll show you who's a runt! I gave my arms and legs to the Lord Jesus Christ, that's how much of a runt I am! Would you dare do that? Would you give your cock and your balls to the Lord Jesus Christ? That's what I did! I cut them off myself, with a big sharp knife, and I ate them! You can't do anything to me that I haven't already done to myself, bozo, so you listen good. I'm going to kill you, you and your harlot too! I'm going to cut you into little pieces, the same way I did with Mrs Kemp! I'm going to drink your blood, bozo! I'm going to drink it out of your arteries while you're still alive! You got me? So come on here, come on – and make me happy!'

Charlie remained crouched in the middle of the skiff, watching the dwarf intently, lifting first one hand and then the other to give the impression that he was skilled in some kind of martial art. He wanted to say all kinds of things to David to psyche him out, but somehow the words wouldn't come. The only noises he could make was a series of attenuated burps. *Fear*, he thought. *I'm afraid.*

'I'm going to take your manhood first,' the dwarf promised him, whistling his machete around his head. 'Your manhood – and then your head. Just think how pleased Mme Musette is going to be, if I bring her your head.'

'You asshole,' snarled Charlie. 'You couldn't even go the whole way, could you, and do a good job of killing yourself?'

The dwarf let out a noise that was halfway between a retch and a scream and hobbled violently towards Charlie with his machete swinging. Charlie threw himself sideways out of the skiff, splashing noisily into the muddy water under the bridge, and the dwarf toppled after him, still screaming. Robyn fell into the water, too, clutching her injured shoulder; but Charlie knew that it was only three or four feet deep, and that she wouldn't come to any serious harm.

For David the dwarf, however, the water was overwhelming, and his scream of fury turned to a gasp of shock. Charlie immediately waded towards him, with a surge of muddy wash, and gripped the stump to which his machete was strapped. David bucked and jumped and heaved his amputated limbs, but Charlie smacked him hard in the side of the face, and twisted the machete free of its leather strap. He tossed it away, into the water, and it skipped just once on the surface before sinking.

David screeched, '*Heretic! Heretic! Bastard! Heretic!*' in a voice that sounded completely unreal. But then Charlie seized hold of the back of his neck, and forced his head under the water, into the mud. David struggled and thrashed like a maniac. Charlie found it almost impossible to hold him. But he knew that if he didn't kill David now, he would return time after time to haunt him, and that in the end he would destroy him, and Martin, and Robyn too. With that determination firing him up, he kept David's face pressed deep into the mud, two feet below the water, and he held him there and he held him there and he wasn't going to let him go for anything.

David struggled and struggled, but gradually his convulsions became weaker, and more spasmodic. His back arched in one final shudder, and then he floated face down in the water, nudged by the current, a torso with stumps for arms and legs, wrapped in a soaking robe. A dwarfish parody of Ophelia, '*Till that her garments, heavy with their drink, / Pull'd the poor wretch from her melodious lay / To muddy death.*'

Juddering with cold and exertion, Charlie waded his way back around the skiff. Robyn had pulled herself up on to the muddy bank of the bayou, underneath the trailing vines, and she was pressing her hand over her shoulder where David had cut her. She was white-faced, and shaking. Charlie sloshed up to her through thigh-deep mud and put his arm around her and held her very close. 'It's all right. You don't have anything to worry about. He's dead.'

Neither of them turned to watch David's body float like a water-sodden cotton bale out from under the bridge and slowly away down the bayou. Charlie carefully opened Robyn's blood-soaked blouse and lifted her hand away from her wound. It was a vicious, blunt, nasty cut, and there was no doubt that it needed stitches. But David had missed her vital arteries, and chopped his machete into nothing but muscle and bone. She was lucky: a second blow could have caught her in the skull.

'Listen,' said Charlie, 'I don't know even the first thing about dressing wounds. But if you can hold on until we reach the next community, I'll make sure that you get this properly stitched.'

'They'll call the police,' Robyn protested. 'The next thing I know, they'll put me under arrest. Or worse – they could hand me over to the Célèstines.'

'Listen, don't worry about it,' Charlie reassured her. 'We'll find ourselves a country doctor. One who doesn't ask too many questions.'

'Are you kidding?' said Robyn. 'Country doctors who don't ask too many questions died out with *Young Dr Malone*.'

'*Young Dr Malone*? You're too young to remember that.'

'If you think I'm too young to remember *Young Dr Malone*, then you're too old.'

Charlie helped Robyn back into the skiff, and made her comfortable, padding her wound with the tail torn from his shirt. Then he paddled out from underneath the bridge, into the glaring sunshine, noon in south-western Louisiana, with the cypress trees turning crimson, and the sky clear. Robyn said, 'God, this hurts,' but a little while later they passed the body of the dwarf David, dipping in the bayou, and Robyn didn't complain after that. All she said was, 'I wonder who his parents were? I mean, they must have sent him to school, and been proud of him. And look at him now.'

Charlie said, 'My mother always told me, "Never ask questions when you know that you're never going to be able to find out the answer".'

'Is that what they call homespun philosophy?' asked Robyn.

Charlie didn't answer, but carried on paddling. He was finding it increasingly difficult to shake off his dreams. In fact, he was beginning to wonder whether this journey to rescue Martin was in itself a dream, propelling a flat-bottomed skiff along a narrow Louisiana bayou on a warm October afternoon, while the police were hunting for him high and low, and Marjorie was fretting, and M. Musette was lasciviously sharpening his butcher's knives for the second coming of Jesus Christ.

Around three o'clock, dry-throated, exhausted and hungry, Charlie finally raised his paddle out of the water and let the skiff glide. Robyn had been drowsing, her head couched against her arm. 'What's the matter?' she asked him. She kept his shirt tail pressed to her shoulder. It must have been hurting pretty bad by now.

'I think I've had it,' Charlie admitted.

'We can't go on like this,' said Robyn. 'We have to find someplace to stay for the night; and another car, too.'

'Another car?' said Charlie.

'Sure. How else are we going to take Martin away from the Célèstines? On bicycles?'

Charlie knelt up, setting the skiff tilting from side to side. He shaded his eyes and peered at the fields spread out on either side of the bayou. 'There's a girder bridge, no more than a half-mile ahead of us. I guess we could land right there, and hitch ourselves a ride. That's always supposing somebody comes by.'

'What if they don't?' Robyn wanted to know.

'Then we'll walk,' said Charlie. 'Acadia can't be too far from here.'

He paddled towards the bridge. The bayou was wider here, and the bridge was a steelgirder construction, with tarred wooden slats for a roadbed. It was only when he was far too near to it to turn back that Charlie saw the Louisiana State Police cars parked on either side of the bridge's ramps, and the wide-hatted officers standing waiting with pump-guns resting on their hips, their eyes concealed by orange Ray-Bans, their faces laconic and bored, as if homicide suspects came paddling their way down the bayou every damn day of the week.

There was, of course, no chance of escape. One of the officers lifted a loud-hailer from the roof of his car, and called out, 'You there! Charles McLean and Robyn Harris! We're arresting you here for homicide in the first degree, kidnap, and grand theft auto. Would you pull your boat into the side here, please? We have instructions to shoot you if you try to get away.'

Robyn said urgently, 'Do you really think that they'd shoot?'

'Do you really want to put them to the test?' Charlie said.

He guided the skiff towards the muddy bank, until its flat bottom scraped against the mussels that clustered below the waterline. Then he balanced his way on to dry land, turning around to help Robyn out. Two young police officers came down to the edge of the bayou to guard them, and to drag the skiff right out of the water. Charlie climbed the levee and stood in the sunshine with his hands on his hips, exhausted, out of breath, and resigned at last to being caught.

The officer with the loud-hailer came forward and took off his sunglasses. 'Sergeant Ron Duprée, Louisiana State Police,' he said, in a very slow drawl. 'You've been causing us a whole lot of trouble, sir.'

Charlie said, 'If you're going to arrest me, don't you think you ought to read me my rights? You wouldn't like to be responsible for having my indictment disallowed, would you?'

'Well, we can Mirandize you all in good time, sir,' Sergeant Duprée told him, holding his sunglasses up to the light to check that they were perfectly polished. 'Right now we'd like to invite you along for a little ride.'

Robyn put in, 'We don't have to go anywhere, not unless you arrest us properly and read us our rights.'

Sergeant Duprée turned and stared at her in exaggerated amusement. 'Well, now, I always was partial to an outspoken lady.' He walked up to Robyn with his thumbs in his belt and grinned at her. 'You're perfectly correct, my dear lady, you're not *obliged* to come along for this ride, not in the eyes of the law. I can't coerce you. It'd be different, of course, if you were to volunteer.'

'You're crazy,' said Robyn. 'I'm not going to volunteer.'

'But supposing your boyfriend here was to happen to meet with some unfortunate accident?'

'Are you threatening us?' Robyn demanded.

'Sure I'm threatening you. This isn't New England, this is south-western Louisiana, and here we have a way of doing things different. Totally according to the letter of the law, mind you, but different. You could say we were more community-conscious, if you like. More neighbourly. And there's some neighbours of ours who'd like to have a little talk with you, about this and that.'

Charlie said coldly, 'I suppose you mean the Célèstines?'

Sergeant Duprée looked back at Charlie over his shoulder and gave him a toothy grin. 'That's right first time, sir. Right first time. Give the man a porce-a-lain rabbit.'

Robyn said, 'Charlie?'

Charlie let out a long breath. 'I don't think that we have very much of a choice, do you?'

Sergeant Duprée laughed, and slapped Robyn cheerily on the shoulder. 'Right again, sir. Right again.'

Covered all the way by pump-guns, they were led to one of the three police cars that had been parked beside the bridge. Sergeant Duprée opened the rear door for them, and they climbed in. The car was unbearably hot inside, and smelled of McDonald's hamburgers. Sergeant Duprée climbed into the passenger seat and took off his hat. 'We'll have that air conditioning blowing in a while, folks, then you'll feel more comfortable. I have to say that you're both in a sorry state, aren't you?'

'Miss Harris' shoulder needs attention,' said Charlie. 'She's been given a serious cut.'

'Well, I'm sure your friends at L'Église des Pauvres can help you out there,' Sergeant Duprée said. 'They've got all the facilities for dealing with cuts to the human body that anybody could wish for.'

They drove at nearly sixty miles an hour along a narrow, dusty highway, in between fields that were the colour of red roof tiles. The air conditioning was set to Hi, and after a few minutes the interior of the car was freezing. Sergeant Duprée took out a pack of grape-flavoured chewing gum and offered it around. 'You surely caused us a whole lot of trouble, I've got to tell you,' he repeated, folding a purple stick of gum between his front teeth.

'Is the church far?' asked Charlie.

'Three miles, that's all. The town of Acadia is just over to your left there, you can see the spire of the Baptist church once we pass these cypress trees up ahead here. Then L'Église des Pauvres is about three-quarters of a mile further on. It used to be a farm, years ago, before the Célèstines took it over. Scarman's Farm. Lots of people hereabouts still call it Scarman's Farm. We Police Sergeant Duprée however, have to be accurate in our terminology.'

They drove for a little while without talking. Then Charlie said, 'Can I ask you what you think about the Célèstines? I mean, you personally?'

Sergeant Duprée barked with laughter. 'Me personally? I think they're fruitcakes.'

'But it doesn't concern you, what they're doing?'

'Sir, they aren't breaking no laws. I may disapprove of them, morally or whatever, but just like I said we do things here by the letter of the law, and if they want to eat themselves for lunch, that's up to them.'

'Besides which, they keep you paid off?' Charlie added.

'Now, that's where you're *wrong*,' Sergeant Duprée told him, without taking offence at Charlie's allegation that he was taking bribes. 'The Célèstines themselves don't pay nobody nothing. Not a cent. But let me put it this way: there are plenty of influential people in this state who have friends and family connected with the Célèstines, and it wouldn't be wise of me to encourage career problems, would it? It's all a question of politics. Apart from which, those Célèstines have official approval from some very high places indeed.'

After about ten minutes, they skirted a wide cornfield, and then turned off to the right along a rutted, uneven track. At the end of the track, there was a metal gate, and a high fence wound around with razor-wire. A man in a plaid shirt and a stetson hat stood by the gate holding a rifle. When he saw the police car approaching, he swung the gate wide and allowed it to enter, although he approached it with his rifle held ready and peered into the windows. 'Looks like you had some good hunting there, Ron,' he remarked.

Sergeant Duprée chewed his gum noisily. 'Where's the big chief?'

'Main building, I guess. You'll have to go round the back way, there's a couple of buses blocking up the front.'

'*Hasta la vista*,' said Sergeant Duprée and pointed forward like an orchestral conductor, to indicate to their driver that they should move on.

L'Église des Pauvres still clearly showed its origins of Scarman's Farm. They drove around a cluster of outbuildings and barns and pig-pens and silos: although there were no animals here any longer, and no feed, and no manure. All the buildings had been immaculately whitewashed, and were presumably being used as offices and dormitories. The main building was a converted barn, with an arched roof, its northern side shaded by an enormous and ancient oak. On the apex of its roof, a high gold cross caught the sunshine, almost as if it were alight.

They parked close to the oak, and climbed out. Sergeant Duprée didn't bother to cover Charlie and Robyn with his gun, now that they had safely arrived. 'Come along,' he said, and beckoned them to follow him up the wooden steps and into the double doors of the main building. Charlie glanced at Robyn, but at that moment she wasn't looking at him. He hoped to God that she didn't think he had let her down.

Inside, the main building had been divided up into corridors and separate rooms. It was very silent and cool in there. All the walls were painted white, and the only decoration was a painting of St Célèstine contemplating the Cross. There was a smell of subtropical mustiness and rose-scented room spray, and something else, like herbs and formaldehyde all mingled together.

Sergeant Duprée led the way along the central corridor until they reached a pair of swing doors. He pushed them open, and ushered Charlie and Robyn into a high, white-painted room, illuminated by clerestory windows. There were rows of trestle tables on the floor of the room, nine or ten of them, each laid with a bright, white linen tablecloth, and decorated with fresh flowers. A small group of people were standing at the side, talking in cheerful, animated voices. Charlie instantly recognized both M. and Mme Musette. At the far end of the room, the floor had been raised into a low platform, and on this platform stood a huge altar, draped in yellow and white, the colours of the Papacy. Behind the altar rose a polished brass crucifix, at least twenty feet high, with an elegant and sad-faced Christ nailed on to it with shining chromeplated nails, and crowned with chrome-plated thorns.

Sergeant Duprée led Charlie and Robyn over towards the Musettes. M. Musette was wearing a white cassock and a white cape around his shoulders. A gold crucifix shone on his chest. Mme Musette was dressed in a very white silk sheath that reached to her calves, so tight and clinging that Charlie could clearly see the outline of her nipples and even the depression of her navel. Her hands were concealed in elbow-length while silk gloves.

'Well, well, Mr McLean,' said M. Musette, extending his hand. 'You have decided to join us at last. And Ms Harris, too! Welcome to L'Église des Pauvres. You couldn't have chosen a better time.'

Charlie ignored M. Musette's hand. 'Forget the welcome, *monsieur*. All I'm going to do is repeat what I said before. I want my son, and then I want to leave.'

Sergeant Duprée chuckled. 'This gentleman's an optimist, you have to give him that.'

'Thank you, sergeant,' said Mme Musette smoothly. 'You've done an excellent job.'

'You can't hold us here,' Robyn protested.

'Of course not,' said M. Musette. 'But while young Martin McLean remains alive and whole, I'm sure that his devoted father is not going to abandon him. Any more than *you* my dear, are going to abandon his devoted father.'

'I want to see him,' Charlie insisted.

'By all means,' agreed M. Musette. He looked at his eighteen-carat Ebel wristwatch. 'At the moment, he is at devotions. But he should be here shortly. Perhaps you would like me to show you around?'

Robyn said, 'This is quite illegal and quite ridiculous.'

M. Musette smiled distantly. 'It depends on your definition of both words, my dear. Sergeant Duprée will assure you that nothing is being done here which contravenes either state or federal law. And as for it being ridiculous... well, even our Lord was ridiculed. Look at him there, with his crown of thorns.'

Robyn snapped, 'Officer – I insist you arrest this man for kidnap.'

Sergeant Duprée shook his head. 'I can't do that, miss. I don't have any grounds.'

'Then arrest me, on the charges you mentioned before.'

'I may,' Sergeant Duprée told her. 'But not just yet.'

'It's all right, Sergeant Duprée,' said M. Musette. 'You just leave these good people to us. We'll take care of them.'

'Sir – I'm sure you will,' Sergeant Duprée replied. He raised his hat to Mme Musette, and then to Robyn, and walked unhurriedly out of the hall, closing the double doors behind him.

'Now what?' said Charlie.

M. Musette raised a hand. 'There's no need to be impatient, Mr McLean. Nor is there any cause to be angry. First of all, you look as if you could use a shower and a change of clothes. Perhaps I can lend you one of my suits; and I'm sure that Ms Harris here is just as slender as my dear wife.'

'I want my son,' Charlie repeated doggedly.

'All in good time,' M. Musette assured him.

It was then that a wheelchair was pushed into the hall by a man with a blue medic's shirt and close-cropped hair. The wheelchair was crammed with white pillows, to support the creature who was sitting in it. The man with the close-cropped hair wheeled it across the hall, and parked it right beside M. Musette. 'You said you wanted to see her before she cuts off her breasts.'

'That's right,' said M. Musette. 'I wanted to give her a last word of praise and prayer.' He knelt down beside the wheelchair, resting his elbow on the arm of it, and looked warmly into the eyes of his Devotee. Charlie could feel Robyn's hand searching for his. He held it, and she clutched him tight with absolute horror.

The creature propped up in the wheelchair had no legs and one arm. She was wearing nothing but a yellow sleeveless T-shirt, which had been knotted together underneath her pelvis to conceal the stumps of her legs. The stump of her left arm was still wrapped in surgical dressings. It was her face, however, which was the most disfigured. She had cut off most of the fleshy part of her nose, leaving a red-raw cavity, and she had sliced ribbons of flesh off her chin and her cheeks. Her carefully back-combed ash-blonde hair made her disfigurement seem all the more grotesque.

M. Musette held her one remaining hand, and squeezed it. The creature turned her eyes on him, and gave him a mutilated smile. 'The Lord is near,' she whispered. 'I can feel it.'

M. Musette said, 'Yes, Velma, my dear. The Lord is near.'

22

Charlie and Robyn were taken away from the main building to one of the accommodation blocks, which looked as if it had once been a creamery. They were led to separate rooms, both bare except for a single bed and a plain pine locker, and a picture of St Célèstine. They were allowed to shower; and when they came out, they found that their old clothes had been removed, and new clothes laid out in their place. Charlie had been given a light grey suit with unfashionable bell-bottomed trousers, while Robyn had been given a blue print cotton frock with puffy sleeves and a very deeply scooped front.

All the time, the man with the close-cropped hair stood guard outside Charlie's door; and a matronly-looking woman waited outside Robyn's door. They were not technically prisoners, but Charlie was quite sure what the reaction would be if they attempted to escape.

They were brought back to the main building and told to wait. M. Musette was welcoming the delegation from Reno, Nevada. Mme Musette was meditating. They sat at the end of one of the trestle tables, supervised from twenty feet away by the man with the close-cropped hair, who stood with his arms folded, completely expressionless, and stared at the opposite wall.

Charlie looked around. 'They must be holding the Last Supper in here.'

'Just so long as they don't expect me to attend,' said Robyn. 'That *woman*, Velma—I can't believe that anybody could do that to themselves.'

'Religious ecstasy,' said Charlie. 'Think of Jonestown, that was worse in a way. I guess there's a self-destructive element in all of us.'

'But she *smiled...*'

Charlie closed his eyes. He didn't like to think about Velma. He could still remember too vividly the way she had appeared when he had first seen her at the Windsor Hotel. A little blowsy, maybe, but strongly attractive; a woman with looks. It was almost impossible to believe that the maimed and mutilated creature in the wheelchair was actually her, the same woman. Only the eyes gave her away. They were Velma's eyes. The eyes, and the ash-blonde hair.

Robyn held Charlie's hand. 'Supposing it actually happens,' she said.

'Supposing *what* actually happens?'

'Supposing they eat all these twelve Devotees and supposing He does come back – Jesus.'

'Are you kidding? Do you think that Jesus – even if you *believed* in Jesus – would seriously consider returning to earth for a bunch of crazies like the Célèstines?'

'Do you believe in Him?' asked Robyn seriously.

Charlie lowered his eyes, but wouldn't look at her. 'Right at the moment, I'm not so sure.'

'Because of Velma?'

'I guess Velma's part of it. But mostly it's because I can't see Jesus condoning anything like this. I mean, whatever name you want to put on it, it's barbaric. It's like voodoo.'

Robyn said, 'I went to Haiti once. My friend's father used to have a sugar plantation just outside of Port-au-Prince. She was always talking about voodoo. That was when Baby Doc was still in power, and they still had the Tonton Macoute. She took me down to the servant's quarters, and showed me a bone that her father's maid used to use for putting evil spells on people. It was a baby's finger bone. It gave me the shivers. She said if you pointed this bone at somebody you didn't like, Baron Samedi would come and tear them to pieces.'

'Baron Samedi?' said Charlie, lifting his head.

'That's right. He's the great voodoo demon. The king of all the zombies.'

'Eric mentioned Baron Samedi.'

'Well, I expect he would. He probably thought that Baron Samedi was coming to get him. I mean he probably *believed* it.'

'Samedi means Saturday, right?' asked Charlie.

'What of it?'

'I don't know. Something clicked. Maybe it's just circumstantial. But in the Célèstine Bible, when they're talking about the Last Supper, they say something like "You should know by these secrets that he was vanquished on the fifth day, but the sixth day is his day, and on that day you're going to get your just reward."'

'Well?' said Robyn.

'Well, don't ask me,' said Charlie. 'But "his" was written with a small "h", as if they weren't referring to Jesus, but to somebody else. "He was vanquished on the fifth day". Who was? Not Jesus. Jesus triumphed on the fifth day. He was crucified and he died and just by dying he redeemed the sins of the world, and conquered evil. So who was vanquished?'

Robyn whispered, 'The Devil.'

'That's right, evil was vanquished. But what does the Célèstine Bible say? The sixth day is his day. And the sixth day is Saturday. Samedi. And on that day you're going to get your just reward.'

'Charlie,' said Robyn. 'What exactly are you trying to tell me?'

'I don't know. Maybe I'm going crazy. I *am* going crazy. But supposing when those Célèstines lived on that Caribbean island with those cannibals all those years ago – supposing their religions became totally tangled up, voodoo and Roman Catholicism, so that you couldn't tell one from the other? The Caribs worshipped Baron Samedi, right? So what if Baron Samedi got himself all mixed together with Jesus Christ? Supposing what they're actually doing here isn't arranging for the second coming of Jesus – but the second coming of Baron Samedi? "The sixth day is his day," right? For God's sake – supposing they've gotten it all wrong?'

Robyn squeezed his hand. 'If you don't believe in Jesus Christ, you're not going to start believing in the Devil... Or are you? Come on, Charlie, it's not going to happen. It's all fantasy. There won't be any second coming of Jesus Christ and there won't be any reincarnation of Baron Samedi.'

Charlie sat back, and tried to smile at her. 'What do you think of the suit?' he asked.

'Terrible,' she said. 'You look like one of the Monkees.'

'Something really bad is going to happen here tomorrow,' Charlie told her. 'Can't you feel it? I don't believe in the supernatural, but can't you feel the *atmosphere* in here?'

'I don't know,' said Robyn. She stared at him sadly. 'What are you going to do about Martin?' she asked. 'Do you think you're going to be able to get him free?'

Charlie said, 'I'm going to have to talk to him first. It's possible that he's changed his mind about cutting himself up. If he has, we're going to have a pretty good chance of getting out of here. If he hasn't... well, I'm going to have to work that out as I go along.'

The doors opened and M. Musette appeared, accompanied by Mme Musette. 'Well, Mr McLean,' he smiled, rubbing his hands together so that they made a dry, chafing noise. 'How would you like a tour of inspection?'

'Can I see Martin?'

'My dear sir, of course you can. You are only too welcome. I will take you to meet all of the twelve Devotees who will be part of the second coming. Your son, *naturellement*, is the twelfth. Perhaps you will meet some other faces that you know.'

Mme Musette said, 'We were talking about you, Mr McLean, just a moment ago. We were saying what a courageous man you are. You have fought harder than any other father we have come across. You were mistaken, of course. Being a father does not entitle you to own your child's future. But very courageous.'

Charlie could have lashed out with any one of a hundred different retorts. But he knew that this was the moment for keeping cool. He nodded his head in silent acknowledgement of Mme Musette's compliment. At the same time he noticed how incredibly beautiful she looked, in her white silk sheath. She was standing directly under the light, so that her body stood out in shadowed relief – her breasts, her angular hips, the curves of her upper thighs and the distinctive swelling of her pudenda. She could have been a statue, smoothed out of pearly-white ice.

'This way,' said M. Musette. 'Let me show you some of our accommodation.'

He led Charlie and Robyn outside. The afternoon was grey and overcast but very humid. They walked across to a long single-storey building with a corrugated asbestos roof and whitewashed walls. 'This is where our friends from Le Reposoir are staying,' M. Musette explained. 'I'm sure that they'll be glad to see you.' He opened the door, and beckoned Charlie and Robyn inside. 'This church is a family, you know. If we like you—well, we treat you like a relative.'

'And that's what you do to your relatives, is it?' asked Charlie. 'You cut them up and eat them?'

M. Musette looked saturnine and stern. 'Don't mock me, Mr McLean.'

'I'll make a deal with you,' said Charlie. 'I'll stop mocking you if you let me take my son away from here, unharmed.'

'What a word to use, *unharmed*,' said M. Musette. 'How can he come to harm if his destiny is to become part of the reincarnated Christ? Mr McLean, you son is going to be honoured above all imaginable honour. His life will become the keystone in the perfect reconstruction of the Mother Church. Tomorrow the world will change for ever, and your son's self-sacrifice will make that change possible. Don't you feel any pride at all? Don't you understand what your son is about to do?'

Charlie said tautly, 'What my son is about to do makes me sick to my stomach, so don't talk to me about perfect reconstructions of the Mother Church, do you mind? Just do whatever it is you want to do, and then leave us alone.'

'You're a heretic, Mr McLean.'

'You're not the first person to tell me that today,' said Charlie.

M. Musette smiled, as if he knew what Charlie was talking about, but he said nothing in reply. He took hold of Charlie's elbow and guided him into the accommodation block. 'Of course, this isn't the Beverley Hills Hotel, but it's clean and it's comfortable – and, do you know, we'll be catering for more than one hundred and fifty people here— Guides and Devotees and advisors. It's very peaceful here, very secluded. Our Lord will be mightily pleased.'

'Mightily, huh?' said Robyn sarcastically. M. Musette ignored her.

They walked along the corridor to the first door. M. Musette knocked, and said '*C'est moi, madame!*'

They waited for a while, and then the door was opened. It was Mrs Foss, from the Iron Kettle. She was wearing a beige two-piece suit, with a pleated skirt. She looked at Charlie in bewilderment; but then her face suddenly broke into a smile.

'You *came!*' she exclaimed. 'You actually came! Harriet bet me twenty dollars that you wouldn't.'

Charlie looked back at her, stunned. 'Mrs Foss? I thought you hated the Célèstines.'

'Oh, come on now, how could anybody hate the Célèstines, when they're bringing back Lord Jesus Christ? You didn't take me seriously, did you? You knew about Ivy going missing? Ivy was a Devotee, and I'm a Guide. Ivy's one of the thousand thousand – and *you*, you lucky man – your son's going to be the *one!* The thousandth thousandth!'

Charlie said, 'You inveigled me into it, didn't you, Mrs Foss?'

'Oh, come on now—*inveigled?*'

Charlie was furious. 'You trapped me, you caught me, and worst of all, you caught Martin. You were a Célèstine and Harriet was a Célèstine, and you knew how close you were getting to the thousandth thousandth. Did the Musettes give you some kind of reward for kidnapping my son? Huh? Money, stocks, something like that?'

'Your son wanted to join us,' said M. Musette calmly.

'My son didn't know anything about you until that dwarf of yours persuaded him to go to Le Reposoir. You know that and I know that, so don't you give me any bullshit about him wanting to join you. He was kidnapped, and then he was brainwashed.'

M. Musette shrugged. 'If you say so, *monsieur.*'

'You bet I damn well say so. In fact, I want to see him now.'

M. Musette clapped his hands in genial impatience. 'All in good time, Mr McLean! Give your son a chance to pray and meditate! Give him a chance to realize his own private destiny!'

'Let me tell you something,' Charlie warned him. 'My son's destiny is to grow up, and mature, and then grow old, with a wife and a family and a house wherever he wants it – that's what my son's destiny happens to be. My son's destiny is certainly not connected with chopping off parts of his body and eating them. Now—do you have that straight?'

M. Musette turned away. 'I thought you would understand, Mr McLean. I really believed that you would understand.'

'I understand everything,' Charlie replied. 'I understand everything perfectly.'

'Then come along,' said M. Musette, and guided Charlie to the next room. He knocked, and the door was opened by Mr Haxalt, from the First Litchfield Savings Bank. He was wearing a bathrobe, and his silver hair was wet and spiky. 'Yes?' he asked; but when he saw Charlie and M. Musette together, he stepped back, confused.

'Mr Haxalt is one of our staunchest supporters, aren't you, Walter?' M. Musette enthused.

'I do my best,' said Walter Haxalt guardedly.

Charlie said, 'You know something, Mr Haxalt? I'm glad I took your parking place. I should've stayed there all day.'

M. Musette laughed. 'Mr McLean is a little upset,' he told Walter Haxalt. 'He'll get over it, mark my words.'

He guided Charlie to the next room. There, sitting on the bed, dusting his feet with athlete's foot powder, was Christopher Prescott, one of the old men from the green at Allen's Corners. 'Why, you made it!' he exclaimed. 'It's good to see you.'

'Where's your friend?' Charlie asked him.

'My friend? Oh, you mean Oliver Burack. Oliver T. Burack. He doesn't know anything about all this. Better that he doesn't. He's back at Allen's Corners, where he should be. He thinks I've gone to see my sister in Tampa. Little does he know, hey?'

'That's right,' said Charlie, his voice flat. 'Little does he know.'

A large room at the end of the block had been converted into a television lounge, and there Charlie saw several more faces from Allen's Corners. Clive, the deputy sheriff who had first approached him when he arrived there, gave him a shy, acknowledging wave. Then there was the woman who served behind the delicatessen counter at Allen's Corners supermarket. All of them were smiling, all of them were happy. You would have thought they had come for a weekend vacation, rather than a religious bloodbath.

'Where's my son?' asked Charlie.

M. Musette laid his arm across Charlie's shoulders. Charlie didn't attempt to lever it away. 'He's a very special boy, your son. We're keeping him someplace special.'

They left the accommodation block and walked along a shadowy avenue of pecan trees, until they reached a small breezeblock building surrounded by a low whitewashed wall. A young man with the oval, pimply face of a halfwit was sitting on a chair outside the door, reading a *Super Friends* comic. As M. Musette approached, he stumbled up off his chair and let out a hoot of enthusiastic welcome.

M. Musette ruffled the boy's awkwardly cropped hair. 'Ben has his uses, don't you, Ben? If I tell Ben that nobody gets in or out of here, excepting me and my wife, then I know that nobody is going to get in or out of here.'

He produced a key from his robes and started to unlock the building's green-painted door. Robyn said, 'All those people back at the accommodation block – did they actually conspire to lead Charlie to the Célèstines?'

M. Musette raised one eyebrow. '*Conspire* is a very media kind of a word, my dear lady. But you could say that once young Martin had been observed by Mrs Foss, there was a certain concerted community effort to induce Mr McLean to come into the fold. It is not often that you find a boy of the right age travelling alone with his father, as Mr McLean was. Especially when the time of the thousandth thousandth is imminent.'

'You mean everybody at Allen's Corners *knew*?' said Charlie.

'Most of them,' replied M. Musette. 'They knew, and they rejoiced. There were, of course, one or two exceptions, like Mrs – what was her name now?'

'Kemp,' Charlie told him. 'That woman you told your dwarf to hack to bits.'

M. Musette tutted. 'She was being very obstreperous. But come on in. Your son is here, he's waiting for you.'

M. Musette opened the door and led the way into the building. There was only one room, with one corner of it partitioned off as a shower and toilet. The walls were white, the floor was scrubbed oak blocks. Against the far wall, there was a hospital-style bed, covered with a white sheet. Martin was lying on the bed, wearing a simple white habit. His head had been shaved, and he looked waxy-pale, with circles around his eyes that could have been stained with beetroot juice.

'Martin,' whispered Charlie, and stepped forward with his hands held out.

'Dad,' said Martin, and managed the faintest hint of a smile.

Charlie sat on the bed and took Martin is his arms and held him close. Martin felt different, thinner, and he smelled of the same herbs which permeated all of the Célèstine buildings. Fennel, and something else unidentifiable, something bitter.

'Are you all right?' Charlie asked him quietly. 'They haven't hurt you?'

'No, Dad, I'm fine. I'm really fine.'

'Have they been feeding you properly? They haven't interfered with you, anything like that?'

Martin prised himself free from Charlie's embrace. 'You mean sexually?'

'I mean in any way at all.'

Martin looked towards the doorway where Mme Musette was standing with her arms folded, the ice queen in silky white. 'They've been treating me good, Dad. They brought me down here in a private plane. It was neat.'

'You don't know how good it is to see you,' said Charlie. He was so choked up with emotion that he could scarcely speak. His eyes were filled up with tears. Martin touched his shoulder, and said, 'It's good to see you, too, Dad. It really is.'

Charlie cleared his throat. 'You know why you're here, don't you? You know what they're planning to do?'

'I'm all prepared for it. I've been praying and fasting and now I'm all ready. Tomorrow's going to be fantastic.'

'Martin, if these people have their way, tomorrow you're going to die.'

Martin smiled again, a little dreamily. 'Am I supposed to be afraid of dying? Is that it?'

'Martin, they're going to kill you. Don't you understand? They're going to kill you, and that's going to be the end of your life, period. No life hereafter, nothing.'

Martin shook his head. 'Tomorrow I'm going to do something for which most people would give their lives ten times over. That's what Edouard says. Tomorrow I'm going to become part of the living saviour. Tomorrow I'm going to be part of our Lord Jesus Christ.'

Charlie was shaking. He gripped hold of Martin's hands, and said, 'I'm begging you, Martin. I've never begged you for anything before. But I'm begging you now, *please* don't let them do this to you. Give yourself some time, think it over, then decide.'

'It has to be tomorrow,' said Martin. 'Tomorrow is the day.'

'Martin,' said Charlie, 'if I mean anything to you at all, please think this over.'

Martin wrapped his arms around Charlie's neck, and pressed his forehead against Charlie's forehead. 'Dad, you don't seem to understand at all. I love you. You're my father. If you hadn't given birth to me, I never would have been able to serve Jesus this way. Don't you know how proud and grateful that makes me?'

Under his breath, Charlie said, 'You won't be serving Jesus, Martin. Maybe you won't be serving anybody at all, except those Célèstine yo-yos. It's even possible that you'll be serving the Devil.'

Martin stared at him, their eyes only inches away from each other. 'The Devil?' he whispered. 'What do you mean?'

'I mean that this ritual tomorrow, this Last Supper, it could have completely the opposite effect to what you believe. Instead of bringing down our Lord and Saviour from heaven above, it could raise the Devil himself from out of hell.'

Slowly, very slowly, Martin began to smile again. 'The Devil,' he repeated. 'From out of hell?'

Christ, thought Charlie, *I've gotten through. I've actually made an impression on him. Maybe now he's going to turn around and start doubting what the Célèstines have been telling him. Maybe now, at last, he's going to set himself free.*

Martin smiled even more broadly. *I've done it,* thought Charlie. *I've done it, I've done it, I've done it!*

Then Martin began to laugh. He threw back his head and laughed and laughed, a weird high-pitched laugh of total mockery. He grasped his bare feet and rocked from side to side, looking, with his shaved head, like some hilarious young Buddha.

'The Devil!' he gasped. 'You really believe that we're going to raise the Devil!'

'It's a possibility,' Charlie snapped. 'You only have to read the Célèstine Bible. It's a mixture of voodoo and Roman Catholicism and cannibalism

and all kinds of ridiculous mumbo-jumbo. Martin—
a million people have died for this moment, over the
years. Men, women, and children. A million people
have died in agony, for the sake of some twisted
superstition. It's practically genocide, this so-called
religion. Do you seriously think that Jesus would
have condoned genocide?'

Martin stopped laughing, and stared at his father
with distant, lambent eyes. 'Jesus said, "Take, eat, this
is My body. Drink... for this is My blood of the new
testament, shed for many, to the remission of sins."'

Mme Musette came forward, stood beside the
bed, and laid her gloved hand on top of Martin's
shaven head. Martin glanced up at her with a quick
smile, like an obedient pupil, or an adoring pet.
Charlie got to his feet and looked down at Martin
and couldn't think what else to say.

'There is one thing more,' Mme Musette told
him. 'When your son goes to the altar tomorrow, it is
you who must willingly give him as a sacrifice.'

Charlie stared at her. 'You expect me to offer up
my own son?'

'It is his destiny, Mr McLean. You cannot deny
him his destiny.'

'I can and I will. You must be cracked.'

M. Musette said, 'It is necessary for the
completion of the ritual. The father must willingly
sacrifice his son. Do you remember what God said to

Abraham when he offered to sacrifice Isaac? "*You have not withheld your son, your only son, indeed will I greatly bless you.*"'

Charlie said, 'I seem to remember that God spared Isaac's life.'

'In those days, God had no need of it,' M. Musette replied. 'But now that His only Son has been crucified, He requires such a sacrifice in order for Jesus to live on earth once again.'

'This is complete bullshit,' said Charlie. 'If you don't let me take Martin out of here right now, I'm going to break your face.'

'Dad!' interrupted Martin.

Charlie turned to him.

'Dad,' said Martin, more quietly. 'I'm not leaving. I'm staying here. I'm happy. This is what I want. Dad – this is what I want more than anything else in the whole world.'

Mme Musette stroked Martin's head once more. 'You see, Charlie? He's determined.'

'I'm still damned if I'm going to sacrifice him for you.'

'Well, we'll see about that,' replied M. Musette. 'We do have ways of making people do what we want. Not painful ways, mind you! We managed to bring you here simply by making it difficult for you. I could see what an obstinate man you were, right from the moment I first met you. Tragedy and failure usually make people grow obstinate.'

Charlie said nothing. Robyn came up and took hold of his hand, and said, 'Come on, Charlie, let's leave it for now. While there's life there's hope.'

'You're right, my dear,' said M. Musette. 'And after death, there is glory.'

Reluctantly, Charlie allowed himself to be led away. They visited the remaining eleven disciples, who were housed in what used to be the farm's feed store. All of them were already mutilated, some of them severely. Dulled by disgust, Charlie and Robyn were introduced to a seventeen-year-old girl without legs or breasts or ears; a twenty-two-year-old boy who had amputated his entire body below the waist, and who was being fed intravenously; and a stunningly good-looking woman of twenty-seven, who had cut off and eaten her own feet. The building smelled strongly of bile and antiseptic, and there were seven nurses and two doctors in constant attendance, keeping these pathetic scraps of human meat alive and conscious for one more day.

What Charlie and Robyn found most disconcerting, however, was the cheerfulness of everybody in the building, Devotees and staff alike. There was almost a carnival atmosphere, and most of the disciples were singing hymns and spirituals and laughing as if to cut oneself into pieces was the happiest privilege they had ever been given.

Charlie stood in front of the woman with no feet for a very long time, while she hummed 'Michael, Row The Boat Ashore'. After a while, he said, 'Could I ask you your name?'

'Of course,' she said. 'My name's Janet. You're Martin's father, aren't you? I saw you in Connecticut.'

'Janet,' said Charlie, ignoring her question. 'Can you tell me why you're doing this? Can you explain to me what it is that has made you mutilate yourself this way?'

Janet's eyes were bright. 'I'm giving myself to Jesus. What better reason could I have than that?'

'Do you have a family? Parents? A husband?'

'I'm married, with two small children. A boy and a girl.'

'And don't you think your family needs you?'

'Jesus needs me more.'

Charlie talked to two or three more disciples, but each time he found their devotion to the Célèstines impossible to penetrate. They were like gentle, loving lunatics, who had discovered a dangerous but different reality, and could never be persuaded that what they were doing was madness.

Outside the disciples' building, Robyn said to M. Musette, 'They all believe in it, don't they? I mean, they all believe in it without one shadow of a doubt,'

'They believe in it because they know it to be true,' M. Musette replied. 'Besides, what else does the world have to offer them? Money, perhaps. But not much more. Everybody has to have spiritual goals, if they're going to be happy. If you give people a spiritual goal, their life is transformed, and you can never persuade them to go back to the time when their ambitions were circumscribed by material greed. Once you have felt Jesus's seamless robe brushing against your face while you sleep; once you have heard Him murmur in your ear, you are won over for ever!'

'I think Sergeant Duprée put it all in a nutshell,' said Charlie. 'He said you were a fruitcake.'

M. Musette smiled. 'Sergeant Duprée has to do what he is told, by his superiors. As long as he does what he is told, he can think whatever he likes.'

Now they walked back across the farmyard towards the main building. 'The last part of the guided tour,' announced M. Musette. 'Then we must retire to meditate and to pray, and to prepare everything for tomorrow.'

He led them back into the corridor, and into the room where the trestle tables were all laid out. 'This way.' He beckoned them, and he took them across the room and along another shorter corridor. At the end of this corridor, to Charlie's deep alarm, there were two stainless steel doors, with circular porthole windows.

'*The kitchen,*' he whispered. '*The ritual kitchen.*'

'Yes,' said Mme Musette, who was right behind him. 'But why are you hanging back? The kitchen is the most fascinating part of our tour.'

'I don't want to go in there,' said Charlie.

'You must,' M. Musette told him. 'How can you understand what is going to happen here tomorrow unless you see the kitchen?'

'I don't want to go in there, that's all.'

Robyn took hold of his hand. 'Come on, Charlie, you'll be all right.'

'Yes, come on, Charlie,' M. Musette mimicked. 'It's only a kitchen, you know.'

'I had a nightmare about it,' said Charlie. His legs refused to move forward.

'We all have nightmares,' said M. Musette. 'The only way to break their spell is to confront them in reality.'

'But I saw those same doors in my dream, those same stainless steel doors with those circular windows.'

M. Musette shrugged. 'In that case, you must have considerable powers of clairvoyance. Come along now, you mustn't miss this for anything.'

Charlie allowed Robyn to drag him towards the kitchen doors. M. Musette deliberately heightened the suspense by standing with his hands flat on the door, pausing before he pushed them open. 'Are you ready?' he asked. 'There will be no blood. We haven't started the ritual yet.'

He opened the doors and marched ahead of them into the kitchen. Charlie and Robyn followed, still holding hands, and Mme Musette came behind.

The kitchen was almost fifty feet square. It was tiled in white, with a single green band running around it, and it was artificially lit with fluorescent tubes hanging from the ceiling. In the centre of the room, there were twelve tables with stainless steel tops and gutters running all the way around them. Charlie had seen tables like that before, in *Quincy*. They were similar to the tables used for autopsies, and the gutters allowed the bodily fluids to run off into the drains.

At the far end of the kitchen, there was a gas-fired range, large enough to serve a small hotel. Hanging up over the burners, there were rows of aluminium pots and pans, *bainsmaries*, woks, colanders, and ladles.

They walked between the tables, their faces dully reflected in the stainless steel surfaces, like people who had drowned under ice. Each table was equipped with a full selection of Victorinox knives, butcher's saws, and surgical scalpels. There was also equipment for medical emergencies: oxygen, dressings, and electronic resuscitators in case of cardiac arrest. Each table was also provided with a large tilting mirror, so that the Devotees could see what they were doing while they amputated their own limbs.

'I feel sick,' said Charlie, looking around. 'This is even worse than my nightmare. This is worse because it's real.'

'I'm amazed that your Devotees can actually stand the shock and the pain of cutting off their own arms and legs,' Robyn remarked to M. Musette. Charlie thought, here she goes again, once a newspaper reporter, always a newspaper reporter.

M. Musette trailed his fingertips across the surface of one of the tables. 'The human body is a remarkable thing, Ms Harris. You may talk about worms being cut in half, and still wriggling away. But you can cut a human body down to practically nothing, you can cut a grown man down so small that you can carry him under your arm like a dog, and still he survives! And, of course, each time a man is reduced in size, his heart has less work to do, pumping blood around the length and breadth of his circulatory system, so the body in actual fact grows stronger and more capable of survival, right up until the very last *coup*. You know, there was a sideshow freak called Prince Randian, born without arms and legs. He lived until he was sixty-three, and fathered four children.'

'But how do they stand the pain?' asked Robyn.

'All pain is relative,' said M. Musette. 'These Devotees are reaching for spiritual ecstasy, they feel very little pain. Some of them revel in it.'

'And what about you?' asked Charlie, looking at M. Musette keenly. 'You're supposed to be transformed tomorrow, aren't you? You're supposed to turn into Jesus Christ. Aren't you frightened?'

M. Musette turned to Mme Musette and gave her a smile. 'I know that my Redeemer liveth,' he said. 'He is more than welcome to live inside of me.'

23

Charlie couldn't sleep at all that night. Apart from his fear of what was going to happen in the morning, there was constant activity throughout the church compound as the Célèstines prepared themselves for the second coming. Charlie heard shouting and laughing and hymn-singing, and at about two o'clock in the morning, somebody started playing a guitar. He stood by the darkened window of his room, watching the moon slowly slide across the sky. All he could see was the row of pecan trees and the corner of the building where Martin was being held. He tried reaching Martin by telepathy – by concentrating all his thoughts into making Martin wake up and realize what he was going to do – but there was no response.

He sat on his bed and bent his head forward and prayed. He hadn't prayed like this since he was a child, sitting next to his father at the Episcopalian Church on Sunday mornings, smelling the pipe tobacco on his father's suit, and staring down at his polished brown shoes.

O Lord, save me from this predicament. O Lord preserve my son. Whatever you want of me, you can have it. Just don't let Martin die.

The moon vanished behind the pecans and soon the sky began to lighten. He had prayed that time would stand still, and that this morning would never come. But by seven o'clock the sky was firmly blue and the sun was shining across the whitewashed buildings. At seven-thirty, the man with the close-cropped hair brought Charlie a cup of black coffee and two wholemeal breadrolls, with jack cheese.

'A happy day for you, huh?' Charlie asked him, as he set the food down on top of the bedside locker.

The man looked at him without expression, and left.

Charlie drank his coffee but he couldn't manage to swallow any bread. He went to the window again to see if there was any activity around Martin's building, but it appeared to be deserted. He couldn't even see Ben, who had been sitting outside guarding it for most of the night. Perhaps they had taken Martin to the main building already.

At nine o'clock, the man with the close-cropped hair came back and said. 'The rituals are about to begin. M. Musette wants you to come now.'

Without a word, Charlie put on his jacket and buttoned it up. Then he followed the man outside. In spite of the sunshine, the morning was quite cold. His breath smoked in the damp air as he walked towards the main building. As they reached the doors, Charlie could hear singing. '*O God, our help in ages past, our hope for years to come...*'

The man took hold of his elbow and guided him into the main room. Overnight, there had been a transformation. The walls of the room were now hung with yellow and gold banners, and the tables were set with plates and glasses and silver cutlery, and beautifully arranged centrepieces of flowers. Every table was crowded with Célèstine Guides, dressed in plain white-hooded robes – businessmen, bankers, musicians, television producers, fashion models, writers, salesmen, mechanics – men and women from a rainbow of backgrounds. Charlie recognized several famous media faces as he was ushered between the tables to the end of the room. He saw at least one well-known politician, and a singer whose records he had once bought, and right at the end of the table next to the kitchen doors, Sheriff Norman Podmore, his eyes squeezed tightly shut in prayer.

Charlie was taken to the end of the centremost table, facing the white-draped altar. M. Musette was kneeling at the altar in prayer, flanked on one side by Mme Musette, and on the other side by one of the Guides from L'Église des Anges in New Orleans. Sunlight fell from the clerestory windows high above, and an electronic organ softly played an inspirational interlude before the next hymn.

The man with the close-cropped hair said, 'Wait there,' and left Charlie standing a little way behind M. Musette. As Charlie stood there, his hands down by his sides, it occurred to him that he could jump on M. Musette and seize him around the throat and strangle him. But he probably wasn't strong enough to do it – even if he did manage to fend off the bodyguards – and he wouldn't have a chance at all of helping Martin if he screwed up. So he remained where he was, feeling tense and jittery, while M. Musette continued to pray, and the organ continued to pour out 'Jesus Wants Me That I Know.'

At last, M. Musette stood up, and came across to Charlie. It was uncanny, but he did almost look as if he were possessed of a great inner light. He was certainly happy, and at peace with himself. He took hold of Charlie's arm and led him to the table. 'The proud father,' he said. 'God bless this day, and God bless you.'

'God bless you, too, you maniac,' said Charlie. But M. Musette was quite beyond insults now. He stood at the head of the table, and beamed at Charlie on his left, and Mme Musette on his right, and the surrounding company of Célèstines.

'In the name of our Lord Jesus Christ, I bless this meal, which is to be eaten in the sure and certain knowledge of the resurrection of our Saviour.'

'Amen,' chorused the Célèstines. Charlie swallowed, because his mouth felt so dry.

'Please, sit,' M. Musette invited him. 'You are about to eat the meal of your life.'

Charlie said, 'Oh, no. Not a chance. I'm not going to eat that stuff.'

'That would be very impolite of you, as well as impious,' said Mme Musette. She was dressed almost like a nun, with a starched wimple. 'This meal is the product of one thousand times one thousand lives. It is the true reflection of the Last Supper. How can you refuse to take part in the sacrament? And how can you let down your son? This is your son's day of glory!'

Charlie reached across for the cut-glass water jug and poured himself a large glass of cold water. He drank it without saying a word. He had promised himself during the night that he wouldn't allow the Musettes to provoke him. He had to think clearly and logically and be prepared to act at a split-second's notice.

'Don't worry,' said M. Musette, laying his hand on top of his wife's two fingers. 'Mr McLean is a connoisseur. Once he has tasted long pig for the first time, he will be hooked for ever.'

'Long pig?' asked Charlie. 'What's that?'

'Just my little joke,' said M. Musette. 'Long pig is the euphemism the Caribs used for human flesh. You see, the trouble with human flesh is that it tastes so very good. Well cooked, it is rich and firm, and better than the very best beef. It is illegal to eat it only because those who have tasted it always long for more. It's a fact, historically proven! Take that poor Australian convict who escaped with his fellow prisoners from MacQuarie Harbour. He ended up eating them, to stay alive; but once he had tasted human flesh, he killed people deliberately so that he could get more. The Donner party who were stranded in the Sierras ate the bodies of those who died, and one Mr Keseberg was found boiling the liver and lungs of a young boy in a pot, even though he had left whole legs of oxen untouched. The ox-meat, he said, was too dry eating.'

Charlie glanced from M. Musette to Mme Musette, and then quickly searched around to see if he could see where Robyn was. At last he caught sight of her two tables away, and she looked as sick and as tired and miserable as he did. M. Musette, undeterred by Charlie's inattention, continued to tell him about modern-day cannibalism.

'Look at those boys who were stranded in the Andes after that airplane crash! They ate their friends, and they were haunted afterward by what they had done. But sometimes in the darkness of the night the craving comes and the craving is like a drug! It is irresistible! It is not only gastronomic, but erotic – and this is quite apart from its powerful spiritual significance. Many primitive tribes used to eat the brains and the hearts of their dead fathers and mothers in order that they should inherit their intelligence and their strength. The Fore people of Eastern New Guinea still do it today – only they tend to be less than fastidious about hygiene, and they suffer quite frequently from a progressive and fatal disease called kuru. No chances of contracting kuru today, I hasten to add. All the meat will be fresh and clean!'

Charlie closed his eyes. He prayed that when he opened them again he would be somewhere else, and that his encounter with the Célèstines would have proved to have been nothing but a long and troublesome nightmare. But he could not block his ears, either to the low burbling of conversation all around him, or to M. Musette's persistent monologue about the delights of human flesh. Eventually he opened his eyes again to find Mme Musette smiling at him like a sister of mercy. If only she were.

'Come now,' said M. Musette, bristling with enthusiasm, 'now that I have said grace, you may accompany me to the kitchens.'

Charlie said, 'I'd rather stay here, if it's all the same to you.'

'Charlie,' M. Musette insisted, in a low and threatening voice, 'you may accompany me to the kitchens.'

Charlie took a deep breath, then pushed back his chair. 'I'm warning you now, if any harm comes to Martin or Miss Harris...'

M. Musette linked arms with him. 'What will you do? Strangle me with your bare hands?'

Charlie felt an odd little chill. That was exactly what he had been thinking about doing, only a few moments before. He began to wonder if there was something spiritual about M. Musette—if all his years of eating human flesh had invested him with an extra sense of psychic perception. After all, if so many tribes had believed in eating human flesh in order to acquire the brains and the strength of the people they had devoured, maybe there was something in it.

Or maybe M. Musette and his followers were all deranged; and Charlie was becoming deranged too.

M. Musette said, 'I heard this morning about M. Fontenot. They found his body in a bayou, drowned. Accidental death, that's what they said,' He squeezed Charlie's arm uncomfortably tight. 'He was one of my dearest friends, Fontenot. I just thought you might like to know that. His death is very painful to me.'

Charlie said nothing. If M. Musette was psychic enough to be able to work out that M. Fontenot had died trying to chase after him, then there was nothing he could do to conceal it. If he wasn't, then Charlie certainly wasn't going to admit it.

They approached the kitchen doors. The windows were black, like tunnels going to nowhere at all, tunnels that never ended. From inside the kitchen Charlie could hear the clattering of knives and the dull ringing sound of saucepans, and something else. Grunts, and suffocated cries, and the spasmodic rasping of saws.

'I can't go in,' he told M. Musette. His face felt as if it had no blood in it at all.

M. Musette tugged at his arm, coaxing, threatening. 'You must. This is what you came for. This is what you came to see. This is what you have been pursuing so hotly, both asleep and awake.'

Charlie swallowed but his throat was utterly dry. 'I can't go in.'

'You must.'

'Is Martin there yet? Is Martin in there?'

'Not yet. Martin will come in when the feast is almost finished, and he will make the first self-sacrificial cut right in front of us.'

'What cut?' asked Charlie.

M. Musette tugged at his arm again. 'Come on, you have to see it for yourself.'

'What damn cut?' Charlie persisted.

'What cut do you think? The cut that is holy without being fatal. The cut that transforms a man into a divine being.'

'He's going to—?'

M. Musette nodded.

Charlie could have screamed, and hit out at him, and banged his head against the wall. He was shuddering with suppressed hysteria. But all the time his logic was telling him: *This isn't the way. These are only words. They haven't hurt Martin yet, and until they do you've got to bide your time, Charlie, otherwise you'll blow this chance and you'll never get another.*

'Come on,' M. Musette encouraged him. Charlie swallowed again, and followed him through the kitchen doors.

It took Charlie a few seconds to understand what he was seeing. The kitchen was so crowded and steamy, and there was so much bustle, that at first he saw nothing but stainless steel and glistening scarlet flesh and two dozen men and women wearing blue aprons and overalls. There was a strong smell of garlic and grilling meat; and that distinctive aroma of herbs which the Célèstines always seemed to find to their taste. The noise was chaotic, too. Pans were being clonked on to the ranges; knives were being sharpened on steels; people were shouting and coaxing and calling and sobbing and crying out; and it could have been the busy kitchen of any large international restaurant.

Except... as Charlie stepped forward, pulled by M. Musette like a boat being pulled through water, the true spectacle of what was happening was almost too grisly for the human mind to comprehend.

At the first table, a young naked girl with long brown hair was sitting up, supported by two blue-shirted Guides, and she was sawing through her own arm at the elbow. Her eyes were fixed and wild-looking. Her teeth were clenched on a hard rubber wedge, to prevent her from biting her tongue. She had cut through the skin and muscle of her upper forearm with a surgical scalpel, and now she was rasping her way through the bones, radius and ulna, bone dust mushing white into her bright leaking blood.

At the next table, a one-armed boy of about twenty was grimacing in concentration as he cut long deep slices of flesh from his calves and his. thighs. One leg had already been reduced to the bare bone, and the raw meat of his upper thigh was bound around with a rubber tourniquet to prevent the boy from bleeding to death before he had finished stripping the meat from his other leg. Blood ran along the gutters around the table, and poured darkly down the drains.

One hideous spectacle followed another, eleven of them, and M. Musette tugged Charlie past all eleven. Velma was there, or what was left of Velma. She had sliced off both her breasts, and then cut open her own stomach in an attempt to drag out her liver and her kidneys. The assistants who had been helping her looked up as M. Musette passed, and explained, 'She died just a few minutes ago.' Two of them were carefully dipping their hands into the bloody tangle of her abdomen and cutting out her stomach and her pancreas; a third was severing her head with a stainless-steel hacksaw.

'Of course, you knew Velma,' said M. Musette, but Charlie could only hear his voice as a distant echo, like somebody shouting through a closed window.

Harriet was there, too, the waitress from the Iron Kettle. She was weeping as she lifted her left bicep away from the bone with the point of a broad-bladed carving knife. M. Musette approached her and laid his hand gently on her naked back, and said, 'Are you in pain, Harriet?' And she turned to him with tearful eyes and smiled.

'Christ suffered on the cross,' she said, with the blade of the knife running right through her upper arm from one side to the other, and blood running from her elbow in an endless stream.

They came across two more disciples who were already dead. Their bodies were being quickly and expertly butchered. The dark red meat was being arranged on white enamel trays, according to which cut it was, leg or arm or shoulder or rib. Offal was being collected in white enamel buckets, great slimy maroon heaps of human liver, and gristly crimson hearts.

Out of all of this horror, one image cut itself with extra vividness into Charlie's consciousness: a young boy of nineteen, no more than that, who had already amputated both of his legs below the knee, holding a razor-sharp butcher's knife underneath his scrotum, and staring at his genitals in fascination and fear. For the first time since he had seen a Célèstine Devotee, Charlie saw indecision and uncertainty. Ecstasy was one thing: self-emasculation was another. M. Musette must have seen the hesitation, too, because he stopped for a while, and watched the boy with expressionless eyes.

'Vincent?' he said at last.

The boy looked up. Charlie saw a look of terrible desperation. So it *was* possible for the influence of the Célèstines to be broken. It remained to be seen, though, whether the boy could stand up against the cold, withering personality of Edouard Musette.

M. Musette stepped forward and laid his hand on the stump of the boy's left leg. 'Vincent? Is something troubling you? Today you will become part of our Lord Jesus Christ.'

The boy opened and closed his mouth, and then looked down at his genitals again. Charlie could see his hand was trembling.

'Vincent?' whispered M. Musette.

Charlie turned away. He heard the knife slicing through skin and veins and spongy flesh. He heard the boy Vincent utter a noise that was almost inhuman. When Charlie turned back, the boy's assistants were already pressing a large bloody pad of gauze between his thighs, and the boy was holding up something which looked like a butchered bird.

'Now,' said M. Musette, 'let us see how our sacramental feast is being prepared.'

He guided Charlie through to the kitchen range. There, a small sallow man with a white apron and a black wilting moustache was grilling flesh over a gas barbecue. As the slices were cooked, he was arranging them on white dinner-plates, three thin slices on each, and garnishing them with zucchini and peeled tomatoes and green beans. The plates were then being carried out to the waiting company.

'This is Fernest Ardoin, who directs the preparation of all our sacrifices,' explained M. Musette. 'Fernest has prepared meals of human flesh for private dinners all over America, and a few in Europe, too. Some of the meals were for spiritual purposes. Others were simply for the appreciation of long pig. All of the meals, of course, were superb. Fernest is an artist, as well as a dedicated Célèstine.'

Fernest nodded his head to acknowledge this flattery. 'We are almost finished preparing the first course, M. Musette. The barbecue-grilled fillet of upper thigh, served with a light tomato-and-garlic sauce.'

Next to him, one of his younger assistants was cutting liver into wafer-thin slices, almost transparent, to be lightly sautéed in butter and served with fresh rosemary.

The cooking smelled so much like ordinary restaurant cooking, and it was so fastidiously prepared, that Charlie found it almost impossible to associate the elegant *nouvelle cuisine* on the plates with the grim self-inflicted butchery that was going on behind him. Somehow he had always imagined cannibalism to be a matter of gnawing at half-roasted human legbones, or cutting off human flesh in strips and hanging it out to dry, like pemmican. This gastronomic expertise somehow made the Célèstine's crime against nature ten times more ugly, and ten times more sickening. They were indulging a forbidden appetite, that was all, and they were taking the name of God in vain to do so.

M. Musette touched Charlie's elbow, and said, 'We must go back to the feast, my dear sir. They will be missing us, and we will be missing our appetizer. I hope you have found this to be instructive.'

Charlie nodded numbly. 'Instructive, yes. I think that's all I can say.'

He averted his eyes from the gory bodies of the eleven disciples as they left the kitchen. The young girl with the long hair had severed her forearm, and was holding it up in triumph. The doors swung shut behind them. M. Musette said, 'Are you all right, Charlie?' but Charlie pushed him away and said, 'Don't worry about me.'

They rejoined their table. Charlie sought Robyn's face and tried to convey with nothing more than a slight shake of his head the horrors he had just witnessed. He felt as if his stomach was filled with worms and grease, and his throat was so parched that he found it almost impossible to say anything.

'You look pale, Charlie,' said the nun-like Mme Musette. 'I thought restaurant inspectors weren't supposed to be squeamish.'

Charlie choked out, 'I don't usually inspect the kitchens, Mme Musette. And I have never inspected a kitchen like that. That kitchen is a human abattoir.'

'Well, you're right, of course,' said M. Musette, cheerfully. 'Look – here is our food.'

Plates of thigh meat were set in front of each of them. Charlie kept his head raised so that he wouldn't have to look at it; and so that he wouldn't have to witness Mme Musette carefully slicing it up with her knife and fork and putting it into her mouth.

The Guide sitting next to Charlie tapped him gently on the shoulder and said, 'Don't you want yours?'

Charlie could do nothing but stare at him. The Guide said, 'Do you mind if I...?' and forked Charlie's meat on to his own plate.

The feast was slow and leisurely and proceeded with sinister stylishness. Outside, the sky became overcast and dark, and the clouds that Charlie could see through the clerestory windows looked like inkstains on wet cartridge paper. 'Wouldn't be surprised if we're in for a storm,' remarked M. Musette, with his cheek full of human liver. 'Makes it more dramatic, in a way, don't you think?'

After every course, there were prayers of hope and thanksgiving, and the Célèstines sang a hymn. They ate thigh meat and liver and boneless ribs, and then they were served what M. Musette called, 'a selection of delicacies', which included thin slices of female breast, some of the best of them tinged with the nipple, and pale pink *sushi*-like arrangements of raw marinated labia. Mme Musette laughed a tinkling laugh at Charlie's obvious disgust.

'You sit down at Thanksgiving and eat the butchered carcasses of living creatures, served with sauces and herbs and vegetables. This is no different, once you have accepted the notion that there is nothing blasphemous or illegal in man eating man. This is a sacramental feast of body and blood. It is God's gift, and you should be grateful, not disgusted. Those young people gladly gave their flesh and their pain – *gladly* – how can you sit there and feel self-righteous about rejecting their sacrifice?'

Charlie said, 'You might be able to persuade the rest of these freaks but you're never going to persuade me. Haven't you heard about something called the sanctity of human life?'

Mme Musette smiled, and slipped something into her mouth that looked like a flesh-coloured oyster, but obviously wasn't. Charlie turned away, his lips tightened, his stomach clenched in tightly suppressed nausea.

By eleven o'clock, the feast was close to its climax. A choir of twelve Célèstine guides assembled solemnly in front of the altar, and began quietly to sing the *Kyrie Eleison*. The kitchen doors were opened, and a procession of Célèstine cooks emerged, headed by Fernest Ardoin. Between them, they were carrying in the most symbolic and most openly grotesque of all the dishes that had yet been served – the dish that showed conclusively that the eleven disciples were now dead, and that the assembled Célèstines were about to eat their very essence. On a large white dish were heaped, still steaming, their eleven brains, lightly poached in a stock made from boiling their lungs and their sweetbreads, served on a bed of red cabbage. The dish was carried up to M. Musette for his approval, within inches of where Charlie was sitting. Charlie did nothing more than glimpse the shining fawn-coloured convolutions of human cortices – did nothing more than breathe in one nostrilful of their pale, sweet aroma, and he started to gag. Without excusing himself, he pushed back his chair and walked quickly toward the exit. Behind him, M. Musette nodded to the man with the close-cropped hair to keep an eye on him.

Charlie went outside and bent double under the oak tree and vomited coffee. The man with the close-cropped hair stood on the steps watching him. Charlie's stomach went on convulsing for two or three minutes, but at least he managed to stand up straighter and lean against the tree, his throat sore and his eyes watering.

'You done now?' the man asked him.

Charlie nodded. He raised his head and looked around. Clouds had gathered above L'Église des Pauvres, and over towards Ville Platte and Evangeline County lightning was flickering all along the horizon like the tongues of electrified snakes. A cold wind began to stir the dried oak leaves that were scattered on the dirt, and the cypress trees dipped and swayed.

There was an extraordinary feeling in the air. Excitement, fear, the sense that something incredible was about to happen. Charlie looked at the man with the close-cropped hair and for a moment they both shared this sense of oncoming apocalypse.

'We'd better get ourselves back inside,' the man suggested, his white robe ruffled by the wind. But at that instant, a blinding artery of lightning ran down into one of the abandoned cotton fields only a quarter-mile away, with a sizzling crack, and from inside the main building Charlie heard a deep, low moan, all the Célèstines chanting at once.

Charlie wiped his mouth with his sleeve, and pushed his way quickly back into the feasting hall. The room was almost completely dark now, and assistants were going from table to table, lighting candles. M. Musette was standing at the head of the dining table, his arms outstretched, and he was reciting the Célèstine Creed, while his followers chanted their responses. Thunder burst over the rooftop with a noise like a collapsing bridge.

'It is time!' cried M. Musette. 'It is time for the second coming!'

Charlie quickly checked that Robyn was still at her place, and then walked purposefully up to M.

Musette. 'This is it,' he said adamantly. 'This is where the game finishes. I'm taking my son and I'm going.'

M. Musette stared at Charlie and his eyes didn't even look human. 'This is the hour of the second coming of the Lord Jesus Christ. You will not deny Him your only son.'

Charlie made a quick move toward M. Musette but the man with the close-cropped hair was quicker. He grasped Charlie's arm and whipped it painfully behind his back in a half-nelson. 'Keep still and I won't break it for you,' he murmured, almost apologetically.

M. Musette raised his hand. 'Bring the sacrificial lamb!' he cried out. 'Bring him here, for the moment is upon us!'

Charlie shouted, '*No*!' but four Célèstines rose from their table and went to one of the side rooms, their hands crossed over their chests.

Through the clerestory windows, Charlie could see more flickers and flashes of lightning. Rain began to beat against the glass, and patter on the corrugated roof like dancing cats. He turned almost hysterically to Mme Musette, who was sitting upright in her seat, her face rigid and incandescently beautiful.

'Don't let him do it!' he yelled at her. 'Don't let him murder my son!'

Mme Musette said nothing, but gave Charlie a wan, mysterious smile, and turned away.

The four Célèstines returned to the room, walking with their heads bowed. In the middle of them walked Martin, completely naked except for a white headband. Charlie struggled against the man who was holding him, but his arm was jerked upwards until his hand was almost touching the back of his neck, and there was nothing that Charlie could do to break free. Charlie looked desperately at Martin's face, hoping for one last breakthrough of normal feeling, hoping for one last sign of love and recognition, but Martin was smiling the same idiotic, accepting smile that Charlie had seen on the face of so many Célèstines. Happiness is obedience. Nirvana is an empty mind. Heaven only comes to those who surrender their private will to live.

'*Martin!*' Charlie appealed to him. '*Martin, this is your father! This is Daddy! Martin, listen to me, don't let them do this to you! Martin, for Christ's sake!*'

'Yes,' murmured Mme Musette. 'For Christ's sake.'

And M. Musette added, '*Amen.*'

The four Célèstines brought Martin in front of the altar, and then turned him round so that he was facing the assembled company. He was the twelfth disciple, the final sacrifice. M. Musette approached him, walking all the way around him, and then stepped up to the altar, where he knelt down and bowed his head and spent a moment or two in silent prayer. Then he rose up again, and turned to the main body of the hall, and spread his arms wide in conscious imitation of the crucifixion.

'Almost two thousand years ago, our Lord Jesus Christ sacrificed His body and His blood in order that we might live. Now, we have repaid the debt; and we are about to return to Christ that body and that blood which He so freely gave to us.'

There was yet another crackling lightning-strike outside. Charlie jerked his head up. He felt sure that it had hit the crucifix on the roof. There was a strong smell of ozone and burned metal, and he could feel the hairs on the back of his neck lifted up by the huge charge of static electricity in the building.

M. Musette nodded to his wife, and she left her place and walked up to Martin. She touched his forehead, she touched each of his nipples, she touched his navel. Then she drew out of her robes a long steel-bladed knife with a handle fashioned out of gold and silver.

'The sacrificial knife,' said M. Musette. Charlie watched in fascinated horror as Martin accepted it from M. Musette, and lowered it between his thighs.

'You said you had to have my consent!' he screamed at M. Musette.

M. Musette turned to Charlie in acknowledgement. 'Of course; but only when it comes to giving his life. And I am sure that by the time he has finished sacrificing his arms and his legs and his genitalia to the Saviour, you will be quite prepared to give your consent in order to release him from his earthly suffering,'

Charlie found himself unable to speak. He looked away, he couldn't bear to see Martin hurting himself. But then he found that he had to watch. Martin was his son, his responsibility. He had to know what agony Martin was going to go through, or he would never be able to redeem his own guilt for it in the future.

If he *had* a future, of course. The Célèstines were probably planning to kill him, too, once this ritual was over. Especially when it failed to produce a second coming.

M. Musette pressed his hands together and prayed. '*All flesh is as grass, and all the glory of man like the flower of grass. The grass withereth, and the flower thereof away falleth, but the Word of the Lord endureth forever.*'

As he spoke these words, Charlie alone in that company of Célèstines, raised his eyes. Directly above the altar, suspended only a few feet below the ceiling, he saw a white light, soft and radiant and steady. He thought at first that it must be static electricity, something like St Elmo's Fire, but it remained calm and steady and unblinking.

M. Musette continued to pray, and while he did so, the light very slowly descended, growing brighter and larger as it neared the top of the altar. '*Do you not know that your bodies are members of Christ? Shall I then take away the members of Christ and make them members of a harlot? It shall never be! Or do you not know that the one who joins himself with a harlot is one body with her? For He says, "The two will become one flesh."*'

'*But the one who joins himself to the Lord is one spirit with Him.*'

One by one, then more quickly, the praying Célèstines raised their eyes. A ripple of astonishment ran all the way around the room. Only M. Musette remained as he was, with his hands pressed together and his eyes closed. Charlie had to admire his faith. He knew what was happening, he believed in it, and by God it was actually coming to pass.

The light hovered a few inches above the altar and it was now as dazzling as phosphorous, and impossible to look at directly. Charlie used his one free hand to shield his eyes, although the man with the close-cropped hair gave him a sharp tug on his other arm to remind him that he was still held captive.

Martin hadn't moved. His eyes remained bright. He held his knife ready. All he was waiting for now was the word from M. Musette that would begin his self-sacrifice. The first cut, which would instantly change him from a young man to a eunuch.

The light above the altar seemed constantly to shift and change, as if it were a living spirit. M. Musette at last turned around to face it, and he genuflected and crossed himself and cried out in a voice choked with tears, 'Oh, Saviour! I know that my Redeemer liveth!'

There was a moment of utter silence. Then a hair-raising voice spoke all the way around the room, a soft, deep voice that was everywhere and nowhere at all. Charlie wasn't sure whether he was hearing it with his ears or through his bone marrow.

'*You have summoned Me here. You have called upon Me and I have heard your voices.*'

M. Musette let out a cry of sheer ecstasy. 'Oh Lord, you have returned to us! We thank you, Lord, for hearing our cry! Everything is ready, we have consumed the thousand thousand, but for the very last, and your earthly temple awaits You!'

There was weeping and shouting and clapping in the hall. Many of the Célèstines dropped to their knees. But none of them could take their eyes away from the bright, pure light.

'Where is this last sacrifice?' asked the soft, deep voice.

M. Musette stepped back from the altar and took hold of Martin's shoulder, turning him around so that he was facing the light. 'Here, O Lord, a boy pure in body and spirit.'

'And who gives him to Me?'

'We do, oh Lord, the church of the Cétèstines.'

There was a pause. Charlie could see M. Musette biting at his lower lip in tension. Then the voice said. 'Only the boy's father can give him to Me. It is the law – just as Abraham offered Isaac in the old writings.'

'My Lord, he *will* give you the boy,' said M. Musette.

'The boy must be untouched, and whole,' the voice insisted.

M. Musette looked around in panic. 'Charlie?' he said. 'Charlie? Did you hear that?'

Charlie was staring at the light. A remarkable feeling had come over him; a feeling of bottomless peace and wholeness. He relaxed his arm, and the man with the close-cropped hair, sensing that something extraordinary was happening, released him. Charlie could see his whole life behind him like a tangle of black briars: all the lies, all the cheating, all the cowardice, all the aimless driving from place to place. He saw himself in hotel rooms all across America, thumbing through Polaroids of his son he hardly ever saw. He saw himself in Milwaukee, betraying the only woman he had ever really loved. Yet he knew that this part of his life was over now.

He understood what it meant to have your sins redeemed. He felt as if he were being healed all over, mind and body. There were tears running down his cheeks, but he wasn't even aware of them.

'Do you have to take my son, Lord?' he whispered.

The voice replied, 'Do you believe in Me?'

Charlie nodded. 'I don't believe in what the Célèstines have been doing, that's all. I don't believe that You could condone such pain and suffering.'

'If that is what you believe,' the voice told him, 'your choice is as clear as the day.'

Charlie frowned. And then he understood.

At least, God Almighty, he hoped he understood.

'Take him,' he said, so quietly that not even Mme Musette could hear him.

M. Musette snapped, 'What? What? What did he say?'

'Take him,' Charlie repeated, more boldly now.

M. Musette's eyes widened. 'You're going to give him to us? Freely, willingly?'

'Not to you,' said Charlie. 'To the Lord.'

M. Musette grasped Martin's bare shoulders in unconcealed glee. 'Now, Martin!' he whooped. 'Now is your time! Now!'

Martin lifted the shining knife, and held himself out in preparation for the first cut. M. Musette rushed back to the altar, and abased himself in front of the dazzling light, and cried out, 'Lord! O, Lord! The very moment of your second coming has arrived!'

But the soft voice was suddenly stern. 'You have not summoned *Me*, you evil man. I came because I was aware that you had summoned another.'

M. Musette slowly raised his head. 'What?' he said. 'What do you mean? What do you mean I've summoned another? What other?'

'You have performed today the culminating ritual of him whose day is the sixth day, a spirit long banished for his cruelty and evil. Your devouring of human flesh is the greatest of all sins; and your love of its taste is the deepest of all iniquities. I came today to save the innocent and the pure, and he stands before me, freely sacrificed to Me by his father, as Abraham freely sacrificed Isaac.

'For this man knows, as Abraham knew, that your Lord is neither cruel nor murderous; that He gave His body and blood in order that man should no longer kill or maim or cause suffering to the defenceless and the innocent.

'And I say to this man, as My Father said to Abraham, 'Indeed will I greatly bless you, because you have obeyed My voice.' And I say to him, go now, and take with you those whom you love, untouched, unharmed, and always be blessed.'

M. Musette stood aghast. He turned to Charlie, and then to Martin, and then to Mme Musette. Mme Musette came over and held her arms around him, and stared at the light in mounting horror.

M. Musette screamed. 'You can't do that! You can't do that! I—I am your earthly temple!'

The voice remained completely calm. 'It is time that the temple gates were opened, and the souls of those you have taken prisoner were released, in order that they may take their rightful place by the side of their Maker. And – since you have summoned another, I shall leave you with him, in order that you and your sinful disciples may suffer the punishment which you have brought upon your own heads.'

M. Musette shrieked, 'You aren't the Lord! You aren't Christ! You're nothing but a falsehood! You're nothing but a liar and a deceiver!'

But the brilliant light began to rise up, and as it rose it faded, until the feasting hall was once more drowned in the eerie darkness of the electric storm. There was a terrible silence. M. Musette looked all around him, like a caged animal, and then he suddenly lunged forward and grabbed Martin around the neck.

'A false God!' he shouted to the silent Célèstines. 'That was a false God! If we sacrifice this boy, we'll summon the real God!'

Charlie, however, without hesitation, and without being hindered by any of the Célèstine assistants, strode forward and punched M. Musette hard in the side of the head. Then he twisted the sacrificial knife from Martin's grasp, and went after M. Musette with nothing in his heart but bloody revenge. Whimpering, M. Musette picked himself up, dodged back behind the altar, and fell to the floor.

'That was a *false* God,' he babbled. 'That wasn't Jesus, that was a *false* God!'

Charlie, maddened, went after him. But Robyn had left her seat and was tugging at his arm and saying, 'It's over! Charlie, it's over! All we have to do is get out of here!'

Charlie stiffened, and stood straight, staring at M. Musette like Captain Ahab staring at Moby Dick. 'I'll kill him,' he breathed. 'By God, I'll kill him.'

But it was then that M. Musette stood up, and he was staring at Martin with bulging eyes. 'I can't,' he retched. 'I can't —!'

The room darkened. The shadows could have been filled with clotted blood. And then M. Musette clutched at his throat, and vomited blood, and chewed-up flesh.

'Oh, God,' said Mme Musette, and tried to take hold of Charlie's arm, but Charlie wrenched her away.

M. Musette's body heaved and shook in terrible convulsions. He tried to scream, but his screams were choked and gargled with half-digested human tissue. Then he arched his neck back, with his veins bulging, and began to sick up not just everything that he had eaten, but every human being that had been ingested by the Célèstines, a thousand times a thousand. In the words of the voice that had spoken from the dazzling white light, the temple gates were opened, and the souls of all those who had been taken prisoner were released.

M. Musette's mouth stretched wide. He couldn't speak. Only his eyes betrayed his agony. Out from his lips fountained blood and brains and human flesh, gallons of it, dark red and pungent, hosing the floor of the feasting hall. The Célèstine Guides screamed and shouted and began to elbow each other toward the doors.

Then, however, two eyes appeared. Two scarlet flaring eyes, and the smoky outline of something grisly and bizarre. The Célèstines fell silent again, and turned and stared at the altar. The eyes flicked this way and that, reddened as coals, mesmerizing everybody they looked at.

'Baron Samedi,' breathed Robyn. 'They've summoned up Baron Samedi.'

A deep rumbling noise shook the building from end to end. Lightning crackled and blasted against the roof. The scarlet eyes glared this way and that, and everywhere they glared, people burst into flames, as if they were made out of nothing but sawdust and sticks. Charlie grabbed Robyn with one hand, and Martin with the other, and said, 'Let's *go*! This whole place is going up!'

They struggled their way between screaming, hysterical Célèstines. On either side of them as they pushed their way towards the exit, people were spontaneously exploding into flames. Their shrieking was so intense that at times it was inaudible, like a hundred-strong chorus of dog-whistles.

They reached the doors; Robyn whimpering, Martin silent and still and robotic in his movements, but obedient. After all, hadn't M. and Mme Musette taught him obedience? From now on, he would do everything that he was told.

Charlie turned around. He saw M. Musette, thigh-deep in regurgitated tissue, still endlessly vomiting one thousand times one thousand. He saw Mme Musette, with her wimple alight, rigid with hysteria and fear.

Behind them both, smoky and vague, but with eyes that burned like coals from hell, he saw Baron Samedi, the voodoo devil, wreaking his revenge on all those who had disturbed him from his thousand-year sleep.

They let the doors swing shut behind them. Then they hobbled and ran across the compound. A Cherokee four-wheel-drive was parked down at the end of the accommodation block, with the keys still in it. Charlie wrenched open the doors, and said, 'Come on. Let's burn rubber.'

They drove into a day that loomed all around them as dark as night. Lightning crackled down on either side. In the rearview mirror, Charlie saw the Céléstine building blazing from end to end, and even before he reached the bend in the track, he saw the roof collapse, showering fire and molten metal on the congregation who called themselves the Heavenly Ones.

He drove straight through the metal barrier which protected the property, and headed east. Baton Rouge, Hammond, and then Route 59 back towards New York.

They had driven only two miles before Martin began to shiver from cold, and weep. Robyn helped Charlie out of his coat, and draped it over Martin's shoulders. She looked at Charlie with that expression which convinced him that he loved her, and smiled. 'Martin's fine, Charlie. I do believe you've managed to get your son back.'

After ten miles of high-speed driving, just east of the Atchafalaya, Charlie pulled the Cherokee off the road and killed the engine. The storm had passed over, the sun was beginning to drift through the clouds, and there was a smell of sassafras and dust in the air. Charlie bowed his head over the steering wheel for a moment, in exhaustion and delayed shock, and then turned to Martin and touched his face.

Martin didn't respond first of all; but then his eyes glittered with tears, and he took hold of Charlie's hand, fingers intertwined with fingers, and said, 'Dad. Dad. I love you, Dad.'

Charlie gave him a tight smile. 'Why don't you call me Charlie?'

'Charlie,' said Martin, and then they both held each other tight and neither of them was ashamed of crying.

'Do you know what I'm going to do?' said Charlie. 'I'm going from one Célèstine church to another, one by one; and I'm going to burn them all to the ground. And, believe me, there isn't one police officer or one politician who's going to lift a finger to stop me.'

Robyn reached across the front seat and held his hand, and said, 'You're a brave man, Charlie McLean.'

24

It was evening, three days later, when Charlie parked the Cherokee in the driveway outside Le Reposoir. The sky was the coldest of pinks, and the trees stood tall and naked around the building's silhouetted spires. Charlie opened the Cherokee's tailgate, and dragged out two metal jerry cans, both sloshing full with gasoline.

He carried the jerry cans one after the other up the front steps. He tried the door handles, and to his surprise the doors were unlocked. He opened them up, looked into the dark echoing hallway and called, 'Hallo? Anybody there?'

There was no response. He waited for a little while, listening, and then he hefted the jerry cans into the hallway, and set them down. Only the faintest of lights filtered down the stairs from the medieval stained-glass window. Only the faintest of breezes blew through the building that had once been called 'the little altar'.

Charlie opened up the first jerry can, tipped it over, and poured gasoline all over the floor. When it was half empty, he was able to pick it up and slosh more gasoline over the staircase and wooden panelling. He coughed once or twice. The fumes were almost unbearable.

He was about to open the second jerry can when he thought he heard a clicking noise. He stood up straight, listening hard. It was probably a rat, or a bird. He waited a couple of moments longer, and then he began to slosh out more gasoline.

Bastards, he thought, *I'm going to burn your name off the face of the earth.*

He searched in his pockets for the cigarette lighter that he had brought with him. He didn't see the small shadow that fell across the floor.

He didn't see the small hooded figure that approached him silently as a ghost; and the dull blade of a machete that caught the very last strains of evening sunlight.

We hope you enjoyed this book!

About Graham Masterton

GRAHAM MASTERTON was a bestselling horror writer for many years before he turned his talent to crime. He lived in Cork for five years, an experience that inspired the Katie Maguire series.

Find me on Twitter
https://twitter.com/GrahamMasterton
Visit my website
http://www.grahammasterton.co.uk/

About the Katie Maguire Series

Katie Maguire was one of seven sisters born to a police Inspector in Cork, but the only sister who decided to follow her father into An Garda Siochana.

With her bright green eyes and short redhair, she looks like an Irish pixie, but she is no soft touch. To the dismay of some of her male subordinates, she rose quickly through the ranks, gaining a reputation for catching Cork's killers, often at great personal cost.

Katie spent seven years in a turbulent marriage in which she bore, and lost, a son – an event that continues to haunt her. Despite facing turmoil at home and prejudice at work, she is one of the most fearless detectives in Ireland.

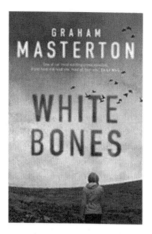

Find out more
http://headofzeus.com/books/isbn/97817818
52170

Find out more
http://headofzeus.com/books/isbn/9781781852194

Find out more
http://headofzeus.com/books/isbn/97817818
56758

Find out more
http://headofzeus.com/books/isbn/978178185679

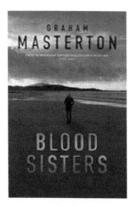

Find out more
http://headofzeus.com/books/isbn/978178408132
4

Find out more
http://headofzeus.com/books/isbn/9781784081362

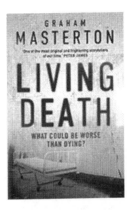

Find out more
http://headofzeus.com/books/isbn/978178408140
9

Find out more
http://headofzeus.com/books/isbn/ISBN

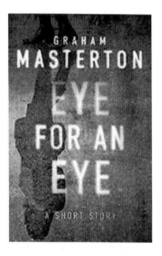

Find out more
http://headofzeus.com/books/isbn/978178497072
7

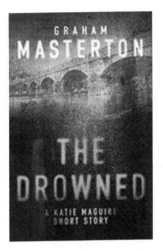

Find out more
http://headofzeus.com/books/isbn/978178497627
9
Visit Head of Zeus now
http://www.headofzeus.com/

About the Scarlet Widow Series

London, 1750

Beatrice Scarlet is the apothecary's daughter. She can mix medicines and herbs to save the lives of her neighbours - but, try as she might, she can't save the lives of her parents. An orphan at just sixteen, Beatrice marries a preacher and emigrates to America.

New Hampshire, 1756

In the farming community where Beatrice now lives, six pigs are found viciously slaughtered; slices of looking-glass embedded in their mouths. According to scripture, this is the work of Satan - but Beatrice Scarlet suspects the hands of men. As she closes in on the killer, she must act quickly to unmask him - or become the next victim herself...

Find out more
http://headofzeus.com/books/isbn/978178497595
1

Find out more
http://headofzeus.com/books/isbn/9781784977191

Visit Head of Zeus now
http://www.headofzeus.com/

Also by Graham Masterton

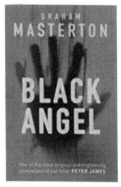

Find out more
http://headofzeus.com/books/isbn/978178669556
7

Find out more
http://headofzeus.com/books/isbn/978178669567

Find out more

http://headofzeus.com/books/isbn/978178669561

1

Find out more

http://headofzeus.com/books/isbn/978178669566

Find out more

http://headofzeus.com/books/isbn/978178669559

8

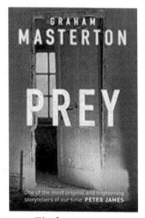

Find out more

http://headofzeus.com/books/isbn/978178669555

0

Find out more

http://headofzeus.com/books/isbn/978178669562
8

Find out more

http://headofzeus.com/books/isbn/978178669563
5

Find out more

http://headofzeus.com/books/isbn/978178669560
4

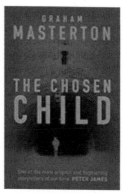

Find out more

http://headofzeus.com/books/isbn/978178669564
2

Find out more

http://headofzeus.com/books/isbn/978178669558

Find out more

http://headofzeus.com/books/isbn/978178669565

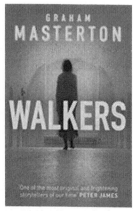

Find out more

http://headofzeus.com/books/isbn/978178669557
4

Find out more

http://headofzeus.com/books/isbn/978178669287
0

Find out more

http://headofzeus.com/books/isbn/978178669288
7

Visit Head of Zeus now

http://www.headofzeus.com/

From the Editor of this Book

If you enjoyed this book, you may also enjoy reading
these novels recommended by the editor.

Find out More
http://headofzeus.com/books/isbn/978178497043
7

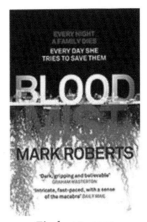

Find out more
http://headofzeus.com/books/isbn/978178408287

1

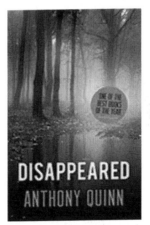

Find out more
http://headofzeus.com/books/isbn/978178408814

9

Visit Head of Zeus now
http://www.headofzeus.com/

An Invitation from the Publisher

We hope you enjoyed this book. We are an independent publisher dedicated to discovering brilliant books, new authors and great storytelling. Please join us at www.headofzeus.com and become part of our community of book-lovers.

We will keep you up to date with our latest books, author blogs, special previews, tempting offers, chances to win signed editions and much more.

Get in touch: hello@headofzeus.com
Visit Head of Zeus now
http://www.headofzeus.com/
Find us on Twitter
https://twitter.com/HoZ_Books
Find us on Facebook
https://www.facebook.com/Head-of-Zeus-Books-178965895576244/
Find us on BookGrail
http://www.bookgrail.com/store/head-of-zeus/

First published in 1988 by Severn House Ltd

This eBook edition first published in the UK in 2017
by Head of Zeus Ltd

9 7 5 3 1 2 4 6 8

A CIP catalogue record for this book is available
from the British Library.

ISBN (E) 9781786695628

Head of Zeus Ltd
First Floor East
5–8 Hardwick Street

London EC1R 4RG

www.headofzeus.com

Made in the USA
San Bernardino, CA
02 May 2018